ANVIL DARK

J.N. CHANEY
TERRY MAGGERT

LAS VEGAS, NV • PORTLAND, TN

Copyrighted Material

Anvil Dark Copyright © 2021 by Variant Publications

Book design and layout copyright © 2021 by JN Chaney

This novel is a work of fiction. Names, characters, places, and incidents are either products of the author's imagination or used fictitiously. Any resemblance to actual events, locales, or persons, living, dead, or undead, is entirely coincidental.

All rights reserved

No part of this publication can be reproduced or transmitted in any form or by any means, electronic or mechanical, without permission in writing.

1st Edition

CONNECT WITH J.N. CHANEY

Don't miss out on these exclusive perks:

- Instant access to free short stories from series like *The Messenger*, *Starcaster*, and more.
- Receive email updates for new releases and other news.
- Get notified when we run special deals on books and audiobooks.

So, what are you waiting for? Enter your email address at the link below to stay in the loop.

https://www.jnchaney.com/backyard-starship-subscribe

CONNECT WITH TERRY MAGGERT

Check out his website
http://terrymaggert.com/

Connect on Facebook
https://www.facebook.com/terrymaggertbooks/

Follow him on Amazon
https://www.amazon.com/Terry-Maggert/e/B00EKN8RHG/

JOIN THE CONVERSATION

Join the conversation and get updates on new and upcoming releases in the awesomely active **Facebook group**, "JN Chaney's Renegade Readers."

This is a hotspot where readers come together and share their lives and interests, discuss the series, and speak directly to J.N. Chaney and his co-authors.

facebook.com/groups/jnchaneyreaders

CONTENTS

Chapter 1	1
Chapter 2	15
Chapter 3	33
Chapter 4	47
Chapter 5	67
Chapter 6	83
Chapter 7	99
Chapter 8	119
Chapter 9	137
Chapter 10	151
Chapter 11	171
Chapter 12	189
Chapter 13	201
Chapter 14	217
Chapter 15	227
Chapter 16	239
Chapter 17	253
Chapter 18	263
Chapter 19	277
Chapter 20	287
Chapter 21	303
Chapter 22	313
Chapter 23	325
Chapter 24	341
Chapter 25	357
Chapter 26	371
Chapter 27	385
Chapter 28	401
Epilogue	411

Glossary	415
Connect with J.N. Chaney	419
Connect with Terry Maggert	421
About the Authors	423

1

I gripped the antenna mount, then pulled myself up and over the edge of the weld between two of the *Fafnir*'s applique armor plates. The tether unspooled neatly behind me, but I barely noticed it anymore. Unlike my very first spacewalk, which had been terrifying and wondrous, this one—my fifteenth—was just work.

"Okay, I have *definitely* joined an elite club among humans today," I said.

"And what club would that be, mighty space warrior?" Perry, his voice humming through my helmet's headset, replied.

"The one consisting of people that find spacewalks tedious. Even kind of a pain in the ass." I pulled myself up toward the antenna array itself, just a couple of meters above me.

"Van, have you ever heard of James Voss and Susan Helms?"

I frowned, trying to place the names. I couldn't.

"Don't think so. Why?"

"Because they are two NASA astronauts who, while on mission

STS-102 aboard the space shuttle *Discovery*, did an eight hour, fifty-six minute spacewalk to make some changes to the International Space Station. You've been outside just over eleven minutes."

"It's been a long eleven minutes, though."

I stopped myself in front of the upper scanner array and inspected the transceiver. Sure enough, stars gleamed through a ragged hole about the size of my hand, fingers outstretched, that had been punched through it.

"That would explain why the data from it is so fuzzy," Netty said.

"Wonder what caused it? Some battle damage we missed, maybe?" Torina put in, obviously watching the imagery from my helmet cam.

"Hard to miss something like this," I said, pulling myself around the transceiver to look at the hole from the other side.

"Probably a micrometeorite." The speaker was the newest member of our happy little gang, Icrul, or Icky for short. She was a Wu'tzur, a four-armed alien, and one *hell* of an engineer. Having her on board had already saved us thousands of bonds in labor and parts and headed off at least two major system failures.

I put my gloved hand through the hole. "Nothing very micro about this."

"It doesn't take much of a rock to blast a hole like that, believe me. Depending on how fast it's traveling, maybe the size of a—"

The next word was something in native Wu'tzur that tripped up the translator. Before I could ask for clarification, Perry was on it.

"The edible seed of a plant native to the Wu'tzur home world, similar to Earthly peas, grown as a staple crop."

"And the bird comes to the rescue," I muttered

"As usual."

I smiled, then thought about the patching kit slung on my harness. It consisted of heavy-gauge metal foil that could be bonded over the hole with vacuum-adhesive. It wasn't a permanent fix, but it would bring the scanners up from their roughly seventy-five percent accuracy to... something better than that, at least until we could make a permanent fix. The trouble was that whoever made the patch kit hadn't contemplated a hole this big. I was going to have to try to rig two patches to cover it and was discussing the details with Icrul when Netty cut in.

"Van, we've got a problem."

I froze. "The words *problem* and *spacewalk* don't play nice together, Netty."

"No, they don't, and neither do *spacewalk* and *incoming missile*."

I thought I'd already tensed up, but Netty's chilling reply tightened up a few more muscles, including a couple I hadn't even known about until now. I immediately looked around, as though that was going to make any difference. Something the size of a missile wouldn't be visible to unaided sight until—well, until it detonated, probably. And then it would be all *too* visible.

Briefly, anyway.

"Netty, who the hell is shooting at us? How did anyone even get close enough to shoot us without—"

"Van, two things. One, there are two ships, both of which looked like normal outbound traffic from Spindrift until they started shooting at one another. We just happen to be downrange of their fight. And two, that's not really the problem."

"Then what the hell is?"

"Uh, the fact that you're outside? That we can't maneuver at more than a walking pace without you being ripped off the outside of the ship?"

"But if we're not the target—"

"Doesn't matter," Perry said. "If that missile decides it can't track its target, it's going to detonate anyway, so it doesn't become a navigation hazard. And, on its current trajectory, it's likely to do that close enough to the *Fafnir* to be a serious problem. For all of us, not just you."

I was already pulling myself back toward the airlock. "I'm coming back inside—"

"Van, you won't make it," Netty said flatly.

"Why? How long have I got?"

"Two minutes. Maybe."

"Well, shit."

"Indeed. I don't think it's going to detonate close enough to do serious damage to the *Fafnir*, but you won't have armor between it and you when it does."

"Your b-suit is good at protecting you from radiation, Van—but not that good," Perry said.

Torina cut in. "Van, I'm going to try and shoot the damned thing down before it gets too close. Make sure you're clear of the laser mounts."

While she was speaking, the turret sporting the upper laser emitters slewed around and elevated. I instinctively followed the sight line but still didn't see anything, of course. Too far, and space was *big*.

"Van, your best bet is to try to keep the bulk of the *Fafnir* between you and the blast, if and when this thing detonates," Icky said. "That should block most of the radiation and any chance of you getting hit by fragments."

"Okay. Which side of the ship should I head for?"

"We're… not sure, yet."

"Damn it! I thought space was supposed to be too big for this sort of shit to happen!"

"It is, Van, right up until it isn't," Perry replied.

I let my eyes wander in hope of finding a solution, discarding ideas as quickly as they came to me. Nothing worked. I also checked the laser mount to make sure I didn't inadvertently get in the way of its beam and get bits of me puffed to vapor. My gaze skimmed across the stern of the *Fafnir*, just beyond the laser, kept going, then snapped back.

"Netty, is there any chance of that missile detonating directly astern of us?"

"It's not likely, no. Why?"

"Because I have an idea. Oh, and an order."

"What's that?"

"Do *not*, under any circumstances, fire up the main drive!"

"Okay, I'm in," I said. The reply that came back crackled with static.

"Roger—stand by—thrusters—maneuver to keep—"

I think it was Netty, but it might have been Torina. Or Icky. It didn't matter, though. I got the gist of it. They were going to use the thrusters to rotate the *Fafnir*, keeping her nose pointed toward the missile. I, in the meantime, was going to huddle in place.

Where I was, jammed inside one of the *Fafnir*'s three drive bells, the flaring constructs poking from her stern that spewed incandescent plasma while her main drive was operating. Made of a dense, heat-resistant alloy, they were specifically designed to shield the ship from the furious thermal and radiation effects of her own exhaust. Ironically, short of the shielding encasing the reactor itself, they were probably the most durable and radiation-resistant part of the *Fafnir*.

They were also my only real hope for survival. Torina had tried, and failed, to shoot down the missile at range, and now it was less than thirty seconds from detonating. Either she or our point-defense system might yet manage to blast the damned thing apart before it blew, but it was doubtful. The inbound missile was military-grade, incorporating enough stealth tech to make it an even smaller, more elusive target than it already was.

Not that it was even remotely comfortable. The drive bells were only a meter and a half or so in diameter at their open end, and narrowed down to the actual exhaust port, which was only about as big as my fist. Moreover, a magnetic collimator, a device intended to keep the plasma exhaust focused into a stream as it exited the port, protruded about halfway into the bell. It left me crunched up in a space about the size of the trunk of a typical sedan—not to mention squashed against a device that, when operating, pushed about thirty thousand degrees Kelvin. A grim part of me wondered just what would happen if someone fired up the drive right now. An even grimmer part realized that I'd never know the answer to that question.

The *Fafnir* began to vibrate in staccato bursts. It was, I realized, the mass drivers of the point-defense systems firing.

"Guys? Any updates?" I asked.

"—seconds—" was the only reply. The drive bells did a good job of blocking comm signals, too. Again, though, I got the gist of it and hung on as the starfield began to slew sideways. Netty, or whoever was piloting the ship, was rotating her to face—

A dazzling flash erupted outside the drive bell, a pulse of searing light that came and went. The headset crashed with an ear-splitting blast of static.

—to face that, the detonation of the missile's warhead. I instinctively braced myself for the impact of the shock wave.

Which, of course, never came, there being no atmosphere and all.

"—Van?" Perry's question was hesitant, hopeful.

I tentatively stuck my head out of the drive bell. A fading sphere of glowing gas marked an explosion that looked terrifyingly close to the *Fafnir* but was probably kilometers away.

"Van, are you okay?"

"I'm still here." I checked my suit's heads-up. "And I'm much less irradiated than I might have been."

"Van, you're still breaking up," Perry said. "You said you want us to activate the main drive?"

I winced, then scowled as I pulled myself out of the drive bell. "No, I said I wanted you to run the AI bird through the trash compactor—a couple of times."

Icky laughed, a jumble of notes that were pure joy. "Firing up Bird Smasher 9000 now, boss."

"Is that real?" I asked, laughing.

Icky paused, thinking. "Not yet. But I am an excellent engineer."

We cautiously approached the remnants of what had been a particularly vicious battle—with me safely back inside the *Fafnir*—and scanned the area. One of the ships, a heavily armed cutter used by the Cloaks, the Spindrift security force, had been left a drifting wreck and was unlikely to be holding survivors. The other ship, a class six workboat, had fared better. Its drive was out and most of its other systems were offline, but it was still substantially intact.

I pointed at its icon on the tactical overlay. "So that's the bad guy, right? It's hard to tell without a program."

"Depends how you define bad," Perry replied.

Torina frowned at the overlay, then shrugged. "Theoretically, the Cloaks are the good guys. But, as you might recall, they're as corrupt as sin. So this might have been a legitimate law enforcement action, or the Cloaks may have decided to make a little coin on the side."

"Well, that Cloak ship isn't much more than scrap. This workboat might have some salvage value, though," Icky said from her jumpseat in the back of the cockpit. We'd rigged it up for her, along with a repeater panel giving her access to the *Fafnir*'s critical engineering functions. It was enough to let her monitor the ship and keep track of what was working properly and what wasn't. It was a long way from being an actual flight engineer's station, but that was still a major upgrade away, so it would have to do in the meantime.

I glanced back at her. "There might be, you know, survivors, too."

"Yeah, I suppose," Icky said, idly scratching with three of her arms. The fourth tugged at her ear as she worked up to saying something.

Torina lifted a brow. "You sound disappointed."

"Well, yeah. Survivors mean no salvage claim."

"Wow, that's cold," Perry said. "And also not quite true. If that ship was doing anything illegal, then we can impound it and claim salvage."

Icky brightened at that. "Sweet!"

I resisted shaking my head. Perry was right. Icky's attitude was frosty. But I had to remind myself that she'd grown up with essentially no one but her father for company, aboard his big, refurbished battleship, the *Nemesis*. She was a brilliant engineer, able to read meaning into the tiniest flicker of an instrument reading, or the most minute change in the harmonic vibrations of a fusion drive. But when it came to reading social cues and just general interpersonal relations, her isolated upbringing showed.

"Netty, is there a usable docking adapter on that workboat?" I asked.

"Topside, near the bow, there seems to be an intact UDA. We should be able to make a seal there."

Torina, always the voice of reason, cleared her throat. "Uh, Netty, what are the chances of that ship just blowing up in our faces?" She glanced at me. "I'd hate for poor Van here to have survived a missile detonation only to end up vaporized anyway."

"Poor Van would hate that, too," I said.

"Minimal chance of that. That workboat's drive is basically just a bunch of spare parts now, and its reactor has scrammed and shut down. Of course, there could be scuttling charges."

I sighed. "People out here do love their explosives, don't they?"

"Space is mostly explosions, Van. Every ship's drive, a controlled explosion. Every star, just one big explosion that goes on and on. Ever—"

"Yeah, yeah, I get it." I sighed again and unstrapped from my seat. "I guess it's time for another trip outside."

Perry gave me an amber-eyed stare. "Look at it this way, Van. Another couple of spacewalks, and you'll beat out that record I mentioned to you earlier, set by those space shuttle astronauts. Of course, they did it in one go."

"Yeah, but they didn't have to dodge missiles while they were doing it, now did they?" I said, pushing past Icky to gear up.

"Seriously? You think somebody was firing missiles in Earth orbit?"

"Since discovering a spaceship in my barn? Let's just say I don't think it's *not* possible, Perry."

"Sheesh. Next thing we know, you're going to imply the Tunguska Event and the Vela Incident were both missiles that went astray."

"I—what? Do you mean—?"

"Chop-chop, Van! You've got a ship to salvage, remember?"

TORINA, Perry, and I made the crossing to the disabled ship, about a hundred meters away from the *Fafnir*. We did so with great care, since scuttling charges were generally conventional explosives— highly energetic ones, but nothing the *Fafnir* couldn't handle at that distance. The chances of a nuclear scuttling charge weren't zero, but it was much less likely.

Of course, if we were wrong, we'd never really have the chance to complain about it. Boom, it's over, and thanks for playing.

We entered through the intact airlock and found ourselves in a ship that probably hadn't been in the best or tidiest condition even *before* it had the shit kicked out of it. Decks were caked with grime and corrosion, fluid conduits showed signs of long-term leakage, greasy stains streaked the bulkheads. A few power transfers were pocked and blackened by arcing from bad cabling. Some of the emergency lights, specifically meant to come on when power failed, were themselves burned out.

Torina took it in, then shook her head. "This ship was an accident just waiting to happen."

I touched a gloved finger to a resinous splash of—something—on a bulkhead. The glove stuck slightly as I pulled it away. "Just one accident? I'm thinking a whole bunch of accidents, myself."

Cradling The Drop, I started forward. Perry ranged ahead, scouting corners and junctions, while Torina watched the rear. We'd only gone a few paces when a loud clang rattled down the corridor ahead of us.

It might have just been a battle-damaged component failing. But another followed, then another. Another. They had a deliberate rhythm to them, like sounds being made and not just happening. I raised The Drop and carried on behind Perry, who peered through a hatchway just ahead.

A loud crack split the fetid air, and sparks erupted from the hatch coaming just a few centimeters from Perry. He ducked back and turned to me.

"Found a bad guy."

"No shit."

I moved up to the hatch and activated my suit's external speaker. "You in there! This is Peacemaker—"

A pair of shots banged off the bulkhead across the corridor

from the hatch. I killed the speaker and turned to Torina. "Somebody doesn't want us to go in that compartment."

"Yeah, I kind of gathered that from all the shooting."

"Van, I'll activate dazzle mode, you follow me in," Perry said.

I gave him a thumbs-up. In dazzle mode, Perry would emit radiation across the EM spectrum, flooding it from mid-ultraviolet, through visible light, into far infrared. He also emitted one hell of a racket, some combination of high-frequency squeal with infrasound undertones. It was meant to confuse and disorient its targets and had proven handy more than once. In essence, he became as loud as a group of teenagers, but on a broader bandwidth.

Perry paused a moment, then leapt through the hatch in a sudden blaze of searing white light. I could feel the impact of his aural emissions even through the b-suit and helmet. Gripping The Drop, I followed him, using his massive distraction to gain entry into the compartment. As soon as I stepped through, he shut his dazzle mode down and leapt aside, out of my way.

I found myself confronting a Yonnox that was standing three meters away. He had his eyes averted and an arm flung up to shield his face. But his other hand swung and smacked a control. A round hatch about a meter across slid closed, then the whole ship shuddered. It took me a second or two to recognize it as a missile tube, and that we were standing in the ship's forward magazine.

"Netty, missile launch!" I shouted.

"I see it. We're not the target, though. That missile just twisted away."

"It—what?"

"A missile with a twist drive? That's got to be something valuable," Perry said.

I cursed and crossed toward the Yonnox, meaning to take him into custody and get some answers out of him. He just spun toward us, though, laughing, and started shooting blindly, apparently still dazzled. Slugs clanged off the deck, against the bulkheads. One smacked into another missile, still in its storage rack. One grazed my shoulder and glanced off my b-suit.

I raised The Drop and fired, point-blank, center mass. The Yonnox froze, stopped laughing, then slumped against the bulkhead behind him. He leaned there for a second or two, then slid to the deck in a heap.

"That thing does have a stun effect, you know," Perry said.

I nodded. "Yeah, a stun effect that works *most* of the time." I gestured at the missile the Yonnox had hit and its ruptured casing. "And *most* of the time, a hit like that won't make a missile detonate, right?"

Perry glanced at the casing, then bobbed his head. "I see your point."

Torina poked her head around the hatch coaming. "You guys all done in there?"

I looked at the fallen Yonnox. "Yeah. Sorry, Torina. Looks like the party ended before it even really got started."

"No apologies necessary. I'm always good with not being shot at."

2

"So what kind of missile has a twist drive?" I asked, settling back in the *Fafnir*'s pilot's seat.

"Typically, none of them. They aren't necessary, they take up a lot of internal space, and, most of all, they're really, *really* expensive," Netty replied.

"Suggesting it wasn't actually a missile at all, just a vehicle for carrying something away that Yonnox didn't want us to find," Torina added.

"Yeah, I'd say that's a safe bet. Perry, any luck with anything you gleaned from that ship's data core? You know, incriminating lists, detailed outlines of evil plans, that sort of thing?"

"Sorry, Van, that guy's data core was as much of a mess as the rest of his ship. Oh, and porn. Lots and lots of porn."

"Um. *Yonnox* smut? Please tell me it was only Yonnox smut," I asked with dwindling hope.

After a gravid pause, Netty said, "Sure. Let's go with that."

Torina sniffed. "And here I was thinking our friend over there couldn't get any less appealing."

We'd managed to at least retrieve the ship's registry data from its transponder, only to find it was using a spoofed identity, data cloned from a ship that had been decommissioned and scrapped almost two years ago. And there simply wasn't much else of note. A bit of salvage value, and that was it.

Well, except for the mysterious super-luminal missile, that is. And about that—

"Okay, Netty, how are you doing with tracking that thing to... wherever the hell it went?" I asked.

"Actually, the one to ask is Icky. She has some innovative ideas for tracking things that twist," Netty replied.

Torina, Perry, and I all turned to Icky. She gave us a self-conscious glance, then shrugged. "They're not actually my ideas, they're my dad's. He theorized that you could measure the compression of space-time around an operating twist drive, then based on the vector sum of the gravimetric—"

I held up a hand. "I believe you. And your dad. The rest of your explanation will, I'm afraid, be lost on me, not being big into... theoretical physics, I guess."

Icky nodded. "Sorry. Netty and I really got into a discussion about it."

"A really interesting one. I must say, she's a delight to have aboard," Netty put in.

"Glad to hear it. Now, did your really interesting discussion lead to any conclusions?"

"Halcyon," Icky replied.

"Halcyon."

"Yeah. That's the most likely destination for that missile. Or, at least, somewhere along that trajectory, but Halcyon's the only known habitation it intersects."

I thought for a moment. The memories I had implanted when I was inducted into the Peacemakers provided me with a thumbnail sketch. Halcyon was another deep-space habitat, similar to Spindrift and Crossroads. It was a remote one, though, sitting within the general boundary of known space, but on its own. Halcyon was like the kid no one wants to sit near in the cafeteria.

I had Netty bring up the chart, centered on Halcyon. The station was located in one of the better-known star systems among Earth astronomers, Altair. It was a big, bluish-white star almost twice the mass of Sol, and one of the brightest in the terrestrial night sky. And that made me immediately curious about something.

"Why is a star that big and bright so unpopulated? Given the profusion of rinky-dink little red dwarf stars, you'd think something like Altair would be a lot more popular."

Netty had the answer—of course. "Altair is rotating fast, as in, not too far from just flying apart at the seams. That causes some weird interactions between its stellar wind and its magnetic field— anyway, bottom line, there simply aren't any habitable planets there."

"Okay, then let me flip my question around. If it's that inhospitable, what the hell is this Halcyon station doing there?" I asked.

"There are several inhabited systems on the… far side of Altair, for lack of a better term. It makes for a long twist. Halcyon was originally established by a shipping consortium as a combination navigational waypoint, refueling station, and general layover location."

"Ah. Kind of like a roadside rest stop back on Earth."

"Essentially."

Icky narrowed her eyes. "Netty, I notice you said it was originally established for this stuff. That implies it's doing something else now."

"I think I can answer that," Perry put in. "Halcyon has changed owners several times in the hundred or so years it's been around. The most recent owners are the Children of Resplendence."

"Huh. Kind of sounds like a cult."

"That's because it is a cult."

"Oh."

Torina shrugged. "Look at this way, Van. They can't be any weirder than space hippies, right?"

I held up a finger. "Torina, hold that thought. Because every time I don't think things can get weirder, they do."

WHILE NETTY WORKED on our twist to Altair, I pored over the Peacemaker file on the Children of Resplendence. It was hefty. Supposedly, they were a *psionic collective* whose members were all part of something called *The Resonance*. It seems that The Resonance is a specific psionic frequency shared by all sentient beings, and that the Children's particular initiations and rituals—collectively called Tuning—allowed those who engaged in them to become aware of The Resonance. Through The Resonance, the Children of Resplendence achieved a harmonious, unified existence.

Blah, blah, blah. It was pretty clear from the laundry list of malfeasance and wrongdoing that the Children of Resplendence were, indeed, a cult devoted to the harmonious separation of gullible people from their money. By calling themselves a religious organization, they claimed, with varying degrees of success, exemptions from various tariffs and fees and things normally levied under interstellar commerce laws. And, as if that weren't all sleazy enough, they'd cleverly taken control of what amounted to a choke point between the bulk of known space and the nearest inhabited systems located beyond it. The isolated systems were mostly quiet, agrarian worlds that didn't see a lot of trade activity or interest, so the Children even managed to avoid antagonizing any large commercial interests.

Somebody had really thought this particular scam through. I was kind of impressed, in the way that one can admire a predator on the hunt.

We made the twist, and Altair suddenly popped into existence ahead, a searing, blue-white glare, oddly shaped into a fat, bulging disk. Netty had said the star rotated fast, so much so that it hugged the edge of simply flying apart at its equator. The result of all this was an inner system lashed by violent stellar storms, driven by a magnetic field that was twisted like an over-tightened spring. Halcyon orbited just outside the danger zone but was still hit by the occasional errant blast of stellar plasma, forcing everyone aboard to take cover in heavily shielded safe zones.

We contemplated bending the law and approaching the station with our transponder malfunctioning, but I finally decided against it. I was curious to see what effect the arrival of a Peacemaker might have. I especially wanted to see if any ships suddenly felt an urgent need to be elsewhere.

There was no particular scramble to depart, though. Two ships on outbound courses plodded on, as did one inbound, a big freighter. As we approached the station, we scanned another five ships at dock, including one registered to the Nesit homeworld.

"Now *that's* interesting," I said, eyeing its registry data.

Torina nodded. "It is. I wonder what a Nesit ship is doing way out here."

"Maybe they're here to join themselves into the peaceful harmony of The Resonance," Perry suggested.

I gave him a look. So did Torina and Icky.

He shrugged back at us. "Just saying."

"Well, let's find out," I said, requesting a comm channel to their traffic control system. As soon as I did, the true nature of the Children of Resplendence leapt into stark clarity. In a scroll of data, we received an automated list of docking fees, surcharges to docking fees, various administrative charges, and something called a 'navigation tariff'. I glanced at Torina, trying not to grind my teeth.

"Got your credit card handy?"

She blew out a breath as she scanned the list. "They're asking for almost a thousand bonds just for the privilege of docking?"

"It gets better. I've just received a list of freight tariffs and handling fees. Basically, if we offload or take on any cargo here, they claim tariffs and customs charges equal to about a third of the gross value. Even if you're just moving cargo *through* here, they still want a twenty percent cut," Netty said.

"It's just a *little* bit cheaper than the fuel cost of twisting right past these assholes," Perry put in.

Icky sniffed. "Well, fancy that. I'll bet their rates are tied to the price of fuel, too, so if it goes down, so does their cut, so they can stay competitive."

"Yeah, well, we're not paying a thousand bonds just to dock," I said, then switched back to the comm.

"This is Peacemaker Van Tudor. I've got a counteroffer. We'll pay a standard docking fee, the usual hundred bonds or so, and you'll be happy with that. Or, I will go away, and I will come back with a few more Peacemakers, and we'll start inspecting cargo going in and out of this system. So you—"

"That's extortion," a voice snapped back over the comm. "It's harassment. We'll lodge a complaint with the Peacemaker Guild—"

"Let me get them on the comm for you," I said and closed the channel. It took a few minutes, but I was able to get Lunzy on a long-distance comm relay and explain the situation to her. She laughed.

"Sure, put me through."

I did, and all the humor fled from Lunzy's voice. "This is Peacemaker Lunzemor Nyatt, official rep of the Guild Masters. I understand you wish to file a complaint about Peacemaker Tudor? If so, then I'll dispatch an investigative team to take statements, gather evidence, interview potential witnesses—"

"That's… fine. Just a misunderstanding. We're happy to accommodate Peacemaker Tudor, who is, of course, exempt from any charges related to the performance of his duties."

"Are you sure? We take matters like this very seriously. I've got three Peacemakers I can send right now—"

"That won't be necessary. As I said, it was all just a misunderstanding."

"Very well, then. I'm glad we've resolved this to everyone's satisfaction," Lunzy said.

"Except theirs," Icky muttered, chuckling.

Lunzy signed off, and we docked the *Fafnir* without further ado. I left Perry and Netty to do a discrete but detailed scan of the station's exterior and every other ship. I also reminded Perry to watch out for things being planted on the *Fafnir*, since attaching various types of tracking or sabotage devices seemed to be quite popular among the reprobates out here in the deep.

After all, we'd done it ourselves.

TORINA, Icky, and I made our way into the station, which tried to portray itself as a cross between an airport terminal and a spa. Potted plants, concealed lighting, and white paneling mounted to the bulkheads made the place seem luxurious, at least until you looked closely. Then you noticed that the plants were droopy, the concealed lighting flickered, and the white paneling looked like some interstellar version of cheap particle board.

"A veneer of respectability," Torina pronounced.

Icky and I both nodded.

"Layered over a core of immorality," I said, then sighed. "Is there anywhere in this damned galaxy that *isn't* all about greed and corruption?"

Torina raised an eyebrow at me. "My homeworld?"

"Okay, yeah, fair point."

"Also Schegith's planet? Null World? And how about the music school centered around the Synclavion—?"

"Alright, I surrender. You're right. There are decent places out here."

"Yeah, well, I don't think this is one of them," Icky huffed, nodding at a small group of figures clustered around an airlock, one that corresponded to the Nesit ship. "Doesn't that gang of miscreants look awfully, ah, miscreant-ish?"

I shot Icky a bemused glance. "Miscreant-ish?"

"What can I say, I like playing with the language."

We ambled toward the group gathered around the Nesit airlock, looking as inconspicuous as we could. I had no doubt that they knew I was a Peacemaker, despite my trusty spaghetti-western style duster coat. But I hoped that if we didn't express much interest in them in particular, we'd at least be able to get close enough to get some sense of what was going on.

Icky came to the rescue. She saw a slender alien with bluish skin wearing otherwise nondescript clothing, but with a blue surcoat embroidered with fancy golden filigree and dangling doodads. Her face lit up, and she aimed herself toward him.

"Excuse me!"

I glanced at Torina, who shrugged. We both followed Icky as she beelined toward the alien in the fancy outfit.

"Excuse me," she said again.

The alien turned, offering a beatific smile. "Yes, my child?"

"You're one of them, aren't you? One of the Children of Resplendence?"

"I—am, yes." The alien gave her a doubtful look. "Can I help you in some way, child?"

"Yes!" Icky said, then babbled on about wanting to join the Children, to become part of the Resonance, become harmoniously enlightened, and so on, and so on. I wondered what she was doing, since I couldn't imagine that she had any real interest in joining this usurious cult. But then I noticed that she'd intercepted the fancy alien just within earshot of the group gathered around the Nesit ship's airlock. Torina got it, too, and gave me a knowing look. We both then stood, watching and listening intently as Icky and the alien delved deep into the requirements to join the Children of Resplendence, what the Resonance was all about—basically anything that would give us reason to stand where we were.

I tuned out their babble and concentrated instead on what was being said near the airlock. I noticed that several crates had apparently been unloaded from the Nesit ship and seemed to be the subject of some intense discussion—

No. Wait. Not discussion. *Bidding.*

We were witnessing an impromptu pop-up auction.

I turned to face away from the small crowd so I could speak to Torina. As I did, I saw Icky shoot me a quick glance. I gave a slight nod back, and she pushed on with some deep, surprisingly insightful questions about the nature of the Children of Resplendence, the Resonance, and—and actual existence, I think. I had no idea she was so philosophical. I also had to correct my earlier assumption that her relatively isolated upbringing meant she didn't know social cues very well. It turned out she did, at least when she wanted to.

In fact, she had this particular Child of Resplendence as firmly hooked as the hefty speckled trout I'd caught during a business trip up to Canada, my one and only fishing triumph. She carefully kept seeding her conversation with hints that she had money, and a lot of it, and didn't really understand its value—music to the ears of a grifter. I actually had to tear my attention away from her.

"So that's an auction," I muttered to Torina.

She pretended to read something on a data slate. "It is. I wonder what's in those crates they're bidding on."

"Good question. We should have brought Perry and his super-sensitive directional hearing with us."

I nodded. That was a definite note to self.

We briefly mused about getting closer, or even joining in the bidding, but decided against it. We didn't want to spook them and pass up some potentially valuable leads. On the other hand, they might have just been auctioning off old spaceship parts, and there was nothing of interest to us going on at all. I shifted, sighing my frustration—

A small shape swept around a nearby corner, spread its wings, and settled onto the rim of a big plant pot a couple of meters away. That got the attention of Icky's new friend, who looked at Perry, then at us, then back to her, and quickly excused himself. Icky tried to keep him engaged, but he just waved her off and hurried away.

"I think he made us," she said.

"Sorry, did I arrive at a bad time?" Perry asked.

I shrugged. "Maybe? We've been keeping an eye on that little auction going on over there, but we don't know what it's all about, or if it's even of any interest to us."

"Ah, then I arrived at exactly the right time."

"What are you talking about?"

"Well, that detailed scan Netty and I were running picked up lots of potentially interesting things, but the most interesting was a signal characteristic of something of terrestrial origin."

"Something from Earth? Here?"

"Yup. It was faint, just a few specific isotopic ratios associated with Earthly metals manufactured since you guys detonated your first nuke. And it didn't last long. We picked it up somewhere in the general vicinity of that Nesit ship, so I figured I'd come and check it out."

"So there's an Earthly artifact in one of those boxes."

Perry bobbed his head in a nod. "The one furthest to your right, in fact."

I glanced at the case in question. It told me nothing, of course, just being a standard, small cargo crate, identical to hundreds of thousands, maybe millions scattered around known space. A pair of squat, lumpy, somewhat lizard-like aliens were in the process of picking it up and heaving it away. In fact, it looked like the whole auction was breaking up, all of the crates being lugged away by their new owners. The whole thing lasted maybe ten minutes.

"Perry, can you find out where that case containing the Earthly whatever is being taken? I'm assuming another ship, so which one, where it's going, if you can manage it—"

"On it, boss," Perry said and leapt into the air. He followed the two lumpy aliens as they carted their new purchase along the docking concourse and passed out of our view.

"What do you want to do about the Nesit? I can't imagine they're going to hang around here for very long," Torina said.

Icky nodded and pointed out a nearby viewport, where we could see part of the Nesit ship. "He's fired up his running lights and hazard beacon. I'd say he's planning on leaving right now."

I nodded back and walked toward the airlock, where the Nesit was obviously hurrying to finish up his business. A Yonnox held out a data slate, probably to make payment on whatever he'd bought, but there seemed to be a disagreement underway. The Nesit saw us approaching, obviously decided that discretion was the better part of business, thumbed the data slate with a quick nod, then turned and hurried toward the airlock.

I pulled open my duster. "Excuse me! Peacemaker here! I need—"

The Yonnox yelped, grabbed the case containing whatever he'd purchased, and heaved it onto a small cart to wheel it quickly away. We ignored him and rushed to catch the Nesit before he got the airlock closed. We almost made it.

I stopped short at the closed door. "I am disappointed."

Icky crowded up beside me. "Permission to do a little bit of petty vandalism?" she asked.

Inside the airlock, the Nesit shot me a smug look, then turned toward his ship. "If it'll wipe that shit-eating grin off that bastard's face, go for it."

Icky turned and swung one of her bigger, more muscular upper arms against the airlock control. She did it again and bent the faceplate enough that she could rip it partly open. Then she reached in with the fingers of her smaller, more delicate lower arms and fiddled. An alarm sounded, and the airlock door slid open again.

A mechanical voice intoned, "Airlock integrity compromised. Please evacuate now."

I spun on Icky, bracing myself for an explosive decompression. "What the hell did you do?"

She waved a hand. "Relax, boss. The airlock thinks the outer door is unsealed, so it wants to evacuate anyone inside it, then seal the inner door. Which"—she fiddled a bit more—"it won't."

Which left the Nesit standing and gaping at us.

I smiled at him. "Well, hello there. I guess you didn't hear me when I said I wanted to talk to you."

"What do you want? I haven't done anything wrong."

Torina smirked. "You know, in my experience, whenever anyone says *I haven't done anything wrong*, it almost always means that they have done something they shouldn't have."

I held up a hand to the Nesit. "I don't really care about your little auction. Or, I do, but I care more about one of the items in it. It was the one from Earth."

"I don't know what—"

"Okay, maybe I do care about your little auction," I said, striding toward the alien. "Maybe I care about that, and whatever cargo you have on your ship right now, and all of your ship's paperwork, and whether it's using the right transponder code, and—"

"Alright, fine," the Nesit said, raising his own hands. "One of the lots was from Earth. So what?"

"I'm from Earth."

"So are lots of humans."

Torina shook her head and sighed. "If this is your idea of cooperating, then I'd hate to see you being obstructive." Her expression suddenly turned poisonous. "No, wait. I *am* seeing you being obstructive, and it's pissing me off."

I gave Torina a sidelong glance. *Nice tactic.* I was buying her anger.

But it worked. The Nesit eventually coughed up the identity of the Earthly item he'd sold. He showed us an image of a small spherical device about the size of a big grapefruit, with six protruding antennae. I recognized it right away from when I was a kid enthralled with space. I'd thought I'd known everything there was to know about spaceflight, spacecraft, and space exploration.

Turns out I was wrong.

But it came in handy now. "That's Vanguard."

Torina and Icky both frowned at me. "Vanguard?" Torina asked. "Any relation?"

"Any relation—?" I smiled. "Ah. I get it. *Van*guard. Ha-ha. No, it's not. Still, we are both handsome devils, now that you mention it. So we have that in common."

Icky stared at the image. "It's a ball."

"With sticks coming out of it," Torina added.

The Nesit nodded. "I know, right? It's amazing what people will pay—" He stopped, seeing all of us glaring at him. "I would like to remain silent now."

"That *ball with sticks coming out of it* was only the second artificial object the United States ever put into space, and one of very first humans put into space, period. It's a historical artifact, at least as far as we humans are concerned, and it's supposed to still be in orbit around Earth. That was its enduring claim to fame, in fact, that it was the oldest object still in orbit."

I spun on the Nesit. "So imagine my surprise at seeing it being sold in some sleazy pop-up auction way the hell out here."

The alien shrank back from what, I realized, was genuine anger. Greedy assholes were plundering humanity's heritage like ravens collecting sparkly things, and it pissed me off. The Nesit could obviously tell.

"I'm just a middleman! All I know is that it's one of three highly prized relics originating from your homeworld!"

"What are the other two?"

"I don't know—seriously! All I know is that they're unavailable, owing to security issues."

"What the hell does that mean?"

The Nesit shrugged. "Whatever they are, they're both in orbit around your homeworld, and they're being watched closely by several interested parties. Parties that will blast one another to bits if any of them try to make their move to grab—whatever they are." He held up his hands again. "And that's *all* I know."

"Fine. Torina here is going to collect every bit of information you have about your sellers and your buyers." Torina nodded, but the Nesit looked panic-stricken.

"These are very... discrete people. If word gets out that I've said things I shouldn't—"

I slammed the Nesit back against the airlock's outer door. "You've already said things you shouldn't. Things like, that artifact is a priceless piece of your race's history, but we put a price on it anyway. Things like the fact there are scumbag aliens hanging around my homeworld, waiting to plunder even more of my past. So you are going to tell Torina everything you know, and you're going to do it now, or so help me, I will heave you out this airlock myself. Do—you—understand—me?"

I was surprised at how angry I was. I could tell that Torina and Icky were, too. I guess treating my history as a commodity was a button I never even knew I had.

Perry's voice rose behind me. "Van, we just—" He paused. "Oh. Did I come at a bad time again?"

"Torina, he's all yours. If he utters an *ah* or an *um* or anything that even remotely sounds like hesitation, feel free to take appropriate action."

"He means throw him out the airlock," Icky hissed in a stage whisper.

"Yeah, I got that," Torina said, stepping forward with her data slate poised. I stepped back, whereupon Perry pulled me aside.

"Did you find out anything about that ship carting off part of humanity's early spaceflight history?"

"Yes. Some stuff, anyway. And Netty's tracking them so she can try out Icky's technique for tracking ships when they twist. But that's not the priority right now."

"Oh? And what is?"

"A general call from Anvil Dark for all Peacemakers, for an emergency hostage retrieval."

"*That* sounds critical. Let's file all this stuff about Vanguard for future investigation, in which my close *personal* attention will be showered on anyone involved." I shot the Nesit a withering look, and it was clear he understood. "Now, who was taken hostage?"

"One of the Peacemaker Masters. They were taken right on Anvil Dark and carried away."

3

THE MISSING Master turned out to not be Groshenko, or any of the others that I'd come to at least recognize, if not actually know. The Master who'd been kidnapped was named Yewlo, a taciturn, blue-skinned, scaled race called the Gajur. I'd never actually met Master Yewlo and only recognized him from images, including a portrait hanging in the foyer to the Master's Table on Anvil Dark.

Lunzy briefed Torina, Perry, and me on the situation aboard her ship, the *Foregone Conclusion*, which was docked at Anvil Dark just three slots away from the *Fafnir*. "The surprising thing is that Yewlo was probably one of the least controversial Masters. Maybe *the* least controversial. The Gajur have a reputation for doing things slowly and deliberately, based only on the facts of a situation. Master Yewlo seemed to pretty much epitomize that. He was always fair and even-handed."

"That might have been the problem," Torina suggested.

I had to nod at that. "Somebody might have explicitly *not*

wanted fair and even-handed, and when that's what they got, they took action."

"How does snatching Master Yewlo help fix that?" Perry asked.

I shrugged back at him. "It doesn't. But it might not have been meant to. Somebody might have just wanted him out of the way."

"Which means that Yewlo might very well be dead now. So maybe this wasn't a kidnapping. Maybe it was actually an assassination," Torina offered.

"Have there been any demands? Ransom, or anything like that?" I asked Lunzy.

But she shook her head. "None. Not even a whisper of communications. All we know is that Yewlo's personal skiff went missing, then turned up drifting, on minimal power, about sixteen light-minutes away from here. It doesn't seem that anything in his personal quarters was disturbed or taken. Same for his office. His personal secretary saw Yewlo, still in his office working, when he clocked off work yesterday. And as far as we can tell, that's the last time anyone saw him."

"How the hell do you get someone out of the Peacemaker's home turf without being seen?" I asked.

Torina leaned forward. "I was wondering the same thing. Surely Anvil Dark is riddled with surveillance and security systems."

Lunzy nodded once, and brusquely. "It is."

"So did they record anything useful?"

"They didn't."

I waited for Lunzy to go on. When she didn't, I gave her a narrow-eyed stare. "Lunzy, what aren't you telling us here?"

She locked stares with me for a moment, then leaned back and sighed. "What I'm not telling you is how much of an uproar this has caused. Anvil Dark *is* lousy with security systems, and none of them picked up a damned thing. Zero. None. That's more than just embarrassing. It's a public relations catastrophe."

"And the Peacemakers are worried about their public image?"

It was Perry who answered. "Of course they are, Van. In case you haven't figured it out by now, it's not force of arms that lets the Peacemakers do what they do. You might have noticed that we're frequently outgunned. And sure, the Guild can amass a potent force if it needs to, but that still pales in comparison to the firepower of an actual military fleet."

"Perry's absolutely right. Believe it or not, a significant chunk of our authority is strictly of the moral variety. We're seen as one of the preeminent forces for—if not *good*, then at least *order*, in known space. Even the people who hate us tend to at least respect us because we have a reputation for being competent and fair. Well, mostly fair, anyway."

"So if word gets out that a Master was snatched right out of Anvil Dark, our reputation takes a hit. And our credibility takes a hit along with it," I replied.

"Exactly right. And with less credibility comes less respect, and it makes our jobs that much harder to do."

"So what's the official story?" Torina asked.

"That Master Yewlo has departed the station on urgent business of an extremely sensitive nature, and that any rumors of his being kidnapped are just that, malicious rumors."

As Lunzy spoke, it struck me we'd been sitting in the room with a hitherto unnoticed elephant, who refused to be ignored any longer.

"Um, Lunzy, is it possible that that's true? I mean, not necessarily the urgent and sensitive business stuff, but is it possible that Yewlo just, ah... left?" I asked.

"It would explain why the security systems didn't raise any alarms," Torina said.

Lunzy spread her hands in an elaborate shrug. "I have no idea. Nor does anyone else. And you're right, it might actually make more sense. Yewlo probably could have circumvented any security systems that might have gotten in the way. He is a Master, after all."

She sighed again. "Anyway, that's what we want you and any other available Peacemaker to find out. Discreetly, of course. The Guild has posted a reward of five hundred thousand bonds for information leading to Yewlo's return, and that's increased to two *million* bonds if it's accomplished within thirty standard day-cycles."

I whistled. Perry just muttered, "Wow."

"What's so special about thirty days?" I asked.

"The Guild believes that the chances of Yewlo's recovery become very, very low after thirty days," Lunzy replied.

"Or zero, if the good Master has already been spaced," Torina said.

I couldn't resist. "Thrown into space? That's cold."

Perry stared amber disapproval at me. "Too soon, Van."

But I just shrugged as I stood. "I'll read the room next time. Either way, I guess we're on our way to find out which."

THE LOGICAL PLACE TO start looking for evidence was at the site of Yewlo's abandoned ship. The trouble was that we were far from the only Peacemakers that thought so. When we did the minute twist to reach the coordinates, we found six other Peacemaker ships already there. All of them were hanging in space, apparently waiting.

I drummed my fingers on the armrest of the pilot's seat. "Am I missing something here? Are all of these other Peacemakers actually doing something? Is there something we should be looking at?"

Icky spoke up from her jury-rigged jump seat. "None of them are using active scans. They're all just kind of here, doing nothing." She shifted uncomfortably. "By the way, can we invest a bit of the reward if we get it, in a bigger chair? I'm a bit thick for the current model."

"It's on the upgrade list, Icky," I said. "Didn't know my engineer would have a furry dump truck, but I'll take it up with Human Resources."

"Dump Truck?" Icky looked back at herself. "If only I had wheels. Very efficient."

Torina raised a finger. "Icky has a point. Everyone here is just waiting for something."

I stared at the tactical overlay for a moment, then nodded. "Yeah. They are. Everyone's waiting for one of the other Peacemakers to do something that might suggest they found some evidence."

"Sounds kind of desperate," Icky said.

"In a way, it is. Notice that all of these other ships are *Dragonet*-class, without many upgrades. These are all either new-ish Peacemakers, or ones that have fallen on hard times and need a big infusion of cash," Netty said.

Torina suddenly laughed.

We all looked at her.

She shook her head. "Sorry, I was just thinking back to my graduation from advanced schooling. I had no end of fellow classmates sucking up to me, asking me to go out to dinner, etcetera, etcetera. This reminded me of that."

"Why?" I asked.

"It's like Netty said. They were desperate. They were all launching brand new careers, facing who knew what kind of future, and they knew I came from money. They were the ships, and I was the reward they were after."

"That actually sounds pretty pathetic," Icky said.

"Not to mention pretty damned insulting," Perry added.

"Oh, it was very much both," Torina replied, then turned to me. "Anyway, that amounted to nothing for any of them."

"Which is what you think this is," I said.

"Well, what do you think?"

I glanced again at the tactical overlay. Torina was probably right, but before I could say so, Perry spoke up.

"There's nothing on any scan to suggest there's anything here but a bunch of Peacemakers wasting their time. I smell bullshit, Van. This is a setup."

"You *smell* bullshit? Do you even have a sense of smell?" Icky asked, grinning.

"I have an olfactory sensor that uses mass-spectrometric discriminators to distinguish various airborne chemicals, so yeah, I smell bullshit."

I leaned back. "Perry's right. There's nothing here, and there never will be. This is a distraction."

"From what?" Icky asked.

I glanced back. "If I knew that, I'd be telling Netty to start plotting a course to go somewhere."

"We can always go back to chasing after that Vanguard probe of yours," Torina suggested.

"We can, but you know what? I have a better idea. I think we need to take a couple of days to mull over all the bits and pieces of evidence we've got and get a little R and R while we do it. So what say we head to your homeworld, Torina, and spend a couple days languishing there. I wouldn't mind spending some more time with Cataric, honing my Innsu skills, as well."

"Sure. Mind you, Icky and I might just sit around and drink wine while we ponder our leads. You do drink wine, don't you, Icky?" Torina asked, craning her neck around.

"Wine? What's that?"

We both stared, and Icky burst into laughter. "You know, for people in a job that just begs you to be suspicious by nature, you guys can be pretty gullible. Anyway, Torina, to answer your question, I don't drink wine, no."

"Oh."

Icky grinned. "I guzzle it instead."

I WATCHED INTENTLY, waiting for any sudden shifts in weight, any tensing of muscles that would telegraph an impending attack. It was like watching stone, waiting to see it crack. But I maintained my Focus and—

There.

A flicker, a tiny shift, utterly invisible if you weren't looking for it.

I dodged right and struck left, swinging the knife across my body and attacking from my off side. I caught a blur of movement coming at me but slammed my foot down, reversed my momentum, and drove myself backward again. Thanks to long practice, I knew exactly how much weight that knee, my defective one, could bear, and I applied *almost* that much force. The blur changed direction, the strike narrowly missing me. It gave me a half-heartbeat of opening, and I seized it, driving a strike back. My opponent dodged *into* the strike, using a free hand to deflect my blow. I knew a counterblow would follow and was ready for it, spinning and slashing out again as I leapt past my opponent to attack from an unexpected quarter.

It worked. My practice blade hit something solid. I let my momentum carry me another couple of steps—almost tangling my feet, which would have left me victoriously sprawled on my ass—and stopped.

Cataric, the Most Deliberate Learner and master of the Innsu academy on Torina's homeworld, beamed a broad grin at me and dropped to his knees in the fine, clean sand covering the training hall's floor. The gloriously intricate sand drawing he'd made had been obliterated by our feet, which was the point. As victor, I would now make my own marks in the sand, which would last until the next bout, when a new victor made theirs. It was meant to demonstrate the impermanence of things, including our victories and achievements. It was humility through art and combat, and my respect for the place grew with each passing moment.

I acknowledged Cataric's submission, and he stood. "Excellent, Van. You've mastered the Seventh Form beautifully. And I applaud your variation on Falling Star Style. Most innovative."

"Thank you. I wasn't sure how much latitude I had to make changes."

Cataric raised an eyebrow. "You speak as if there are rules to follow."

We padded to the side of the hall, where I retrieved a clean towel and wiped away sweat. "Aren't there? Isn't that the point of these forms and moves and styles?"

"If you had the opportunity to adjust one of the laser weapons on your ship, to make it more efficient and effective, would you do so?"

"I—well, yes, of course I would."

"Despite that clearly not being what the manufacturer had intended?"

I smiled. "Point taken."

"Everything I've been taught, and have been teaching you, is only the beginning, Van. It is all just a starting point on a journey that only you can complete."

I hung the sweaty towel back on the rack. "Again, point taken. Still, it would be nice to have a map to consult. Something to help plan ahead."

Cataric narrowed his eyes slightly. "Would you be up for another bout? I'm intrigued to see if you can integrate your mastery of the forms and styles we've covered so far, with the changes you've chosen to make in them. After all, it's one thing to change a part, like your laser, but if it has other effects on your ship, then it might not be an advantageous change at all, would it?"

"Excellent point, sir. And I'd be honored with another bout."

We moved to the middle of the hall. I had to take a moment to rake the sand around me, applying unique patterns and flourishes that came off the top of my head, to make it mine. All of it would be wiped out in a moment, but once again, that was the point. I kind of liked the symbolism. It was somehow... comforting.

I put the rake aside and assumed my stance, facing Cataric. We once again fell into our Focus, observing and waiting for our opponent to move—or choosing to move ourselves.

Seconds ticked by. Again, Cataric remained so wholly immobile, I found myself staring at his ribs as they rose and fell with glacial slowness.

And then my own thoughts cleared from inactivity to... a choice.

Strike without thought.

It was an instant, based on raw instinct, when Focus abruptly became action. I drove out a straight-armed strike, at the same time leaping into it and turning, ready to dodge the counterblow. But something cold touched the side of my neck.

Cataric stood with his knife against my flesh, a certain killing blow. I dropped to my knees, Cataric acknowledged my concession, then I stood again.

He smiled at me. "That was well fought, but in a sense, it was not fought at all. In fact, our conflict never truly occured. Do you understand?"

I frowned. "Well, I guess I was trying to vary Reed in the Wind by adding a strike—but that most certainly did occur, Master." I looked up and away, stretching my vision beyond where we stood. I knew there was a lesson, I just didn't know—

"I lost before we ever began."

He smiled, slightly, an invitation to continue.

Now it was my turn to smile, and this time, it was in open admiration. "Your offer. Of another bout. It came with… suggestions."

He put a hand on his chest. "Surely you're not suggesting I shaped your intentions merely by telling you what I wanted? Van, you're an excellent student. You wouldn't be that"—he searched for the word, then pierced me with a mirthful gaze—"malleable."

"That's a very kind word for—for me being taken by such obvious bait," I said, sighing.

Cataric slapped my shoulder with affection. "I shaped your thinking. I said I wanted to see your innovations, so you tried to show me one. Your thoughts were, therefore, a tiny fraction of an instant *behind* your movements, instead of ahead of them, where they always should be."

So he'd defeated me before the battle had even started, and now—

I put my hands on my hips and grinned. "They want us to think we've lost."

"I assume you're no longer talking about me. A problem at work?"

"Yes. But not anymore. Thanks to you, Most Deliberate Learner, I have a new angle, and a clear path for a problem that is… not of this kind, and yet, it is. Thank you again. I'm humbled and energized."

"Innsu is more than just a martial arts style, Van, but you know that. It's science and logic and life. You may find it applies to more than merely thrashing about in the sand now and then."

I nodded, looking at the practice knife I held. It led me to another idea.

"So if Innsu is actually a way of thinking, an approach to life, then it doesn't only have to be fought with knives like this one, does it?"

"Not at all. The knife is customary, but it's really just a tool of convenience. Why?"

"Because I'm thinking of doing some more innovating. And it starts with this blade."

I'D LOST track of time. By the time I'd finished up my final bout of the day with Cataric—which I'd won, meaning I'd also had to take time to rake my particular shapes and imprints into the sand—it was getting dark. I enjoyed the cool dusk air on the short walk back to Torina's family estate, where I found her and Icky sprawled lazily on a veranda. It looked across the rolling hills and fields that had been rehabilitated by the space hippies, the scene an absolute embodiment of harmonious, pastoral bliss in the fading light.

Torina blinked up at me, her expression a little dreamy from the combined effects of the peaceful setting, the warm, slightly muggy evening air, and a glass or five of cracklefruit wine. It was a local concoction, made from the fruit of the same name, an apple-like thing that split and dripped sweet fluid as it ripened, giving its name. The golden wine had a taste like tart apple pie and a kick like a blast of fusion exhaust in the face.

"I see you two have been busy," I said, pouring a glass for myself.

Icky lazily held up an empty bottle. "Hey, this stuff doesn't drink itself."

Torina sat up. "You've got that look."

I glanced at her. "That look?"

"Yes. That look. The one you get when you have an idea."

"I didn't realize I had a *look*."

"I didn't realize he had ideas," Icky said, grinning. I stuck out my tongue at her.

She clicked her tongue. "There are some races that would consider a gesture like that deeply insulting, worthy of a blood feud."

"Is yours one of them?"

"Oh, no, not at all. See?" She stuck out her own tongue, which looked both funny and slightly frightening on her simian face. "I was saying, some races don't like it."

"I'll keep that in mind." I sipped at the wine, savoring its sharp flavor. "Anyway, yes, Torina, I've had an idea. I think it's time to take another trip. I've got a hunch."

"Oh? And what *hunch* is that?"

"Yeah, where're we going, boss?" Icky said, giving her empty bottle a mournful look, then sighing and standing.

I smiled as she wobbled on her feet. "Right now, nowhere, except to bed. Tomorrow, though, we're going to answer a question—where, exactly, does a Guild Master come from? Well, we're going to find out."

Icky sighed and looked at the bottle again. "It was nice while it lasted."

But I grabbed a full one, still sealed, and hefted it.

"Tell you what. We'll bring this one with us and drink it on the way. I know you're not supposed to drink and drive, but hey, we've got an AI who can *fly*."

4

I STARED at the time displayed on the *Fafnir*'s panel, curling my lip.

"Netty, is that time right?"

"In comparison to what?"

"Uh—in comparison to real time?"

"Now, that's an interesting question. What defines the standard for *real time*—?"

"Netty, focus."

"I keep the *Fafnir*'s chronometer synchronized to standard time beacons and run regular error-checking routines. So, yes, that time is right."

"Then my sense of time is off due to being downplanet. That, or the cracklefruit wine. Regardless, where are we with the depot?" I asked.

"We've received clearance from the fueling depot to do our final approach," Netty went on.

I acknowledged and let her handle the flying. We were going to dock and refuel the *Fafnir* at a depot—essentially an orbiting gas station—in the outer part of the Tau Ceti system. It was, I thought, not too different from the gas stations set up for truckers back on Earth, on the outskirts of cities, so they didn't have to get embroiled in downtown traffic just to gas up. I watched as Netty deftly slid us into a berth, nosing the *Fafnir* into a holding port that would keep her relative to the depot. She then worked out our refueling scheme with the depot's AI, mechanical arms smoothly rotating into place, locking in magnetic conduits carrying anti-matter, and more conventional ones pumping regular deuterium for fusion fuel.

"Well, well, look at that," Perry said, hopping onto the armrest of the copilot's seat Torina had just vacated. I'd unstrapped too and was about to make my way back to the head, but I stopped and followed Perry's gaze.

A Nesit ship occupied a berth three slots away. It was exchanging cargo with the ship next to it, a nondescript workboat displaying no name, just a registration number.

"Well, that looks shady as hell," I said.

"It does. Seems like the Nesit are rather busy being sketchy," Perry said.

Torina, who'd stopped at the rear of the cockpit when Perry spoke up, peered back out the canopy at the Nesit ship. "You know, there might be a big underground operation going on that we could consider disrupting."

Icky, still in her seat and watching as the fuel levels rose on her engineering panel, nodded. "Especially since they're considerate enough to keep doing shady things right where we can see them."

I'd started to stand but sat back down.

"Netty, we're still doing detailed, passive scans of every ship that comes in range of us, right?"

"I scanned for any emissions or signatures that might suggest stolen identities on chips, yes. That's what you wanted. Did you want to change that?"

"No, I don't. Having said that, we haven't actually detected anything unusual for quite some time, have we?"

"Depends on how you define *unusual*, but in terms of stolen identities, no."

"But we *do* keep running across suspicious Nesit."

I had everyone's attention now. Torina leaned back into the cockpit.

"There's that look again. What are you thinking, Van?"

"I think we're being fooled. Played for fools, even."

"Fooled? How?" Icky asked.

"By having the stuff we are looking for, like stolen identity chips, directed away from us, and us from them, like water flowing around a rock. And the rock in question is the Nesit."

"You think that someone is arranging for us to keep running into Nesit trading in stolen artifacts and the like, to keep us away from other things they don't want us to chase?" Perry said.

"Right. So that means we're probably meant to get involved with that Nesit, get sucked into a whole morass of legalities, charges, penalties, paperwork—"

"So what do you want to do, Van?" Torina asked.

"Well, first we finish gassing up. And then, we fly."

As we continued our journey to Master Yewlo's homeworld, it struck me that I might be getting a little paranoid. Some conspiracy involving tracking our movements and ensuring that there'd be Nesit evident along the way—it felt like a stretch the more I chewed on it. But I recalled some of the hacking jobs I'd been involved in back on Earth, some of which involved huge amounts of misdirection, deception, and quiet, low-key, behind-the-scenes actions. When I did, the idea of us being misdirected didn't seem quite so farfetched.

If anything, it was plausible, and for one simple reason: there was money involved.

We arrived at Yewlo's former home, Gajur Prime, one of two habitable planets in the Teegarden's Star system. The other was Falaax, a rustic planet noted across known space for its artistry, proving that two *very* different cultures could rise and grow in the same system—as long as they didn't share the same planet.

As we approached Gajur Prime, it quickly became clear that this was not a very nice planet at all. The side lit by Teegarden's Star glowed a dull brownish-grey, apparently the result of extreme atmospheric pollution. Where there were gaps in the fetid cloud cover on the dark side, sprawling patches of light suggested cities, big ones, and everywhere. In other words, Master Yewlo's homeworld was a polluted, overpopulated mess, heaving with people and the detritus of a planet that was tired. Used up. Maybe on the verge of that long slide into senescence, where the world doesn't die with a bang but a sigh.

As we entered orbit, I found myself brooding over the noxious cloud top below, pale brown with nitrogen compounds. "Can't help but wonder if this is what Earth's going to look like in a few hundred more years."

Perry rotated his head toward me. "A few hundred?"

"Sooner?"

"Well, every advanced civilization goes through a couple of filters. The first one is nuclear power. If they don't wipe themselves out that way, then it's polluting their planetary environment, mainly because of all of the energy they can generate. And if they survive *that*, well, then they're golden."

"So you're saying Earth is somewhere in the middle of step two."

"Firmly, I'd say."

I looked back down at the planet below and wondered if these people would emerge into that golden age Perry mentioned. But my thoughts quickly focused. That wasn't the important question. I had one issue to investigate—what did growing up here mean for Yewlo? What had it done to him? For him?

How had it affected the way they viewed the world? What his family was like, and what sort of friends, and more importantly enemies, he'd made along the way.

In short—what kind of person did the smog and crowds create, and how did that person escape the murk to become a Master?

As we settled into orbit, I reached for the comm to contact traffic control and get put through to some information directory, somewhere we could begin to track down Master Yewlo's family. My fingers hadn't quite reached the controls when Netty suddenly spoke, at the same time a warning alarm sounded.

"Van, we're tracking an incoming missile, launched from a platform ahead of us and in a lower orbit."

"What? They're *shooting* at us?"

"They are. One missile only."

"Must be a mistake," Torina suggested.

But Netty didn't think so. "We were pretty deliberately lit up by a fire-control scanner. Unless we're talking rogue crew or a malfunctioning AI, I'd say it's clearly intentional."

"So they must have us confused with someone else—" Icky started, but Perry cut her off.

"Might I remind you all that there is an incoming missile?"

I nodded. "Good point. Netty, weapons-free on the point-defense systems. Torina, can you stand by to do your magic laser show?"

"Already on it," she replied.

The missile closed fast. Torina finally decided against shooting at it with the *Fafnir*'s main armament, since the relative movement of our ship, the missile, and the platform meant any miss was going to come close to hitting the latter. Instead, the point-defense batteries made short work of it, blasting it to orbital scrap.

"Well, that was fun," Icky said.

"Bit of a stretch to call it fun, but sure," I said, finally activating the comm. I broadcasted our Peacemaker credentials, and an incoming channel lit up.

"You're a Peacemaker. Big deal. I don't care. You're just human scum. Get away from this planet and this sector. *Now*."

Torina leaned back. "Either someone has a real problem with authority figures, or they've been scarred by a run-in with the law."

"There is another possibility. Maybe they're just assholes," Perry suggested.

"Was Master Yewlo an asshole?" I asked.

But Perry shrugged. "You know as much about the good Master as I do."

"I thought we were told the Gajur were fair and even-handed and all that," Icky said.

"No, we were told that Master Yewlo was fair and even-handed. And maybe Mister Missile out there is the lone wolf, the wacko xenophobe that's wholly unlike his people." I rubbed my chin and considered the tactical overlay. "Netty, if we descend over one of the poles, we'll be farther away from any of these orbital platforms, right? At least, once that one there"—I touched an icon on the overlay—"moves further along in its orbit, right?"

"That's correct. That's going to use more fuel, but it's actually a good idea otherwise."

I grinned. "I'm really blooming into my role as a navigator. Gonna need some ribbons or medals."

"You are. Soon, we'll have you doing twist calculations by hand," Perry said.

"Really?"

"No, not really. You'd have to constantly solve thousands of equations for thousands of changing variables, then translate those results into fractional changes in the twist drive's harmonics. And you'd have to do it thousands of times a second."

"Then I respectfully yield to Netty."

"Superb choice, boss. You hear that, bird? I'm his *favorite*."

We made an uneventful descent from orbit over the north pole of Gajur Prime, our fiery reentry sputtering out just about the time we touched the first cloud tops. Netty flashed up a warning that we were only five to seven reentry cycles away from having to replace the *Fafnir*'s ablative shielding. I made a mental note of it, and also to shop around for a good price. There was lots of competition to do it, it being the spaceship equivalent of changing the oil in your car or putting on winter tires.

We continued plunging toward the planet's north pole. Perry gave one of his rather eerie little mechanical laughs. "Next stop, Santa's workshop!"

Icky spoke up from behind me. "Who's workshop? Wait, I thought we were going to track down the family of Yewlo. Who's this Santa?"

I glanced at Perry. "I choose Unfamiliar References to the Earthly Zeitgeist for five hundred, Alex."

Perry glanced back at Icky. "Sorry, Van's right. Santa's a prominent cultural figure on his home planet, a friendly, jolly figure who travels to every dwelling on the planet in one evening to reward young humans who have been good throughout the year with gifts."

"Sounds kind of judgmental, actually," Icky replied.

"Not to mention supernatural," Torina put in.

I nodded. "Some of both, actually. Anyway, much as I'd love to keep discussing the only sanctioned serial home invader of my home planet, we did come here for a reason. Perry, have you had any luck—"

"Yes."

"—tracking down Master Yewlo's—" I did a double-take. "His family? Really?"

"I did. Interestingly, it took a fair bit of digging and access to a database or two that isn't generally available to the public."

"You hacked them."

"*Mea culpa*, and stop sounding so disapproving, Hacker Boy. Anyway, his family lives in Equatorial Urban District Forty-Two. I've put an icon on the overlay."

"Equatorial Urban District Forty-Two. Doesn't that just give you a warm fuzzy," I said.

Torina nodded. "They need to work on their tourism marketing, yes. Beats the only restaurant I found referenced near their building. Charming little place called *Almost Good*."

"Make reservations for later then. I'm sure it's busy."

Perry coughed a mechanical laugh as Netty threw us into a hard banking maneuver to the south, punching through banks of miserably drab clouds. Rain and occasional bouts of hail rattled across the *Fafnir*'s canopy. We'd tried, without much success, to get official descent clearance from Gajur Prime traffic control, who alternated between hostile and disinterested, apparently depending on who we were talking to. We eventually just descended anyway until we were flying through airspace that was *technically* controlled but without any actual clearance. We had to rely on the scanners to ensure we maintained separation from other traffic, of which there was a lot. But that didn't seem to matter.

"This is the most slipshod control system I've ever seen," Netty said as we slalomed like a downhill skier around other ships, ranging from little workboats to big bulk carriers. But the space-going traffic was quickly eclipsed by the atmospheric sort as we approached the solid belt of cities that girdled the planet around its equator. These airborne hazards came in nearly every flavor, from high-performance craft zipping about, to ponderous airships plying their stately way through the clouds.

At one point, we emerged from a wall of mist to see soaring towers looming against the pale expanse of the next rank of clouds. The open space between us and it seemed almost alive with airborne craft wheeling and whirling and zooming around in a furious dance that bordered on chaos. I'd once gone hiking in Vermont and had quickly attracted a cloud of bugs that swarmed around my head. It was like that, except these weren't little insects, they were flying machines weighing thousands of kilograms hurtling about with no apparent rhyme or reason. I let Netty do the flying, given that she could react faster than any of us mere biologicals.

After a few spicy minutes of dodging collisions, we reached our destination, a slender spire hundreds of stories tall. It was only one of a multitude sprawling both east and west, the furthest fading from view in a driving, misty rain. It reminded me of those famous opening scenes from the movie *Bladerunner*, depicting a futuristic, cyberpunk-ish Los Angeles, except even grimmer and grittier, and with fewer product placements.

"No neon," I muttered.

"Too expensive for these people. This is real poverty," Torina observed, her eyes never leaving the cheerless urban sprawl.

We finally settled onto an expansive platform perched on the very pinnacle of our destination tower and powered down the ship. As we did, I couldn't help noticing some sketchy-looking figures pausing in loading or unloading other aircraft and giving us some ominous looks.

"Eyes open, kids. I don't like the attention we've garnered," I said.

"Must be my plumage. It's tough to be this—"

"If you say beautiful, I'm spray painting your feathers olive green."

Perry paused, then continued. "The word I chose was dignified."

"Nice save. You can stay shiny black."

He flicked a wing at me as we disembarked, our senses on high alert. We decided that we'd all make the trek down the tower to visit Yewlo's family, reasoning that Netty was more than capable of looking after herself. She kept the point-defense batteries powered up and obviously swiveling around, as though looking for targets. Interstellar law allowed her to use lethal force to protect the *Fafnir* if requisite warnings weren't heeded, but I much preferred she didn't start spewing rapid-fire shots around the city. Hopefully, simple intimidation would be enough.

"Everybody remember where we parked," I said as we sliced into the relentless deluge of rain. Torina and I were fully suited up, looking sleek and menacing in our b-suits and helmets, but we didn't have a set for Icky yet. She had to be satisfied with some body armor, my duster coat, and the fact that she outweighed every alien in sight by at least fifty percent. We were watched intently as we strolled toward the banks of elevators, but no one tried to bother us. In addition to her size, Icky had a natural gift for glaring, an ability that I encouraged her to use.

The elevator ride down eighty-one stories to the three hundred and eighth floor was an adventure unto itself. The car was dimly lit, with one light flickering inconstantly. Corrosion and graffiti stained the walls, and a puddle of something too viscous to be water pooled the floor. The whole contraption shook and rattled as it descended.

"Charming, and by that I mean a death trap," I said.

"Please. No talking." Torina closed her eyes tightly, and I reached out to take her hand.

"We're okay, it's… is that elevator music?" I asked as a tinny speaker above began playing insipid yet catchy alien music. Naturally, it was *easy listening*, proving that some things, like rednecks, hippies, elevator music, and bureaucracy—were truly universal.

"This way," Perry said, flying a few meters down the corridor.

I was smacked by more *Bladerunner* vibes, with dripping walls, grimy doorways, and a pervasive aura of despair. We had to step over a Gajur sprawled on the floor and snoring, then scrub filth off of a sign posted at a cross-corridor to see which way we had to go.

Perry finally stopped in front of a door that looked identical to every other one we'd passed.

"This is it?" I asked.

Perry hopped a few centimeters to get out from under a steady drip from above. "So it would seem."

"Can you guys smell anything with those helmets on?" Icky asked.

Both Torina and I shook our heads.

Icky scowled. "Count yourselves lucky then."

"So this is where a Peacemaker Guild Master comes from?" Torina asked.

I shrugged and moved to the door. "Local boy makes good, I guess." I touched a pad beside the door, sounding a sad, truncated chime. When the door opened, I knew many things, simply from the scene that unfurled before me.

Poverty has a weight to it, and it was crushing the people inside that apartment. Yewlo's family were poor to the point of being destitute. Perry reported that Yewlo's father, despite his age, still slogged away in the metallic hell of a metal foundry, while the other adults present all held down menial jobs or didn't do much of anything at all. And there seemed to be an awful lot of adults for what was supposedly a single-family dwelling. I wasn't sure who they all were, assuming they were probably siblings and cousins and other extended-family members. There were a few kids, too, who just peered at us around corners and vanished if we actually made eye contact with them. In seconds, as Yewlo's dad stood looking at us with dull suspicion, I counted no less than twenty people.

"Sir, I'm Peacemaker Van—"

"Don't care."

That brought me up short, although it wasn't unexpected. I tried a new tack. "I'll get right to the point. Master Yewlo is missing, and we're trying to find him. He's a person of some importance and—"

Yewlo's father stood forward, close enough to let me get a whiff of the metallic tang that clung to him. He flicked a glance over his shoulder, then scratched idly at what passed for his chest. Flakes of debris fell away with each *skritching* sound, and I schooled my features into something that passed—I hoped—for pleasant, non-threatening interest.

"You got the wrong place," he said.

Another person—Yewlo's mother, I was betting—looked away as I tried to make eye contact.

I did the math, realized our chances were nil, and stepped back, making a small bow. "My sincere apologies. If I do see your son, do you have any message?"

As his father slammed the door, he growled, "Yeah. Tell him don't bother coming back."

"And I thought I had family problems," I said. "That was more awkward than the shittiest Thanksgiving dinner ever."

"What's Thanksgiving?" Torina asked as we started back to the elevators.

"A holiday where people have too much to drink and tell their family what they *really* think of them."

Torina coughed with laughter. "Like the—oh, we call it the *Bright Fight*."

"The what?"

"It's actually the Feast of Stars, but we just call it the Bright Fight. Everyone cooks too much, drinks too much, and settles scores with family members they only see once or twice a year."

I was stunned into silence, shaking my head in amazement. "Yet another identical cultural trait we share. I'm starting to think our cultures originated from the same playbook."

"Sure sounds like it. There's nothing like the Bright Fight for truly cringeworthy family drama. It's my favorite night of the year," Torina admitted.

"I saw thirty-one people arrested on Spindrift during a Bright Fight meal. They did almost twenty thousand bonds worth of damage to the place after someone told an auntie her soup was bland," Perry enthused. "A truly magnificent confirmation of my superiority as an AI."

I gave him a sidelong glance. "Not sure I can argue with that logic. Solid. Still, feels like we wasted a trip here."

"It might not have been a breakthrough, Van, but we did learn something useful," Torina said as we threaded our way past the sleeping Gajur again.

"Oh? And what was that?"

She stopped. "Yewlo has no connection with his family. Like, none whatsoever."

"Hmm. Okay, that's a point. He didn't just leave them behind." I glanced back the way we'd just come and thought about his extended family members who apparently didn't even know who Yewlo was. "He erased them from his past entirely."

Torina didn't answer. Instead, she stared at something over my shoulder, behind me. Her hand creeped toward her sidearm.

I turned around.

Two Gajur had just stepped off the nearest elevator, sporting weapons—one a truncheon made out of what looked like an old piston, the other a rusty axe.

"Van, look the other way," Perry said. Sure enough, two more Gajur with nasty-looking weapons stepped around the corner and started toward us.

We were hemmed in between them, stuck with nowhere to go.

I CONSIDERED DRAWING The Drop but immediately decided against it. We'd seen people unexpectedly emerge from apartments and step into the corridor, and I didn't want to risk catching someone with a stray shot.

"No guns, folks," I said, drawing the Moonblade instead.

Because of how we happened to be standing, Icky and I squared off against the first two, who'd exited the elevator, while Perry and

Torina pointed themselves the other way. I noticed that none of our assailants had firearms, either. After a mutual moment of belligerent silence while we sized each other up, I opened my mouth to order them to stand down and get out of our way.

I'd only just drawn breath when they charged, bellowing profanities and a colorful description or two of what anatomically terrifying things they meant to do to us. A few seconds after that, battle was joined.

The corridor was too narrow to get fancy, but fortunately, my recent bouts of Innsu with Cataric came in handy. I dodged into my opponent's truncheon swing, and the haft of the weapon slammed against my shoulder. I felt the impact, which probably would have pulverized bone if I hadn't been wearing my b-suit. Instead, I winced at a brief, dull flash of pain but kept going, driving the Moonsword in a whistling upward stab. I really didn't want to kill our attackers if we could avoid it, but they might not leave us much choice. The Moonsword slid across the inside of my foe's bicep, provoking a yelp and another swing from the club. I dodged back, and it clanged against the wall.

Beside me, Icky drove herself forward and met the charging Gajur with the axe in mid step. She had the advantage of four arms, so she stopped his axe-hand with one of her bigger upper limbs, grappled him with the two smaller ones, then swung something that cracked against his head with a glorious thump. I caught a glimpse of crystal and realized Icky wielded an empty cracklefruit wine bottle. But I didn't have time to dwell on it. I stepped to absorb my own opponent's next attack, and took a solid hit to my helmet. It knocked my head sideways and wrenched a muscle in my neck. I replied with another stab that this time creased the

Gajur's side. Blackish blood erupted, adding more gooey stains to the walls.

The Gajur stumbled back, shouted something, then broke and ran. Icky's opponent had fallen to his hands and knees, moaning and vomiting onto the floor. Concussion, I thought, turning to see how Torina and Perry were doing. One of Perry's wings hung limp, and Torina had taken a cut on her right forearm that had almost penetrated her b-suit. But, just as on our side of the fracas, one of their opponents was down, and the other was beating a hasty retreat.

"Everyone okay? Perry, that wing looks bad."

He tried to lift it, servos whining faintly. It barely moved. "Nothing a bit of time on the hoist can't fix."

Torina checked her arm, then scowled at our fallen attackers. "What the hell was that about?"

"I guess they don't like Peacemakers," I suggested.

But Perry shook his head. "No. There's any number of criminal things going on all around us right now. I mean, there's an obvious drug deal unfolding in that left-hand side corridor. I suspect this was just meant to keep us busy."

I glared down at the Gajur Icky had dropped. "Yeah, well, I've got no interest in whatever sordid little schemes these assholes are peddling." I said it especially loudly, so my b-suit's speaker would carry it through the corridors and apartments around us. Then we moved to the elevator and started back up to the landing pad on the tower's roof.

Once again surrounded by the scratchy tones of the elevator music, I glanced at Icky. "A wine bottle? Really?"

She shrugged. "Torina mentioned it was made of ultra-high

impact stuff. It's got a good heft to it for its size and weight—" She shrugged again. "Never let a bottle of wine go to waste, full *or* empty."

"I HAVE to admit that this is not a place I'm in a hurry to come back to," Torina said as we lifted from the roof and started climbing back to orbit. The towering spires of Equatorial Urban District Forty-Two almost immediately vanished into the endless rain and shifting mists.

"Maybe Equatorial Urban District Forty-One is a lot nicer. You never know," I said.

We flew on in silence for a few minutes, choosing a departure path that would take us to orbit, and then break it, as fast as possible. On top of everything else, I really didn't want to get into an altercation with some bored and belligerent traffic controller or planetary defense officer with his finger on the firing button. As we climbed, Perry went to the back, so Waldo and Icky could help him repair his damaged wing.

I looked at Torina. "So why do you think Yewlo divorced himself so thoroughly from his family?"

She glanced back at me with a mildly surprised look. "Because he's ashamed of them?"

"You think that's it? Doesn't say much about him, does it?"

"No, it actually makes him as big an asshole as anyone else we've met, and maybe even bigger. He had the financial means to take his family out of that shithole, or at least make it far easier for them to live within it. Instead, he just left them behind without a backward glance."

I pulled at my lip in thought. "Could his shame about his upbringing be behind why he's missing?"

"You're thinking he was afraid he was going to be found out? Then what?"

"I—don't know. What impact would his, um, humble upbringing back there have on his reputation?"

"Honestly, not much. At least, I don't think so. If anything, you'd think he'd be proud at having risen above his past."

I nodded along as Torina spoke. "Okay, so maybe shame isn't really his motivator. But the kind of guy that would actually erase his family from his own existence has what I'd call a weak character. And that can open him to even more powerful motivators."

"Like greed," Perry called from the back.

"The bird has good ears," Torina said.

"Damn right I do," Perry replied.

I smiled, rubbing my neck where it still ached from the sudden wrench of the truncheon impact. We passed through the cloud tops into a clear day, the sky ahead of us starting to purple as we gained altitude.

"The bird also speaks wisely," I said. "Shame might be a powerful incentive, but greed? Yeah, greed is *way* more powerful."

5

We returned to Anvil Dark without fanfare—or any further insight into Master Yewlo's disappearance. But we weren't alone in that.

"This just gets more embarrassing with every day that passes," Lunzy said over the comm. She was aboard the *Foregone Conclusion*, outbound from Anvil Dark, while we were just in the process of docking. "We're not any closer to finding out where Yewlo has gone, despite having half the Guild trying to find him."

"Has word got out to the general public that he's missing, yet?" I asked.

"No, but it's only a matter of time. Our cover story about him being on special assignment won't hold up forever."

"Why don't you just say that he died on that special assignment? Then no one would have any further reason to wonder why he's missing, right?" Icky asked.

"We've considered that. And it's a great plan, right up to the point when he reappears. Then, not only do we have to explain how we got it wrong, but it's also going to smack of a cover-up," Lunzy replied.

"Right, but if he doesn't reappear, at what point do you accept that he's not coming back—either because he won't, or he can't," Torina persisted.

"No idea. But until then, it remains an active and *secret* case."

"We found his family. There were almost two dozen people in a squalid tower apartment, and to say they hate him is an understatement. Their feelings for Yewlo are—actually, scratch that. They don't have any consistent feelings for him. He doesn't exist, at least not in any real way. He abandoned them, and they've passed into the realm of numbness, sprinkled with occasional flickers of disgust."

"I had no idea he came from such, ah, humble beginnings."

"I don't think anyone did. And I think that's the point," I replied.

We signed off, docked at Anvil Dark, then—

Then, I sank back in my seat. "Is it just me, or are we now officially out of leads?"

Perry lifted his head. He'd been fiddling with his wing servo, making him look like a bird preening itself. "I'd say we're officially out of leads regarding Yewlo."

"But?"

"But, we've still got our stolen identity case and your rock."

I frowned at that. "My rock? What the hell are you talking about, Perry?"

"Your rock. Remember, the stream flowing around it, and all that?"

"Oh. Right. The Nesit, who we think are trying to distract us." I sat up, a little more enthusiastic. "That's a good point. Netty. You got detailed scans on those Nesit ships we encountered, right?"

"I could tell you the ratio of uranium to lead in each one of their individual hull plates, to two decimal places. Which is actually interesting, because you could probably track each one back to its manufacturer that way."

"I'll take that as a yes." I hesitated. "Although, is that uranium-lead thing useful to us?"

"Probably not. You said to gather detailed info, and I did. It is interesting, though."

"I suppose."

"I'm a spaceship, Van. I have to take my fun where I can find it."

I held up a hand. "You're also a nerd. How about this-- there any way of tracking the Nesit ship, or ships, that have been hanging around so obviously near us?"

"Well, by using Icky's space-time compression idea, I have a pretty good idea where that last one we encountered at the refueling depot went. And that was only just over two days ago."

I sat up a little more. "Oh? Where?"

"Wolf 424."

"Ah, our old friend where the mining never stops," I replied. We'd been there a couple of times, most recently to rescue the Nesit, Tand, from his chip-based slavery aboard a big ore processing barge. At least, we'd thought at the time it had been Tand, but it apparently hadn't. That made picking up the trail at Wolf 424 again almost poetic.

I looked around the *Fafnir*'s cockpit. "Okay, let's do the fastest turnaround we can here. If you've got business to do on Anvil

Dark, do it. Netty, you get us refueled and ready to fly in, say, two hours?"

"Copy that, boss. Two hours."

As the others started making their way to exit the ship, I had to stop and face another of the stunning moments of unreality.

I was giving orders aboard a spaceship to a mix of humans, aliens, and artificially intelligent mechanical constructs, and they were happy to carry them out.

How the hell did I *get* here?

The moment didn't last. I knew one thing to be true, no matter how surreal the realization.

I was meant to be in space.

WE ARRIVED in Wolf 424 at the far edge of the Kuiper Belt, then remained in silent-running mode, taking some time to watch what was going on. The system was busy with an array of automated craft of all sizes, frantically chewing up asteroids and planetary fragments to produce commodities of significant value. It was all very purposeful—

It was also a dead end, unless something interesting lurked among the spiraling rocks and drive plumes of the robotic fleet.

"Well, if we can't pick up the trail here, then I'd say we're dead in the water," I watched the tactical overlay fill with data as Netty collected it. I'd already resigned myself to returning to Anvil Dark and looking for more jobs to fill up our time and bank account. It wouldn't hurt for me to take a week or two off Peacemaking and put in an appearance on Earth, either. My extended vacation excuse was wearing thin, and I did have clients back on *terra firma* with whom I still had open contracts—

"Van? Netty and I have been comparing transponder signatures, traffic control data, and the like, and we might have found something interesting," Perry said.

"What's that?"

"It might be nothing."

"Okay, so what is it?"

"I just don't want everyone to get their hopes up—"

"Perry!"

"Okay. There are ninety-two distinct commercial interests that hold a total of four hundred and sixteen mining licenses in this system."

"So?"

"So, only one of them is registered as a corporation on Nesit, and it holds a single mining license."

Torina sniffed. "That doesn't seem suspicious at all, does it?"

"Where is it?" I asked.

Netty highlighted a point about a four hour flight away if we just flew as normal. If we wanted to be stealthy about it, she'd plot an alternate path that took advantage of other orbiting bodies to conceal much of our way. That would take us at least fourteen hours—longer if we wanted to look truly unremarkable and plod the whole way.

I wasn't keen on spending the better part of another day just flying, but this remained our only half-assed solid lead. So I leaned back in the seat and sighed. "Unless anyone's in a hurry, we've got some time to kill."

Icky leaned forward. "More wine?"

"If we're going to end up going into some horrible, dangerous situation, I'd rather do it sober, thanks."

Icky's expression turned decidedly mischievous.

"Why?"

I just smiled back at her. I have to admit, she did have a bit of a point in there somewhere, though.

WE'D MANAGED to get the *Fafnir* to within a few hundred klicks of the Nesit mining operation and took up station behind a chunk of rock the size of a small mountain. The problem was that we couldn't gather any more direct imagery or scanner inputs without moving the ship out of the rock's shadow and risking exposure. Perry came up with the answer, one that he'd occasionally used while working with Gramps.

He got out.

It was sometimes easy to forget that Perry was a machine, so exposure to hard vacuum, searing cold, and hard radiation didn't bother him. He had no active scanners to speak of, of course—nothing that was meaningful over more than a few hundred meters range at most, anyway. But he did a pretty good job as a passive sensor, gathering data and images while hanging in plain view of the Nesit operation. He was simply too small, his emissions too weak, to even tickle a full-blown spaceship scanner.

Over the next couple of hours, he hung there, relaying data back to the *Fafnir* and watching the Nesit and their supposed mining concern.

"That's the third ship that's showed up, transferred some cargo, then zipped away, all in the past one hundred and two minutes," he said as another of the ubiquitous and nondescript workboats accelerated away from the object of our interest, a small orbital station fastened to another asteroid by a rickety-looking gantry of beams and cables. A Nesit ship, the one we'd encountered just a few days ago, or one just like it, had been docked to it.

"And I suspect none of that cargo has been ore or mining equipment," Torina said.

"In crates that small? Nope, I'd say that's a good bet."

I nodded. "You've gotta hand it to them. So industrious."

"With other people's things," Icky pointed out.

"There is that. Okay, so what's that Nesit doing now? Fueling? That looks like a fueling coupler."

"I think so. He's probably met all the customers he's intended to and is topping up before getting underway again," Perry said.

"Okay, so that means we need to do whatever we're going to do, and soon." I glanced around the cockpit. We'd been mulling over various ideas but hadn't landed on anything yet. We no longer had the luxury of *mulling*, though, and had to start with the *doing*.

"Head straight in? Him being hooked up to that fueling coupling is going to buy us some time," Torina suggested.

And her suggestion was a good one. If he was just taking on regular deuterium to fuel his fusion reactor and main drive, he could literally just do a pump-and-dash and zoom away. He'd lose some fuel and probably have some repairs to do, but it meant he could bolt as soon as we showed ourselves. But Perry's imagery showed a much bigger, more massive fuel coupling, of the type used to transfer anti-deuterium, deuterium's evil, anti-matter twin, which was used to power the twist drive. That sort of refueling operation had to be shut down in a very particular way to avoid turning you, your ship, and everyone in the vicinity into elementary particles.

"Van, I think I've got a stolen person here," Perry said with some urgency.

"A chip?"

"Yeah. It's a weak signal but a characteristic one. I've just detected it, and only because I was specifically looking for it. It came online when whoever's over there cycled the airlock that seems to connect the station with the asteroid it's attached to."

"Another robot stuck with some mindless, tedious chore? That shit is just too sad," Torina said, shaking her head.

"Actually, it's even worse than that. I think this poor bastard is tied *into* that airlock specifically," Perry said.

"Wait. Are you saying they made some enslaved consciousness the operating system of a damned airlock?" I could only shake my head, almost impressed, for lack of a better word, by the sheer and casual cruelty of it.

"So it would appear. The signal came online in tandem with the airlock's cycling and dropped off again at the same time. At least, that's the way it seems, but as good as I am, we are talking pushing my scanners right to the limit."

"What do we do here, Van? Swoop in and arrest them all?" Torina asked.

I gripped the armrest. "Much as I'd love to do that, we've got no idea what's over there. And I don't just want to start a gunfight with them, because we might end up killing the poor sod stuck in that airlock." I looked around. "That's my way of saying, any ideas?"

"Actually, Van, I've got one," Netty said.

I blinked at that. I had all the faith in the galaxy in Netty when it came to reliably implementing ideas, but she didn't often put them forward herself. "Okay, Netty, let's hear it."

It didn't take her long to explain it, and by the time she was done, Torina, Icky, and I were all on board.

I held up a finger when she stopped speaking. "A point of clarification?"

"Yes?" Netty asked.

"You're *sure* about putting the bird—well, you're sure about all this?"

"Totally, boss."

I gave a slow smile. She wasn't just a superb pilot. Netty was *devious*.

"Simple and direct. I like it," I said as we accelerated around the rock concealing us and started for the Nesit station. "Perry, you okay out there?"

"Piece of pie, Van. I've ridden on the outside of this ship a bunch of times."

"I think you mean *piece of cake*."

"No, pie. A cake's just a sweetened construct of gluten fibers and air. A pie, on the other hand, is full of filling, like fruit or coconut cream."

"Well, sure, when you call it a sweetened construct of gluten fibers and air, of course it sounds kinda gross. Besides, you're a machine, it's not like you eat. At all."

"No, but if I did, I'd definitely be pie over cake."

Netty cut in. "If I can interrupt your discussion of baking, the

Nesit ship is powering up. No targeting scanners, though. At least, not yet."

"I conclude they either have no weapons or don't intend—" Icky began, but Netty cut in a second time.

"I take it back. Targeting scanners just came online. And… we've got a pair of missiles on the way."

We were close enough to actually see the missiles' exhausts as they accelerated away from the station, barreling toward us. Torina immediately shot one to pieces. The second turned to fragments when our point-defense battery found the range.

"Those are antiquated missiles, with guidance systems at least two generations old," Netty said.

"Someone hasn't bothered investing in the good stuff," I said but still had to frown. "Correct me if I'm wrong, but the closer we get, the less the guidance system is going to matter, right?"

"At close range, even an unguided rocket is potentially deadly," Netty agreed.

I clenched my jaw and waited. It would take us only minutes to cross the gap between us and the station. But, with every second that passed, we got closer to the launcher, which was probably reloading.

Torina switched the lasers back into standby mode and turned to me. "Van, those missiles will be coming straight at us from the station. If I shoot and miss, I'm going to hit it. Are you okay with that?"

I pressed my lips together and went with my gut reaction, which was—

"No. We'll leave it to the point-defense systems. Perry, you ready out there?"

"I'm perched on the cargo winch. Netty, you can start playing it out."

This was going to be insanely dangerous for Perry. The *Fafnir*'s cargo winch was a kilometer of monofilament tether, nearly unbreakable line about half a centimeter thick. Perry was going to pull it to the airlock and hook it up as we passed the Nesit station, whereupon we'd simply yank the whole airlock assembly away. He'd then ride the extracted airlock as we winched it back to the *Fafnir*. It was simple, sneaky, and vicious. A triple play in my book.

But that didn't mean it couldn't go horribly wrong.

"Two more missiles inbound," Netty said at the same time we saw the launch. The point-defenses opened up immediately, tracking one missile, shooting it down, then the other. The second actually detonated only about five klicks away.

"Shit—Perry, you still there?"

"Yup. That was spectacular, by the way. Mind you, I could do without *spectacular*. Just plain *effective* would be nice."

"We'll see what we can do." I turned to Torina. "Can you get a clear shot on that launcher?"

She reactivated the laser controls, then peered intently at the targeting display. "It's just a few meters away from the airlock, mounted on the surface of the asteroid. I—" She shrugged. "I don't know. Probably? As long as the *Fafnir* doesn't do anything but fly in a straight line at a constant speed?"

"If we don't disable that launcher, Van, the next two missiles, which should be reloaded and ready to fire in about fifteen seconds, are going to be too close to reliably engage with the point-defense—"

"Torina, do it."

She nodded and focused on the laser controls. I braced myself and felt Icky do the same behind me. She'd have one opportunity, and if she blew it, there was a good chance she'd obliterate whoever was slaved into that airlock.

She fired.

She actually hit the launcher while it was in the midst of firing. One missile launched just a fraction of a second ahead of her shot, while the other died, along with the launcher itself, halfway out of its tube. It still left one missile hurtling straight toward us, threatening impact in less than ten seconds.

"Perry, hang on!" I snapped.

"Already kinda doing that—"

Running on nothing but hope and instinct, I gave the *Fafnir* a full-power burst from her main drive. She shot forward, suddenly moving far too fast for the missile to properly track. It passed astern of us and plowed straight into our exhaust plume. When it emerged from the other side, it had been half reduced to glowing slag.

I cut the drive. "Perry, you okay?"

"What did I say about *spectacular*, Van?"

"I'll take that as a yes. Netty, how badly did I screw this up?"

"You mean that whole extra chunk of delta-V I hadn't planned on? Pretty badly."

I braced myself to scrub the whole thing, but Icky suddenly leaned forward, staring at the instruments.

"Put your helmets on," she snapped.

I turned. "What—?"

"Put your helmets on!"

Torina was already doing it. I joined her. I was still snapping the clamps closed when Icky suddenly spun back to her own engineering controls and punched in a rapid-fire sequence of inputs.

An instant later, everything around me vanished into a howling gale and a wash of vaporous white.

IT DIDN'T TAKE LONG for the *Fafnir* to completely depressurize, maybe five or six seconds. A column of vapor streamed from her forward airlock, and a slight shock passed through the ship. Mister Newton made his presence felt, the action of the venting atmosphere becoming a reaction that slowed the *Fafnir* slightly.

"Well, that worked. Eleven seconds to closest approach," Netty said.

"Okay, start spooling out the winch, Netty," Perry said—unnecessarily, and only for the benefit of us mere humans, since he and Netty could communicate perfectly well electronically.

"Icky!"

Torina had turned around. I did likewise. Icky sat motionless in her seat, her eyes glazed over, unmoving.

"Shit, Netty, repressurize—"

"Already on it."

The forward airlock sealed, and Netty started refilling the *Fafnir* with air from her emergency supply. There was enough to fully repressurize the ship once. But it would take a moment, and for that time, Icky was without a suit.

Torina unstrapped. "I'll take care of her, Van. You just focus on flying."

I pulled my attention back to the instruments and the situation around us. Perry, using his limited internal store of thruster propellant, had aimed himself at the latch on the end of the winch at the airlock. As we swept past, he hooked it onto a stanchion protruding from the airlock, then hung on for dear mechanical life.

"Okay, Netty, any time," he said.

Netty applied the brake to the winch and gradually let it go taut. I felt a slight shudder as the winch stopped spooling out altogether, and the *Fafnir*'s momentum ripped the entire airlock assembly free. Another explosion of vapor erupted from the gaping hole left behind, atmosphere venting both from the station and whatever was inside the asteroid. The latter seemed to be quite a bit, given how long the decompression went on.

"Netty, reel 'er in!" Perry said.

She did, but she had only gotten Perry and the airlock halfway back to the *Fafnir* before a laser shot slammed into us, boiling away a cloud of vaporized armor. The Nesit ship, still hooked up to its antimatter fuel coupling, had finally opened up with its laser battery.

I thought about returning fire but just fired the glitter caster instead, surrounding the *Fafnir* with a cloud of bright, reflective chaff. The Nesit took a few more parting shots, one of which managed to blow off our left side maneuvering thruster; another damaged the scanner transceiver I'd only recently repaired.

"Ouch. Wallet ouch, not physical ouch," I said.

"Both hurt in different ways, boss," Netty agreed.

We finally got both the airlock and Perry back aboard and were able to fire up the drive and get back underway. Only then did I turn back to Torina and Icky, expecting the worst.

But I was stunned to find Icky blinking at me. "I really hate the way vacuum dries out your eyes. They sting like hell for hours afterward."

The *Fafnir* reached full atmospheric pressure again, so I yanked off my helmet. "You've done that before?"

"What? Exposure to vacuum?"

"Yeah."

"Well, sure. You don't help an old man refurbish a battleship on a budget without the odd mishap. I mean, this wasn't even close to my personal best for time spent in vacuum." She grinned. "Hell, I've managed almost two full minutes. This was nothing!"

6

"Freeze, asshole! You're under arrest!"

I stared at Waldo for a moment, mesmerized by the fact that our maintenance bot sounded like an actor from some 70s cop show.

"Does he say anything else?"

"Only variations on that general theme," Perry replied.

"So we rescued Mannix?"

"WHO THE HELL'S MANNIX?" Icky boomed. She'd recovered from her exposure to vacuum with no apparent ill effects, aside from stopped-up ears that tended to make her shout. I gestured for her to, once again, take the volume down a notch or two.

"It's an old television program about a cop. On Earth. Before my time, actually, but I hacked a guy once who was super into it. He had every episode on his hard drive and ran an online fan club. He also had—" I curled my lip. "He had some fan fiction."

"Go on," Perry said.

I shook my head. "I'd rather not. Anyway, what's going on with our friend here? We're almost back at Anvil Dark, and we haven't been able to get anything out of him but bad cop-show dialog?"

"'Fraid not, Van, sorry. The last couple of chips we plugged into Waldo just immediately meshed with his operating system. This one, though—defective, maybe?"

"We'll bring him to Steve, see what he can do. In the meantime, if you can think of anything else, well, give it a try."

I left Perry with Waldo and whoever the hell he happened to be this time around, and returned to the cockpit. Icky followed me.

"MAYBE IT GOT DAMAGED WHEN WE—"

I turned and put a finger to my lips.

Icky gave a doleful smile. "Sorry, Van. Maybe it got damaged during our recovery op. It was one hell of a ride for it."

I sighed as I clambered back into my seat. "Yeah, I hope not. I'd feel awful if we did that to him. Imagine spending the rest of your life able to say nothing but things like, *freeze*, *asshole*, or *go ahead, make my day*."

Torina shrugged. "Sounds like he'd make a great Peacemaker."

"I've got catchphrases in *reserve*. I'm clearly better suited to this."

Torina inclined her head. "Fair enough. But pace yourself. It's a long career."

"I sure hope so."

We flew on, entering Anvil Dark's traffic pattern and starting our final run in toward the station. Perry reappeared, reporting little more success.

"Right now, he—whoever *he* is—is stuck in some sort of mixed-up identity. There are three major sub-programs all vying for processor time, but that might be an artifact of some damage to the logic system. I can communicate with him—sort of, anyway. Do you want me to tell him the cavalry's on the way?"

"Sure. Tell them to sit ti—er, never mind, they're not going anywhere." I shook my head. "I can't wait to hear what kind of shitty grudge led to this. But we're going to have to, since right now, he's got a pretty limited vocabulary to work with, it seems."

"Maybe they're just really dumb," Perry suggested.

"So dimwitted, and threatening to arrest everyone in sight?" Torina said, arching an eyebrow at me.

I made to snap something back at her, but Icky leaned in between us and beat me to it.

"YAY! VAN, THIS IS A GREAT DAY! WE FOUND YOUR MISSING TWIN!"

WE BOOKED some hangar time to repair the damage to the *Fafnir*. It had actually been more extensive than we'd first realized. The Nesit ship must have packed a potent laser because its beam had punched almost completely through an applique armor plate on our starboard stern quarter, spalling molten alloy that had scoured the hull plate beneath and damaged some internal systems behind it. Most egregiously, it had wrecked a power coupling for the ship's auxiliary power system, so we had the main, and that was it—no backup if it went down. That made the *Fafnir*, at least for the moment, unflyable.

So I spent the next day in greasy coveralls, working with Icky to repair that damage, as well as the demolished thruster assembly and the wrecked scanner transceiver. Our little venture had proven costly. In fact, it had been the single most expensive clash we'd faced. And all that damage had been done by a stationary Nesit workboat stuck at dock, refueling.

I took a breather while Icky used an overhead derrick in the hangar to lower a new armor plate into place.

"So we'll get this fastened back in place, then it's just the transceiver, and we're done," I said, wiping my hands on a rag.

Netty spoke up, her voice humming out of the comm I kept clipped to my tool harness. "Van, I've got the final bill. Including hangar time, we're out eighty-six thousand bonds."

"Holy shit!" I sighed. "We need to pick up a paying job soon, before our cash reserves start getting too thin—"

"Van, Torina here. I'm with Steve. It looks like we've managed to start communicating with Kwazalein."

"Kwazalein? So we have an intact identity? That's good news."

"We do. And then some."

"I—what?"

"Easier if you come here."

I glanced at Icky, who just nodded. "I got this."

"Okay, Torina. On my way."

Steve, Torina, and Perry intercepted me before I entered the workshop where they'd been trying to restore—Kwazalein, apparently. That made me frown.

"Is something wrong? Something's wrong, isn't it?"

"Not wrong, as much as… complicated," Steve said.

"How so?"

Perry answered. "Remember how I said there were different sub-programs competing for processor time? Well, that was a simplification, but it turns out to have been pretty accurate, actually."

"Kwazalein actually consists of three separate identities," Steve said. "Essentially, three people, sharing one physical existence."

"So… like a split personality thing? Although I guess the better, more modern term is actually associative identity disorder," I said.

"Yes and no. A dissociative identity disorder is, well, a disorder. It's something that shouldn't be happening. In Kwazalein's case, though, it seems to just be the way his species rolls," Perry said.

I stared. "How does that work, exactly? Is it like—what, time-sharing a condo?"

"What's a condo?" Steve asked.

"Oh, I know. It's a bird, on Earth. A big one."

"That's a *condor*, Torina. And I'd like to point out that bigger doesn't necessarily mean better," Perry said.

I waved them all away. "So are you talking to all three of Kwazalein's identities? Do they have different names? Do they switch at will?"

Steve raised a hand. "Yes, maybe, and I don't know. This is a new species to me, too, Van. All that I can tell you at the moment is that there are three versions of this person, each of them is equally valid, and only two of them get along."

I decided to proceed with care, since this was, in a sense, a family fight. It was just happening inside one being.

"So exactly how different are these three personalities?" I asked.

"How different are you, Torina, and Perry? Well, aside from the obvious man, woman, AI bird differences?" Steve answered, reasonably.

"Very. For one, the AI bird is smarter, faster, and much more charming than the other two," I said—except it wasn't me, it was Perry, mimicking my voice. I scowled at him.

"I seem to remember you making some remark about not being a mimic, like parrots and ravens."

He cocked his head at me. "I'm not. Technically, that wasn't mimicry."

"He did sound just like you, though," Torina said with an impish smile.

"I'll point out that if he can sound like me, he can probably sound like—"

"Torina? Sure, I can do that," she said, except it was Perry again, of course.

Torina's smile flicked off. "I'm with Van. Enough with the impressions, bird."

Steve had watched the whole exchange with a bemused smile. "There you go. Three different individuals, and one's a wiseass, one's mischievous, and one's just an asshole." We all opened our mouths to speak, but Steve went on, cutting us off. "I'll let you guys figure out which is which."

But he turned serious. "Anyway, two of three personalities that make up Kwazalein seem to be older, more balanced, and generally more thoughtful. One comes across as more assertive, even a little aggressive, while the other seems more, ah… bookish, for lack of a better word."

"What about the third?" I asked.

"Think human adolescent, on the order of fifteen or sixteen standard years of age."

"Oh. Shit. I feel sorry for all three of them."

"But mostly the two older ones. I mean, I *was* a human adolescent, and even I didn't like me sometimes," Torina said.

"So you see the problem. Debriefing him—or them—is going to be a laborious process. It took us this long just to figure out what was going on and then who was who, and then to get them to stop bickering long enough to say anything useful at all."

I sighed. This might just be another dead end. I mean, I was glad we were able to rescue Kwazalein from a life as an airlock, but aside from frustration, I wasn't sure they'd be helpful at all, at least any time soon.

"And I can tell from that crestfallen look, Van, that you don't think Kwazi is going to be able to help you," Steve said.

I shrugged. "A teenager and two older guys, inhabiting the same identity? I'm sure we'll be in for hours of enlightened discussion."

But Steve triumphantly held up a data slate. "In that case, let me move us along straight to some actual results. I knew what you'd be after, so I was able to get them to focus long enough to provide this."

I took the data slate. It gave a thumbnail summary of where and how Kwazalein was first taken. Apparently, he'd been attending yet another remote refueling depot, which allegedly also functioned as a multi-species brothel.

I shook my head. "Talk about full service."

But Torina, reading over my shoulder, pointed. "Van, right there. Kwazalein says they were there for, um, refueling—"

"Let's just assume they mean actually getting fuel, for the sake of my delicate sensibilities."

Torina snorted. "Sure. You're a fragile blossom, all right. But they weren't the only ones taken, apparently."

My eyes widened as I read on. Kwazalein claimed that two others had gone missing from the place, apparently just before they arrived. One was, of all things, a Schegith. Together with Schegith herself, and the handful of her people that we rescued previously and returned to their home planet, Null World, this made the eighth known member of the race. Moreover, they were apparently royalty, or at least had a name that translated to Prince Splinter.

The other individual kidnapped from the refueling depot-slash-brothel was even more curious. It was a Trinduk, a Sorcerer, one of the beings we assumed to be behind the whole stolen identity operation, or at least intimately involved in it.

"If the Sorcerers are the bad guys in all this, then why would they have taken one of their own? For that matter, how do we know they were taken and didn't just, you know, leave?" Torina asked.

"All very good questions, which the Masters would like you to answer as quickly as you possibly can," Steve said, reaching over and tapping the data slate to open another document. It was a search-and-seizure warrant, freshly issued, along with a variety of clearance forms and other documents that, taken together, suddenly gave us an urgent mission.

"I routinely report things like Kwazalein in there to the Masters, and this came back from them almost immediately," Steve said.

I glanced at Torina and Perry. "Someone wants this dealt with in an awful hurry. Not that I'm complaining, mind you, because it's a solid lead. But why are the Masters suddenly so interested in this? I thought Yewlo was the crisis of the moment."

"Maybe they think there's some link between them," Torina suggested.

Perry nodded. "Maybe they have reason to believe Yewlo was seized and chipped the same way as these other poor bastards."

I almost winced at that. I'd started to pretty much assume that Yewlo had gone missing out of choice, for reasons of his own. Coming from abject poverty the way he had, he might have taken advantage of his position as Master to skim money off somewhere to enjoy a life of idle luxury in some remote place with no extradition treaties for the Peacemakers, or anyone else, to enforce. I'd seen it happen often enough back on Earth. I'd had a few jobs, in fact, tracking down people who'd come from nothing, gained lots, and now simply didn't want to be found. So I certainly understood the psychology.

But if Yewlo had been taken and chipped, then it represented a security catastrophe for the Peacemakers. Every piece of information, every detail of every past and ongoing operation, intimate knowledge of the internal structure, politics, and general goings-on of the Guild would be potentially laid bare.

Perry downloaded the contents of the data slate, and we started back toward the *Fafnir*, leaving Steve to undertake the painstaking and probably frustrating process of continuing to debrief Kwazalein. I hit my comm as we strode along.

"Netty, you ready to fly?"

"Icky's still working on a few systems."

"Tell her to stuff everything back into place and start doing the preflight. We've got a job to do."

WE MUSED over our many questions during the flight. Whoever the identity thieves were, why did they seem to have a particular fixation on the Schegith, to the extent that they'd kidnapped all of the known surviving members of the race? Did they have anything to do with Yewlo's disappearance, and if so, what were the implications? How much of a dent had we put in their organization when we took down Axicur, Icky's mother, who had seemed to be an important part of it? Were the Nesit and their dabbling in stolen artifacts part of it, and if so, how? Who were the Sorcerers, and had they turned against one of their number, treating him as just another identity to steal? If so, and we found this Sorcerer, would that give us a window, or maybe even a door, into this shadowy but apparently powerful network of dealers in stolen people?

We kept coming back to the same answer every time, though.

We don't know.

"I have to admit that this is all very intriguing," Torina said as we completed the twist into the system hosting the refueling station that was our destination. "It's kind of like... a puzzle, I suppose. We can see individual pieces, and can even recognize what some of them are, but we still haven't yet started putting them together into a complete picture."

"I didn't know you were a puzzle aficionado," I said, eyeing the tactical overlay as Netty updated it. There were four ships in transit, two inbound, and two outbound. None of them even remotely matched any that interested us, but I told Netty to collect as much data as she could on each.

"I'm not. I'd rather just see the whole picture right up front. Still intriguing, though," she replied.

I tapped the overlay, bringing up the data on the refueling

station known as Xublu's Folly. Technically, that was the popular name for the whole star system, which in the Earthly star catalog was designated TZ Arietis. The titular Xublu was a Mustilar, a species apparently famous for an almost pathological tendency to wanderlust. Mustilar explorers were at the forefront of pushing back the boundaries of known space, and doing it not for recognition or riches but because of something hard-coded into the race. Xublu actually had many claims to fame, but his name had stuck to this system because it had proven so profoundly hostile to permanent colonization. TZ Arietis was a flare star, periodically brightening and vomiting great gouts of radiation through the system. Xublu, when he'd declared the system ideal for habitation, apparently hadn't known that, so the first attempt at colonization had ended disastrously.

It hadn't done Xublu's reputation any good, either. Despite many achievements, the one he was remembered for was this particular miss. It just proved the old adage, *you're only as good as the last time you screwed up.*

Ultimately, though, TZ Arietis had proven to be a good location for a refueling depot, not too different from some of the others we'd visited. This one apparently provided a much broader range of services to its patrons than those others had.

I rubbed my chin as I read the entry in a window that had popped open on the tactical overlay. "So... this place is owned by some nondescript consortium. What a surprise." I glanced at Perry. "I'll bet if we run this down, we'll find that this consortium is just a front for a shell corporation, that's owned by another shell corporation, that's owned by some investment fund, that's operated by some commercial bank on behalf of yet another consortium—"

"I see you've heard this tune before," Perry replied.

"Many, many times, and it always comes down to the same thing. Do you have the patience to thread your way through all these Russian nesting dolls, or will you just throw your hands up and forget it before reaching the rich, corruption-filled center?"

"Is this your way of saying you don't care who's behind this sordid little operation out here?" Torina asked, smiling.

"Yes. Yes it is. Unless, of course, it's implicated in our identity-theft ring, in which case I swear that I will happily dig until we finally hit bottom."

RIGHT AWAY, it was apparent that Xublu's Folly was much more than just a refueling depot. For one, it was much too large. For another, the four ships in transit, and those docked at the station itself, were far more traffic than a remote refueling stopover would readily warrant. Add to that the fact that most of these ships weren't just standard workboats or freighters but sleek, luxurious runabouts and pleasure craft, and you had all the makings of a *wink-wink-nudge-nudge* sort of refueling business going on.

I decided that we'd play it low-key, keeping our warrants tucked away, at least for now. When traffic control started asking some pointed questions about the arrival of a Peacemaker, I did my best to sound kind of seedy.

"Let's just say that Peacemaking is stressful. And sometimes, you just wanna burn off some stress, if you know what I mean."

"So you're saying you're off the clock."

"Off the official one, yeah. But I still feel the need to… refuel."

Torina grimaced. "Is it just me, or did it just get a lot sleazier in here?" she whispered.

I shot her a look. The station's traffic control finally relented, mainly because I agreed to pay their various fees without trying to throw any Peacemaker weight behind getting any sort of discount. I guess they decided I was desperate enough to dock and board their station that I'd just say to hell with it and pay full price rather than keep trying to barter.

In any case, I wanted to sound as much as possible like a guy anxiously looking for a good time. Hopefully, that would let us fly below the suspicious social radar that would no doubt be beamed our way, at least for a while. In economic terms, trying to come across as a *lonely spacer* was going to end up costing us a chunk of bonds, but given that this was our only solid lead, I figured it was worth it.

Fortunately, corrupt Peacemakers of days past had bravely paved the way for us. Our arrival, while noted warily by patrons of the station, didn't seem to ring any alarms.

While Netty arranged to actually make use of the place's refueling services and get the *Fafnir* gassed back up, I led Torina, Icky, and Perry into the station. As we exited the airlock, we were walloped by yet another sprawl of palatial luxury—more thick carpeting, recessed lighting, and overstuffed furniture. I was starting to realize there were essentially two types of interior spaces in known space—dank, scuzzy shithole, and the tacky luxury den. Anything in between squalor and opulence was rare. I was starting to appreciate the tidy, functional utility of the *Fafnir* a little more with each ship, station, or planet we visited.

"Wanna bet there are a bazillion criminal endeavors that have been suddenly put on hold?" Icky said, looking around at everyone trying so obviously to not look right back at us.

"Yeah, I know." I sighed. "I'm starting to think that ordinary, law-abiding folks are the minority out here."

Perry hopped onto the back of a chair. "Survivor bias."

We stopped as though getting our bearings and deciding where to go amid the riot of shops, eateries, and spas sprawled around us, a ring of seedy commerce around a central, hub-like atrium. "What about it?"

"You're experiencing it. Or, not survivor bias itself, obviously, but something like it."

I frowned at him. I'd heard of survivor bias, sure. One of the best known examples was the efforts made to armor airplanes during the Second World War to protect those parts of them observed to be most shot up when they returned from missions. It took some time, but it eventually became clear that those were the *least* important parts of the aircraft to protect, because they were the ones damaged in *other* areas that were actually failing to return from missions. Since the only damage anyone ever actually saw, though, was to the less-critical parts of the planes, it was wrongly assumed that these were the parts that needed to be armored.

"You're saying that I'm drawing the wrong conclusions," I said to Perry.

He bobbed his head back at me. "You're a Peacemaker, Van. It's your job to go where all the criminal stuff is happening. It means you run into a lot of criminals, doing a lot of criminal things. You're forgetting that for every station like this one, with maybe a couple of hundred people doing naughty stuff, there are whole cities in places like Tau Ceti and Epsilon Eridani, where millions of your *ordinary, law-abiding folks* live out their *ordinary, law-abiding* lives."

"Thank you, Perry, for restoring my faith in the okay-ness of the universe," I replied.

"On the whole, known space really is reassuringly *meh*," Torina agreed.

7

We carried on and were met by a simpering robotic attendant who immediately deluged us with salvos of innuendo. Everything was described in outwardly innocuous terms, but if the bot had had elbows, they'd have been pointedly poking me in the ribs by now.

The bot's sensor cluster swept around, taking in Torina and Icky. "Of course, the gentleman seems to have no lack of opportunities for *ongoing maintenance* while in space. So perhaps some new, *non-standard parts* are in order, no? Perhaps some with less… bilateral symmetry? With more available *open ports* for—"

"Actually, the gentleman is interested in some very particular services. In fact, I can show exactly which ones," Perry cut in.

The bot turned to me, and I shrugged. "He knows what I like."

Perry hopped off, and we followed. The station's bot kept up its suggestive chatter all the way, throwing in a few advertising blurbs for shops and restaurants for good measure. We stopped in front of

—to my utter surprise—a noodle bar. Perry pointed with a wing at a nearby suite.

"The gentleman wants to have what's available in there."

The bot took in the door Perry had indicated, then swung its sensors back on me. Despite them being nothing more than alloy and crystal, I couldn't help feeling I was getting a look of surprise. "Really? The gentleman *is* adventurous. Please, give me a few minutes to get everything ready, including a breathable atmosphere."

"Breathing is, ah, sort of my thing. Among other pursuits," I said with a winking leer that made Torina wince.

"I'll also ensure that medical services are standing by for when he has completed these particular, and rather drastic, *system upgrades*."

The bot trundled off, apparently to make the necessary arrangements.

"Perry, just what the hell have you signed me up for?" I asked him.

"No idea, Van. But I'm detecting a signal from that door that conforms to one of our stolen identities."

"Ah." I breathed a sigh of relief. I'd dedicated myself to my job, but I had my limits, and *drastic system upgrades* that unnerved a *robot* were probably somewhere on the far side of them. We decided to just watch the door until the bot returned to see who, if anyone, entered or exited.

In the meantime, I turned to the noodle bar. It offered a surprisingly wide array of items, including noodles of nearly every imaginable color and a spread of containers holding a dizzying array of condiments and sauces. Some were marked with icons representing different species with X's through them, indicating they'd be toxic to those particular customers. X'd out humans appeared on a lot of them.

I finally settled on my order, and leaned over the bar to point. "Think I might try some of the yellow. No, not the blue. You can skimp on the blue, friend."

Holding a bowl of spicy and surprisingly tasty noodles, I joined Perry. Torina and Icky both decided to try noodle bowls of their own.

"Anyone coming or going yet?" I asked, shoveling noodles into my mouth.

"Nope. Whatever's behind that door, it isn't exactly what I'd call high traffic."

By the time the others had returned and we'd all finished our meals, our robot guide delivered a *work order* specifying certain *procedures* I wanted *performed* as part of a *maintenance regimen*. I accepted the upload and rolled my eyes as the bot trundled away.

"Really? Do I look like the kind of guy that would enjoy that?" I said, pointing at one of the items on the list.

Icky, peering over my shoulder, pointed at another. "Or that? I mean, who the hell would be into something like that?"

"I can't imagine how that one's even possible," Torina said, indicating yet another, then giving me a once-over. "At least, not with human anatomy, anyway."

"So which one of these things do you plan to do first, Van?" Icky asked me, her grin sly.

"The one where I tell Perry to delete this list—no, wipe it entirely, so no one ever finds it and gets the wrong idea." I glanced at the mysterious door. "Having said that, though, Perry, don't do that quite yet. Whatever's beyond that door is on the list—the fourth item down, I think. And, since it is—"

I put down my empty noodle bowl, then ambled over to the doorway. Icky and Torina followed at a discrete distance, surreptitiously watching my back.

I stopped at the door, noting a wide-eyed and somewhat disgusted stare from an alien who happened to wander past.

"Please provide the security code you were given, in order to access this particular workshop," a voice said.

I glanced at Perry, who was on the floor beside me. "Workshop. They're really milking this whole service station thing, aren't they?"

"They are that."

I lowered my voice. "So is that our guy? The one who just spoke?"

"Nope. That's truly just an AI. Our guy came online at the same time we were scanned, probably for weapons and contraband. I suspect if you actually give that access code, you're going to be told that you can't bring your weapons inside there."

That wasn't a problem, since I had absolutely no intention of passing through this door. Instead, I pretended to study the list the bot had given me.

"So our guy is somehow connected to the weapons scanner?"

Perry bobbed his head. "So it would seem. The logic module seems to be behind that access plate halfway up from the deck, to the right."

"Number five, Van!" Icky called.

I glanced at her. "What?"

"Number five on the list! Do that one first!"

She said it loudly enough to turn a few heads. It struck me that she was trying to maintain our cover but doing it in a way that let her continue being a smart-ass.

I checked number five on the list and grimaced back at her. "Ewww."

Perry hopped to a point beneath the access plate he'd mentioned. "Yup, it's inside there. I'd say it's probably a standard E4045, based on the type of system."

I glanced at him. "Meaning?"

"Meaning that, if you'd like to do this low-key, we could swap that module with one from our spare parts stock on the *Fafnir*. If we preload a basic AI template onto it, it might be enough to keep the system happy until we're gone."

I nodded. Not raising the alarm would be nice, yes. It wasn't that I particularly cared about being discreet or having regard for the other patrons and their… interests. Rather, I didn't want to make a big scene everywhere we went because it would make going back awkward. It was the same reason I generally left many of the systems I hacked alone, as long as they didn't contain stuff that was too egregious. Should I wish to make future visits, then never having shown any sign I'd been there in the first place was a definite benefit.

While Perry retrieved a spare E4045 module from the *Fafnir*, I worked out our plan of attack with Icky and Torina. Icky figured it would take about thirty seconds to get the access plate open, swap the modules, and close it up again. So, we needed a distraction that long.

Torina smiled at me. "Van, take your top off."

"What?"

"Take your top off. You're going to be the honeypot."

I blinked at her. "You, my dear, are out of your *mind*. I'm not going to start parading around here half naked, no matter how truly magnificent I am in the buff."

Torina snorted. "Humble *and* hot. A win/win for us all. Look, I'm not saying you should get naked. What I *am* saying is that we need something guaranteed to draw everyone's attention away from the door. So, here's what I'm thinking."

She told me, asking me to nod with each embarrassing step as the plan—using me as bait—took shape. Step by step, from my shirt off to making a scene, I felt my scowl deepen until she waved grandly, indicating that her brilliant plot was complete. I exhaled in resigned disgust. The plan she'd suggested was utterly ridiculous, bordering on humiliating. Even worse, it was a good plan.

I sighed. "Fine. There's Perry, with the spare module. Before we do this, though—"

I ambled back to the door.

"Please provide the security code you were given in order to access this particular workshop."

"Keep your panties on."

"I don't wear panties. The code, please."

"It's just a—never mind." I consulted the data pad, found the access code that had been assigned to me, and read it back.

A new voice spoke up. "Please be advised that weapons aren't allowed in the workshop—"

I cut in, *sotto voice*. "How would you like to sail the undersea with the Schegith again?"

A moment passed. Something like a burst of feedback erupted from the speaker, then a faint voice.

"What? How?"

I looked back at the others and gave a slight nod. This was our guy, alright.

I wandered back.

Perry was staring at me. "Torina just told me what you guys have planned for your distraction," he said.

"And?" I glared. "Go ahead, bird, say whatever smart-assed thing you're going to say."

"Van, I'm offended. I just want to applaud you for such devotion to your duty that you'll risk public humiliation to carry it out."

I gave him a narrow-eyed stare of suspicion, but he just stared back. That was the trouble with him being a machine. His expression literally never changed, because it effectively couldn't.

"Okay, well—thank you, Perry. I appreciate it."

"And if it doesn't work out, then Torina could spank you. Or, wait, isn't that part of the distraction too—"

He dodged aside as I aimed a kick at him. Even if I'd connected, I wasn't going to damage a construct intended for combat. It just would have felt damned good.

He and Icky angled their way toward the door, while Torina and I moved to the far side of the noodle stand. Once we were in place, she grabbed me and pushed me against the wall.

"Van, I have been waiting to say this since we got here. You don't need any of this. You've got me." She almost shouted it, then pressed herself against me, pushed her hands under my duster coat, and shoved it off my shoulders, into a heap around my feet.

"Torina. We… we work together. Why didn't you say something—"

She yanked open my tunic, then worked on my shirt. "Don't

care. I told you my kink, but you were too busy making money. I'm not gonna be ignored now. It's happening. Right here."

Despite knowing it was staged, I felt... flushed. People were taking notice and gathering around. Torina was climbing me like ivy, her hands fluttering across my chest as I realized I was wearing fewer clothes.

"Nice trick," I murmured.

"Just getting started," she said in my ear with a torrid whisper.

She pulled my face to her and leapt up *on* me, her legs wrapped around my torso like a python, and raised her voice. "Now. The real you. Not some—some *machine*, made in there. Just you, like I've wanted all these months." Her tone was a sensual rasp, and I saw dozens of people stop to listen and watch the show. Hell, I would have done the same. Torina was *selling* the fiction.

Over Torina's shoulder, I saw Icky open the access plate and switch units with the nerves of a jewel thief. She was big and strong but worked with a silken delicacy. When she was done, she gave me a thumbs-up with one arm as the other three finished the task.

I looked back at the door, gave a decisive nod, and took Torina's face in my hands. "You're right."

"I know I am. Back to the ship?" she asked, her voice full of promise.

"Back to the ship."

I pulled my shirt and tunic back into place and picked up my duster coat, then we made a quick retreat back to the *Fafnir*, parting the crowd to an array of smirks and knowing glances.

Once inside the airlock, we looked at one another and then began to laugh.

"The spin was a nice touch. I'm guessing that randy humans aren't a common thing out in the corridors," I said.

"Or near a noodle bar. Then again, carbs *are* delicious. I can see how they might fire the passion of a lonely spacer. Or two," Torina said.

Icky and Perry stepped through the airlock. Perry looked at Torina, then at me.

"You guys need some privacy?"

Icky held up the logic module in triumph, then turned sly. "If you guys are going to go and satisfy your unrequited passion, might I recommend item seven on your list?"

I lifted the pad and found item seven. Torina looked at the screen along with me.

Then we both turned to Icky and spoke in perfect unison.

"Ewww."

WE PLUGGED the data module containing what we assumed was Splinter, our Schegith Prince, into Waldo. Once he booted up, we were able to confirm his identity.

"This one can't begin to express their gratitude to you," he said. His voice caught and broke with raw emotion.

"It's what we do, Splinter," I replied, then explained we needed to deactivate him again. "You have my word, this is to save you. To protect you. We have another person to free, and—"

"This one wishes to believe you, but it has been a long time in the darkness," Splinter said.

"I'm sorry, Splinter, I can't imagine what you've endured. I'm asking you to believe me—to believe us, as friends of the Schegith. A little more oblivion, since we need Waldo to check on the other person we're going to free. Then you can begin living. Again, you have my word."

After a long pause, Splinter spoke. "This one—this one will believe, then."

"Thank you, Schegith." I turned to Perry. "Speaking of our other wayward soul, the apparent Sorcerer, have you managed to track them down yet?"

"I haven't, but I think Netty's made some headway," he replied.

"Really. Netty, whatcha got for us?"

"I've been scanning the hell out of this station, looking for the sorts of emissions that seem to be typical of these memory chips we've been hunting. I detected some, albeit very weak, and they were intermittent, appearing for a while, then disappearing."

"So it's being activated for short periods of time, then deactivated again."

"That was my original thought, yes. But I was able to get a direction on the signal and found it was coming from a section of the station at the far end of it, relative to where we are now. There's a shielded module down there that resembles an antimatter storage pod."

"Resembles?"

"Resembles. But it's not. Perry and I did a little digging into this station's comm logs, we did some cross-referencing with our own intelligence databases, and got a hit. We think that module has actually been repurposed to house an operation called the Fracture Room. It's a place for high-value metals and other commodities to be stripped out of stolen goods."

Icky nodded. "Sometimes components, especially damaged ones, are worth more for the stuff they contain than as the components themselves. Precious metals, rare earth elements, fissile materials, it can add up to a lot of bonds."

"So it's a chop shop," I said, shaking my head. "You know, the more you leave home, the more home comes to you."

"It's a discreet chop shop, too. No one thinks twice about heavy shielding on an antimatter pod, so they hack away at them—but there's a local effect. Whenever someone accesses it, opening any sort of portal, airlock, that sort of thing, they briefly let emissions from inside leak out," Netty replied.

"Which also wouldn't be much of a problem for them, except we've been scanning for a certain type of emission," Perry added.

In the cockpit, Netty put imagery of the station, along with a rough schematic, onto the screen. Then she superimposed the data, bringing the entire situation into focus. We all studied it, brows furrowed.

"It looks like the only access to this chop shop is from outside?" I traced a finger over the schematic of the pod, noting that the emanations Netty had detected seemed to correspond to a point on its exterior.

"The only access that's currently being used, anyway. I'd note that the ship docked closest to it is a supremely bland workboat," Netty explained. "It seems intentionally plain, I might add."

I sat back. It made sense. If you wanted to discreetly move stolen goods around, carting them through the populated part of the station didn't make a lot of sense. And ships at dock often had crew working on and around their exteriors. It wouldn't be hard to unobtrusively move things from the ship's hold to an exterior airlock on the chop shop while keeping the entire operation effectively isolated. It might be awkward, but sometimes awkward had a value all its own.

But it meant that accessing it was going to be awkward for us, too. Hunting around inside the station for some sort of access that might not even exist wouldn't only waste time, it would also risk attracting attention.

I drummed my fingers on the armrest as we considered everything from an outright, head-on assault, to just saying to hell with it and leaving this supposed Sorcerer to a fate he no doubt deserved. But he might also have valuable information, and might even give us a window into our shadowy opposition.

Icky finally spoke up. "Why don't we just cut our way in?"

I raised a brow at her. "Bold. But would it work? Isn't this pod heavily shielded? Made of tough stuff?"

"Yeah, I don't think we want to hang around, slowly cutting our way into it with a torch. I mean, they'll probably catch on when they start losing atmospheric pressure," Torina added.

But Icky brandished a data slate at us. "When dad and I were restoring the Nemesis, we needed to do a lot of cutting through old structural components, hull plating, and the like. If we'd used torches, he and I would still be there with a half-restored battleship. We came up with a way of cutting using shaped charges that we made from old missile warheads."

Torina sniffed. "You're lucky you didn't go boom."

"We had a few mishaps while we got the bugs worked out, but before long, we had it down to a science."

"Think you can rig up some sort of shaped charge to bust our way inside?" I asked.

Icky nodded. "It'll take me a couple of hours, but I don't see why not."

I polled the others for objections.

Torina spoke up. "We're talking about explosively decompressing that module, Van. We might end up hurting, even killing some people."

I had to admit that was possible, and a grimace crept over my face. Running a chop shop might be a distinctly villainous thing to do, but it hardly warranted a death sentence. Perry offered a solution that was less violent and final.

"You know, if they got a fault warning from their airlock, they'd suit up."

"Can we make a fault warning happen on cue?" I asked.

He shrugged his wings. "Sure. Why not? As long as you can stick around long enough to pick me up afterward, that is. It's a long way back to Anvil Dark otherwise."

WE HAD A PLAN. Icky would rig up our breaching charge, a series of shaped charges she cobbled together out of two of our missile warheads. Once she was ready, Perry would make his surreptitious way to the chop shop's airlock, while we departed and ostensibly got underway. Perry would trigger the fault alarm, while we came back, planted the charge, blew it, then used the confusion to retrieve the Sorcerer. We'd then recover Perry and be on our way.

Simple.

And with about a hundred possible points of failure, we weren't likely to come up with anything better.

"You do realize this is going to blow a hole in your noble policy of not burning any bridges, as you say on Earth?" Torina asked.

I shrugged. "Omelets and eggs, right?"

"What?"

"Omelets. Eggs. You can't make one without breaking—never mind. It's another saying from Earth, but—I'll give you a demonstration next time we're back in Iowa."

Icky declared her contraption ready—and a contraption it was. She'd rigged up a rough rectangle from light structural beam stock, with a series of shaped charges mounted on one side of it. A pair of magnetic clamps scavenged from our spare parts store would hold it against the module's hull, so when we activated it, the focused blasts of the charges would cut out a rectangular section big enough for us to gain access.

"Okay, then, folks. Let's give it a try."

Perry raised a wing in salute. "Stirring words, Van. It reminds me of Nelson, at Trafalgar, and his famous message to the British fleet. *England expects every man to, you know, give it a try.*"

I rolled my eyes at him. "Sorry. Next time I'll be sure to compose a rousing motivational speech."

Perry departed and started making his way toward the chop shop, staying close to the station's exterior so as to not come up as debris on its scanners and trigger a cleanup. We gave him five minutes, then departed ourselves, backing away from Xublu's Folly. We turned about, as though to enter the departure pattern, but told traffic control we needed a few minutes to deal with a minor problem. They were content to wait.

"Okay, folks, I'm in position at the airlock, and I've accessed its controller," Perry said. "He's just a dumb, off-the-shelf AI. Not much of a conversationalist."

"Can you convince him that there's a fault? To raise the alarm?" I asked.

"Van, I could convince this guy that water isn't wet if I wanted to. Just say the word."

I glanced around the cockpit. We'd all suited up, ready for our part of the operation. Torina and Icky nodded.

"We're good to go, Perry. We'll be in position in about five minutes."

Even as I spoke, Netty started easing us toward the chop shop. Traffic control asked us what we were up to, and I responded that we were just testing our thrusters, then ignored any further calls from them.

As Netty nudged us into place, Torina, Icky, and I made our way to the *Fafnir*'s airlock, opened it, and waited, watching as the hull of the module crept ever closer.

"We're in position," Netty said, her voice humming in my helmet.

"And the alarm has been sounded, so I'm on my way back," Perry put in.

"Okay, looks like we're on," I said. Icky and I pushed off and drifted the ten meters or so to the module. Torina exited the airlock, cradling a slugger. She hooked her foot in a stanchion, ready to give us covering fire in case anyone decided to start taking potshots at us.

Icky planted her makeshift breaching charge on the hull and locked it into place with the mag clamps. "You won't want to be near this thing when it blows," she said, and we both backed away, her moving left, me right, until we were both a good five meters away.

She counted down, then triggered the charge.

Nothing.

I scowled. "Are you shitting me?"

The radio detonator had failed, so Icky made her way back to the charge, plugged in a cable, then spooled it out. It left her alarmingly close to the charge, only about three meters away. I clenched my jaw. If the charge didn't detonate this time, we'd probably have to scrub the whole thing, since station security would start getting interested.

Icky counted down, then again triggered the charge.

This time, it blew with a flash. An instant passed, then a ragged section of hull plate blasted off into space, trailed by a column of frozen air, bits of debris, and robots.

Lots and lots of robots, all tumbling off into the void.

ACTUALLY, six robots, as it turned out, along with the other jetsam, including, to my utter surprise, a bowler hat. I'm sure there was a story behind that, but we didn't have the time or inclination to inquire.

"Netty, is one of these robots giving off our signal?" I asked.

"Yes."

"Which one?"

"One of them."

"Netty—"

"Sorry, Van, but I can't specifically tell. There's a lot of electronic background noise around this station. The best I can do is say that one of those robots is the one we want."

I sighed. "Okay, better get all six and see which one complains the most. If it's an asshole—"

"Then it's a Sorcerer. Got it, boss," Icky said and deftly launched herself toward the scattering robots and debris. She had more than a thousand hours of working in no-g vacuum, compared to my paltry twelve or so, so she quickly maneuvered each of the robots back to the *Fafnir*, using economical bursts of thrust from a maneuvering unit. I just returned to the ship and entered, then got ready to fly away.

"Van, there are four incoming comm calls," Netty said as I settled into my seat.

"Put them all on hold. With music. Make it *The Girl From Ipanema*. An instrumental version. Oh, and every thirty seconds or so, tell them how important their call is to us, and to please wait for the next available representative."

"Really?"

"Sure. It'll be nice to be on the other side of that for a change."

WITH THE ROBOTS recovered and everyone back on board, we were ready to get underway. Another ship, one of the ubiquitous workboats, had detached from the station and immediately lit us up with fire control scanners, while continuing to transmit increasingly assertive messages to us.

"Folks, I think we have officially overstayed our welcome here," I said, applying power and accelerating the *Fafnir* away. The workboat came after us, but after a brief stern chase and a few traded shots, Torina landed a solid railgun hit that left them decompressed. They gave up after that and turned back for Xublu's Folly.

"Well, I guess that's another place we can cross off our vacation list," I said, sinking back in my seat.

"Just show up with a stack of bonds next time. You'd be surprised at how quickly large sums of money will cause all to be forgiven," Perry said.

Icky finally appeared, pushing into the cockpit. "I've got our robotic passengers stowed and locked down back there."

"Any idea which one's the asshole?"

"Two of them are only semi-autonomous, like Waldo, so they've got nothing especially interesting to say. As for the other four, take your pick. They're all bitching, pretty much nonstop."

I could actually hear distant chatter coming from behind us. I decided to just let them all stew a while, and said so, when Icky produced a small, oblong metallic device.

"I also found this amid that debris. It was giving off an interesting signal, so I figured I'd grab it."

"Huh. Any idea what it is?"

"Nope."

"I recognize it," Torina said, and we all turned to her, surprised.

She grinned and shook her head. "Sorry, it's not exactly some arcane, esoteric knowledge. Do you remember the Srall?"

I thought about it and nodded. "The desert people. We rescued their princess from chip slavery on one of their sand-ship thingies."

"That's right. While we were there, I noticed one of them had a couple of those slung on his belt."

"Really? Well, that princess made us part of her family. When we get a chance, we'll have to drop by for a reunion."

8

WE CONTACTED Lunzy and let her know what had transpired. She, in turn, let the Schegith know that we'd recovered another of their people. They immediately arranged for a new body from the Spindrift Flesh Merchants, while committing to a generous one hundred thousand bond payout to us. That made me breathe a little easier. We weren't getting close to broke by any stretch of the imagination, but ongoing costs had been steadily eating into our funds. The Schegith reward would recoup all of those costs and then some. We still had a way to go before we could afford to upgrade the *Fafnir* from *Dragonet*-class to a full-blown *Dragon*, so I was watching our funding pretty closely.

The Schegith also sent along an image, that a bemused Lunzy relayed to us. "I hope it means something to you, because I don't get it," she said.

I laughed as soon as the image came up. So did Torina. It

showed a new boat floating just off the beach in the Null World undersea, with lettering on the hull in English, *Vacation Rental*.

"Lunzy, send a message back to them for us. Make it, *we accept, and do you take reservations?*"

Lunzy curled her lip. "Nearly thirty years as a Peacemaker, and I get to play glorified courier for cryptic messages I don't get."

"I'll tell you all about it, Lunzy, I promise. Hell, I'll even take you for a boat ride."

"You're on."

As we made our way back to Anvil Dark, we decided to check out our erstwhile robotic passengers. Icky had removed all of their logic modules, and we tried plugging them into Waldo, one at a time.

"This unit is non-standard. I demand to be plugged into a unit with the following minimum specifications—"

Icky unplugged the module when I shook my head. "Annoying, but that was no Sorcerer."

We tried the next one.

"Well, hello there, sexy. Give me a few minutes to figure out how this unit's manipulators work, then I'll bring you the sort of pleasure you can only—"

"Easy, big shooter. I'm not in the market for love. Okay, so that one's definitely not a Sorcerer," I said, nodding at Icky to plug in the next module.

"Your skin will be peeled from your body, your nerves boiled in acid, your—"

Icky unplugged it.

"Yeah, this is our guy. Is there any way to shut this prick up?"

"Yeah. Gimme a second." Icky fiddled with Waldo's internals, then nodded. "Okay, he'll be in listen mode. He'll hear, but he won't be able to speak."

"Heh, I can think of more than a few people I wish I could stick into *listen mode*," Torina said as I gestured for Icky to replace the module. She did, then pointed at me when she finished.

"Pay attention. Two options. Flash something if you understand."

A long, surly beat passed, then Waldo's work light flicked on and off.

"Good. Option one. We buy you the body of—" I paused, trying to recall a bit of implanted memory but wasn't quite able to get hold of it. "Shit. Torina, what's that race that's all about sensation, that has the, you know—the—" I mimed wiggling arms, trying to look the way a spasmodic squid might if it had too much coffee. Torina stared blankly, then snapped her fingers and laughed.

"So you're *not* having a seizure. That's good. I think the race you're referring to is the Tsssht. Their entire body is a nerve receptor, but why would you… ohhhh."

She turned to the Sorcerer, shaking her head in mournful apprehension. "Oh, my friend, I do feel bad for what's about to happen to you. Well, almost, anyway."

I nodded to Icky. "Let him speak."

She fiddled with Waldo's interior again, and a harsh voice erupted from his speaker.

"My nerves will not survive for even one day in a Tsssht. We aren't compatible."

"Really? So you'd last less than a day… as a perfect receptor of pain. Wow, that would *truly* suck. Of course, it doesn't have to be that way, which brings us to option two. That would require you to—what's that word, Perry?"

"Capitulate wholly to our needs as an organization and crew, without bitching about it, or we'll just end up melting you, or—?"

"Thank you, Perry. That was more than one word, but still quite accurate. Anyway, you get the picture, ah—what's your name, Trinduk? I mean, I don't want to be rude."

Another long, silent moment passed, then the tinny voice spoke, a little more subdued.

"Kent."

I wasn't sure what I'd been expecting, but it certainly hadn't been that. "Kent? Really?"

"It's actually Kinumaskwatuno'k, but I was called Kent by the guild."

"Holy shit, did your mom get paid by the letter?" Torina asked.

I gave her an approving smile. "Solid joke, Torina. Works well in any culture."

"Not mine," Kent snapped.

"Oh, trust me, Kent, you'll think that joke was high art after you hear what we've got planned for you. But first, you need a body, and not because I especially care one way or the other, but because I want Waldo back. Therefore, I'm going to get you one."

"I assume there are conditions."

"Look at you, all insightful and such. Hell yes, there are conditions, and they are as follows. Once you have a new body, if you try to run, we'll hunt you down and you'll die. If you commit a crime, you'll die. If you do anything *but* cooperate—guess what happens to you? And before you ask, no, you're not a slave. Unlike you and your people, I won't abide forced servitude of any kind. But you *are* in legal custody. So, you'll give us information on specific things we want to know, and then you'll answer to the Peacemaker Guild. You'll get your day in court, whereupon you're no longer our problem."

Another of those long pauses followed. I half-expected Kent to go tell us to pound sand, which wouldn't leave us with many options, aside from deactivating him again. I was hoping, though, that his desire to be restored to a body, and then eventually gain his freedom again, would outweigh any intention of being an uncooperative asshole.

When he finally spoke, though, the dispirited resignation in his voice was clear. "What kind of things do you want to know?"

I gave Torina a triumphant glance. "You'd better limber up Waldo's manipulators, Kent, my friend, because you're going to write it all down."

Kent proved to be surly but reasonably cooperative on the trip back to Anvil Dark. He'd occasionally lapse into threats to *slowly flay us alive* and *impale us on red-hot spikes* and similarly fun stuff, but we just cut his external audio until he fell back in line. In the meantime, we were able to slowly pry information out of him, proving his value as an intelligence gold mine.

Even so, I was tired enough of the guy that, on our third day with him, shortly before our last twist back to Anvil Dark, I was more than ready to shut him down completely.

I took a break and clambered back into the cockpit.

Torina, who'd been on watch, gave me a thin smile. "How's our passenger?"

"He's a miserable, cantankerous, pumped-up scumbag. From the way he goes on, you'd think he was loaded into some high-end combat bot and not—well, Waldo."

"So no change? No character growth at all?"

"I won't be inviting him to my next birthday party, if that's what you—"

"Van, we've got a contact. Correction, two contacts. Two ships, inbound at a high rate of acceleration," Netty cut in.

I cursed and swept my gaze over the tactical overlay. We'd popped into an uninhabited star system to do our last navigational fix before twisting to Anvil Dark. The system hosted a Saturn-like gas giant, complete with a spectacular set of rings whose atmosphere was enriched in deuterium compared to similar planets. It was essentially free fuel, with minimal filtering or processing required. And the *Dragonet*-class included a fuel scoop and processor as standard equipment. We'd therefore detoured and entered orbit around the gas giant, low enough to skim the top of its atmosphere. Our tanks were almost full, but it meant we were well out of position to try to twist away. Moreover, the two incoming ships were traveling fast and would overtake us long before we could break orbit and put any appreciable distance between us and the big planet.

In other words, we were stuck.

"Who are they? Do we have an ID on them?" I asked Netty, while Torina brought the weapons and fire control systems online. We also suited up, then Icky moved into the rear of the ship and readied herself to do any necessary damage control.

"They're non-standard designs, one class eight, and one class five. Their best fit is with Sorcerer designs we've encountered previously."

I exchanged a stunned glance with Torina. "Sorcerers? How the hell did they find us?"

"They must have had some way of tracking Kent," she replied.

"Or communicating with them," Perry suggested, then stopped and turned as Waldo slowly clattered his way into the back of the cockpit.

"You fools! I was able to gain access to your comm system and call for help, and you didn't even know it!"

"Netty, is that true?"

"I have no records of any extraneous comm traffic, but I suppose it is possible, if he was able to cover his tracks well enough."

"Haha! You pathetic idiots have no idea what I've done to your ship!"

I shot Perry a nervous glance, but he just shrugged. "Personally, I think he's just blowing smoke. Unless he came preloaded with viruses and a cascade program, which I doubt, because he'd likely have used them back in the chop shop."

"No! I was just biding my time! And now you are trapped and have no way to escape!"

Torina turned and stared at Waldo. "So what you're saying is that you've brought the very people that did this to you here to—what, rescue you? Do you really think they're going to be happy to see you, that it'll be some joyful reunion?"

"Actually, they're probably more interested in knowing what he's told us," Perry said.

I nodded. "Good point. Let's save them the trouble. Netty, open a comm channel to those Sorcerers so I can share with them exactly what Kent has revealed to us. I'm sure they'll be very interested—"

"No, wait. I—was lying. I didn't do anything to your ship. Really—"

He went silent as Icky came up behind him and deactivated his speech processor again.

She smiled and shrugged. "I thought you guys might not want this asshole distracting you while you're doing space combat stuff."

Space combat stuff. I'd already learned about it and was constantly learning more. But those were all nuances because the basics were simple. Space battle ultimately came down to acceleration—specifically, who had more of it. If you could change your velocity faster than the other guy, you had an edge. Going faster was better for overtaking and made you harder to hit, but it limited maneuverability, because the faster you went, the longer it took to change your direction. Going slower made you much more maneuverable, the ultimate limit being a dead stop, which allowed you to spin around in place and point in any direction. But it also limited your options and made you easier to hit.

So that was space combat 101. Space combat 102 was knowing how to use acceleration to adjust your velocity and maintaining that perfect balance between going fast and being able to maneuver to fit the circumstances. And that was all very good and interesting stuff, until you were starting in orbit, in a deep gravity well like, say, that of a gas giant. Your ability to accelerate was grossly limited by the need to climb your laborious way out of that gravity well—kind of like someone literally climbing out of an actual well, with guys at the top waiting to start beating on them, aka you were at a massive disadvantage.

That was us. Caught skimming the top of the gas giant's atmosphere to refuel, we were stuck at the bottom of that well and had to climb out before we could even start maneuvering.

"Sorry, Van, there simply are no tricks available here. That painfully slow acceleration curve you're looking at is thanks to the immutable laws of physics."

"The only laws that enforce themselves," Torina said, smiling sweetly.

I shot her a glare. "You're awfully chipper for someone who's staring down the barrels of two ships less than ten minutes away from opening fire on us."

She shrugged, then crumpled her face into a dejected frown. "I can do despair instead, if you'd prefer." She put her hands together like she was praying and managed an excellent quaver in her tone. "Do tell momma and poppa I'll miss them so, won't you?"

"Okay, that's a decent Scarlett O'Hara, but I'd rather have ideas. Whatcha got?"

"While I like that name, I'm not sure I can pull off a true Georgia accent—no, don't glower at me, I know about the south. And biscuits. Anyway, we do have *one* advantage. We've got a full load of fuel, so we can afford to be a little generous with using it."

I tilted my head in thought. That was a good point. Acceleration might be king in space battles, but its reign was based on fuel. You had to run it through your engines and thrusters, and inject it as reaction mass, to invoke Newton's Third Law about actions and reactions.

I frowned at the tactical display for a moment. "Netty, correct me if I'm wrong, but for a ship far away from this planet to stay directly above us while we orbit, it would have to be really cooking in terms of speed, yes?"

"Yes. And the further away it is, the faster it would have to go. Eventually, it would reach a point at which it couldn't change its direction quickly enough to keep a constant distance from the planet and would keep getting further and further away."

"Interesting."

Torina looked up from the display that showed the two Sorcerer ships about five minutes away from firing. "I smell something burning. You must be thinking."

"While I appreciate an unprovoked insult, this isn't the time. Save it for when we're at dinner. Makes for more awkward chat."

"I do appreciate an awkward meal."

"See? I care. Now then." I tapped a finger on the arm of my chair. "Perry, how long would it take to get help, in the form of other Peacemakers?"

"No idea. We know where the nearest Peacemaker ships are supposed to be operating, but whether they are or not—and whether there might be others as close, or even closer, we don't know. All we can do is put out a general distress call."

"The point being that if we don't know, then our friends out there don't either, right?"

"Uh… presumably not, no."

I nodded. "So we can put them on a clock. Or, at least, make them think we've put them on a clock."

"To what end, Van? We're still stuck in orbit, at the bottom of a very deep gravity well."

We were. It made me think back to my own mental analogy, about the guy trying to climb out of the well while facing bad guys waiting to pound the crap out of him at the top. That would, of course, be a very tough and dangerous, possibly fatal thing.

So what if that guy never climbed out of the well at all and just stayed safely down at the bottom of it? The bad guys could try dropping things on him, of course, but the guy at the bottom could dodge them. Eventually, if the bad guys really wanted to make sure they'd gotten him, they'd have to climb down into the well themselves.

"Netty, the orbit we're currently in isn't stable, is it?"

"Not one bit. It's too low to be stable, and add atmospheric drag to that—let's just say I was about to raise this point myself. Why?"

"Because I want to accelerate and raise our orbit until we're going as fast as we possibly can without actually breaking orbit, or at least breaking it very quickly."

I turned to Torina. "Broadcast a general distress call on our standard Peacemaker emergency channels. Make it seem like you're specifically asking for help from—I don't know, Larry, Moe, and Curly—three other Peacemakers, anyway, all of whom can be here in, say, a few hours."

I turned back to the tactical overlay and eyed the two icons representing the approaching ships. My grin was anything but friendly. "Here, kitty kitty."

"—AND decaying fast. Tanks are damned near dry and we're in a massive gravity well. Get here. Get here *yesterday*. Comms are weak with the field from this gas gi—"

Torina waved a hand, and Netty cut the comms, but not before adding a fuzz of static.

Torina was a natural actor. As she implored other Peacemakers, both actual and made-up ones for help, she managed a trembling edge of near-panic in her voice that made *me* want to help her. In the meantime, Netty started a long, high-power burn of the engines, steadily raising our orbit—exactly what the Sorcerers would expect us to do since we had to break orbit to flee.

Minutes passed, the two Sorcerer ships flying on implacably above us, closing the range. They'd already reached firing range for standard missiles but hadn't opened up yet. I wondered about that, but Netty had the answer.

"They want to get into laser range before they start committing themselves. Lasers are the only weapons that won't be affected by the gravity and radiation of this big ol' planet."

"Torina, they're going to expect us to shoot back. Feel free, anytime," I said.

Her hands were already busy. "I'll do my best," she said, sparking up the fire control system and swinging the lasers into firing position.

We were now playing a game of what amounted to chicken. The Sorcerers' ships began to fall behind us—we were now orbiting faster than they were able to track us without accelerating themselves. I suspected I knew what they were going to try and made a bet with Torina. A bet I won when the larger of the two ships abruptly decelerated and fell rapidly toward us as the gas giant's gravity pulled it inexorably in. The smaller ship opened fire, snapping a surprisingly intense barrage of laser fire at us, while also loosing a salvo of missiles.

"Hate to say it, but you're learning space warfare," Torina said, acknowledging my win.

I shrugged. "I've started to realize it's really all about logic, based on rules. And that's all computers are, really. So I guess I've kind of been training for years to do this, haven't I?"

"That's all computers are? Logic based on rules? Really?" Perry asked with his usual degree of affront.

"Unless they're shaped like birds or spaceships. Then they verge into the realm of *stylish*."

"Nice recovery, boss," Perry allowed.

We raced along in orbit, exchanging fire with the bigger Sorcerer ship. Between Torina and the point defenses, we dealt with the incoming missiles, destroying the closest nearly ten klicks away. As we sailed along, I had Netty spin the *Fafnir* about and apply short, hard burns to accelerate us in different directions, causing us to speed up, slow down, and veer side to side. It made targeting harder for the Sorcerers, and they weren't able to do the same anywhere near as effectively, simply because they were moving so much faster. Plus we had fuel to burn and could just fall back to the edge of the gas giant's atmosphere and scoop up more. Every time they fired up their drive, their tanks crept closer to empty.

"This almost feels like cheating," Icky said, poking her head into the cockpit. She'd been standing by to do damage control, but we'd only taken a few minor hits.

"That class eight ship is starting to worry me," Torina drawled.

"He's dropping into an orbit dead astern of us, and higher. That could be trouble."

I grunted my agreement. The class eight was the bigger threat by far. It outgunned us and was rapidly settling into a position where it could bombard us at leisure, without us being able to do much about it. As comfortable as the current situation seemed, it was a false comfort.

I rubbed my chin. Torina had landed several solid hits on the class five, meaning it would soon either have to withdraw or risk critical damage. But it had done its job, setting its companion up for continued offensive action. We needed a way to deal with it decisively, and we needed it—I checked the various bits of data portrayed on the overlay—sometime in the next ten minutes. Otherwise, all of this cleverness would amount to nothing but prolonging the prelude to our eventual defeat and destruction.

I looked around the cockpit, hunting for inspiration. Nav, powerplant, engines, thrusters, comm, other basic ship functions, none of them offered any ideas. I looked back at the weapons panel. Everything was charged up, and we still had a full load of missiles. But it wouldn't matter if we—

Wait.

A full load of missiles.

"Netty, do we have to actually *shoot* our missiles?"

"As opposed to what, exactly?"

"As opposed to just dumping them into space."

"You can dump anything into space. All it requires is an open hatch and a push."

"No, I mean, can we fire our missiles, or eject them, or whatever, without having their motors kick in?"

"I... suppose. If we deactivated their drives and let the launch charges kick them out of the tubes, they would very slowly pull away from the ship, at least until we started maneuvering."

"Exactly. They'd be more like mines then, wouldn't they?"

Torina sat up. "I think I see where you're going with this, Van. It's a nifty idea, but even as small as they are, they *will* detect the missiles from far enough away to destroy them."

I shot her a grin. "Not if we use my secret skill."

"What's that, boss?" Icky asked.

"I'm a *sneaky* bastard."

"Van, I must admit, this is such a cool plan, it's one *I* could have come up with," Perry said.

I glanced up from the overlay. "So why didn't you?"

"Hey, you're the one still climbing the learning curve, not me."

I chuckled and watched as the class eight closed in behind us. Torina had finally driven off the class five, sending it packing and leaving a trail of debris behind it. But it had distracted us enough that the class eight was now less than a minute from slamming us with the full weight of its fire. It would no doubt swamp our defenses and probably bring my career as a Peacemaker to a quick and definitive end.

"Icky, how much longer?"

Her voice came from behind the cockpit, where she was digging around in the guts of the fire control system. "Believe it or not, missiles aren't *meant* to launch themselves, then kind of float around.

The manufacturer goes to great lengths to make sure that *doesn't* happen, in fact—"

"Icky, we've got about thirty seconds, and then it's plan B."

"What's plan B?" Torina asked.

"Probably erupting into a ball of plasma and slowly becoming part of this gas giant, molecule by molecule."

"Plan B sucks."

"Which is why—"

"Okay, Van, I've got three missiles set to go," Icky said.

"Torina, if you please," I said.

Torina nodded and fired the glitter caster, enveloping the *Fafnir* in a scintillating cloud of chaff. I then pitched the ship slightly downward, while Icky triggered the missiles. Three dull *whumps* shook the hull. What typically happened next was a blur of exhaust flare as the missiles fired up their drives and leapt away toward their targets. Instead, they simply hove gracefully into view, one by one, and slid away from the *Fafnir* at a quick jogging pace.

As soon as the third came in sight, I pitched the ship's nose upward and applied thrust, sending us sailing out of the glitter cloud, away from the missiles still enclosed within it.

Icky, festooned with tools, pushed her way into the cockpit and stared out the canopy as I flipped the *Fafnir* around. "I had time to crosslink the drive and the proximity fusing of two of them. The third one's just along for the ride, unless that bastard gets close enough to trigger it."

"Here's hoping," I said as we all watched intently. I swear that even Perry was holding his breath, and he doesn't breathe. All we saw, though, was the cloud of glitter falling away behind us as we continued to accelerate. We couldn't see through it, so we had no idea what the Sorcerer was doing. If he was smart, he'd be braking like mad rather than just sailing into a cloud of chaff. That should at least buy us some time as we raised the ship toward breaking orbit and made a run for it. But if he wasn't—

He wasn't. Evidently unwilling to give up his velocity advantage over us, he braved streaking through the chaff cloud and was quickly bracketed by a trio of explosions as the missiles detonated. When he emerged from the chaff, he was decidedly worse for wear, trailing tumbling bits of debris and leaking atmosphere. Of more immediate concern, his main power flicked off, briefly on again, and then off, where it stayed. It left him wide open to *our* attacks.

Torina grinned. "Shall I finish him off?"

I narrowed my eyes at our damaged opponent. As long as he got his drive online again, he could climb away from the gas giant. If he didn't, though—

"Netty, if he never fires his drive again, what's going to happen to him? Will he just stay in orbit?"

"No. This planet is surrounded by a cloud of ionized gas molecules kicked out of its atmosphere by stellar radiation and its own magnetic effects. Friction with it will cause his orbit to slowly decay, and that decay will accelerate the closer he gets to the planet, and I think I know where you're going with this and you're an evil bastard, Van."

"I'm not the one that murders people, encodes their identities onto chips, and sells them into digital slavery for fun and profit."

"Good point."

"Torina, take out his engines, please," I said.

She gave me a frosty look. "Really."

I thought about the poor bastards we'd already rescued,

including most of the surviving members of an entire race, the Schegith. And that was only the tip of the proverbial iceberg.

I nodded.

"I'm sure. Oh, and let's bring Kent back online to see it. And then we can resume our discussion about—what was it? Oh, right. Smuggling routes used by the Sorcerers."

Perry bobbed his head. "As I've always said, space is a harsh and unforgiving place."

9

WE HANDED Kent's chip over at Anvil Dark, putting him into the custody of the appropriate Peacemaker authorities who would decide what to do with him. According to Lunzy, he'd likely be given a robotic body, not too different from Waldo, then stand trial for a variety of crimes. More importantly, I was able to hand over to her a treasure trove of information about the Sorcerers that Kent had seen fit to spill to us—probably to try and curry favor and win himself some leniency.

"It's amazing how quickly you can abandon your principles and beliefs when you, you know, don't have any," Lunzy said. We were lounging aboard her ship, the *Foregone Conclusion*, currently docked at Anvil Dark. In truth, I'd been surprised to find her here. I'd assumed she'd be out looking for Yewlo.

"Yeah, that effort has been scaled back. I think the idea's taking hold that he wasn't kidnapped or captured and simply chose to take his leave of us," she said.

"But we don't know that for sure," Perry replied.

"No, we do not. And before you ask, no, I don't really believe it either. But as more and more systems are secured, and whatever he knows gets more and more obsolete with no one obviously taking advantage of it, I think the general feeling is that he's just less and less important."

"So it's a comfortable sort of fiction that he's scarpered," Perry said.

I gave him a raised eyebrow. "Scarpered? How very British of you."

"I'm an eclectic bird."

I gestured to the data slate we'd handed over to Lunzy that contained everything we'd gleaned from Kent. "Anyway, it's all there. I have to admit, for all of their impenetrable secrecy and compartmentalization and shit, the Sorcerers' operation is surprisingly simple. It's basically murder, steal, repeat."

"Simple is good. The fewer moving parts, the better. In fact, it probably explains why their operation is so damned hard to penetrate. Remember The Stillness?"

I did, of course. A sophisticated criminal organization, it had been the subject of one of my first major cases. We'd taken some of the wind out of their unlawful sails, but they weren't gone by any means. Intelligence reports suggested they were just reconstituting and reorganizing prior to resuming their malfeasant ways. I was still keeping a close eye on those, since The Stillness had been a particular thorn in my grandfather's side and his great unfinished business.

So I grunted in assent. "Yeah. Of course."

"*Way* too complicated an operation. Too many moving parts.

That's what made them vulnerable. If they're smart—and we have to assume they are—they'll simplify things before they let themselves end up back on our radar," Lunzy said.

I managed a disgusted sigh, then filed The Stillness for another day. The more immediate one was loaded into the data slate in Lunzy's hand.

I gestured at it. "What bothers me most about the Sorcerers is the trail behind Kent's boss, the guy, or gal, or whatever, called Terminus. If you scroll down, you can—"

"I'm reading it now," Lunzy said, holding up a hand.

When she was done, she leaned her head back and sighed. "This Terminus, who or whatever it is, is connected to senior levels of the Eridani Federation, the Seven Stars League, and about a dozen other major powers in known space. Great." She looked at me. "Don't suppose you could get an actual identity out of him?"

"Nope, because he claimed he doesn't actually know who or what Terminus is. All of his communications with him, or it, or—anyway, all of his communications were done through dead drops, or heavily encrypted messages routed through intermediaries," I replied.

"Figures. It hints at someone or something with a military or intelligence background. That is, if you believe him?"

I glanced at Torina, who just nodded. "We do, actually. When we consigned that Sorcerer ship to an eventual plunge into that gas giant, he really opened up," I replied. But I leaned forward, again pointing at the data slate.

"There's another thing that concerns me, though. Check out the link between Terminus and the so-called Source Mirror."

Lunzy studied the slate, then sat up. "Kent thinks that this

Source Mirror is the *Starsmiths*?" She scowled. "The Starsmiths are above reproach, Van, and have been for centuries."

I understood Lunzy's discomfort with the idea that the Starsmiths might be compromised. It wasn't that they played an especially mission-critical role in the Peacemakers. The loss of Moonswords and their upgrades wouldn't really end up affecting the Guild very much. But the Peacemaker Guild, and its parent organization, the Uniformed sect of the mysterious Galactic Knights, thrived on customs and traditions, many going back well over a thousand years. And one of the oldest and most revered was the relationship between the Peacemakers and the Starsmiths.

A shared history was powerful. Traditions still in practice even more so.

It would be, I thought, like Earthly military forces giving up their banners and standards, their medals and awards and regimental histories. It wouldn't stop them from being just as lethal and effective, but it would still be a loss of something deeply enmeshed in their very culture. The unintended consequences and long-term effects were difficult to envision.

"I think we need to look into it regardless," I said.

Lunzy shot me back a hard look. "Considering the source here, Van, this could just be an attempt to sow discord and start us chasing our own tails."

Torina came to my aid. "I don't think so. Right up until those two Sorcerer ships bounced us, Kent was being a miserable, uncooperative asshole, sure. But once it became clear that they weren't there on some grand rescue mission, that he'd earned some sort of final redemption from his former—ah, colleagues, I guess—he kind of deflated."

"Being chipped and stuck in a bot, stripping scrap wire from old components, wasn't enough to convince him his friends didn't like him anymore? Really?"

"Yes. Really. He's a Sorcerer. He knows the ins and outs of the whole chip thing. I think he assumed that he was doing some penance for however he'd transgressed but would eventually be forgiven. Then, he finds out that no, the Sorcerers are quite happy to kill him."

I nodded. "Finding out your coworkers are quite happy to murder you without a second thought *would* constitute a pretty hostile workplace, I think. Gotta think their Human Resources Department is run by a minor demon or three."

Lunzy brooded over the slate for a moment, then sighed. "You're right. It guts me to think that the Starsmiths might be implicated in this somehow."

"The idea that one or more of the Masters might be didn't?" Icky asked.

Lunzy waved a hand. "Masters have been heroes and villains, sinners and saints, and everything in-between throughout the Guild's history. We've had Masters that have been noble, inspiring forces for good, and we've had Masters that have been mean-spirited, narcissistic wonks. But the Starsmiths have always been exactly what they are, no more, no less."

I could see discomfort twisting behind Lunzy's eyes. She'd been doing this a lot longer than I had, so the idea that the Starsmiths might be compromised hit her hard, in a very personal place.

Lunzy sighed again. "Van, you've done damned fine work so far and haven't ever given me any reason to doubt your intentions." She gave a wry smile. "Or maybe you're just really, really good at covering your tracks."

"Electronically? Digitally? You bet I am. In person? Well, I—"

Torina snickered. Icky shook her head. Even Perry muttered something.

I looked from one to the next. "What?"

"Van, you've got exactly one deceptive version of yourself, the one you slide into whenever you put on your duster. Other than that, you're about as devious as a supernova," Torina said.

"I can be sneaky. Sort of."

Perry put his wing on my shoulder. "No, Van, you can't," he said, shaking his head sadly.

"It's one of the big reasons we like working with you. None of that crooked, hypocritical bullshit," Icky added.

"A ringing endorsement if I'd ever heard one, and really what I was about to say myself. So, Van, go check out the Starsmiths. See if you can find out what's going on—if this is real," Lunzy went on. "But be discreet about it. Hell, get your Moonsword upgraded while you're there. No one will even blink at that. I'll even spot you the bonds. Within reason, of course."

"And what if we turn something up? Something we don't like?"

Lunzy's reply was flat and toneless. "For the sake of the Guild, let's just hope that you don't."

"So what's the next recommended upgrade?" I asked.

Linulla, the Starsmith, held my Moonsword in his claw and slowly turned it, examining it closely with his eyestalks. "I would suggest one of two. The first would add a component to the blade's substance that could catalyze a reaction with a range of gases, resulting in an energetic, exothermic reaction producing not just heat, but light."

"So, fire," Perry said.

"That's right. The other option would be to lengthen the blade to whatever maximum best suits your particular anatomy. It would give you additional edge and reach, making it more useful for, say, cutting through a secondary hull. But it would also change the blade's balance significantly, meaning you would need to retrain yourself to wield it effectively."

I crossed my arms. "Well, as much as the teenaged Dungeons and Dragons player in me would love to brandish a flaming sword, I'm not sure that's very practical."

"It wouldn't work in a vacuum, either," Linulla said, then gave as good an approximation of a human shrug as his crab-like body would allow. "Frankly, it's a gimmick. Peacemakers who specialize in working on lower-tech worlds, and especially more superstitious ones, like using the effect to wow an audience. Or they just like flaming swords, like your Dungeons and Dragons teenager."

I stared for a moment. "Wait. You got that reference? To Dungeons and Dragons?"

"You're not the first human Peacemaker to muse over the flaming sword function, Van Tudor. So, yes, I get it. In fact, I even know what THAC0 is, and how to calculate it."

"Holy shit."

It left me stuck in a moment of bemused unreality. That a giant crab-like alien who did smith work on a planet orbiting a distant star didn't just know something about table-top role-playing games, but actually knew obscure things about them—

I wondered what my old D&D group would have thought of *this*. Especially that whiny snot Bradley, who always played a rogue, always wanted to be the center of attention, and once screwed my character out of a freakin' +5 vorpal sword—

I shook myself. Now was *not* the time to start brooding over the theft of imaginary stuff over a kitchen table.

I'd do that later.

"Let's lengthen it," I said.

Linulla agreed and took some measurements of my body using a scanner gizmo. He then had me take the Moonsword and run through some swings, stabs, and blocks, and recorded it all with the same gizmo. Then he consulted its display.

"We're going to add about twelve point five centimeters to the blade," he announced.

"So that's about—five inches," I said. Being an American who traveled a lot, I'd got used to quickly converting between metric and Imperial in my head. "You're going to add five inches to it?"

"That's right," Linulla replied.

I heard Torina and Icky, both standing nearby, mutter something between them, then snicker. I turned to them, curling my lip as contemptuously as I could.

"Let me guess. Jokes about length."

Icky giggled. Torina shrugged, a stupid smirk on her face. "Men and their… swords. No matter what they've got, they're always wanting more."

"Efficiency. Thank you, Torina, the Starsmith will take it from here."

While Linulla set himself up for the job, I decided to gingerly start asking some questions. I kept them as indirect and circumspect as I could, trying to slowly nudge the conversation with the Starsmith toward what Kent had told us and how it seemed to implicate the Starsmiths generally. Linulla answered them while selecting suitable bar stock for the Moonsword's lengthened blade, then subjected both it and the bar stock to scans, presumably to confirm their respective metallurgies. After placing the scanner down, he turned to, I expected, shoo us out of his forge while he got to work. Instead, he focused all of his eyestalks on me.

"Van Tudor, are you asking if I, or any of my colleagues, have indulged in corrupt practices?"

I blinked. Okay, maybe the others were right. Maybe I *wasn't* as cunningly deceptive as I thought I was. I decided to forego subtlety and get right to the point.

"Actually, Linulla, I'm trying very hard *not* to ask that," I said, then went on to explain the disquieting information we'd obtained from Kent that at least suggested that the Starsmiths might be compromised or implicated in some way.

I braced myself for outrage, or disappointment, or even shame. But Linulla seemed utterly unperturbed.

"Oh, yes. We get asked to produce forgeries, counterfeits, and otherwise falsified things all the time. The pay that's offered for this can be quite generous."

I exchanged a frown with Torina. "That—wasn't an admission, was it?"

"An admission that we get asked, yes. An admission that we agree to any of that, absolutely not. In fact, if you look back through your Guild's records, you'll probably find many instances when Starsmiths have reported such nefarious proposals. I can't say that every instance gets reported, but—"

"That's okay, Linulla. I believe you," I hastily replied.

But Icky spoke up. "Just curious here—how much do you get offered to do this stuff?"

"I believe my record is—" Linulla paused, obviously thinking about it. "I think it would be three point five billion bonds to duplicate a unique article of statuary considered sacred to a race known as the Tsenjo."

We all just spent a moment gaping.

Torina finally spoke. "Three point five—"

"—*billion?*" I finished for her.

"Yes. Now, of course, most of the *requests* come with offers in the hundreds of thousands, to millions, often into the tens of millions, and occasionally the hundreds of millions. So three and a half billion is rather exceptional."

"You sound pretty blasé about being offered such—I'm struggling to even envision this—such *astronomical* amounts of money. How can you resist?"

"Three reasons. First, look around you. This is my life, Van Tudor. This is what I do. This is all that I do, and I am content to do it. So what need do I have for wealth?"

I nodded at that. He had a point, a very humble, almost poignant point.

"Second, if I were to use my talents to produce a forgery and it was discovered, my reputation and trust others would have in me would vanish, wouldn't it?"

"Instantly and permanently," Perry replied.

"Third, it would be… wrong. Doing such a thing would

diminish the value of the original, a piece that someone labored to produce based on their own unique vision. And, in the process, it would diminish the universe. Certainly not by much, but a finite amount, and I believe that our duty as sentient beings is to *enrich* the universe, to add to the totality of what it *is*. Thus, every work I produce is mine, and mine alone."

"You know what, Linulla? You're a true inspiration, even if you don't realize it," Torina said.

Again, I found myself smiling at the nobility of it all. But I also thought through the list of treasured artifacts I knew about on Earth, wondering how much they would fetch, as forgeries. I'm no art connoisseur by any means, but I knew the biggies—the Mona Lisa, Michelangelo's David, the Sistine Chapel, the Pieta…

I sighed and shook my head "There's a statue back home that is worth billions, if not trillions."

"What is it?" Linulla asked.

"The Pieta. It's—well, it's God, and his mother. Sort of. It's complicated."

"That would certainly do it. Religious artifacts always command the highest values, either as things to be sold for even more, or used in an attempt to influence or manipulate a religion and its adherents. That was the case for the Tsenjo's sacred statue. Those who wanted to duplicate it were contemplating fraud on a truly epic scale. Now, the people who do this and get caught—"

"Let me guess. Torn apart by a mob?"

"It's almost like you were there."

"No, I just know mobs. And fervor."

"More like fever," Linulla replied. "And I stand corrected. Not being torn apart by a fevered mob is a *fourth* reason that no Starsmith, including this humble one, would ever contemplate perpetrating something so—so *monstrous*."

I gave a firm nod. "Linulla, I'm sorry we even had to bring this up."

"Nonsense. It is your job to ask questions like this, to uncover wrongdoing."

"It is. It's just nice to ask them and find absolutely no wrongdoing at all."

The Moonsword seemed like a whole new weapon. No longer a short-bladed weapon suited mostly for stabbing, its lengthened blade now had enough cutting edge to represent a true slashing threat. I spent some time just admiring the workmanship. I had no idea how Linulla had amalgamated what had, just a day earlier, been a crude piece of alloy bar stock, into the sword's blade, and so seamlessly. It was as though the blade had always been this length.

I moved to a clear section of Linulla's forge, made sure no one and nothing was close by, and tried a few practice swings, thrusts, and parries. It was immediately evident that the Starsmith was right. I had to relearn how to handle and wield the thing. All of my technique, even my muscle memory, was just wrong. I was slow and cumbersome, overcorrecting and repeatedly leaving myself wide open. I wouldn't have to start entirely from scratch, but it was pretty damned close.

I felt like a baby with a knife. In a sense, I was. Just taller and a bit more dangerous.

"Take care with that blade, Van Tudor. The third upgrade to a

Moonsword customarily makes it a generational weapon, meant to be passed down to your successor, the way this was to you by your grandfather."

I hefted the blade, admiring it, and actually looking forward to the opportunity to train and test myself with it. "I will. I plan on using it for just that, in fact. To make sure there *are* more generations of Tudors."

10

WE'D BARELY broken orbit from the planet called Starsmith when a high-priority broadcast came across a Peacemaker general channel. It seemed that the Masters had obtained some sort of intelligence regarding Yewlo and wanted all available Peacemakers to proceed to a particular set of coordinates at best possible speed to run down a lead. Netty plotted the given coordinates, fixing them in a nearby star system that only served as another navigational waypoint, yet another of those unremarkable red dwarf stars.

The message was followed up a moment later by one specifically addressed to us, from Lunzy, on a secure, private channel.

"Van, you're one of the closest Peacemakers, so I'd like you to make your best possible speed to those coordinates."

That made me frown a bit. "Already intended to do that, Lunzy. I mean, that was the order, right?"

"It is. But I'd like you to arrive there *first*. I'm going to try and hold back the next two closest Peacemakers, neither of whom I know particularly well. I'll—I don't know, come up with some reason to distract and deflect them."

Perry leaned forward. "This all has a definite conspiracy vibe to it, Lunzy. What's up? As in, what's *really* up?"

I'd been wondering the same thing, and it looked like Torina had, too.

"Let's just call it an abundance of caution. If they were Peacemakers I knew, like Alic or K'losk, I wouldn't hesitate to have them rush to join you. But they aren't, and while I'm not saying they're anything less than honest, dependable Peacemakers, I'm also not one hundred percent sure. And I'd really like nothing to happen to whatever evidence might be there before you arrive."

"Understood. Netty's plotting the twist now. We'll be there in—um, Netty?"

"Eight hours, plus or minus ten minutes."

"Sounds good. Lunzemor out."

I turned to Perry. "Is this normal?"

"What, flying through space? I'd have thought you'd have figured out by now that it's kind of what we do—"

"No, you smartass space chicken. What I mean is, is this sort of paranoia normal? Deliberately distracting Peacemakers you don't want potentially fiddling with evidence or interfering in an investigation? Not trusting Peacemakers you don't personally know well?"

"Well, there's always an element of this sort of stuff, sure, especially on jobs with a lot of money involved. Peacemakers can be pretty competitive, and the Masters and senior ranks naturally have their favorites and protégés. And may I add, *bawk bawk*."

"That's not bad. As to the rest, but… "

"But, it's not normally this—well, pronounced. There's a definite undercurrent to all of this, that there's some sort of corruption festering away deep inside the Guild. Or is that just me?"

I glanced at Torina, then we both spoke in unison.

"It's not just you."

I settled back in my seat. Perry's undercurrent was, to me, running pretty close to the surface. We had the disappearance of Yewlo. We had definite suspicions about Master Yotov, who signed off on the sketchy terraforming operation where we recovered the identity we'd thought had been Erflos Tand. We'd had a few hints of malfeasance that potentially implicated Groshenko. And then we had my cousin, Carter Yost, who'd been set up as a Peacemaker and kept gaining standing in the Guild, despite being an utter moron and shitty at doing anything but moussing his hair and being wealthy. I still had no idea who'd been behind that, or why.

I unbuckled and made to leave the cockpit. "Torina, over to you. Since we've got a few hours of flying ahead of us, I'm going back to my cabin to practice with my sword."

Torina lifted a brow as Perry turned to me, his eyes fairly pulsing with an oncoming insult.

But Netty struck first. "I'm told it's all in the wrist, Van."

I drew myself up like the gentleman I am. "And to think I called you cultured."

As soon as we twisted into a point close to the coordinates, we knew there was trouble.

Not a threat, per se. Despite hammering away with our active scanners at full power and in all directions, we didn't detect any other ships. Or, at least, any intact ones. What we *did* detect was a whole lot of debris.

"There's one larger ship, about class ten. That's probably a freighter. And two smaller ones, about class seven. Workboats, which mean they could be anything," Netty said.

"Mmm-hmm," I mumbled. Calling a ship a workboat was like calling a car a sedan. It didn't say anything about what the car was being used for. After all, a personal car, a taxi, and a police cruiser could all be sedans. Workboat was the same sort of thing.

We eased our way closer. The three ships just hung in space, one of the workboats slowly tumbling end over end, all of them a few tens of klicks apart. Each ship was badly damaged, both by explosions—probably missile warheads—and the characteristic clean, circular through-and-through hits from hypervelocity mass-driver slugs. Debris filled the space around them, all of it recognizably spalled off by battle damage. It was what we didn't find, though, that was most intriguing.

"No bodies," Perry said.

Icky leaned forward like an eager kid in the backseat of a car, but with four arms and five times the mass. She was close enough that her breath tickled my ear in a warm rush. It was a lot like having a pet bear, but the bear was a superb engineer with two extra arms. "Maybe none got ejected, and they're still aboard."

But a closer inspection of the damage proved that unlikely. There were several instances of hull damage that would have explosively decompressed portions of the ships. That, in turn, would have flung bodies, cargo, and debris into space. We found the debris but not a single body or cargo pod.

"It's almost as though someone cleaned up the site of this

battle," Torina said, watching as a fragment of hull plating slid past the *Fafnir*.

I suppressed a frustrated sigh. "You know, conspiracies aside, I'm getting awfully tired of feeling like somebody is always one step ahead of us."

"Kind of makes you wonder what evidence the Masters had that drew their attention to this random spot in space, doesn't it?" Torina asked.

"Yeah, it does." I glared at the scene for a minute, then unbuckled again.

"You know what? Screw it. Let's check out these ships more closely. I want to see just *how* thoroughly this particular crime scene has been scrubbed."

WE SPENT the next four hours suited up, boarding each of the ships in turn. Neither of the workboats turned up anything useful, leaving me gnashing my teeth in frustration. My mood had become particularly foul by the time we started searching the bigger ship. I honestly expected to find nothing, and would have to be consoled with submitting what would still be a decent salvage claim.

And then we found that whoever tried to clean things up made a mistake.

"Right there," Perry said, pointing into an access panel he'd asked Icky to open. His wingtip indicated a small, black rectangle about as big across as my thumb was long.

"That's a maintenance logger. It's intended to record data about ship operations, reactor efficiency, engine performance, that sort of thing," he said.

"And that interests us how, exactly?" I asked.

"It interests us, at least potentially, because ships licensed to carry cargo normally copy their manifest from each trip they make to this little gadget. It's so that things like total mass and its distribution across the holds, center of gravity, axis of thrust, and similar bits of data that can affect a ship's performance are available."

"Wait. You're saying the cargo manifest is contained on that module?"

"Yup. We've got the same setup on the *Fafnir*, though it's obviously a lot simpler, since we don't routinely carry cargo."

I had to narrow my eyes in suspicion. "Hold up. Wouldn't our bad guys be likely to have known that? Can we trust anything we find on it?"

"Not necessarily. Outside of maintenance and engineering circles, not many people know about this at all. The maintenance logger is rarely pulled or consulted, generally only during refits, or if there's been a problem of some sort, obviously," Icky put in.

My suspicion faded. I recalled instances on Earth when crashed airplanes hadn't yielded anything useful from their so-called black boxes, the flight data and cockpit voice recorders. Investigators had turned to other recorders, like engine performance monitors, that collected at least a few useful parameters. I recalled this because I'd retrieved such data on behalf of a joint government and corporate client, who'd been prevented from properly investigating a crash in a hostile country.

"Well, let's pull it and see what it tells us."

We took the logger back to the *Fafnir* and plugged it into a sandboxed reader so Perry could scan it for malicious code. It came up clean, so we passed it over to Netty to read.

Sure enough, the ship's final cargo manifest, including things like masses and loading schemes, had been captured and retained by the little device. It didn't offer much detail about each cargo pod, unfortunately, beyond its mass and where it had been located in the ship, but there was at least some identifying information. We were able to quickly filter out the ones of no obvious interest, which left us with only one pod worthy of follow-up. It was a shipment of Yonnox origin, but it was being shipped by a shell corporation whose majority owner was the Srall.

"Fascinating. That's the second time we've bumped up against the Srall in just a few days," I said.

"It is. We've still got that module from one of their sand skimmers. Maybe we need to take it home," Torina said.

"What a *delight*. I've missed being—um, what's the word?"

"Treated with frosty indifference?" Perry offered.

I snapped my fingers. "Yeah, that's it. Anyway, let's take the Srall their data core and maybe take the opportunity to ask a few questions. We can presume upon our close relationship with their princess, and hey, I've been meaning to see a desert, anyway."

"Really?" Icky asked.

"No. But I like pretending we're going somewhere interesting."

"Or at least chatty," Perry said.

I flashed him a grin. "Oh, I think you've got *chatty* pretty much covered, Perry."

"If this is leading to some stupid, *Polly wanna cracker, who's a pretty boy* bullshit, I swear I'll start playing nonstop Kalusian thrash metal. Then you'll be *glad* to hear the dulcet tones of my voice again."

I looked at Torina. "Kalusian thrash metal? Is it bad?"

"Not at all. If you like the sound of spaceship parts being fed into a reclamation grinder, it's great."

I'd been looking forward to a visit to the Srall, actually. Not because I particularly liked the Srall themselves, because they were insular, humorless shits whose lives revolved around a complex, quasi-religious belief system I really didn't get. For instance, they seemed to believe that there was really only one electron in the entire universe, that effectively filled the role of all electrons by being in all places electrons were, and doing all things electrons did, simultaneously—and that electron was an aspect of their god. I was well-traveled enough back on Earth to know I should just nod and smile and look understanding, even if I wasn't.

No, the reason I'd actually been looking forward to visiting the Srall was because of So-metz, a young noble whose family had actually had her killed and chipped, then installed in one of their sand runners to forever pilot the thing across the shifting dunes of her homeworld. It was a punishment for her being *sacrilegious*, insofar as she loved to have friends, party, and generally behave like a teenager —which she was. We'd rescued her and arranged to have her restored to a new organic body, and she'd actually made Torina and I members of her family.

But our request to speak with So-metz when we arrived in orbit over the Srall homeworld was a disappointing one.

"The Radiant So-metz, Princess of the Crimson Dunes, is

currently off-planet," a dour Srall replied. He'd introduced himself as Tik-mar and was apparently her great uncle.

Well, shit. So-metz was the only Srall we actually knew. We'd been hoping that, based on the scant information we had, we could get her help in identifying who was behind the company that funded the mysterious and missing shipment from the wrecked freighter we'd found. But her off-world trip was apparently a diplomatic one, which Perry helpfully interpreted as *she's off partying somewhere*.

"That's what turned her family against her the first time. Isn't she worried she's just going to rile up even more Srall with her sacrilegious debauchery?" I grumbled.

Torina smiled. "She's the equivalent of a human teenager, coming from a rigid, restrictive social hierarchy. I mean, *hello*." Her smile became a grin. "I say go get it, girl, because the realities of life as a princess are soon going to overtake her life. And at least she's taken her partying off-planet this time."

"Preferably somewhere without a lot of security cameras," Icky mumbled.

"You have experience with, ah… difficulties? Because of being caught on film?" I asked, smiling blandly.

"Can't go back to Rigel Center," Icky said with a small shrug.

"And what is Rigel Center, pray tell?" I was being *so* helpful. Torina snorted, then shot me a look.

Perry interjected. "A… what you would call a waterpark. But in orbit over a gas giant. Lots of kids go there to raise hell, but I've never heard of anyone actually being *banned* from Rigel Center. What the hell did you *do*, Icky?"

"A cannonball. Well, if you want to be technical, a cannonball from a twenty-meter platform. I, ah, directed the splash—"

"You targeted someone with a huge wave of water," Perry added, again being helpful.

Icky smiled sheepishly. "Turned out to be a diplomat filming a promo video. I kind of… ruined the camera system. And his data slate. And the logistics planning for an entire system's worth of trade." She paused. "For a year."

I clapped my hands. "Well. Done. I mean, if you're gonna make a splash—"

"Make a *splash*," Torina finished, adding to the applause.

I looked at Icky with newfound respect. "You really are a hooligan."

"Thank you. Should we talk about the princess, though?" Icky asked, eager to shift the conversation away from her youthful hilarity.

"We should. We've got no champion to connect us to the Srall, really," I observed.

"Call the uncle again?" Netty chirped.

"Can't hurt. Connect us, if you please," I said.

He answered immediately and began to speak. "I certainly don't approve of her rather wanton ways, but I likewise think that her immediate family's response to them was… a little extreme," he said.

I fought back a string of rich, loud invectives. "Killing her and encoding her personality onto a chip and subjecting them to a future of unending digital slavery? Yeah, I'd call that a little extreme."

"The Srall have only had trans-luminal space flight for a little over one hundred standard years. It takes considerably longer than that to change a culture as based on custom and tradition as ours."

He said it like it was the final statement to be made about it, which I took as a signal that further discussion would be unwelcome. Fair enough.

We arranged with Tik-mar to descend to a spaceport apparently controlled by So-metz's family, where we would meet with a delegation consisting of—

"Consisting of who, again?" I asked Perry as we entered the airlock. It slid open, admitting the scalding, dry heat of the Srall day.

"Various faction heads gathered into a sort of committee whose members come from every Srall family with territory bordering So-metz's. Every family has such a committee, called a Gathering, which harkens back to their ancient nomadic ways."

I sighed, the slow noise of unpleasant acceptance. We were going to meet with a bunch of what amounted to diplomats, each focused on the narrow interests of their particular family, all in the context of a rigid, theocratic society that didn't like outsiders.

Frankly, I would have preferred to be at a water park, even if we were banned from doing cannonballs.

WE WERE MET by ground transportation, a ground-car that rolled along on massive balloon tires that I could see being handy for traversing both hard surfaces and soft, shifting sand. It took us past the spaceport terminal and into a small town a few klicks beyond. It was apparently one of So-metz's family holdings and included facilities to receive off-world visitors. It amounted to something like an Earthly hotel and conference center, climate-controlled toward what the Srall considered to be the cold end of the temperature scale—that is, uncomfortably hot instead of brutally hot.

Torina, Perry, and I were led into a comfortable room with a large conference table, decked out with a spread of Srall art, including sculptures, wall-hangings, and paintings that somehow managed a strikingly 3D look, no matter the view angle. All of it was rendered in shades of brown, brown and red, brown, red, and soft grays, and for a little pizazz, the odd hint of rust.

"They sure do have a distinct color palette," I muttered.

Torina made a face. "It's um… vibrant." She smiled so rigidly I had to stifle a laugh, and then we were swept along past the art, into the presence of our liaison.

Tik-mar, So-metz's great uncle, introduced us to the Gathering, a sudden barrage of names and titles and family origins I absolutely didn't remember beyond the guy sitting across from me being named Kel-arnus… or maybe Arn-kelnus. When we were given the floor, I explained how we'd come into possession of the data core from one of their sand skimmers and placed it on the polished wood table in front of me with a soft clunk. A sudden collective gasp rose from all those assembled.

Tik-mar reached over and hastily retrieved the core. "We thank you for the return of this item, but please, nothing may touch the Gathering table except for food and drink and the vessels that contain them."

"Which you would have known had you done any reasonable background research on our culture before coming here," one of the Srall down the table said.

I was tempted to inform them that their ocean of customs and traditions came across as bitchy, churlish, and doctrinaire, and that

I'd spent hours reading about their culture. All those hours—wasted, I might add—taught me that Srall culture came down to one rule. *It's only okay if we do it.*

I'm sure that not putting anything but food and drink on the Gathering table was in there somewhere—along with a million other things no one could possibly remember. Well, except for Perry, of course, him being a machine. But even that didn't help because the Srall didn't recognize AIs as any different than any other tool. As far as the Srall were concerned, Perry might as well be a shovel.

"My profuse apologies," I said.

"Apologies are merely a plea to justify bad behavior," one of them muttered.

I turned back to Tik-mar, the muscles in my jaw tighter than a piano wire. "In any case, we have another reason for having come here. During the course of a Peacemaker investigation, we came across information that suggested a Srall-owned corporation was involved in the trade of—"

Another gasp.

Now what?

"Matters of crass commerce, or any worldly concern, aren't supposed to be discussed until after the celebratory Feast of Greeting," Perry said, his voice confined to my ear bug.

"I do not believe that this outsider has done us the favor of even attempting to understand our culture," someone said.

"No, it is most insulting—"

I slammed my hand down on the table. "*Tough shit.* Listen up, you preening gasbags! As of this moment, I am no longer here as Van Tudor—who, I might add, *your* princess made part of *her* family. I am now here as Peacemaker Van Tudor, representing the Galactic

Knights Uniformed, conducting a warranted investigation. You will accord me the respect due my rank and station or I'll cuff your asses and haul you to Anvil Dark." I glared at the assembly, which was now staring at me in stunned silence.

When one of the Srall began to speak, I pointed my finger at him like a gun. "Please. *Please*. I'm *begging* you. Give me a reason. Any reason at all. I might not arrest you all, but let me assure you—the first one of you pricks who speaks is the first one put in irons."

Dead silence greeted me at that. Well, other than Perry's stunned whistle—something I didn't remember he could do. Torina just stared, which was fine. I didn't need input. I needed quiet. I'd had enough of diplomacy.

"So, in that capacity, I am going to request a subpoena under Section Four, Article Two of the Interstellar Commerce Treaty, *to* which the Srall are a signatory, for commercial and financial records of each one of you sitting around this table. They'll be subjected to a detailed forensic audit, and any irregularities will be treated as an interstellar commercial crime."

"How *dare* you—"

"How dare I? Like this." I turned to Perry. "Head back to the *Fafnir* and start making the necessary arrangements. Send word back to Anvil Dark that we need a forensic auditor to stand by and a warrant to seize all records—"

"That won't be necessary," Tik-mar said, holding up his hands. "I think we can all accept that you are unfamiliar with our customs and can be forgiven transgressions. In fact, they constitute a learning opportunity, which I believe is something we owe to an honorary member of So-metz's family. Isn't that right?"

He swept his gaze around the table. He got a few defiant looks back but stared each of them down. He finally turned back to me.

"Please, Van Tudor, have a seat, sure in the knowledge that you will *not* be subjected to further criticism. We only ask that you be reasonable in accepting comments and suggestions at the conclusion of this Gathering, which *I* will deliver to you."

"Unacceptable," I growled.

"Excuse me?" Tik-mar managed to say. He'd been expecting some kind of meeting in the middle. I would give him no such thing.

"Was I unclear? I said unacceptable. As in, there will be no *helpful commentary* from anyone at this table. If I have a point of culture I need clarified, I will *ask*. I won't allow you to snipe at me and be emboldened as the meal goes on. That is my offer. You get nothing, and you'll like it." I caught Torina smiling, while Perry flashed his eyes at me.

"You totally nailed that, Van," he said in the ear bug. "I guess your memory works better when you're pissed."

I nodded once, then carried on, speaking into the hum of shocked silence. I explained the derelict ships and the missing Srall shipment—all without a single response from the Srall. Good. They'd earned it, the bastards.

"So, I must ask—is this true? Did a Srall corporation contract a Yonnox broker to ship—well, something?"

"We did," one of the Srall replied.

I had to blink and stare at that. I hadn't expected such a ready answer. The Srall population was hundreds of millions, spread across the planet's equatorial and temperate zones. The chances of us finding someone directly involved in this mysterious corporation right off the bat was, I thought, vanishingly small. But here we were.

The Srall who'd spoken must have sensed my confusion and what it was about. "Every Srall Gathering maintains a seat on the board of directors of our interstellar trade corporation. I am that representative for this Gathering." He gestured vaguely outside. "As you'll appreciate, we are blessed with sand and good manners, and not much else."

Perry's voice hummed in my ear bug. "Well, at least one of those things is true."

I got it. Back on Earth, the British and Dutch East India companies had been respectively bankrolled and backed up by those nations and used as a sort of interface with other economies. This sounded like the same thing, although I could only imagine how complicated that board was, since the Gatherings were made up of representatives of all surrounding families, and these multi-family bodies, in turn, apparently provided directors to this corporation. But I wasn't here to appreciate the niceties and nuances of Srall social and corporate structures, so I just accepted it and moved on.

"Do you do a great deal of business with the Yonnox?"

"I don't know. Such detailed matters are taken care of by our merchants and brokers."

That, I believed. The board of a large corporation wouldn't know the specifics of individual shipments being made by the corporation. We were probably going to have to ask them for their records—

"What were you shipping?" Torina asked.

I glanced at her. Just as I wasn't surprised they didn't know the details of *how* the cargo was being shipped, I assumed they likewise wouldn't know what was being shipped. Not given that it was a single cargo pod.

But the Srall who'd named himself a director of the corporation spoke right up.

"Very simple. We were shipping money."

I leaned forward. "Money? Why?"

"Because the Trinduk do not deal with The Quiet Room or any other banking organization."

I sat back. The Trinduk. The Sorcerers?

"You're doing business with the Trinduk?" I asked.

"Yes. Is that a problem?"

"I—"

Torina cut off what was about to be a tirade. "No, not at all. It's just that there is a sect among them who call themselves the Sorcerers, and they're at the center of our current investigation. So you'll appreciate our interest in this."

I shot her a glance. I was thankful she'd prevented me from tearing into the Srall. For one, notwithstanding how So-metz's family was so obviously implicated in dealings with the Sorcerers, the Srall around this table might very well know nothing about it. To them, the Trinduk could simply be another trading partner. For another, I'm not sure the meeting would have survived a second rant from *Peacemaker Van Tudor*, no matter how righteous.

Tik-mar leaned forward. "Are you suggesting that we're somehow involved with criminals?"

I took my cue from Torina and raised my hand. "Not at all. I mean, I'm sure there are criminals among your people, but I don't simply assume that when I deal with you, I'm dealing with a criminal. I'm sure there are some perfectly nice, law-abiding Trinduk out there."

Somewhere. Maybe.

"I understand. We go to great lengths to ensure that we do not knowingly have intercourse with criminal elements."

His use of the word *intercourse* wasn't wrong, but I wondered if it had the same connotation for the Srall as it did for humans, and if it was intended as a subtle insult. I ignored it, given my earlier diatribe, because we were getting somewhere as the discussion went on.

"That is why we're happy to deal with the Trinduk, as we're unaware of any concerns about them. Besides, they seem to be closely aligned with your own Guild," the Srall corporate director said.

"What do you mean?"

"Ordinarily, the Trinduk send a ship directly here to pick up their payment. This past fiscal month, that wasn't possible. So, given concerns about security, we did not ship all of the money owing to the Trinduk in one shipment. The part that you have discovered is missing from the Yonnox-brokered ship is only one third of last fiscal month's payments—still a cause for serious concern, of course."

"So who carries the other two thirds?" I asked.

"As I said, the Trinduk work closely with your Guild. Each fiscal month, a Trinduk ship arrives to pick up one third of the payment. The other two thirds are picked up by ships that subsequently arrive. Those ships belong to Peacemakers."

AGAIN, I sank back in my seat. Peacemakers? Picking up money from the Srall every month?

I turned to Perry. "Is there any way that could be legit?"

"Sure. You've done extracurricular stuff, Van, like helping Torina's homeworld recover from that illicit mining operation. There's no reason a Peacemaker couldn't function as a money courier. Of course, they're supposed to disclose all fees and such to the Guild, the way you did with all that stuff involving paying the space hippies, as you call them."

I turned back to the Srall. "Alright. Let's put aside the Peacemaker thing for a moment. Do you trust the Sorcerers—er, the Trinduk?"

"They haven't lied to us or given us any reason to doubt them. At least, not yet," Tik-Mar replied.

"What if I gave you another option?"

"Because of your gift, we will listen." He studiously avoided mentioning my volcanic threats. Good move on his part.

"I appreciate that. Just give me a minute, and by a minute, I mean I'll be back as soon as I can. Probably a month or so."

Tik-mar nodded. "We will be here."

"Along with those famous manners of theirs," Perry said in my ear.

11

"Hopefully, So-metz will be here when we next show up. That way, we don't have to run the gauntlet of those oh-so-charming Srall again," I said as we broke orbit. Icky actually sat in the copilot's seat, Torina being in the back taking a call from her family.

"Well, while you were off politicking, I got a lot done around the ship. You should notice a definite improvement in thruster performance. Your roll rate sucked. When was the last time the control valves for those thrusters were taken out and cleaned?" she said, sounding distinctly grouchy.

I smiled. The one sure way to aggravate Icky was to present her with tech that hadn't been maintained to what she considered an acceptable standard. I could tell she'd spent most of her life with only her father for company, because he struck me as the same. It probably meant they were constantly criticizing each other's work. They were both top-notch engineers as a result, but that must have at least occasionally made for some awkward meals.

"I'm not sure. Netty, when was the last time that was done?"

"About six months before your grandfather passed and you inherited the *Fafnir*," she replied.

"Oh." I glanced at Icky. "Is that a long time?"

"The maintenance time is measured in hours of use, Van, not some absolute time. But, yeah, if those valves haven't been cleaned and realigned for that long, then yes, I'd say it's a *long time*."

She sighed. "I'm obviously going to have to go over this ship component by component, nose to tail, to make sure nothing else is in dire need of fixing." She gave me a narrow-eyed look. "I hope you've been keeping detailed maintenance logs."

Her tone was disapproving, but I could see a spark of enthusiasm dancing in her dark eyes. She loved this stuff and couldn't wait to start combing the *Fafnir* for things she could fix or tweak.

"Talk to Netty. She's the expert about—um, Netty."

"The answer is yes, I've been keeping detailed logs. Of course, I also maintain a detailed maintenance schedule, which actually does sometimes get consulted," Netty said. It was her turn to sound disapproving.

I decided to change the subject. "Perry, do you believe those Peacemakers the Srall alluded to are real? That they are legit? Is there any way we can check?"

"Technically, all Peacemakers are supposed to log their time with the Guild. But anything that amounts to 'time off' won't show any associated detail, except for up-to-date contact information, in case someone needs to urgently get hold of that Peacemaker."

"So, no."

"Like I said, Van, Peacemakers do a lot of freelancing. I could see a couple of them taking jobs carrying Srall money to a creditor. It would be seen as secure, and easy money for the Peacemaker."

"That includes the Trinduk?"

"You said it yourself, Van. As far as we know, all Sorcerers are Trinduk, but—"

"Not all Trinduk are Sorcerers. Yeah, I know." I sighed. "It just seems too—I don't know. Too coincidental. We've been nibbling around the edges of Peacemaker corruption for months, and now two of them show up in the middle of our best lead for our own investigation."

I tapped a finger against the armrest. "I can't help feeling there's a picture here, and if we could only see a few more pieces of it, we might be able to figure out exactly what it is—"

Icky stood and clambered out of her seat. "Sorry, Torina, just keeping it warm for you—what's wrong?"

I turned. Torina stood in the back of the cockpit. The expression on her face was one I hadn't seen in a long time. Not since she'd discovered that an illegal mining operation had squatted on her family's lands, and there seemed to be nothing she could do about it.

"Van, can you take me home?" she asked, her voice tight.

"Sure. Netty, a course, please and thank you." I turned back to her. "What's going on?"

I'd expected something like a death in the family. I hadn't expected what she said next.

"It's the land, Van. It's dying again. It's all dying."

I BROUGHT the *Fafnir* down from orbit and adopted atmospheric flight about a hundred klicks from Torina's home. As we raced across the countryside about a thousand meters up, I braced myself for what we were about to see. I felt Torina do the same thing.

It was worse than I'd expected.

In fact, it was worse than ever before, when the strip miners slashed and tore at the ground. That had been an industrial wasteland, brutally clear-cut, soil stripped down to the bedrock, and generally chewed up. This was different. The land beneath us wasn't damaged or even in distress.

The land was *dying*.

Like a tumor, a grey wasteland blighted the lush, green forests, the trees grey and leafless, the grass desiccated yellow. The little ponds and watercourses had gone pale and murky, filled with sludgy runoff from soil no longer root bound by the thriving vegetation and protected from erosion. A fine pall of dust hung over it, a dingy hue that turned the light of Van Maanen's Star as wan and grey as the trees themselves. Even the breeze seemed… tired. Sapped.

Terminal.

Worse, we could see a gradation in the devastation, a clear epicenter, where everything was truly dead, surrounded by a halo of progressively dying land.

Torina sat speechless, just staring out the canopy at the desolation below. I discreetly started to bank the *Fafnir*, rolling her side of the ship upward to spare her having to look at the ravaged landscape below.

"No. I want to see this," she said, her voice utterly toneless.

I glanced at Perry, who shrugged his wings and rolled the ship the other way, deliberately wheeling over the blight. I eyeballed it at maybe two klicks across at its widest. If it continued to spread until it had killed all of the land reclaimed by the space hippies, it would roughly double in size.

If it kept spreading, though…

"Do the, ah, synergists guarantee their work?" I wondered, struggling to find something, anything to break the ponderous silence hanging over the cockpit like a funerary shroud.

But Torina just looked at me, her eyes bright with tears as she began to mourn. I knew that look. Inside her mind—her soul—she was falling, crashing headlong toward the brutal reality that confronted her. The land. *Her* land.

The place where she belonged. The grasses she walked across, barefooted and carefree, as the years passed her by in a cheery blur.

I reached out and took her hand—it hung limp in mine, stricken by the scene she was trying to process—the death of her youth, her life, and her dreams, one devastated acre at a time as we wheeled overhead.

"Go ahead," I told her, my voice as gentle as I could manage over the thrum of our engines.

"Go ahead and what?" Torina didn't turn to me as she spoke. She was captured by the disaster below.

"Cry."

Her head turned, sudden, crackling with anger. "Would you?" There was a bare challenge in each word.

I looked past her, then directly into her eyes. "Yes. I would. This is worth crying for. It's also worth fighting for."

AT TORINA'S REQUEST, we landed the *Fafnir* only a short distance from her family home. We normally grounded at the spaceport, about two klicks away, on the far side of the nearby town where Cataric's Innsu school was located. Torina clearly didn't want to endure any more of this not knowing exactly what was happening, though, so I had Netty set the ship down in the closest open space that wouldn't subject any buildings to blast damage from her exhaust. The blast wash did incinerate grass and fling dirt around and tore some leaves and branches off of trees, but that would all grow back.

Maybe.

As soon as the airlock opened, Torina hurried toward her house. I asked Icky to stay with the *Fafnir* and try to work out a thruster alignment glitch I'd noticed during our atmospheric flight. It wasn't a significant problem, but I frankly didn't want to bring Icky along on what would be a visit awash with emotion and despair. She was coming along, growing out of the solitude that had been most her life until now, but she still had a tendency to be blunt to the point of insensitivity.

I paused before starting after Torina, and turned back to the ship's interior. "Perry, can you go do some investigating, see if you can figure out what's going on? Why everything's dying?"

"They've probably already had experts doing that, Van. You know, biologists, biochemists, botanists—"

"Still. Indulge me. Oh, and can you identify toxins?"

"I can discriminate a few thousand, sure. I can't get fine measurements, but I can tell you if something is above the expected background—why? Are you thinking this was somehow deliberate? The space hippies guaranteeing themselves future work?"

I thought of the singing, dancing, chanting Synergists and how they'd reminded me of old images from Woodstock—the reason I'd dubbed them space hippies in the first place. I shook my head.

"Not them. Someone else, maybe."

"Like whom? And why?"

"No idea. Just—" I shook my head. "Like I said, indulge me."

"Will do."

I turned and hurried to catch up to Torina.

We walked in silence up to her house, to find her mother and father waiting at the sweeping entry. Both looked as stricken as Torina. I hung back, trying to remain discreet as they had a brief, intense, and tearful reunion. Then Torina pulled back and wiped her eyes.

"What happened?"

Her father gave a desolate shrug. "Apparently, there's some sort of delayed toxin in the soil. We don't know what."

Torina stiffened. "Wait. Are you saying this was *deliberate*?"

Her mother nodded. "We received—they were blackmail messages. They demanded payment, or… or they'd poison our land."

"We didn't think anything of it because, as far as we know, everyone involved in that damned mining is—they're dead," her father said.

I raised an eyebrow at that. Dead? All of them? Really? How did *that* happen? But I decided to leave that little tidbit alone.

Instead, I cleared my throat. "Sir, I understand this is—well, I can't imagine what kind of loss you're feeling. But I have to wonder at the cause, since this is all so sudden and total. Have you identified the toxin? Have any clues about how to neutralize it?"

Her mother shook her head. "No. We've brought in a team of researchers, but they haven't been able to isolate anything yet."

"Apparently, the chemistry of the dead plants is so complicated that they haven't been able to pick out anything that's a definitive cause," her father added.

I nodded. "I've asked Perry, my combat AI, to go and take a look. One of his things is being able to detect toxins—for criminal cases."

Torina's father nodded his thanks back to me, his face ashen.

Only there was still something else going on here. Vague hints of deadly retribution aside, there was a subtext that I could feel but couldn't actually place. This was bad, sure. Devastating, even. But Torina's parents were rich, and the Synergists—who I still refused to believe were behind this—should be able to do their singing and chanting and lute-strumming to fix it all again, right?

I was trying to work out how to probe a bit, and do it delicately, in case it was something that was genuinely none of my business. But Torina ended up revealing it.

"How much is it going to cost to fix this?" she asked, wiping her eyes again.

Her parents exchanged a look but didn't answer.

There it was. As was often the case in life, whatever was wrong obviously revolved around money.

Torina just stared. "Mom? Dad?"

"We're finished, Torina. As a family. As an employer—over three hundred families rely on us. As a place." Tears spill down her cheeks. "As a home."

"How much?" I asked.

Torina turned to me. "How much what?"

"To fix it."

Her father shook his head. "We don't know. Preliminary cost estimates are already pretty bad, but the rot just keeps spreading. If it doesn't stop, then the answer to your question, Van, is certainly more than we have available."

I nodded and activated my comm. "Netty, get me the, um, space hippies, would you? Open channel on my comm, please."

"One moment," came her reply.

I stepped back and moved far enough away to give Torina and her parents some time. Netty opened a channel to the Synergists just a few moments later, and I was connected with a senior technician named Lydia-sur, her voice almost musical.

"Yes? I am told this is serious, Van Tudor?" Lydia-sur was around thirty, with streaked blonde hair, high cheekbones, and eyes of cornflower blue. Her teeth were small and even, and she had one dimple.

"I think it's beyond that. Before we begin, know that I don't fault you at all for—for whatever it is that's happening here."

"What *is* happening there, Peacemaker?" Lydia-sur asked.

"I'm having Netty send images, as my explanation won't come close to the reality of what I'm seeing. This land isn't just dying, Synergist. It's being poisoned, with intent."

"I have the images. You say—ah." There was a hint of anger in her voice, then she went on. "Our work is undone. This is, as you say, intentional. Assuming we move quickly, what do you propose we do? Redeploy our teams?"

"In a word, yes. And I'll get to the point. I need a number. A cost. And I need it as soon as possible."

I waited, the hum of anger filling my ears for what seemed a lot longer than seven minutes, but that was all it was—and Lydia-sur reappeared on screen, her face schooled into a neutral expression, and I recognized her as someone about to deliver bad news.

"We… we will do away with any profits, but we must recoup our costs for this as it will take some time. Three local years, in fact."

"Thank you, Synergist. I mean that." I knew she was giving up an enormous sum of money, but I waited for the other shoe—or, in her case, sandal—to drop.

"Four million bonds per year for three years. And this time, we'll leave a team to guarantee and monitor the recovery. This is the best we can do. You have my oath to that effect," Lydia-sur said. "Again, I—"

"Done. When can you start?"

Her eyes went round with shock, then she gave me a slow grin. "This Torina woman is of some value to you, I think."

I felt myself almost blush. "You have me there. And the land is worth saving, too. And her family's interests. Send transfer information about payment to Netty?"

"Done. We will begin preparation immediately."

"Thank you, Synergist," I said, and I meant it.

Her answer was a warm smile, and the connection cut.

I returned to the veranda, where I rejoined Torina and her parents. They stopped and turned as I approached, the dolorous air around them almost oppressive.

I sighed, shaking my head. "Four million a year for three years. The land is compromised, and it's going to take a long time to fix. That's basically their cost, so it's the best they can do."

Torina's mother shook her head. Her father looked on the verge of panic. "We don't have it," Torina's mother said, her voice breaking.

I waved a hand. "I do."

THE THREE OF them stared at me. Torina finally spoke, her voice brittle. "No, Van, you don't. Even if you were to cash in everything the Guild's holding in trust for you, it would just be most of it, not all."

"Maybe not. But I expect to make more money from bounties and prizes, and I need *something* to do with it."

"You've got to upgrade the *Fafnir*."

I smiled and shrugged. "Much as I would like a cabin, that's not my priority right now. We'll get there eventually."

Torina shook her head again. "Van, that's twelve *million* bonds, or maybe more, if this doesn't stop spreading. My parents can't even cover that with our available funds."

"Torina, I've come to think of this place as sort of my home away from home. Trust me when I say I'm doing this for you, but I'm doing it for *me*, too. Besides, isn't it almost—I don't know, poetic that we'll be using a bunch of the proceeds of crime to do something good and beautiful?"

She opened her mouth, but a sudden metallic rustle cut her off. Perry landed on the nearby railing around the veranda and settled his wings into place.

I looked at him. "Well?"

"Do you want the good news or the bad news?"

"Perry, we're not interested—"

"Sorry, yes, I know. I'm sure this is very emotional for all of you. If I actually had emotions, I'd be right there with you."

"What did you find out?" Torina asked.

"Well, the good news is that the toxin seems to be a relatively simple substance, based on glyphosate, a chemical known for its defoliant properties. It shouldn't be that difficult to neutralize with the application of the correct counter agents."

"And the bad news?" I asked.

"The bad news is where it's coming from. The soil is infected with self-replicating nano-scale bots that are manufacturing the defoliant on the fly—basically, they assemble it from hydrogen, oxygen, carbon, and phosphorus from the environment around them. As they copy themselves, they're covering a larger and larger area, manufacturing this defoliant as they do. That's why it's spreading."

"Can we stop them?"

"A sufficiently high-frequency EM charge with enough energy might do it. But that will also completely sterilize the soil. Moreover, it would have to be done over an area considerably larger than that currently affected, because if even one of these little bastards escapes it—"

"It'll start all over again," I said.

"That's right. But—and I'm sorry for this," Perry went on, looking at Torina and her parents, "it gets even worse. This is a dangerous contaminant, as in, measures must be taken not just to control its spread here, but to prevent it from spreading off-world. It would fall under the Interstellar Contagion Treaty, which says some *specific* things about what you have to do to keep this thing in check.

I mean, imagine if this got to another world, spread there, and then kept spreading—"

"Yeah, we get the picture," I said. "So what do we need to do?"

"The Seven Stars League needs to be informed since they have nominal jurisdiction over Helso. They'll have to impose quarantine measures. The number of ships that enter and leave the atmosphere is going to have to be kept to a minimum, and all ships are going to have to be decontaminated before they leave the system. Flying through the radiation field surrounding that big gas giant primary out there should do it."

"We have to prevent it from spreading into other parts of Helso, too," Torina's father said, then pointed. "Look at all that dust out there. It could be carrying those damned things all over the place."

Perry shrugged. "Possibly, although the bots don't seem to like too much oxygen since they need an anaerobic environment to do their shitty thing."

As Perry talked, I could see Torina deflate more and more. I got it. Not only was her home being ravaged, but it had actually become dangerous, and in a pretty fundamental way. I had visions of this defoliation plague spreading to other worlds, and the effect it would have not just on the natural environment, but on food supplies.

I imagined it reaching Iowa.

But not for long. I pushed my attention past that dreary and unsettling image and focused on the here and now.

"Perry, is there someone we need to inform? I mean, this does represent a serious threat—everywhere, right?" I asked. The memories and knowledge the Guild had implanted in me were silent on things like weapons posing existential threats.

I expected Perry to reference some powerful, shadowy organization that dealt with things like this. Like the sorts of organizations from the government that showed up in movies involving aliens and UFOs, wearing hazmat suits and wielding all sorts of cool gadgets with a remorseless, dispassionate intent. But he just shrugged.

"Aside from the Seven Stars League? No, not really. This is bad, don't get me wrong, but in the greater scheme of things, it's not a huge emergency."

I blinked at him. "Really? An engineered plague, basically, that can wipe out plant life? Wait. It is just plant life, right? Or does this thing threaten humans—er, people and animals, too?"

"Well, the defoliant it produces might be toxic, but no, I didn't see anything to indicate that the nanobots themselves were a threat to non-plant life. And there are lots of contagious things out there, Van. Some of them are truly nasty. But there are measures to take, and they're going to have to be taken here, to control this one."

Torina and her parents bowed out, obviously needing some time to mourn, while also getting on with the damage control they now faced. Perry and I returned to the *Fafnir* to find Icky waiting for us.

"Netty didn't want to interrupt you, but you got a message from another Peacemaker, named—uh, Kosk—no. Klok?"

"K'losk," Netty put in. "He sent an encrypted message to meet him on the edge of the Gamma Crucis system. He said it was important but not urgent."

I put my hands on my hips and sighed.

"*Now* what?"

I RETURNED to the house to find Torina and tell her that we had to leave, but to assure her we'd be back. I found her sitting alone on the terrace overlooking her family's dying lands, drinking wine from a bottle.

"Torina?"

She didn't turn, just spoke. "Do you know what the trouble with being rich is, Van?"

I sat down beside her on the couch. "Tell me?"

"You've always got so much to lose." She gestured expansively around. "This is all great, just wonderful, until something comes along and tears it all away."

"I suspect that most people would rather have something to lose… than nothing at all."

She turned sharply to me, face blank—then a single tear slid down her cheek, breaking her façade of iron control. She took a long pull on the bottle and handed it to me—it was damned near empty—and I put it down after a polite sip. It was excellent wine, but what Torina was processing was more important than bright flavors in a bottle.

She blinked at me, sadness being replaced by an array of emotions, each one there for a fugitive moment.

"Torina, we just got a call from K'losk. He wants to meet with us about something privately. I just wanted to let you know—"

She sat up. "Great. Let's get going," she said, then looked at the bottle in her hand and took another drink.

"I think you need to sit this one out."

"Are you—are you firing me, Van?"

"What? No, not at all. I think you should be with your family. With your land, too," I added.

She stared at me. A ghost of a smile appeared on her lips. "You're a good man, Van Tudor."

"I'm trying. Now, as to—"

She caught my wrist as I made to stand. I turned back to her, and our eyes met.

A long moment passed. My thoughts drifted back to the grotto on the Undersea on Null World, where we'd shared a picnic lunch and a moment of unknown possibility. But, by unspoken agreement, we'd shelved those thoughts and returned to the *Fafnir*.

And here they were again. Close, just like she was to me.

"My dad told me to live without regrets," I said into the space between us.

"And?"

I kissed her, and her mouth opened like a flower, tasting of wine and sun and promises. When we broke apart, she was smiling.

"Didn't expect that."

"Yes you did," I told her, and her smile deepened. "You knew. And now, you know. So save that. We've got things to do."

"As I was saying… you're a good man."

"A wide, howling, primal part of me begs to disagree."

"For now."

"For now."

She actually giggled. "So you were tita—title—"

"You're right," she pronounced and clunked the bottle down on the table. She'd pulled off her boots and now started stuffing her feet back into them. "Anyway, you said we need to go."

"Torina, we can manage without you while you help your family."

She shook her head once. "No, you can't. And I can't manage

without you, if I'm being uncomfortably honest." It was as much as we were willing to say, for now, and she kept it brief.

So I nodded and stood, holding out a hand. "Honest is good. Let's go make some money."

She gave a mournful sigh as the moment passed between us, gone but not forgotten. "Right. Space hippies aren't cheap."

12

WE MET K'losk at our agreed rendezvous, in the Oort Cloud enveloping Gamma Crucis, the star system home to Anvil Dark. He'd wanted to meet in person, so we maneuvered our ships together and docked. As I unstrapped from the pilot's seat, I looked out the canopy, then glanced at the nav display.

"Ah, the endless wonder of a random spot in space," I said, noticing that the nearest object to us, a large and ancient comet, lay about a thousand klicks off our port bow.

"And it really does seem like a random spot in space—emphasis on *space*, as in *empty*. So much for Hollywood and its thrilling spaceship chases through these horrifying furballs of hurtling rocks, all smashing together, the good guys missing destruction by mere inches."

"There are places we can do that if you'd like to give it a try," Netty said. "I might be able to find an erratic comet for you to explore. We could even film it—"

"Ooo, I wanna hold the lights," Icky enthused.

"Lights?" I asked.

Icky nodded decisively. "Yes. I've been watching videos from your planet by people who are—what were they called, Torina?"

"Social Media Stars."

"Thank you. Yes. So these, ah, stars all have very bright teeth and good lighting, and some of them wear paint on their faces that change how they look. It's all very much a lie, but I would like to be your light holder. Or whatever that person is called," Icky finished with a wave of two arms.

"As much as I enjoy looking my best and exploring, let's just hold off on the social media for now and focus on this," I said. When Icky's shoulders fell, I added, "If we do social media, you will be my director. Promise."

"I claim assistant status. I'm going to need a byline on your channels, Van. I've got to maintain my brand," Perry said.

"Done, and done. But for now, let's—okay, this appears to be how I like my space, actually. Nice and empty."

I looked in the direction of the comet but couldn't see it, of course. Even at two klicks across and brushed by the feeble light from the distant star, it was still utterly invisible.

"Good call, Boss," Perry said as he examined the scanning data.

We crossed over to K'losk's ship. K'losk greeted us warmly, and I returned the favor. He was one of the few Peacemakers I'd come to trust pretty implicitly, along with Alic, Lunzy, and just a few others.

Perry, however, stopped in the *Fafnir*'s airlock before crossing over.

"Hello, Hosurc'a."

"Hello, Perry."

I glanced from Perry to the subject of his attention, Hosurc'a, K'losk's combat AI. Hosurc'a was, like Perry, in the form of a bird, but something more like a peacock, resplendent—and weaponized—tail and all. They also intensely disliked one another, for reasons no one other than them could even begin to fathom.

I breathed out a theatrical sigh. "Perry, would you and Hosurc'a cut that out."

Perry's amber gaze didn't waver from the other AI. "Cut what out, Van?"

I rolled my eyes and followed K'losk. Torina fell in place, but Icky stayed on the *Fafnir*, struggling to tweak some aspect of her fusion reactor that was bugging her to no end.

Torina had been mostly silent during the trip here from Helso. I'd given her the space she obviously needed, while trying to make it evident I was there for her, no matter what. But she'd applied a thick layer of professionalism over her anguish, so much so that I didn't think K'losk even realized how upset she really was. I had to admit—I admired that. It was something I'd never been very good at, tending to keep my heart beating away on my sleeve, to paraphrase the old saying.

"So, Van, I thought we could compare notes about our missing Master," K'losk said as we settled around his galley table. Like Lunzy, he'd upgraded his ship to a *Dragon*-class. Unlike her, though, he'd eschewed creature comforts, like overstuffed furniture, wood paneling, and even a fake fireplace. But he hadn't done anything notable with his ship, either. In fact, her armament wasn't much more potent than the *Fafnir*'s. I don't know what he did with his money, nor did I feel it my business to ask.

I nodded. "Alright. I'm not sure if you heard, but we actually visited his family."

"Really? And how did that go?"

"A little hairy. But here we are, talking, so not *too* hairy. Anyway, we didn't learn much, unfortunately, aside from just how humble his origins were."

"I'm surprised you were even able to get in to see them."

"Yeah, we had a run-in with his homeworld's orbital defenses but managed to find our way through."

K'losk stared. "Orbital defenses?"

"Yes. A half-assed missile platform firing, well, half-assed missiles."

"I didn't know the Vibariyun even had defenses like that. I thought they just kept everything sealed up," he said.

Now it was my turn to stare. "That who has what sealed up now?"

"The Vibariyun. They normally keep their home warrens sealed up."

"You mean, like, sealed inside their apartment?" Torina asked.

K'losk looked confused. "Apartment? What are you talking about?"

"What are *you* talking about?"

As K'losk frowned, a suspicion began tingling away inside me. "K'losk, we're talking about Master Yewlo, aren't we?"

"Ah, I see." He nodded. "Okay, no, I was talking about the other missing Master."

I exchanged a surprised look with Torina. "*What* other missing Master?"

"Master Proloxus. He went missing a few days ago. Didn't you know?"

WHEN WE DOCKED at Anvil Dark, I headed straight for Lunzy. Or, I wanted to, but she was away from the station. I said to hell with it and headed straight for the Masters themselves.

Torina, Perry, and I strode into the plush lobby that welcomed people to the Keel, the part of Anvil Dark reserved for the Masters. I walked up to the ostentatious desk surrounding Max, the alien who guarded access to them. Max was actually a Commune, several individual beings functioning as a single entity.

I drew up short, taking in the details of Max, because quite frankly, he was a sight to behold.

Max was not *just* an alien squid. He was *two* alien squid with the heads fused together, sporting a forest of tentacles that had suckers and eyes at the end of each. He was a dizzying scene of motion and flickering colors, and he also turned out to be relentlessly cheerful.

"Van, my friend! What can I assist with today?"

I knew a few things about Max—he had a passion for anything incredibly sour and liked Earthly big-band music, to which my grandfather and Master Groshenko had introduced him. He had a tune playing now, softly, as he worked—*In the Mood*, played by Glen Miller. I think. Although Max had mentioned something about preferring Teddy Gray's arrangement—

I cut off the inane train of thought before it could unload its irrelevant cargo. "Max, I need to see Master Groshenko."

"I'm afraid he's—"

"Nope." I held up a hand. "I need to see him. Now. It's urgent."

"Van, I'm sorry, but Master Groshenko left strict instructions he wasn't to be disturbed."

"Why? Because he's missing too?"

Max hesitated, then tapped a discreet button. "Master Groshenko, Van Tudor is here. You need to see him."

The gruff reply was immediate. "Send him in."

Max opened the door to the Masters' inner sanctum. It looked like just another expanse of dark wood, polished to a deep gleam, but that was a veneer over a heavy set of stout blast doors. If the Masters didn't want to see you, then they were *not* going to see you.

Groshenko appeared to greet us in another, smaller lobby. "Van, I understand—"

"Why didn't you tell me another Master was missing?"

Groshenko stiffened. "You're not supposed to know that. Only a small, select group—"

"We've been working on tracking down Master Yewlo. Over the past few weeks, we'd started to assume he *wasn't* kidnapped but had chosen to disappear, and we shaped our investigation accordingly. But if we'd known another Master was missing, we probably would have done things differently. So, I'm sorry, Master Groshenko, but wasting my time is something I will no longer tolerate. I'm a Peacemaker, not a bumbling intern. This shit is real, and you know it can spiral out of control if we don't find answers." I weaponized my anger just enough to bring some heat to the discussion, and the Master leaned back in response.

Groshenko crossed his arms and sighed, a long, slow sound braiding disgust and resignation. "If it had been up to me, we would have told you about Proloxus, Van. You've got to understand that, sure, you've done some amazing things as a Peacemaker. But you're also still new to the Guild. That Peacemaker badge of yours isn't even a year old. In fact, it's that meteoric rise that's actually made some people nervous."

"Why?" Torina asked.

"Because it makes you look ambitious. And a lot of superiors are leery of ambitious subordinates because they might someday end up being peers—or the power dynamic might even shift completely, and the subordinate becomes the superior."

While Groshenko talked, I tried watching his body language, reading his tone and expression, to see if I could work out how much of this he really believed. Unfortunately, this brand of interpersonal sleuthing wasn't my strength. My background had me dealing mostly with people who were just screen names. So, I couldn't see any hints that Groshenko was blowing smoke, but I might just be missing them.

This was, however, Torina's thing. At her suggestion, we'd already worked out a few simple gestures that she could use to surreptitiously pass on her assessment of someone in real time. If she scratched her nose, they were lying, if she rubbed her chin, they were scared. If she drew her weapon, well, things were going badly indeed.

But she sent me no signals at all about Groshenko, and when I glanced at her, I could tell she was barely paying attention—for obvious reasons. Her mind was mired back on her homeworld and its dying ecosystem. That meant I was flying solo.

I decided to keep up the pressure. "Fine. Now, look at it from our perspective. We're deliberately kept in the dark about one missing Master while looking for another. That's starting to edge its way toward coverup territory, or it sure feels like it. In fact, it almost sounds to me like we're getting too close to something that someone doesn't want found out."

Groshenko surprised me by smiling. "That's quite something."

"What?"

"When you're pissed off, I almost feel like I'm talking to Mark, your grandfather. Your tone, the way you hold yourself, all of it, it's almost exactly the same."

That disarmed me a bit. "Ah—okay. Well, I consider that a compliment."

"You should," Groshenko replied, narrowing his eyes at me for a moment. Then he gestured for us to follow him into his office. We did, and he closed the doors behind us.

I'd expected Groshenko's personal office to be as luxurious as the rest of the Keel, but it wasn't. Aside from the wood paneling and the subtly contrasting carpet, there was only a desk and chair, a table with a half-dozen more chairs around it, and a side table sporting bottles and glasses. I recognized one of the former as a popular—and expensive—Earthly whiskey. A big star chart and a few maps of planets I didn't immediately recognize hung on the walls. And that was it.

"Drink?" Groshenko said, moving to the table of bottles and glasses. I accepted his offer, then did so for Torina as well at her discreet nod. Groshenko poured us each a couple of fingers of the whiskey and brought them back to the table, then we all sat.

"Always start a difficult meeting with alcohol," he said, smiling.

I gave him a wintry smile. "Really?"

He smiled. "No, actually, it's a terrible idea. Drunk people aren't as pliant as people seem to think. Quite the opposite, actually. If you're trying to get people to agree with you, give them food."

I held up the glass. "So you're not trying to get us to agree with you, then."

"Or, Van, I could just be offering you a drink of some very fine whiskey."

I sipped it. Again, I wasn't a hard liquor kind of guy. But this particular whiskey seemed to evaporate on my tongue, becoming a rich, malty mist filling my mouth and nose. I blinked at it.

"Superb, and even to my rookie palate. Didn't know they made stuff this good."

Groshenko smiled. "They don't. Not anymore. In fact, I don't think they've made it since, oh, the nineteen thirties, maybe?"

Even Torina made an impressed face. Perry just stood on a chair.

"So I'll just sit here while you biologicals enjoy your yeast effluent, shall I?"

I gave him a surprised look. "Biologicals?"

Perry shrugged his wings. "It's an AI thing."

"*Yeast effluent* must be an AI thing, too," Torina said.

"You should hear what we call cheese."

I turned back to Groshenko. "What's going on?"

"Regarding our missing Masters? That's a good question."

I sighed. "You didn't really bring us in here and ply us with this —yeast effluent—just to stonewall us, did you?"

"No, of course not." Groshenko stared into his drink for a moment, then clucked his tongue in a sound that was oddly remorseful. "I think it's nearly time for me to retire."

Not sure what I'd been expecting him to say, but it wasn't that. I could only stare back at him.

"Okay. Why?"

"Because, Van, I'm honestly tired. Not of the work. I love the work. But I'm tired of having to say no."

I glanced at Torina and Perry, who both shrugged back at me.

"Saying no to what?" Torina asked.

Groshenko considered her over his glass, which he was holding in front of his mouth but not sipping. He finally just put it on the table with a soft tap.

"I'm tired of saying no to the things to which Yewlo and Proloxus stopped saying no." He cocked his head at me. "You might have noticed that there's a lot of corruption in known space, yes?"

"Yeah, I picked up a few hints here and there."

He leaned forward and rested his arms on the polished table. "It doesn't matter if we're talking about humans, or Yonnox, or a Vibariyun, or a Gajun. The members of almost every species are, in the end, motivated by self-interest. It probably has something to do with some need hard-coded into their genetics, that they need to amass as many resources as possible to ensure their well-being, and that of their descendants—" He stopped and shook his head.

"Anyway, I'm no cultural xenopologist. All I know is that, a few exceptional species aside, everyone in known space is pretty much out for themselves. Usually, that includes their inner circle—those people closest to them."

"Where are you going with this?" I asked.

Groshenko gave a thin smile. "Van, I could be fantastically wealthy right now. I could have a fortune that dwarfs that of Howard Hughes, if I'd wanted."

I smirked. "Howard Hughes? You haven't been back to Earth in a while, have you?"

"No, I haven't. Why, are there even richer people now?"

"You might say that."

He waved a hand. "Anyway, it doesn't matter. No matter how wealthy any of them are, if I'd wanted, I could have surpassed them. That I have not has required a supreme effort of will—especially since Mark died."

"My grandfather stopped you from sliding into vice and corruption?"

"More like we protected each other from our worst instincts. I guess we were each other's moral compass. Unfortunately, without his to consult, mine has started to wander. It's only a matter of time before I'm offered something I truly won't be able to refuse. Oh, I'll rationalize it to myself somehow. It's a last hurrah before I retire, and I've earned it, damn it. Or, I'll take this money now and then do good works with it later."

"Or everyone else is doing it," Torina put in.

Groshenko picked up his glass and toasted her. "Exactly."

"So you're saying that Yewlo and Proloxus were both corrupt, and that's what led to them going missing."

Groshenko sipped his whiskey, then nodded. "I'm sure of it."

"What about Master Yotov?"

It was Groshenko's turn to look surprised. "Yes, her too. Although she's more subtle about it and more interested in accruing power and influence than outright wealth."

"So you—just admit it? At least three of the Masters of the Peacemaker Guild are corrupt? That they're on the take?"

Groshenko grinned. "It would be pointless of me to deny it,

wouldn't it? Besides, you're Mark Tudor's grandson. Like I said, you sometimes remind me of him so much."

I held up a hand. "In case this is heading toward me becoming some sort of moral compass for you—"

His grin became a laugh that cut me off. "No, no, of course not, Van. You're still a kid. An awful lot of the Volga has to pass beneath your bridge before you'll be in a position to be anyone's moral compass. Well, other than your own, of course."

Torina raised an eyebrow. "The Volga?"

"A river in Russia, back on Earth," Perry replied.

"Russia?"

"Largest country on Earth, occupies most of Asia—I'll show you on a map when we get back to the *Fafnir*."

I turned back to Groshenko. "I can't help feeling there's more to this than you're letting on."

"Oh, there's a great deal more. But you don't *need* to know any of it, and believe me, you don't even *want* to know some of it. And if you're asking me to connect some dots for you, regarding your current investigation into that sordid memory chip business, I can't. And not because I won't, but because I genuinely can't. You probably know more about that case than I do."

He leaned forward. "But is there some connection between that case and our two missing Masters? Again, I don't know. But my gut tells me there is."

I nodded. "Yeah. Mine too."

13

I LEFT Anvil Dark feeling a little more comfortable about Groshenko, at least. He'd been frank and forthright, and I hadn't sensed any deception in him. Moreover, I'd seen his reaction to something I said to him when we parted.

"It seems to me that Gramps is still your moral compass, even though he's gone."

Groshenko gave a look of wary curiosity. "How so?"

I waved my hand vaguely at his office and the table where we'd sat drinking fine whiskey. "We had this conversation, didn't we? The one where you told us you were being tempted to the point of thinking it was time to retire? You didn't have to tell us any of that. You didn't have to even see us in the first place. It seems to me, anyway, that he's still pointing the way to moral north for you, isn't he?"

Groshenko had maintained that slightly suspicious look for a moment, then his expression softened, and he smiled.

"It sounds like he might be your moral compass, too, Van."

I nodded. "He is. I mean, you didn't think it was *Perry*, did you?"

"I will, once again, point out that I am *right* here," Perry groused.

I smiled as we accelerated away from the station, thinking of Groshenko—and of Gramps.

"What?"

I turned to Torina, who'd asked the question. "What what?"

"You suddenly smiled."

"Oh, I was just thinking about family. How it can be both the best and worst things in your life."

She grinned at that. "Sometimes both at once."

Our next stop was driven by the concept of family. Groshenko had us read into the file regarding Proloxus's disappearance, and although most of it was redacted, it still listed his next of kin. Investigating Yewlo's disappearance might not have broken any cases open, but it did give us some insight into him. Maybe Proloxus's family would do the same. It was at least a place to start.

Perry hopped up between the pilot's seats. "I'm telling you, Icky is more pedantic about numbers than Netty is." He went on in Icky's voice. "It's only ninety-eight-point-six percent efficient, but if I spend another bazillion hours realigning or recalibrating or repolarizing this thingamajig, it'll be ninety-eight-point-seven."

"Did I just hear my own dulcet tones coming from inside here?" Icky said, pushing into the back of the cockpit and settling into her jump seat. "And in an unrelated matter, Van, would you mind if I pursue a personal project, about flying AIs with smart-assed mouths? It's going to involve a lot of hammers and cutting torches and stuff."

Netty cut in. "I would point out that, since Icky has come aboard, this ship's overall systems performance has improved by nearly three percent. At least *someone* takes maintaining me seriously."

I gave the instrument panel the stink-eye. "So working stripped to the waist, drenched in sweat and hatch lubricant, while trying to maneuver a chunk of armor plate into place doesn't count as maintaining you? I'm hurt, Netty. Cut right to the quick."

"I'm sorry, Van. You do an excellent job of operating an overhead crane."

Torina suddenly burst out laughing. Now it was my turn to look at her and ask, "What?"

"You guys. You make me glad I didn't just stay at home and brood like I was no doubt going to."

I flashed her my best smile. "Thank you, thank you. We're here all week."

I HELMED the *Fafnir* to a point about a thousand klicks short of Master Proloxus's homeworld. I didn't enter orbit because there wasn't really anything to readily orbit *around*. At just under a thousand klicks across, Proloxus's home world was an asteroid, about the same size as Ceres, one of the largest back in the Solar System. It was named *Hudecki*, which was apparently a Vibariyun word somehow simultaneously encapsulating the concept of the number twenty-nine, a town, and a family.

"Charming," I said, staring at the drab, grey disk lined with a few sinuous ridges and pocked with craters. It orbited Epsilon

Eridani at about twice the distance Earth did from the Sun, meaning the star's orange-tinged light only brushed its surface, making it dimmer than a moonlit night on Earth.

"I'm assuming all the good, homey stuff is inside, tunneled beneath the surface," Torina said.

I grunted in agreement while noting another ship approaching. It was another Vibariyun, the so-called Invigilator of their various colonies scattered through the system's asteroids. The Vibariyun, as it turned out, had no specific homeworld. Or they had, but their own history, now a mix of fact and legend, recorded their exodus from their planet of origin, and their scattering among the stars. It meant that while the Vibariyun weren't exactly itinerant, they also had no central governing authority. Each of their colonies, called a warren, was a self-governing body in its own right, based around extended family. It made for a lot of inbreeding, but apparently the Vibariyun had turned this to their genetic advantage in a way that, to me, smacked of eugenics. But I wasn't here to judge a race. I was here to visit Proloxus's family.

"Which is going to be a problem," the Vibariyun Invigilator said over the comm. "Their warren has been—" The following word didn't translate.

I shrugged at the Invigilator, a hunched, bulbous humanoid with a multitude of eyes that varied in size and hue, and six limbs I could see. "Sorry, we didn't get that."

"Yes. Right. I'd be shocked if it was in the translator's database. It's an ancient Vibariyun custom that roughly translates to self-exile. A warren might decide to do that, sealing itself off from the outside, for any number of reasons. In time of war or conflict was an obvious one, but there could be others, including a time of—let's call it spiritual cleansing, since I doubt much about it will translate, either."

"So his family is sealed up inside that asteroid?" Torina asked.

"That's right. Our distant genetic ancestors were burrowing creatures, so we still tend to resort to surrounding ourselves with rock and earth when we want to feel safe."

I drummed my fingers on the armrest. "Can we talk to them via the comm?"

"Yes, you could. If they answered. But they haven't answered my calls to them, and looking back through our records, it turns out no one has talked to them in nearly eight standard years."

I looked at Torina. Her expression said what I was feeling.

That's not good.

I turned back to the Invigilator, whose ship had coasted to a stop a few klicks away. "Eight *years*? Isn't that an awfully long time to be sealed away inside an asteroid without ever talking to anyone?"

"Yes and no. In terms of the custom itself, no. Old records show some warrens being sealed for decades. But it is rather unusual for the present day. I don't think my warren's ever been sealed for more than a few weeks, during the Bright Night festival."

"Bright Night? Your people observe that, too?"

"Don't yours?"

"I—no. Well, kind of. We just call it something else." I had to raise an eyebrow. "So what you're saying is that these people have been sealed away for eight years, and you've never tried to check in on them?"

"I have been Invigilator of our Epsilon Eridani colonies for exactly twenty-four standard days. And my predecessor—let's just say that she didn't leave very good records."

I immediately recognized the tone, yet another universal one. It was the aggrieved tone of someone inheriting a mess from a former boss or coworker.

The Invigilator tried again to raise some sort of response from Proloxus's warren. Nothing but dead air answered.

"Now that's unusual. Even when just sealed away for a few weeks, a warren normally maintains comms, in case of emergencies," the Invigilator said.

Netty cut in. "I've scanned the surface of the asteroid pretty thoroughly. There is a comm array down there, near a cluster of domed structures I would assume is the entrance to their warren. And it does seem to be operational. I can handshake with it fine."

"Same here. They just don't seem to be answering," the Invigilator said.

I let a long sigh trickle from my chest. "Okay. What are your people's rules about breaking and entering?"

I'D EXPECTED to have to pull rank or quote chapter and verse in convincing the Invigilator to let us break into Proloxus's warren. But he readily agreed.

"The more administrative headaches I can clear off my agenda, the better," he said, signing off on taking full responsibility for letting us bust into the warren. Like us, I'm sure he thought there was something wrong and just seemed happy to have someone else do the legwork to find out what.

While the Invigilator hung in space overhead, observing, we grounded the *Fafnir* a few hundred meters away from the domes and comm array. The asteroid was far too small to have any atmosphere beyond occasional wisp of gas, so Torina and I suited up. Without a word, we armed ourselves—me with The Drop and the Moonsword, Torina with her trusty sidearm, as well as a long arm, a slugger slung on her back. Perry accompanied us, nudging himself along with brief puffs of his limited reactant supply. Icky stayed back to keep an eye on things with Netty.

Perry reached the domes first, scouted around, found nothing, and perched himself on the comm array. By the time we'd got there, half-walking, half-jumping in the low-g, he'd run a diagnostic on the array.

"Checks out fine. If someone spoke into the other end of this thing, we'd hear them on this channel," he said.

I called out for anyone to answer, then announced that we were coming in.

Nothing.

Torina and I stopped and eyed the domes around us. The largest was the entrance, so we made our way to it and stopped in front of the blast door.

"I have to admit, this is kinda giving me the heebie-jeebies," I said.

"The heebie-what?" Torina asked.

"Is this whole *sealed-up-for-eight-years, dead-silence-on-the-comm* thing making you uneasy? Maybe giving you a few goosebumps?"

"It—is, yes."

"That's the heebie-jeebies."

"Good to know."

We examined the blast door. A fine patina of dust coated it, held in place electrostatically. It suggested that, indeed, this door hadn't been opened in a long time.

There was a panel beside the door, also rimed with dust. I brushed it off with my glove, then tapped it. It remained dark.

"Perry, can you do something with this?"

He launched himself toward us with a gentle burst of thrust. I braced myself against the curved flank of the dome and caught him so he didn't have to spend any of his remaining reactant on stopping.

"If I can get inside that panel, I might be able to hack the door open, sure."

We spent the next ten minutes figuring out how to get the panel open without breaking anything. Icky helped, watching imagery sent back to the *Fafnir* by Perry, and coaching us along. When we finally got the panel open, Perry unspooled a data tether, which we plugged into an open port.

A few seconds passed. "Okay, got it. Whenever you're ready, Van, I'll open it up."

I glanced at Torina. In another of those unspoken moments, we both drew our weapons and leveled them at the door. I dialed The Drop's underslung energy burster to its strongest stun setting but also made sure a round was chambered in the big-bore slugger mounted above it.

"Perry, go ahead."

The door slid silently open.

We looked into utter darkness.

I called the Invigilator. "Do your people live in the darkness? Like, inside their warrens?"

"No, they're normally brightly lit. And since you're asking, I'm assuming that this one isn't."

"It is not."

"Okay, just stay where you are. If anyone's going to intrude into a sealed warren, it should be me."

We followed the Invigilator into the burrow, through an airlock. The interior was pressurized, but we stayed suited up, not knowing what noxious agents, or pathogens or whatever it might hold. Even setting aside the complete lack of light, the place just *felt*—empty. Or, no. Not empty.

It felt *dead*.

We crept along a tunnel until we reached a split, yawning spaces angling off to the left and right. The Invigilator had no map, just a sense of how a typical Vibariyun warren would unfold. For the next ten minutes or so, we followed the Invigilator's lead, looking up tunnels and into excavated compartments, all dark. All disused. All dead. Our helmet lights gleamed off the smoothly annealed rock. We saw furnishings, both practical and decorative. We also saw a few places where things were obviously missing, adding questions upon questions.

At the twelve-minute mark, Perry, who had been taking advantage of the air to move around in powered flight, called us from another side corridor he'd been scouting.

"Van, I found a Vibariyun."

"Alive?" I asked, although I knew what the answer was going to be.

"At one point. Not anymore, though."

We joined Perry and stared down at the desiccated remains of a Vibariyun that was sprawled in a corridor. The Invigilator muttered something, then spoke up and moved away from us.

"I need to report this," he said.

"I doubt that it's going to be the last dead body he reports in here today. This place is a tomb," I said.

Torina nodded. "And, there go those heebie-jeebies again."

According to the Invigilator's records, there had been around eighty-six Vibariyun living here. But a bunch of those might actually have, like Proloxus, left to go to other places and do other things. All we could do was count the bodies as we progressed.

We turned a corner and found another. We'd seen wounds we suspected were from some sort of projectile weapons in several, but this one clinched it. Its head had been blown apart, fragments of skull scattered around it on the tunnel floor.

"You know, I'd been holding out some faint hope that this was some terrible accident, or a disease, or something like that, anyway. But these people have been murdered," Torina said.

I stared down at the body and nodded glumly. "Yeah, that's the way it looks—"

Something moved in my peripheral vision. I glanced that way, along a corridor, but saw nothing.

"Shit."

"What is it?" Torina asked.

"I'm seeing things now."

"More heebie-jeebies?"

I opened my mouth to answer, but something heaved into view, caught in my light.

I'd holstered The Drop. Now I reached for it again—slowly. "Not this time."

Whatever it was, it sure as hell wasn't a Vibariyun. It looked more like an oversized turtle with a gleaming shell, way too many legs, and a flat, triangular head that seemed to be nothing but mouth and teeth.

Then all hell broke loose, and I went into motion.

I snatched out The Drop and snapped off a hip shot as the thing scuttled toward me. The slug smacked against its shell and ricocheted away, but not before spalling a chunk of bone and leathery skin. I cursed and fired the burster, but the energy charge didn't seem to faze it at all. And then it was on me, its mouth snapping shut on my right thigh. I felt the pressure through my b-suit, enough to make me feel like the thing was going to take my leg by simply pinching it off. But the b-suit held, and I opted for the only sensible response.

I bellowed for help.

"Torina! Perry! I'm getting Death By Turtle!"

Torina fired a shot that bounced off the thing's shell and buzzed past my head. I made an uncomplimentary remark about that, then planted the muzzle of The Drop against the thing's head and squeezed the trigger.

The damned thing didn't fire.

"Not my day," I wheezed.

Torina lunged in, banging out three point-blank shots into its neck. The creature grunted, released me, and pulled back, then staggered under repeated shots from both Torina and me, since The Drop seemed to be working again. We backed up the corridor side by side, stumbling over the Vibariyun body and hammering out rounds at the tough, angry creature.

"Bastard won't die!" I shouted, firing again.

Torina changed mags, re-cocked her weapon, and resumed firing. "I've only got one reload after this. Didn't expect a firefight."

Unbelievably, despite the pounding it had taken—the creature charged us again, bone-white palate exposed as it opened up to bite me again.

"Thank you very much," I muttered, jamming The Drop down the creature's throat and pulling the trigger.

Twice.

Gore sprayed backward from the neck and shoulders, and the Turtle of Doom folded obediently, leaking fluid from an array of holes. After a frenetic series of twitches, the beast went still, but not before some gland on its tail cut loose, spraying the wall with a substance so foul it made me gag.

"I... did it just piss on us?" I asked, fighting back bile.

"It tried. Or something," Torina said. Our chests were heaving with adrenaline, and she leaned forward and casually put another round in the creature's head. "Take that, and just because I need to know, what the hell *was* that thing?"

I heard movement behind us and spun around, The Drop raised as Torina lifted her own weapon. "Not again—"

"Woah, Van! Good guys coming to the rescue here!" Perry said.

He and the Invigilator had rounded the last corner and now gaped at the creature filling half the corridor.

I looked right back at the Invigilator. "My colleague here just asked a very pertinent question. What the hell *was* that thing?"

"It would seem to be a—" Again, the word didn't translate. "Apologies. It seems similar to a creature sometimes kept by my people as a companion. They make fearsome watchers," he went on.

I nodded. "Yeah, I'd go with *fearsome*. So it's like a watchdog."

"I get the sense of what you mean, and yes. This one is considerably larger than any I've seen, however."

My heart finally slowed from *frantic rush* to *rapid pounding*. "Okay, obvious question—what does it eat?"

"Actually, they can remain dormant for long periods, their metabolism close to zero. However, they can rouse themselves very quickly, when someone intrudes into territory they consider theirs."

"No shit. Are there likely to be more of them in here?"

"I—don't know. Possibly?"

"All I needed to hear. And, more to the point, I think we've got what we came for," I replied.

"What's that?"

"Some insight into Proloxus's family. Which we've got, as in, they're all dead." I looked back at the corpse whose head had been blown to pieces.

"The question is now, who murdered them?"

THE BEST ANSWER to that question was only too obvious. Proloxus had been made a Master in the Peacemaker Guild eight years ago. He had then made one more visit here, to his home warren, and it had been immediately sealed after that. So he'd either fled who or whatever had killed his family somehow sealed the warren behind him and then never reported it for *eight years*.

Or he'd been the one responsible for the slaughter of his family.

"You know, Van, it is possible the two things are coincidental," Perry noted as we made our way back to the surface—keenly on the lookout for any more *family pets* along the way.

"Sure it is."

"But you don't believe that."

"Don't you?"

"Well, see, it works a little differently with me, being an AI and all. I work off probabilities, not gut feelings and beliefs and emotions."

"Okay, so what are your probabilities telling you?"

"That Proloxus is a murderous scumbag."

When we reached the surface, we found that another pair of Vibariyun ships were inbound. The Invigilator had reported the tragedy that had obliterated the warren, and their own investigative apparatus was swinging into gear.

I turned to the Invigilator. "Do your people perform burials to dispose of your deceased?"

"We do. Why?"

"Because I'm going to give you a stack of bonds to do this one right, with all the honors that you can possibly bestow. These people deserve it. Oh, and a memorial, with a plaque, right about"—I picked out a point a few meters from the blast door—"here."

The Invigilator gave me a many-eyed stare. "Our burials are normally quite discreet affairs. We reserve honorable interments for those who have performed great services for our people."

"Even so. I think it's important. I tried to convince a Yonnox security chief about the same thing once, and he just absconded with my bonds. I had to get his badge made into a memorial. That's how important I think it is."

I locked stares with the Invigilator, which wasn't easy because there were so many eyes to try and meet with my own. I didn't know if he was planning on taking my money and keeping it, but I wanted to make it clear where I stood on that sort of bullshit.

"Very well. I'll make sure this happens," he finally said.

Torina, Perry, and I started back to the *Fafnir*. On our own private comm channel, Torina spoke up as soon as our backs were turned to the Vibariyun.

"You lied to him. Why?"

"Because I wanted to make sure those bonds go to making a big, splashy memorial ceremony and not into a big, splashy pool in that Invigilator's backyard. If they have pools, that is. Or backyards."

"Okay, then that begs the question, why is a big, splashy memorial so important to you? It's not like you had any connection to these people," Torina asked.

"No, but they deserve it. And more than that, I want something about which word is going to get around. Maybe something with some media coverage even."

"Ah. You want Proloxus to find out that the—" She paused. "You've used an idiom about this, something about a dance."

I frowned at her, puzzled. "A dance?"

"Yes. A jig. That's a dance, right?"

I laughed. "Ah, you must mean *the jig is up*."

"That's it. You want Proloxus to know the jig is up."

"I do. And then, well, the ball's in his court. That means—"

"Thanks, Van. I get it."

14

It would take time for the Vibariyun memorial service to happen, and more time for any word of it to get around. Of course, unless he was delusional, Proloxus knew full well that his family's massed death would be discovered someday. That might actually have been what triggered his sudden disappearance, in fact, if he thought we might be checking into the backgrounds of the Masters. Realizing the *jig was up*, he might have just fled.

But, as with Yewlo, we didn't know anything for *sure*, aside from the fact that both had disappeared.

"Could you imagine coming into work every day, overseeing murder cases—hell, even investigating them—while knowing your whole family was lying dead in the darkness? Especially if you were the one who killed them all?" I mused as we accelerated toward our twist point out of the Epsilon Eridani.

"Some people are just psychopaths," Torina said. "After all, who would deliberately seed a delayed toxin into the soil of a place you were illegally strip-mining?"

I glanced at her but saw no more tears, no crushing despair. Instead, I saw anger. And anger was good, if it was put to good use, that is. It gave me some cautious optimism that Torina was starting to work through the devastating shock about her family's home.

Netty interrupted. "Van, I'm missing a piece of data."

"What's that?"

"Well, I know where we are, and that's an important factor in doing the twist calculations. But so is knowing where we're *going*."

I swapped a taken-aback expression with Torina. "Oh. Right. I guess we haven't settled on where we're going next."

"I just assumed we'd go back to Anvil Dark," Torina said.

I curled my lip at that, thinking. While I couldn't think of any particular reason we shouldn't go back to Anvil Dark, I likewise couldn't imagine any reason we should. Again, our trail had gone cold, at least insofar as the missing Masters went. Moreover, there was no guarantee that our memorial service for his family would flush Proloxus out in any way we'd ever know about.

So I called up a star chart and stared at it, looking for inspiration.

"Halcyon," I said as my gaze landed on its icon.

"You want to go to Halcyon," Netty asked.

I held up a finger. I wasn't entirely sure why Halcyon had jumped out at me the way it had. Maybe it was because it was yet another bit of unfinished business. Not that we had any shortage of that, of course, but we'd watched the illicit auctioning of stolen goods happen there, including some terrestrial artifact, probably the Vanguard satellite. And the trade in stolen artifacts linked back to the Nesit, and the identity we'd recovered ostensibly of Erflos Tand, who'd turned out to be an imposter, killed his whole family, and—

And there it was.

"Halcyon, Netty, if you please," I said.

"Why Halcyon, exactly?" Torina asked.

"I was wondering the same thing," Perry added.

I explained my reasoning. "We start back at the beginning. And while you're doing your thing, Perry, hacking into stuff, I'll do mine."

"Which is?" Perry asked.

"Drinking."

"Of course. And the point of that would be…?"

"We need information. The sort of information you can really only get from criminals. So we need criminals, too. And, wherever there's booze, you might very well find both."

"Good point. So much so, I have to admit that I'm troubled by your accuracy."

"Yeah, well, not as troubled as I am knowing I have to drink in a tavern full of fake psychics."

"I take it you'll brush up on your astrology beforehand?" Perry asked, helpful as ever.

"Oh, for—guess I'll have to take a deep dive in their belief structure." I winced because I had to be respectful. And informed.

And I had to make it believable.

After a groan, I slapped my hands on the chair and lifted my chin. "If I'm going to learn about their system, I've got to be an expert."

Perry replicated a tongue click. "That's *just* the sort of thing a Virgo would say."

As soon as we stepped out of the airlock and into the tacky environs of Halcyon, we were accosted by a pair of earnest aliens, both decked out as the Children of Resplendence. I took a deep breath and told them that, thanks to my last trip here, I'd been intrigued by what they had to offer and asked if I could hear more. I glanced back and saw Torina and Icky both grinning. I knew Perry, perched on a nearby bench, would have been grinning at me, too. I tried a quick glower, but that just made them grin even more.

The two Children tried to coax me into a quiet conference room, where they could begin the mystical process of trying to part me and my money. But I sighed.

"You know what I could really use? Something to drink. I have to keep our ship dry because one of my crew is—" I mimed tipping a bottle into my mouth. "You know."

Take *that*, Torina or Icky.

"Ah, of course," one of the aliens, an insectoid creature from the same race with the unpronounceable name as Steve back on Anvil Dark, said. "Right this way. There's a quiet—"

"I've had enough quiet for a while. How about we just get a drink somewhere lively first?"

I saw the two aliens exchange a look. I could tell what they were thinking and didn't need to be enlightened to read their thoughts. In one glance, they weighed trying to get me behind a closed door as soon as possible versus letting me down some alcohol and *then* getting me behind a closed door to begin the initiation, or induction, or whatever they called it. I decided to help them along.

"I don't want to stay there too long. I'm something of a lightweight when it comes to booze to begin with, and I haven't had an actual drink in quite a while now."

"Because of your… colleague?"

"That's right."

"We know just the place," the insectoid said and led me off in the direction of a bustling tavern.

Perfect—almost. If there were some sort of conversation going on in here that was useful, I could drop that almost. At the very least, I hoped I could identify some targets for further investigation.

We settled into the bar and ordered a round of drinks—for the humans. The insectoid either couldn't drink or just didn't and wanted to launch right into the beginnings of his pitch. I had to admit, he was good. He came at the whole matter of me joining the Children in slow degrees, nudging the conversation in that direction without making it obvious.

"We are welcoming to all, but in particular—well, I shouldn't say it, but… " The insectoid let his pitch dangle there, waiting for me to take it.

I obliged.

"Yes? What? What aren't you telling me?" I asked, adding a note of desperation. People generally hated being kept away from secrets, so I let that color my expression as I waited for the next line, which I knew would be *The Pitch*.

That was all he needed. The alien switched to a script he'd memorized, so smooth it was almost believable. But as someone who fended off timeshare sales while at the beach, I was a seasoned veteran of high-pressure hustles. I did what came naturally when faced with a hard sell.

I tuned him out, nodding occasionally as I let him run with his script.

And that was because of Icky, who'd come into the bar a few minutes after me. She wasn't just my backup, either. She wore a sensitive microphone that fed the audio it picked up via an encrypted, short-range comm back to Netty, who peeled it all apart and teased out separate conversations. Netty then fed those results into my ear bug. It had actually been Netty's idea, and it was a good one. I could sit here being inundated with the sale while she wandered around the bar and surreptitiously eavesdropped. Netty preprocessed the feed, listening for any words that might trigger a more thorough examination, whereupon she'd ask Icky to stop and linger a while.

I caught a couple of brief bursts of conversation that went nowhere. In the meantime, I eyed the crowd, picking out individuals that might be worth follow-up. Just as my insectoid friend was starting into a description of the *Third Level of Celestial Understanding*, a new conversation hummed in my ear bug.

—something special. They're so damned hard to please.

They liked that stuff you bought them from—oh, what's that place called? The planet—you know, they think they're all alone in the universe, that actually landing something on another planet is a big deal—

Earth?

That's it. They liked that stuff, didn't they?

Icky turned and looked significantly at a table with two figures hunched over it in a corner, barely lit by a tiny light overhead. One was a Nesit. I couldn't make out the other one, aside from *humanoid*.

Yeah, they did. Don't know why. It's basically just scrap.

No, it's historical artifacts.

They both laughed.

Well, I don't have anymore of those historical artifacts, and Earth is a—

The next phrase didn't translate, but I got a definite pain in the ass vibe from the tone.

—to get to. Last time, after deducting fuel and expenses, I barely made my usual margin.

We need to find someone else who deals in artifacts from that sector.

What, cut in someone else who's going to want a cut? Why?

They'll only get a cut if they're alive.

Heh. Good point.

Their conversation meandered on to other irrelevant matters, then they finished their drinks and stood up to leave. Icky shot me a questioning look, then turned away. A few seconds later, her voice hummed in my ear.

Van, I'll follow the Nesit, the shorter one. If you can follow the other one, make some sort of gesture.

I stood up just as the alien was getting to the part where I handed over all my worldly possessions in order to achieve spiritual clarity.

"Thank you for—" I waved grandly, as if I'd been presented with universal truths that were almost too much to process. "All of this. It's… it's a lot," I said to my erstwhile companions.

I could immediately tell they weren't thrilled with the idea of letting me leave, but I held fast even as they rattled off a series of tactics designed to make me sit down again. The sensation was not unlike getting pinched in the finance office of a car dealer, being sold on rustproofing or some other scam product.

With a mournful nod, I simply stepped away from the pair,

watching Icky follow her mark out of the noisy bar. "With respect, I will now go."

"We will come to visit you this evening. Perhaps we could dine together," the insectoid said, oily as ever.

"Sure, let's do that," I replied, turning away with finality. I thought about what *dining* with a giant grasshopper might look like—and decided I didn't want to know.

Between Icky and I, we were able to link each of our marks back to a ship. The tall alien, of a species I couldn't immediately place, returned to a large freighter, upon which he seemed to be a member of the crew. Icky tailed the Nesit back to a smaller ship, a class four workboat, which he probably flew alone.

"He's our guy," I said, eyeing his ship through a viewport, Icky at my side. "Netty, learn everything you can about that ship. Tell me the last time someone took a dump on board, if you can."

"Really? Because I could try and hack into it, access its waste reclamation log, and—"

"Netty, you're the one member of the crew I count on to not be a wiseass," I said.

Icky shot me a hard glare. "Hey."

"Present company excepted, of course."

"So what do you want to do, boss?" Icky asked me.

"We need to get our hands on something valuable, something this particular buyer, whoever they are, is going to be interested in."

"Didn't you chase down some weird alien song for that very reason?"

I smiled at Icky's use of the word *alien*. But I was an alien to her, too, wasn't I?

"We did. But I don't think we need to get that elaborate. I've got a better idea, one that's going to be a lot easier than tracking down the dying lament of some ancient race."

"What's that?"

"Something that's going to require me to go home. Sort of."

We returned to the Solar System and made a brief stop on Earth, and the first change I noticed was—

The time. It was well into summer, when the corn on my fields was tall, just like the spring calves at nearby farms. The farm was in good order, Miryam having, at my request, leased out the fields to neighbors. It meant I had some Earthly money coming in, which was good, because I suspected bonds wouldn't be considered legal tender when the county tax bill came due. We also made a detour to Atlanta, where I still had an apartment on lease. It was about to come up for renewal, and I let my landlord know I was moving on. I stayed long enough to arrange to have my stuff shipped to the farm in Iowa, and then I told Torina something that still felt strange on my tongue.

"Guess it's back into orbit then."

"Van, you mind telling us what you're planning, other than sorting out your domestic affairs?" Perry grouched.

"Domestic affairs are important. I'd like that farm, the one with, you know, the spaceship facilities in the barn? That one? I'd like it to remain in my hands and not be seized by the county or state or whatever for tax arrears."

"Well, sure. But that's not why we came back to the Solar System, is it?"

"Actually, in part, it was. But it's not the main reason, no. The main reason is that way," I said, pointing toward the Sun.

"What's *that* way?" Netty asked.

"Venus."

"Actually, Venus is over here," she said, painting an icon onto the right side of the *Fafnir*'s canopy.

"I stand corrected. Anyway, that's our next destination."

I felt Torina staring at me. "Why? What's on… Venus? That's the second planet in this system, right?"

"It is. And on Venus is something that will be *irresistible* to a Nesit."

15

We stared down at the cloudscape beneath us. It gleamed pale gold with a hint of green in the brighter light of the sun. From its curved horizon, to the terminator separating day from night behind us, it was just that—featureless cloud. Well, okay, not that featureless, because we could see bands and swirls scrolling beneath us as we orbited, making the effects of winds and the passage of storms in the soupy atmosphere beneath.

"So you're sure we'll be okay descending all the way to the surface?" Torina asked.

I shrugged. "Netty says we will. Right, Netty?"

"Correct. The *Fafnir*'s hull is sufficient to withstand pressure and temperature conditions somewhat higher than the surface beneath us," Netty replied.

Torina gave her mouth a dubious curl. "How much is *somewhat*?"

"We shouldn't exceed ninety percent of the ship's structural tolerance."

"See, there's another of those words like *somewhat*. This time it was *shouldn't*."

Icky gave Torina a curious look. "I know we haven't been flying together long, but you seem awfully out of sorts about this, Torina. You've done things way more dangerous than this."

"First, I know that. But my father has a friend who got trapped aboard an atmospheric skimmer collecting fuel feedstock from a gas giant. The skimmer lost power and fell out of orbit. I had nightmares about what it must have been like for weeks," she said.

"Then, add the fact I've got no control over it and can only sit here while we descend into that—" She shook her head.

"Torina, we can take you back to Earth, and you could wait at the farm," I offered.

But she shook her head emphatically. "No, I'm going to do this. I *need* to do this." She looked at me. "So enough with the waiting already. Let's go. Take me down."

"Okay, then. Netty, you have the coordinates. If you please?"

Netty applied braking thrust, and we began our own fall from orbit.

We entered the cloud tops still traveling fast enough to cocoon the *Fafnir* in a searing flare of reentry. Like putting on high beams in thick fog, the blaze of our passage reflected right back at us from the thick clouds, leaving us momentarily blind, nothing but orange-yellow glare beyond the canopy. But it faded, and everything around us became progressively darker. At the same time, the *Fafnir* shuddered and slewed about even as we pitched in a jarring ride like the most violent rollercoaster in history. The clouds were thick. The winds, savage.

Torina fidgeted in her seat, then stilled when I put a calming hand on her arm. "We're good. Promise."

She gave me a grateful smile. Sometimes, you just need assurance, no matter how much of a badass you might be.

Netty spoke up. "Point of interest—you could survive quite handily outside right now, as long as you had a rebreather or a supply of air. It's Earth-standard atmospheric pressure out there, at just over twenty degrees Celsius."

Interesting, but the thick gloom didn't look any different to me. "Not interested in stepping out for a bit?" I said, offering her a smile meant to be encouraging.

With a mannerly nod, Torina said, "Hell. No."

"Point taken," I said, turning at a furious display of lightning outside.

We continued our plunge. More lightning pulsed around us, ripping through the sky with silvery brutality. A clap of thunder walloped us, hard enough to make Torina yelp. Outside, the pressure and temperature crept ever upward. Twice, the *Fafnir* groaned somewhere in her alloy bones, a deep, slow sound of protest that raised the hackles on my neck. Even though I was in a starship, my lizard brain was still functional, thank you very much.

Despite the raging storms around us, the ship boards glowed cheery green.

Torina spoke in a broken rattle. "If we keep falling—"

We finally broke out of the seemingly endless clouds about a thousand meters above a barren, rocky landscape. I blinked in surprise. Not that it had appreciably brightened—it was a dim glow amid thick fog and shadowy storms. The nightmare around us was muffled by dark, which made it less menacing but still present.

"What *is* this mess?" I asked, staring at the surreal sight below.

Netty's reply was candid. "No idea, Van. Some sort of inversion effect, probably, related to temperature gradients. If you'd like to know more, we'll need to stick around for a while, take some observations over the course of a few days—"

"That's okay, Netty. My interest is just of the slight, abstract variety, kind of like noticing my neighbor painted their house. It's an answer I truly can live without."

We made our way to the coordinates specified for the Venera 12 lander. I let Netty continue flying since there were hills and a few rugged volcanic cliffs all around the shallow depression where the Soviet spacecraft had come to rest. I'd rather let Netty do the flying and not smash us into—Venus, or something smaller but just as deadly, so I could concentrate on looking outside.

I glanced at Torina as we wheeled over the coordinates. "How you doing?"

She looked back at me, pale and taut as a drawn bowstring. "Well, I'm here and haven't been squashed to paste, cooked like a roast, or gotten a lung full of poison—yet—so I'm good, actually."

Icky, who'd been monitoring the *Fafnir* with microscopic care, spoke up without taking her eyes off of her engineering panel. "You know, as phobias go, fear of being crushed in the atmosphere of an alien planet is a pretty good one to have."

Torina scowled. "And just how do you figure that?"

"How often does it come up?"

"Well, since you're asking me that question now, it comes up one hundred percent of the time."

"Yeah, yeah. Try having a phobia about live electrical circuits."

We both turned back at that and looked at her. "Really? You're a *spaceship engineer*, Icky. You practically live and breathe electrical circuitry."

"You can't breathe circuits, Van—at least not without—never mind. But it's true. My phobia, that is. The closest I've ever come to dying was when I managed to electrocute myself aboard the *Nemesis*, helping my dad refurbish her. I *did* die, actually, for a minute or so, until the auto-doc brought me back."

"Holy shit, Icky. I've seen you pretty much tied up in the *Fafnir*'s cabling. Kudos for facing that fear every day," I said.

She shrugged. "I love this engineering stuff, and I wasn't going to let something like death keep me away from it. But it *does* make me a lot more careful."

"So is this the part where I'm supposed to draw inspiration and realize that I can harness my fear and use it in a positive way?" Torina asked.

Icky glanced at her. "Uh—well, if that's what you take away from it, girl, then sure. That was my point all along."

"While you folks have been discussing your *feelings* and all that, Netty and I have been working, Van," Perry said. "And in case you're interested, we're right over the location of that Venera probe. Look out the left side, straight down."

I did and saw nothing but a broad, shallow slope of what looked like gravel. More lightning strobed the air around us.

"There's nothing down there."

"Actually, there is. The scanners suffer a lot of degradation in this atmosphere, but there's a weak metallic response from underneath that pile of dirt," Netty said.

"It looks like the Soviet lander was buried, probably in loose volcanic debris that let go when an earthquake—er, Venus quake—hit," Perry added.

"So we can't get at it. Shit—" A flicker on the scanner display caught my attention. It was a stronger return, from the base of the slope. I pointed at it. "What's that?"

Netty did her best to give us a zoomed and stabilized image, but all we could make out was something metallic gleaming dully in the wan light that filtered through the clouds.

"It must be a piece of the lander that got broken off and tossed there by the landslide," Perry suggested.

I gave a slow nod, then a faster one as another brilliant idea came to me. "Netty, take us down."

"Are you sure, Van? The *Fafnir*'s handling this pressure fine, but that's not all we're facing. It's hot enough to melt lead out there, and the atmosphere is partly made of nitric and sulfuric acid. It's starting to eat away at some of the exterior components," Netty said.

Torina sat up. "Eat away? Which ones? How much? Van, maybe we should leave—"

I touched her arm. "We'll be on the ground for just a few minutes, then it's straight back up into space. I promise, okay?"

I met her gaze and held it, smiling as I did. She settled back in her seat.

"You get us killed down here, Van, and I'll never forgive you."

As awesome as our b-armor was, even it was no match for the fearsome conditions of Venus. And we had no other suits or armor that would fare any better. That meant only one of us could go outside.

I watched Waldo trundle across the rocky surface, rocking as he moved. Netty figured he had about half an hour of useful life outside before the heat, pressure, and corrosive atmosphere got to him and he seized up and died. It should be plenty of time, though.

Should be.

"Just three or four soil samples, Netty, then recover that metal whatsit and bring him back inside," I said.

"Understood."

It went smoothly enough. Waldo was able to dig up three samples a few centimeters deep and dump them into three separate containers we'd tied onto him with monofilament cable. When they weren't braving the horrific conditions of the Venusian atmosphere, they held condiments in our tiny galley.

"I hope somebody enjoys salt, pepper, and—" I shook the container into which the other three had been emptied. "Is that coffee?"

"That brown stuff?" Icky asked.

I closed the container and put it away. "Guess I'm going to be drinking tea until we get back to Earth."

The last thing Waldo did was grab the metallic bit in one of his manipulators, then come stalking back toward the *Fafnir*. He made it a few meters, then abruptly pitched to one side. His opposite side legs kept moving, turning him in a circle, but that was it.

"Something must have failed," I snapped.

Icky nodded. "Yeah, probably a junction box on that side that splits the power to each of his legs."

"Can you fix it from in here?"

"Not a chance, sorry. Waldo doesn't exactly have much in the way of redundancy built into him."

I blew out an exasperated sigh. "And none of us can go out there to rescue him."

"None of *you* can," Perry replied.

I turned to him. "I'm not letting you go out there, Perry. Even if you could fix Waldo, I don't want you exposed to that toxic sludge of an atmosphere out there." I glanced at Torina. "Besides, I made a promise we wouldn't linger."

"Fix Waldo? Are you insane? You can buy a dozen identical units if you want. He's just a machine, after all."

I gave him a bemused look. "Perry, have you been introduced to irony yet? No? Bird, meet irony. Irony, bird."

"Sure, laugh it up at the expense of the AI offering to go outside and save this little mission of ours. Or are you telling me, Van, that you think Waldo, a semi-autonomous maintenance bot, and yours truly are essentially the same? What is it, we all look the same to you, Van—?"

I raised my hands in surrender. "Fine, fine—I'm sorry, Perry. If you can go outside and retrieve the stuff Waldo grabbed, I will forever be in your debt."

His amber gaze shone back at me. "You sure about that, Van? Forever? Remember that you're talking to something that's almost certainly going to outlive you and never *ever* forgets anything."

I patted his head. "Perry, if I have to owe somebody a forever debt, I don't mind it being you. Just be careful out there, okay?"

"Naturally. And Van?"

"If you die out there, I'm not getting a tattoo of your name, weirdo."

Perry sighed. "I had to try."

WE WATCHED INTENTLY as Perry made his way to Waldo. He had to walk, simply because the air resistance was far too high for him to be able to fly, but not high enough that he could actually treat it like water and swim. It seemed to take him a long time to make the roughly twenty-meter trek, which was as close as Netty was comfortable landing lest the *Fafnir*'s exhaust churn the rescue area into an even more dangerous place. It probably only took him a couple of minutes, but it was silent and tense, as Perry was, for once, not being very chatty.

When Perry did speak, I felt an inner relief, mirrored by Torina and Icky.

"Van, you're going to have to be satisfied with this metallic piece that looks like part of a strut, and one soil sample. I can't carry any more than that."

"Whatever you can bring, Perry. Just get your shiny metal ass back in here."

"On the way."

"How are you doing, anyway?"

"Everything's functioning normally, at least so far. But things are heating up for sure. I'm probably, oh, fifteen or twenty minutes away from a heat-induced shut-down."

"Again—shiny metal ass inside, asap," I said.

We watched him pick his way back to the *Fafnir*, the container of soil clutched between his wings, which he'd folded up and across his back, something I didn't even know he could do. He carried the fragment of the Venera lander in his beak.

The moments passed, the silent tension in the cockpit as thick as the atmosphere outside. When a shrill alarm sounded, we all yelped and jumped. I looked wildly around.

"Netty, what the hell's going on?"

"We've had one of our two scanner transceivers just drop offline. Something failed in its controller."

I turned back and looked outside. Perry was only a few meters away now. I clenched my jaw so hard it hurt.

C'mon, Perry. Almost there.

He finally clambered up into the airlock. Netty immediately sealed it.

I waited for the light to turn green. But it didn't. It stayed stubbornly red.

"Netty, what's the holdup?"

"I can't repressurize the airlock. Or, maybe it's more accurate to say I can't *de*pressurize the airlock."

"Van, Perry here. I've had a couple of systems go offline. This atmosphere is really playing hell with—everything."

"I need answers. Netty, what's going on?"

"The airlock is full of Venusian atmosphere. The pumps aren't designed to work against that kind of pressure. It if were vacuum, I'd just open the inner door and do an emergency repressurization, but that won't work either. We'd just fill the ship with that Venusian soup."

"Van, we have to get out of here," Torina said.

"I know, I know. We just need to—"

"No, I mean, we need to get out of here. Into space, or higher up in the atmosphere, anyway, to where the pressure's lower. Then we can vent the airlock."

I gave her a quick and grateful nod. "Good idea. Netty, take us up as fast as you can."

As the drive came to life and the *Fafnir* lifted, I looked outside and stared at Waldo, who was canted forlornly to one side. I kept watching him until he'd vanished into the toxic mist.

"He looks—" I said, but Torina put a hand on my shoulder.

"Lonely?" she asked.

"Yeah. I guess friends can be made out of metal after all."

WE WERE FINALLY able to start venting the atmosphere a few thousand meters up. As we climbed, it vented more quickly, while the outside pressure dropped. At about twenty thousand meters, Netty was finally able to pump in genuine air, then open the inner door.

"Perry!"

He looked up, his amber gaze dull. He still had the condiment container, which was pitted with corrosion, and the piece of the Soviet lander. His normally sleek, dark surfaces were dull, almost frosted.

"Perry, are you okay?"

He dropped the piece of the Venera lander with a soft clack, folded his wings back down, and let the container of Venusian soil roll off his back.

"Nothing that a good sandblasting won't fix."

I knelt by him, my eyes searching his frame for damage. He was a mess, with nearly every feather showing signs of damage. "Sorry about that, buddy. Truly am."

"Does this mean—"

"Perry. For the last time, I am *not* getting your name tattooed on me," I said.

The ship began to rumble as we poured on the power. I saw Perry raise his wings, testing them for damage. "Who said anything about my name? Now, as to my *likeness*—"

16

WE RETURNED to Earth and landed in the barn, then gave the *Fafnir* a good once-over. Like Perry, the entire outer surface of the hull and its applique armor had gone from a satin finish to a matte, pitted disaster. More alarmingly, the extreme conditions of the Venusian surface had eaten deeply into less durable components, including the scanner and comm arrays, and various external sensors. One of the three laser emitters in the battery had failed completely, and the other two would be operating at reduced power because of damage to their lenses, even with the protective covers closed. The mass driver, missile launchers and point-defense all seemed in good working order, though.

After a couple of hours of inspection, poking, and prodding at the ship, Icky and I compared notes.

"There's not much we can do here. I tightened up things as I went and replaced a few small components from our spares. But the big stuff, like the scanners and comms, need complete rebuilds." She grinned. "Don't suppose you can get parts here in Iowa, huh?"

"If the *Fafnir* were a tractor or combine harvester, sure, I could just run into town."

"So that's a no, then."

Perry was in better shape. We kept a set of spares for most of his most critical components, and with Torina's help, he was able to replace his worst-affected parts. His eyes especially needed new lenses since he complained about everything being foggy.

"Bird lasik, coming up," I said.

"I—huh. Can't really argue with the language, but the process will be different. No lasers. Just lenses," Perry agreed. "Which brings me to an awkward question. Mind spotting me a few thousand bonds?"

I raised my brows in surprise. "For the lenses? They're my responsibility."

Perry flexed his wings. "No. Stay with me, here—*chrome*."

Iky snorted. Torina laughed out loud.

I stared. "I'm not letting you turn yourself into a '74 El Camino, you maniac."

"What's an El Camino?" Icky asked, bewildered.

"It's almost a truck, and not quite a car. But in some years, they had *style*," Perry enthused.

"No. No chrome. No pinstriping, no flames, no—"

"Fine. I'll take my lenses and what dignity I can muster, thank you," Perry said, folding his wings with a flick that was pure annoyance.

"I'm glad to see you too," I said.

"Whatever. But thanks," Perry allowed.

Clearly, we needed to get back to Anvil Dark and its maintenance shops. So, after grabbing some more coffee from the house, we lifted and climbed back toward orbit.

But we had something to do first. Actually, two somethings.

"I have to admit, this bothers me," I said as Netty located the two objects we were seeking. It only took her a moment because none of the Earthly tech orbiting the planet was even remotely stealthy, even as far as our degraded scanners were concerned. In fact, in less than a minute, she'd scanned and identified everything in orbit that wasn't completely occluded by the Earth itself.

"Think of it as something you're doing for the greater good," Torina said.

"Huh. I wonder how many awful things have been justified exactly that way through history."

"You're planning on stealing a couple of old satellites, Van. You're not exactly committing genocide here," Perry said.

I nodded. In the earliest days of the American space program, eleven attempts had been made to launch the Vanguard series of satellites into Earth orbit. Only three had succeeded, but all three were still in orbit. Now, nearly seventy years on, they were long dead, and were really more just inert objects than satellites. But they had great historical significance, which I was about to cash in to further our investigation.

I consoled myself that the original designers of the Vanguard satellites probably would have been pleased to know that, someday, their creations could actually help save lives—in this case, from our mysterious identity thieves. But we needed something dramatic that would allow us to crack open the veil of secrecy that shrouded this whole case. And, since someone seemed to have a taste for old tech from Earth's early days of spaceflight, these were the oldest objects, and probably some of the most storied things available.

So here we were. About to commit a cultural theft in the name of justice.

It didn't take long to retrieve the two old satellites. Netty eased the *Fafnir* into a position that would block direct view of the satellite from the surface below, then Icky exited the ship, attached each to a winch tether, and pulled them into the hold. It was unlikely in the extreme that anyone would be looking specifically at these orbiting relics, but if they did, all they would see is that they'd vanished. It was more likely they'd be missed on radar. Some computer down in NORAD headquarters, or some other country's equivalent, would eventually notice that two of the objects they routinely traced in orbit had suddenly just disappeared. If word ever got out that all three Vanguard satellites had gone *poof*, then I'm sure the space nerds and conspiracy theorists would have a field day. The vast majority of people, though, would likely just give a shrug and get on with their day.

We'd just sealed up the hold, securing Vanguard Three, and Icky had just entered the airlock when the comm chimed with an incoming message.

I frowned at that. "Who's calling us while we're in Earth orbit?"

Netty put the message on, and the screen lit up with the image of a Yonnox.

"Why, hello there," he said.

"Uh, hello. What can I do for you?"

"Well, for a start, you can stay right where you are and not change your orbit even a centimeter. And then, you can hand over those two satellites you just picked up."

Netty cut in. "Van, two ships just rose over the Earth behind us, a class five workboat, and a class nine, frigate class. They're catching up to us fast."

"That would be us," the Yonnox said. "And if you want to be alive to see your next orbit, Mister Peacemaker, you'll do *exactly* what we say."

I CUT THE COMM. "How did these assholes manage to sneak up on us? And what are they doing here in the first place?"

"If I had to guess, I'd say they're probably tech poachers. Remember your very first flight off Earth, and the tech poachers we encountered on their way to Jupiter?" Perry said.

Torina scowled as she brought the fire control system online. "They must have noticed us and decided to lay low, right on the horizon behind us, powered down and watching to see what we were up to."

The comm chimed again.

"Van, those two ships have about seventy percent more firepower than we do between them, and that's when our scanners and weapons are working at peak performance. Give them another five or ten percent for the damage done to the *Fafnir* on Venus," Netty said.

Icky clunked her way into the back of the cockpit. "So what'd I miss?"

I gave her a thumbnail summary and gestured at the tactical overlay. She growled softly in her throat in response.

"Bastards. They've got us way outgunned, don't they?"

I nodded glumly. "Yeah, they do."

I reactivated the comm. "Do you really want to have a space battle in full view of Earth?"

The Yonnox laughed. "I've got a better question. Do you? I mean, my colleagues and I, we don't especially care. But this is your home planet, isn't it, Peacemaker? You might have some explaining to do if there's suddenly a bunch of explosions and shit right overhead."

I sank back as he talked. He was, sadly, right. We had a lot more to lose from an obvious battle in Earth orbit than these scumbags did.

Icky sighed. "I'll suit back up, so we can transfer those satellites to them."

But Perry spoke up. "Van, you know what those bastards are going to do once they've got the Vanguard twins back there."

"Yeah, I do. They're going to attack anyway, because not only can they probably not lose, but they've also got nothing *to* lose—"

My voice trailed off. I'd been staring at the tactical overlay, trying to weigh the best way to fight this out. Unfortunately, I had absolutely no idea. We couldn't break orbit and make a run for it since we were already in their weapons range. If we fought, we'd probably be crippled, or even destroyed, during a light show that couldn't fail to attract attention from down below—and of course we were about to pass over the east coast of North America, pretty much right over Washington D.C., just as night was falling. Anyone looking up would likely see at least the detonation of missile warheads.

But the tactical overlay was still crowded with the tracks of all the objects Netty had scanned and identified. I'd been about to ask her to clear it when something tickled the back of my mind.

Things in orbit.

I sat up. "Netty, can you find a satellite called Amulet-Two-Alpha?"

An icon popped onto the screen. It was in a much higher orbit than ours, and a polar one, so it crossed ours at an acute angle.

"That's it, right there. It's catalogued as a mothballed weather satellite," Netty replied.

But I shook my head.

"No, it's not."

A LITTLE LESS THAN a year before I discovered an odd remote in my desk drawer in Iowa and my life spun off into sci-fi craziness, I'd worked a contract for the U.S. Defense Department—specifically, for Space Force. It was a white-hat hacking job, intended to test the security of some particularly sensitive tech. I had to do a bureaucratic limbo to get the necessary security clearance, but it had paid off in the form of one of the best-paying jobs I'd ever done. In fact, I'd envisioned it as the first step into a rather cool career of being paid to try and hack into sensitive government and various public infrastructure systems. The point was to find their security holes and plug them.

And they didn't come much more sensitive than Amulet-Two-Alpha.

"Okay, so it's not a defunct weather satellite. What is it then?" Perry asked.

"For the record, I'm about to violate about eleven different security laws, and if it ever got found out, I'd be spending the rest of my life in a very small room." I took a breath, then let it out. "Amulet-Two-Alpha is an x-ray laser. Basically, it's a one-shot, fission-pumped weapon intended to shoot down ballistic missiles before they can reach their targets."

I was waiting for shock and horror at this admission of the weaponization of space. But I'd forgotten my audience, and the fact I sat in the pilot's seat of a de facto warship.

The only one who spoke was Icky. "That's so *badass*."

"Van, I have to admit, that's a genuine surprise to me, too. Kudos on keeping it such a secret," Perry said.

"Yeah, we usually watch what you guys are launching, and that particular satellite went up without any fanfare on a plain old Atlas V rocket, and from Cape Canaveral, yet," Netty added.

Perry bobbed his head. "I thought you humans were all, *oooh, we can't put guns and bombs in space, we must go forth in peace*! And then you sneak a nuke into space." He clicked his tongue. "Shameful. And useful, you rogues, you."

Torina, though, drew my attention to the comm, where I had yet another incoming message. "I think the only reason they haven't started shooting at us is because they want the satellites we have on board."

I activated the comm. "Listen, Peacemaker—"

"Just—hang on a second. What terms are you offering us?"

"Terms? Well, very simple. You let us come alongside and take those satellites, then you go on your way. Oh, alive. Did I mention you'd still be alive?"

I was really starting to dislike the Yonnox, which was a terrible thing to think. I'm sure that, for every greedy, amoral asshole like this one, there must be thousands of Yonnox who just went about their daily lives without bugging anyone. But the Yonnox who did venture out into known space sure all seemed to be greedy, amoral assholes.

I glanced at the tactical display. The two ships were now just a few thousand klicks behind us and slowly gaining. For the moment, they weren't using their main drives and were just using maneuvering thrusters to gradually slow themselves by dropping from a higher, faster orbit toward us. The display said we had a little under ten minutes until they intercepted us—although they could start shooting any time they wanted.

Less than ten minutes. This was going to be tight.

"Alright, we're standing by," I said and closed the channel. I turned to the others.

"Okay, this is going to be really close. We've got less than ten minutes to break into Amulet-Two-Alpha's control system—"

Perry tried to cut in. "Van?"

I held up a finger. "Just a sec, Perry. Anyway, we've got to break in, reorient the satellite to aim it properly, and then trigger—"

"Van."

I glared at Perry. "What?"

"We're in."

"We're in."

"Yes, we're in."

"In what?"

"Your satellite. Netty and I broke into its operating system right after you blew the cover on it."

"Oh. Really?"

"Yes."

"That fast?"

"Van, we're kind of wasting all that time we gained for you. Trust me. We're in."

I was stunned for a moment, then it was gone. It had taken me *days* of working away to break into Amulet-Two-Alpha. It had been deactivated for the exercise, presumably so that I didn't whimsically decide to see what an x-ray laser looked like when it fired. Still, it had otherwise been fully protected by layers of digital fortification. I figured I had a *shot* at doing it in less than ten minutes, since I'd done it before. But Netty and Perry were hyper-advanced AIs. Even the most robust digital defenses on Earth wouldn't be a match for them.

Holy *shit*. I'd never really considered the havoc these two could wreak across Earth if they wanted. Fortunately, they were on our side.

But not every AI out there was, was it?

But I shelved any concerns for my homeworld's digital welfare and concentrated on the screen that had opened on the center console. It was the control nexus for Amulet-Two-Alpha. From it, I had complete control of the satellite and its functions, including triggering the damned thing.

"Van, you said that's a fission-pumped x-ray laser, right? So it's essentially a nuke," Icky said.

I studied the control nexus. Days. It had taken me *days* to get this far. But I gave Icky a distracted nod.

"Yeah. A nuke."

"So, when you detonate it, it's going to be a touch obvious, isn't it? You know, a dazzling flash and all that?"

Torina went on. "And the EMP is going to damage a lot of these other satellites. Also, it's going to produce a cloud of radioactive debris that's going to spread around the planet, possibly damaging even more."

"The thing is supposedly designed to minimize collateral damage, but yeah, that's a definite issue," I said, sinking back in my seat. I was comfortable, but the horns of the dilemma I was sitting on sure weren't. Firing the damned thing might let us get on with our case, which was all about saving lives. But it would also stand to damage all sorts of space-based communications, imaging and the like, and could very well risk lives down on Earth, even if indirectly.

I glanced out the canopy and watched the glowing sprawl of DC slide beneath. The entire eastern coast of the United States stretched off to my right seemed to be one continuous splotch of light. Brighter spots marked the biggest cities, Baltimore, Philadelphia, and New York.

Not that they'd be immediately affected. Amulet-Two-Alpha was currently over northern Ontario, and the trajectory of its brief but stupendously powerful x-ray pulse would barely skim the top of the atmosphere.

Still—

"To hell with it. Those humorless tools who hired me to break into the damned thing were adamant that the nuke had a limited yield. Let's take 'em at their word. Netty, Amulet normally gets its targeting data from other satellites. Can you feed it data for the bigger of those two ships instead?"

"Done."

Amulet's control system acknowledged the incoming targeting information. The satellite itself, spinning reaction wheels buried inside it, slewed around and oriented itself. I watched our two pursuers for any sign they'd noticed anything. They just kept dropping toward our orbit, though, and were now a lot closer.

Even if they were lying about the effects of the nuke, it was Amulet's accuracy I was more worried about. We'd be *awfully* close to the line of fire.

I tapped the comm. "Is there any way I can talk you guys out of this?"

The Yonnox answered. "Sure. Give us the cash value of those old satellites, and we'll walk away."

"That would be millions of bonds."

"It sure would." The Yonnox tilted his head. "Mind you, I'm curious about something. All this hesitation. Why are you so worried about two ancient satellites anyway? I mean, are you really willing to risk your life for what amounts to some old scrap?"

"Millions of bonds worth of old scrap."

"Yeah. But, I don't know. This doesn't seem right. You think you're up to something, don't you?"

It was now or never.

"You got me," I said, then triggered Amulet-Two-Alpha.

I'D BECOME SO USED to seeing explosions in space that this one, while certainly bigger than most, still didn't seem that impressive. Far off to our right, a sudden searing flash of light pulsed and died. A cloud of vaporous plasma expanded out from what had once been a satellite, then it cooled and faded.

But the x-ray laser part happened in the first few milliseconds of the blast. The fission explosion struck a bundle of boron-alloy rods, surrounded by heavy shielding, which formed the thing's barrel. The rods, when vaporized, gave off stupidly intense x-radiation. The shielding, before it too was puffed away to vapor, collimated that into a fantastically powerful beam-like pulse. Traveling at the speed of light, it struck the bigger ship chasing us.

Most of the ship simply ceased to exist. It was rendered down to vapor, leaving the bow and stern sections tumbling away.

We all just stared in awed silence for a moment. Icky finally broke it.

"I wonder if we could adapt something like that to a reusable system…" Her voice trailed off as she snatched up a data pad and started tapping away at it.

Perry put his wing on my arm. "Van, I must admit, you've restored my faith in humanity. Any race that can build something that kick-ass is going to do just fine when it finally joins the galactic community."

I reactivated the comm. The Yonnox immediately appeared, already in the midst of a tirade. The parts of it that translated were profanity. I suspected most of the rest of it was, too.

He paused, gaping, and I seized the opportunity. "You done?"

"I—"

"My turn now. How'd you like to see another of those go off?"

The Yonnox fixed me with a look of poisonous fury. "You'd better watch your back, Peacemaker," he hissed.

I shrugged. "Terrible revenge? Line forms to the left on that, friend."

I expected the Yonnox to just kick in his main drive and depart in a spectacular, and obvious, blaze of fusion-pumped drama. But he didn't and instead used the much more sedate secondary drive to climb back toward open space.

We all finally relaxed.

"How's that going to play out down there, among command?" Torina asked.

"I suspect the media's going to be reporting on bright flashes in the sky, too," Perry put in.

Icky didn't look up from whatever she was brainstorming on her data pad. "Not to mention that debris out there. That's going to raise a few eyebrows."

"Actually, that debris isn't in a stable orbit. The biggest pieces are going to fall into the atmosphere in a few days. Whatever survives is almost certainly going to end up in the Pacific Ocean."

I nodded my satisfaction at that. "And as for the rest, yeah, there will be more questions, and stonewalling, and pretended ignorance, and someone's going to say it was a big meteor, and someone else is going to claim they're detecting radiation, and it was a nuke, and the American government will deny it—"

I turned and shrugged.

"In other words, just another day on planet Earth."

17

We made a low-speed exit from the Solar System so I could track what was happening back on Earth. As expected, the internet had been flooded with videos capturing the detonation of Amulet-Two-Alpha. And, as expected, there'd been an explosion of media chatter and noise on social media about it. But all explanations seemed to be converging on it being a bolide, a large meteorite that detonated high in the atmosphere. Some of the cannier sorts wondered how an explosion that bright, seen across much of central and eastern North America, could have made absolutely no noise—didn't that suggest it happened in space?

And so the arguing and debating and theorizing rambled on, making so much noise that any signals of genuine thought or concern were quickly buried.

"Leave it to humans to convince themselves they'd just seen nothing of note," Perry said.

But I shook my head. "More like they know they saw something, but every Tom, Dick, and Harry has his own ideas of what it was, and none of them will ever agree."

Torina looked at me sidelong. "Who are Tom, Dick, and Harry?"

I smiled. "I knew you were going to ask that," I replied. "Three names used as average people, so that—"

Netty interrupted. "Again, Van, I need to ask you where you want to sow chaos next. What destination should I be configuring us for? Anvil Dark?"

"Nope. Take us to Starsmith, Netty."

Torina looked up at that. "Starsmith? Why?"

"Because I want to see if I can talk Linulla into reconsidering his stance on forgery."

"I HAVE BEEN DOING this a long time, Van Tudor, and I have been asked to forge many things. Somehow, though, you've managed to come up with something new," Linulla said.

"Because I'm asking you to duplicate an Earthly item?"

"No, because you want me to duplicate it for reasons other than making money."

His eyestalks swiveled, taking in the images I'd brought for him of the Venera 12 lander. "That said, this would be an easy enough item to duplicate. Its design isn't very sophisticated. Is there more information available about its metallurgy, the precise makeup of its various components, that sort of thing?"

"I've given you everything I can find. But that shouldn't matter, at least in the short term. I've actually got a piece of the real thing, as well as some distinctive soil samples from where it's sitting."

Oddly enough, that made me think of Waldo, forever stranded on the hellish surface of Venus, and I found myself dealing with a pang of loss. I retreated into Perry's assertion that he was just an off-the-shelf maintenance bot with no actual personality of his own.

Still. It was Waldo.

Linulla continued to examine the images, then finally turned his eyestalks back to me. "I'll do it. I'll duplicate this device for you, Van Tudor."

"How much?"

"How much profit? That is an easy thing to answer. Since you have assured me that you've got no intent to profit from this, why should I look to ill-gotten gains?" He looked back at the images. "I think my own costs will be minimal. If you could cover those, I'd say, five thousand bonds."

A shock hit my body, and I felt Torina stiffen beside me. We'd braced ourselves for hundreds of thousands of bonds. Five thousand was barely two rounds of docking fees at Spindrift.

With measured tones, I spoke, turning myself to face the Starsmith directly. "Thank you, Linulla. There are no words for what this means."

"You intend to use this as a way of furthering your investigation into that vile enterprise that steals identities. I am happy to be part of that."

"Is it okay if we leave Icrul here to assist you? She's dying to see you at work."

"By all means."

I turned to Torina. "Can you go let Icky know that it's a go? I think she's already packed up."

Torina glanced at the comm that was part of my b-suit's harness. I looked right back at her.

She took the hint, nodded, and left.

When she was gone, I turned back to Linulla. "There is another job I'd like you to do. It's one that I'd like to keep especially quiet."

"And what would that be?"

I told him. Before I could quite finish, though, a pack of smaller, crustacean-like creatures came scuttling and tumbling into Linulla's workshop. They chattered and clattered around until Linulla finally shooed them away.

"My children. Some of them, anyway."

"Some of them? There must have been at least twelve."

"Fourteen, actually."

"Oh. Well, congratulations, I guess?"

Linulla made a grating sound I'd come to realize was laughter. "I will take this second job for you as well. It will be good practice for those of my children who are old enough to learn smith work."

He leaned toward me, in as conspiratorial a way as a giant, crab-like being could. "It also helps keep them out of trouble."

I laughed at the similarities of our lives, even though he was a parent and I had merely watched parents in their wild variations as they raised their kids. We had a different amount of limbs but the same problems. "Kids, huh?"

Linulla gave an alien sigh that tired parents would know, no matter what their species. "Kids."

We returned to Anvil Dark. While Netty and I finally saw to the *Fafnir*'s repairs, Torina got on the comm and put the word out through channels she knew that we had three Earthly relics we wanted to sell—Venera 12, and the two Vanguards. We figured that would take a few days to filter around, so she then threw herself into helping work on the *Fafnir*.

I was worried about Torina, and not just for the obvious reason of the devastating situation her family was facing. She seemed determined to not stop or rest. After a full day of pulling off applique armor to inspect the hull plates beneath them, I was ready to pack it in and go for a drink. She just wanted to keep working.

"Torina, we've still got at least two more days of work before the *Fafnir*'s flyable. We don't need to kill ourselves."

"I'm good," she said, her hands buried in an open access plate, fiddling with something.

"Torina—"

"I said I'm good," she snapped.

I held up my hands. "Okay, fine. I'm just trying to—"

She yanked her hands out and turned on me. "Just trying to what? Make me feel better?"

"No. I'm just trying to get you to pace yourself."

She glared at me for a moment, then turned back to the open access panel. "I'm fine."

At the mention of the *f word*—fine—I turned and walked away, knowing there were certain bridges you didn't cross. Torina was from another planet, but her humanity was a known quantity, at least to me. And *fine* was a nuke. An unexploded bomb.

Fine was… trouble. I left it alone, along with her, and shifted my thoughts to a shower and eating something. Then I figured I'd head into The Black Hole for a drink and—

"Van?"

I stopped and turned back, but slowly.

"I'm sorry." Torina looked abashed but also hurt.

"For what?"

"For—" She waved behind her, as if the bitter words still hung in the air like smoke. "For that."

I walked back to her, then took her hands, a slow smile growing on my face. I knew what it took to apologize. It was more than an admission. It was an investment. "You know, if I had to guess, I'd say that you're determined to keep working until you drop from exhaustion. I'd further say it's because you don't want to stop, because if you do, you're going to start thinking."

She wiped her forehead with the back of her hand, then blew a strand of hair out of her eyes. "I thought you were all about machines, computers, that sort of thing. What made you so insightful about people?"

"Probably hanging around with them. Especially ones I care about."

Her eyes met mine and she smiled—and it reached her eyes.

"Do me a favor?" I asked, letting her hands go. "Close up that access plate. Let's get cleaned up, then I'll buy you dinner."

She peered up into the opening, then stepped away, pushed the plate closed, and latched it. She turned back to me with a grateful smile. "You're on—"

Perry chose that moment to soar into the hangar bay and land on a tool cart. He took us in, then cocked his head. "Did I arrive at a bad time?"

"Why would you think that?" I asked, wondering how an AI could be so good at reading a room. But he quickly dispelled the magic.

"Your respective heart rates are higher than normal, as is your thermal output. Your galvanic skin-current activity is also above baseline, and there's an increased concentration of certain pheromones in the air—"

Torina walked over and wrapped her arms around him. "You had me at galvanic skin currents, you smooth talking bastard."

I smirked. "Yes, Perry, you caught us. We were—we were—experiencing *emotions*." I made a face, and Perry twitched his wings, then laughed.

"Spoken like a true Capricorn," Perry intoned.

"Thought I was a Virgo?"

Perry laughed again, and this time it was vaguely evil. "Yessss. Your research is taking hold. You have a Capricorn moon and—"

"Perry?"

He glanced at Torina, who held her hands up, meaning he was on his own. "Yes, boss?"

"I liked it better when you thought we were going to get naked."

"Oh. Neat. Well, I *still* think that might happen, even if you're resistant to astrology. Being a bird of many talents is—"

"Your burden to bear?" Torina asked.

"Exactly. I'm required to be an expert in your cultural zeitgeist, even if you refuse. Things like astrology, the breeding habits of humans, and—"

Now I interrupted him. "Smut? You're aware of smut?"

Perry looked at me as if I'd been struck mute. "Of course. Netty and I are well-versed in, ah… internet culture."

Torina grinned. "Perry, did you just admit that you watch porn?"

"For the greater good, of course."

"Uh-huh," I said, and I was most certainly judging the bird.

"We think it's hilarious," Netty cut in. "I mean, talk about inefficient. There's presumably some human attraction to it as a concept, but I frankly don't get it."

I shrugged. "Sometimes, I might agree."

"Anyway, if we're done talking about my research, I have news," Perry said.

"What's that, you dirty bird?" I waggled my eyebrows in case my comment was too subtle. It wasn't.

"I'll ignore that for now, because I'm a professional. But in essence, we've got a bite. Guild counter-intel just reported that a broker is setting up a pop-up auction on Halcyon for the Venera and Vanguard probes." He turned to Torina. "You should get word back through your contacts almost anytime."

I raised my brows even higher. "Already?"

"They're hot commodities."

"Like flies to honey," I said, but Perry gave me a sidelong amber glance.

"I think you mean like flies to sh—"

"I like my version better," I cut in.

"Anyway, the auction's being set up for six days from now." Again, Perry turned to Torina. "That's going to be coming to you, too."

I rubbed my chin. We had substantial work left on the *Fafnir*, and then it was at least another day to Starsmith to pick up the fabricated goods, *if* they were ready, and then another day to Halcyon. It was too tight for my nerves.

"You know what, Torina? When you get that word Perry mentioned, push back and tell them the earliest we can be there is ten days. If they don't like it, then screw 'em, we've got other buyers."

"Hardball. I like it," Perry said.

"I know you do. I saw your internet search history."

OUR SECRETIVE AUCTIONEER agreed to the ten-day window, which took a lot of the pressure off. We even had time to make a trip I'd planned to do later, but it didn't really take us very far off our path to Starsmith.

"You want to check in on the memorial service for Proloxus's family? Why?" Torina asked.

"Yeah, have to admit, Van, you seem awfully invested in people you never knew, who died when you were, what, seventeen or eighteen?" Perry added.

"What can I say, I have a big heart. Besides, I filed that as our flight plan yesterday. I'd like to see if anyone follows us today, and if so, who."

18

We departed Anvil Dark with the *Fafnir* in far better shape than it was when we arrived. Like Perry, the ship had a slightly roughed, frosted tone, so she didn't gleam the way she used to. But Netty assured me that the superficial damage etched into the ship by Venus's corrosive atmosphere wouldn't affect performance, nor had it degraded any structural integrity or armor protection. But the scanner and comms arrays, and the other bits and bobs damaged by exposure to Venusian hell, had all been fixed.

Our trip to Proloxus's homeworld was uneventful. Despite the extra fuel, we traveled via Tau Ceti and lingered there for an hour or so, our transponder pinging away in the clear and announcing us to the entire system. No one obviously took the bait, though.

"Maybe they're afraid of us," I said.

Torina and Perry just looked at me. I'm sure Netty did, too.

"Or, yeah, maybe nobody here at the moment is interested in us." I sniffed. "I still like the idea that they're all scared of us more."

"You just keep living that dream, Van. The one where you're so badass that no one wants to cross you," Perry said.

Torina touched my arm. "Someday, Van. Someday."

I practiced glaring, but Torina just smiled. "Not bad. I'm buying it."

"Mission accomplished. Now then, shall we?"

We carried on to Proloxus's homeworld, the asteroid in which he either entombed his family, or at least had them entombed. Either way, the whirling mass was now a cenotaph, if one that had been done on a budget. The Vibariyun Invigilator met us there, happy to show off the somber memorial he'd had erected with the bonds I'd given him.

We grounded a few hundred meters away and bounced our way across the airless distance. The domes were gone, the only remnant of the entrance a square patch of fused rock.

"There were three other entrances. We sealed those up as well," the Invigilator said.

I took in the memorial, a slender pylon three meters tall, made of some bronze-tinged alloy. It was engraved with characters the translator simply didn't recognize.

The Invigilator explained why. "That is the first language of the Vibariyun, an ancient tongue that we now only use for graves and memorials. It seems fitting, doesn't it? To recognize the dead with a dead language?"

I looked around at the desolate surface, broken by only a few jagged ridges and humped craters, wanly lit by the distant star. The pylon stood alone amid hundreds of meters of barren rock. It made me shiver in a way reminiscent of *The Ancient's Call*, the forlorn song of a dying race that we procured as part of our investigation. This was different, though. The *Call* had been a sad lament of a people in their last stages of a long decline. This lonely pylon memorialized lives suddenly truncated, wantonly ended with cold intent driven by greed.

"I have something for you, actually," the Invigilator said, offering over a slim metal cylinder with one of his appendages. I accepted it, and he told me to open it.

Inside, rolled up, was a thin, flexible sheet like glossy plastic. I unrolled it, revealing it to be a still image of a group of Vibariyun, all apparently gathered at or near this spot. A digging machine squatted behind them.

"That is Proloxus's family, or it was at the time that image was captured to commemorate breaking ground on their new warren." He briefly explained how a Vibariyun family would split when an existing warren became too crowded, a smaller faction leaving to found a new one. There were criteria to how it all happened, but I couldn't really understand without knowing the nuances of Vibariyun family structures. It didn't matter, though, because I got the gist of it. Families grew, a small group went forth, and pressure was relieved all while expanding the family reach in a measured—and stable—way.

I stared at the image. "Is Proloxus in here somewhere?"

"No. He was still—let's see. I suppose that gestating is the best way to describe it."

I looked back up at the Invigilator. "Why are you giving me this?"

"Because, Peacemaker Tudor, when you were here previously, you seemed genuinely concerned about these people. And when we discovered their fate, you seemed truly upset. And, of course, you asked to have a memorial erected to them." He glanced at me sideways. "While making remarks about badges being turned into memorials, you might remember."

"I—yeah, I do. Sorry about that. I guess I've just met so many dishonest people in my travels, that, well, cynicism kind of becomes like a greasy film covering everything and everyone you see."

"I understand. I am fortunate, as crime is rare among my people, and that which does occur is usually addressed within the warrens themselves. This tragic event"—he gestured at the memorial—"is unprecedented, certainly within my lifetime. In any case, I wanted you to have that image so that you could see the faces of those about whom you obviously cared."

"I think you did, too. You knew this family, didn't you?"

"I did. I miss them, all the more because the reopening of a warren after a time of closure is a celebration. I must admit that I had been particularly looking forward to this one." He glanced at the pylon. "It chills me to think that while I anticipated the joyful excitement of the reopening, they were all down there, in that quiet darkness…"

He turned back. "In any case, yes, I knew them. Which is why I also know that what happened, in retrospect, isn't completely—unexpected."

"What do you mean?"

"From the time of his immaturity, Proloxus was problematic. He was willful, arrogant, and cold. He clearly never cared for anyone or anything but himself. Even his own family worried for him."

"Are you saying that his family were worried he might commit murder? That he'd murder *them*? And that you knew about it?" Torina asked, her voice taut with shock.

"No, of course not. Nothing so dire. We assumed that he would turn to a life of self-interested sin and vice, not that he would do something like—like *this*."

I glanced at Torina. "And yet, somehow this guy became not just a Peacemaker, but a Master. Perry, don't they do any background screening on these people?"

"Of course they do. It's done with a great deal of diligence, in fact, then all summarized in a report that goes to the Masters."

"And they make the decision," Torina said.

"They do."

I sighed. The implications of that were every bit as disturbing as anything else we'd uncovered in this whole sordid affair. It suggested that all of the Masters, if not actually corrupt themselves, were willing to turn a blind eye to it when it did happen. That, again, implicated Groshenko as well.

I was starting to understand why Gramps decided he didn't want to be a Master of the Guild.

I put the image back into its tube, then slipped it securely under my harness. "Thank you. I know just what I'm going to do with this."

"Van, I doubt that your idea is going to be greeted with much enthusiasm," Perry said.

We'd departed Proloxus's homeworld and were now accelerating to our next twist point, which would take us to Starsmith. I'd outlined my idea for the image the Invigilator had given me, and while Torina had applauded it, Perry had been dubious.

"I think it's very fitting, placing that image on the Peacemaker Wall of Remembrance. These people deserve to be remembered," Torina said.

"They're not Peacemakers, though," Perry countered.

I looked at him. "If a Second, or someone in a Peacemaker's retinue, someone they deputized, dies while on duty, do they get put on the Wall?"

"As Adjunct or Honorary Peacemakers, depending on their specific status, yes. But these people were just the family of a Peacemaker."

"*Just* the family of a Peacemaker?"

"Sorry, Van. I acknowledge that this is all very tragic, but these people just don't meet the criteria to be memorialized at Anvil Dark."

I narrowed my eyes at him. "But Seconds and Deputies and the like do."

"Yes, of course."

"Alright, then I want to make these people part of my retinue. I want to deputize them."

"Which people?"

"Proloxus's family."

Perry gave me a blank stare—which was pretty much the only one he could give, but he still somehow managed to communicate a lot with them. In this case, it was, what the—?

"Van, they're dead. That's a real impediment to being part of a Peacemaker's retinue."

"Why?"

"Because they're—do I need to explain the concept of *dead* to you?"

"Do the policies and regulations specifically disallow it? Does anything?" I asked him, staring straight back into his golden gaze.

"No, but—"

I held up a hand. "So that's a no."

"It is, but—"

"Perry, is there anything official that would stop me from doing this?"

"No. Believe it or not, recruiting dead people has never been an issue the Guild has spent a lot of time worrying about."

"Fine. So I'll deputize all of them posthumously. If I understand this correctly, since they aren't bringing specific skills to the team, they'll be considered Honorary rather than Adjunct Peacemakers. That's fine. And they died as a result of the actions of another Peacemaker." I looked at Torina. "What do you think?"

She nodded with a broad smile. "Sounds perfectly fine to me."

"Me as well," Netty added. "It would hardly be the first time a Peacemaker has found a technicality to exploit, and this time, it's not for personal gain."

"Thank you, Netty."

I turned back to Perry. "Okay, fine, I think it's a great idea, too. I just don't think you're going to get away with it."

"Who's going to stop me?"

"Uh, the Masters? Do you really think they're going to be happy putting up a permanent memorial to a bunch of people killed by one of their own?"

I smiled.

"No, I don't suppose they will. In fact, I'm counting on it."

Our stopover at Starsmith was brief, just long enough to pick up our merchandise and Icky. She seemed disappointed to leave.

"Oh, the things Linulla showed me. I know mechanisms and systems and circuits and stuff, but he knows what's going on right inside the metal, or the crystal, or whatever he's working with. He can practically see the way the forces and loads are acting on it. It's amazing."

I grinned and looked at Linulla. "You might have found an apprentice-in-waiting."

He waved a claw. "That would be nice, but I already have several. And as enthusiastic as she is, I don't think Icrul is ready for, or even particularly wants a life tied to one place, doing the things that one has to do to become a Starsmith."

Icky shrugged. "He's right. There's too much out there that I haven't seen yet. But if I can come back here to visit from time to time—"

"Any time you wish, Icrul," Linulla said.

We inspected the fake Venera 12 probe. It was, of course, magnificent work. As far as I could tell, Linulla had managed to reproduce every aspect of it, right down to specific tool marks on the heavy metal ring that formed the lander's base. I certainly had nothing to offer but my thanks as we loaded it into the *Fafnir*. We loaded the two Vanguard probes as well.

Torina frowned a bit at that. "Why did you leave those two satellites here, anyway? I thought the point was that they are originals, and that will up our credibility?"

"I actually asked him to," Linulla put in. "Since these three spacecraft are all from approximately the same period, I thought I might gain useful insights into the materials science practiced by humans of that time."

It was a good lie, and one that Torina seemed to accept. I decided to seal the deal.

"I've got a backup, anyway, since I really don't want these Vanguard probes ending up in some criminal's living room. Alic is going to be our shill. He's already at Halcyon, posing as a buyer. He's going to buy the Vanguards and then give them back," I explained.

Torina nodded. "Makes sense."

With everything aboard, we said our farewells to Linulla and pressed on to our rendezvous with sleaziness on Halcyon.

"So it doesn't bother you that you're basically plundering your own species' history?" the alien asked. He was, himself, the same species as one of the very first alien criminals I'd had to deal with, a murderous shuttle pilot working for the Salt Thieves, named Koba. Their race, the Druakr, resembled beef jerky layered over a skeleton, their faces covered with goggles and breathing masks that further removed them from anything approaching a friendly appearance.

I shrugged. "These accomplishments are still recorded in our history books. What difference does the actual hardware make? I mean, if that Vanguard satellite had been destroyed in, say, a collision with another satellite, it's not like it would have been erased from our past, right?"

"Very pragmatic of you, Peacekeeper. Maybe a little bit of rationalization in there somewhere, too, eh?"

I thought the Druakr might be grinning under his mask. I couldn't tell and just ignored him. The less of this sort of improv I had to do, the less chance I'd blow it.

Alic, who'd come in plain clothes, stood a few meters away, waiting for his chance to bid on the Vanguard probes. He was the sort of Peacemaker who tended to deal with bigger-picture stuff, his species being renowned for their strategic forethought and overall labyrinthine cunning. As far as his appearance, Alic was completely forgettable.

He was *built* for this kind of operation.

Bidding proceeded on the Venera probe, jerking upward in increments that followed long stretches of silence, punctuated by the auctioneer's *going once… going twice…* Despite the criminality of it all, it was actually weirdly exciting. Crime, I decided, had a frisson all its own.

I had Torina with me. Icky stayed aboard the *Fafnir*, keeping her powered up and ready to fly in case we had to beat a hasty retreat. Perry had parked himself high up among some structural beams, scanning the crowd gathered for the auction and looking for bio-recognition hits. This went beyond mere facial recognition, since for many alien species facial features simply weren't distinct. Instead, this factored in specifics of size, body proportions, angles, gait, and myriad other factors that combined to make someone unique.

The prospects for onerous and inescapable surveillance were frightening. A whole underground industry had developed around defeating this pervasive tech, including actual surgical alterations. I had to admit, I'd need *really* good reasons to fly under the radar before I'd have my limbs removed, then reattached in slightly different positions.

The lead bidder on your Venera probe is a Stillness agent, Perry said in my ear bug.

I shared an uneasy glance with Torina. The Stillness. Shit. We'd given them enough of a beating and compromised their operations enough that we'd expected it would be a good long while before they popped up again. But here they were, apparently once more in business. That worried me. The Stillness and the Peacemakers had a long-lasting mutual enmity of particular intensity. My Gramps had actually confronted them head-on, and although he'd never managed to quite defeat them, either, he'd been a major obstacle for them. I *still* wasn't convinced they hadn't had something to do with my grandfather's sudden illness and death.

I turned to Torina, as though speaking to her, but kept my voice low. "Alic, I'd like this guy bidding on Venera to win. Can you nudge the price up a bit, push some of these other assholes out of the bidding?"

Alic immediately fired off a bid, as though he'd just been biding his time. He was good, I had to hand him that. Most of the bidders, who'd probably been hoping they could luck into a cheap Earthly artifact, slumped in disappointment. I watched the Stillness agent, a human woman who seemed to be made of nothing but flat planes and angles. She didn't bat an eye, and just pushed the price higher. Alic counterbid, and she raised over that. A Yonnox jammed in a higher bid, which Alic, after apparently taking a moment to think about it, bid up again. The Yonnox shot him a poisonous look but shut up.

The Stillness agent coolly bid again. Alic outbid her. I was starting to get worried. If Alic won this, we would have succeeded in accomplishing absolutely nothing here. But the Stillness agent, without even glancing at Alic, simply dropped a counterbid over his.

Twice more, Alic outbid her. The price had gone from high into the stupid range, that rarefied air where money and power converge into a single contested point. The whole crowd had become an audience, watching with fascination as these two competitors for Venera threw increasingly obscene amounts of bonds at the sale.

I was sweating. Actually sweating. And my gut churned.

"Isn't this fun?" Torina asked, her tone sardonic.

"For versions of the word *fun* that include want to puke, sure."

Alic bid again. We were at four million bonds.

The Stillness agent said—

Nothing.

Oh, shit.

If Alic won, it might as well be four billion bonds. He wasn't actually buying, after all, so we weren't actually going to get paid if he did.

"Going once."

I tensed muscles I never even knew I had.

"Going twice."

Shit. All of this for—

"Going—"

"Four point five million bonds," the Stillness agent cut in, each word clipped and precise.

I turned to Torina. "Alic, I think that's—"

"Enough? It is. She's reached her ceiling," came his tinny reply. He'd apparently been talking to a squat, hairy alien I recognized as his Second, although I forgot their name.

The tension drained out of me like an emptying bathtub. If anyone outbid the Stillness agent now, at least we'd score a lot of money.

"Going once. Going twice."

Dramatic pause.

"Sold, to bidder number eleven."

I felt a ripple through my body as muscles loosened, then I turned to Torina. This time, I spoke in a rush of relief. "I could use a drink."

She blew out a breath. "Same. That was… I mean, I *have* money, but that felt like—"

"War?"

She smiled, nodding slowly. "Yep. The personal kind, too."

The rest of the auction was anticlimactic. Alic's amazing brinksmanship, besides demonstrating just how well he could read someone, gave him the perfect excuse to come at the Vanguard probes with a vengeance. He played the thwarted buyer, prevented from acquiring something he wanted, perfectly. It quickly became clear to the crowd that he would *not* lose this time around. Of course, that was a lot easier when you weren't actually bidding real money. But he still had the crowd watching him, bemused, as he almost petulantly flung huge sums of money at the Vanguard auctions. Not surprisingly, he won both, earning another five-point-five million bonds, albeit of the fake, nonexistent sort.

It was time to *go*. Alic paid us a deposit of bonds that were, like his workboat, requisitioned from, and had to be returned to, the Guild. The Stillness agent paid us in full, in cash. Her face might as well have been cast in alloy for all the expression she showed us as she did. More importantly, I didn't see anything resembling recognition.

"You're a credit to your profession, Peacemaker," were the only words she said to me. She laced them with so much cool disdain, I felt a momentary surge of real anger. But Torina intervened, wearing a polite, dismissive smile.

"We'd like to say the same about you."

Not that we did—that we'd *like to*.

Perry spoke in my ear, his tone one of awed respect. "She sure is good at being mean."

19

Now came the next step in our plan—see who came after us. After all, we were laden with bonds, all untraceable cash, and would constitute a definite high-value target.

We'd prepared for this, too. As we sealed up the *Fafnir* and backed away from the Halcyon docking port, Netty spoke up. "K'losk twisted into the system about ten minutes ago and is now inbound."

K'losk had his full Peacemaker identity on open display, right down to the details of his transponder data. We'd already switched to a nondescript transponder code, trying to look as though we wanted to avoid K'losk, who'd ostensibly arrived on other business entirely. He was our backup, though. Our hope was that if anyone did follow us, they'd do so discreetly and at a distance, until they were sure K'losk couldn't intervene fast enough to matter.

We saw Alic, in the meantime, also get underway. He was actually more exposed than we were, carrying the two Vanguard probes, possibly carrying even more money, all of it aboard a lightly armed workboat.

Twenty minutes out, though, and still no sign of any pursuit after us or Alic.

"Well, shit. No bites at all? That's disappointing," I said, scanning and scowling at the tactical overlay.

"You can console yourself by rolling around in that pile of bonds you made from that Stillness agent," Torina said. I could tell that she wanted desperately to ask me what I intended to do with the money, since four-and-a-half million bonds would make a great down payment to the Synergists, the space hippies, to start healing her land. The trouble was that that was all we had—a down payment. We needed another eight million bonds, at least, and didn't have anywhere near that much available.

But her parents had bought some time. They'd hired a nano-chemist, a specialist in assembling new materials virtually atom by atom, who'd managed to come up with a way of stalling the spread of the blight across their lands. It was only a temporary solution, though. The evil little machines turning their lush forests and grasslands to dust and anguish would keep reproducing and would eventually overwhelm the nano-chemist's makeshift defenses.

I opened my mouth to start a conversation with Torina about her family's woes, when Netty interrupted.

"Van, we're receiving an urgent comm message via directional beam from a ship still docked at Halcyon."

I glanced at the transponder code of the transmitting ship. It meant nothing to me.

So I shrugged. "Put them on."

The image of the Still agent flicked open. Her angular face had, if anything, hardened even more, making me think of the business end of an ax.

"Hello, what can I do for—" I began, but she cut me off.

"Spare me. The probe you sold me was a fake. A good one, but a fake. So, you're going to reverse course, come back here, and return my money, and I *might* see fit to let you live beyond the next few days."

I glanced at Torina and Perry, who both shrugged. Icky began quietly bringing our weapons online, while Netty warned Alic and K'losk about what was happening.

For a few heartbeats, I considered just playing the aggrieved seller and throwing this back at her, accusing her of trying to shake us down. But the whole point of this thing had been to find a hook into this shadowy conspiracy—or *conspiracies*, because there might actually be several potentially related ones—that we faced. I'd had a vague idea we'd follow the Stillness agent in some way, a plan I was going to work on with the others as we at least appeared to leave the Halcyon system.

But I was getting a little tired of these intricate schemes and subtle games and runarounds. So I decided, to hell with it, let's see what happens.

"I'll make you a counteroffer. We'll return your money, and you return our missing Masters."

It really was a shot in the dark. I had no evidence this woman even knew about the two Masters who'd vanished. But, as soon as I said it, I could tell from her reaction that I'd managed to hit pay dirt. Her profoundly bland expression cracked slightly, revealing a brief glimpse of surprise, and maybe a little concern. Apparently, we weren't supposed to have associated her with the missing

Masters, and when I did, it had knocked her momentarily off her game.

"I—don't know what you're talking about—"

"Bullshit," I snapped, exploiting the momentary gap in her defenses and driving through it as hard and far as I could. "Honestly, I don't give a rat's ass about the money, which is no doubt the proceeds of all sorts of scummy activities. I was actually thinking of just dumping it somewhere in deep space. But, if you give up those Masters, I'll give it back to you. Or, if you'd prefer, I'll give you the real Venera 12, your choice."

She stared daggers back at me for a moment. I stared right back. One of us was going to back down, and a year ago, it might have been me. But I remembered the campaign Gramps had waged against these pricks and decided it was a mantle I would take up—and run with. I settled into my expression, waiting.

She finally blinked. "I can't give you two Masters. One of them is dead."

"Which one?"

"Yewlo. He had a fit of conscience and was about to reveal his debts to your Guild, then throw himself onto their mercy." She sneered. "He should have. They would have just put him in jail."

I narrowed my eyes at her, trying to read anything in her expression. But she'd restored her social defenses, and I got nothing.

"How much did he owe?"

"At the time of his death, forty-eight million bonds, give or take."

I sat back in my seat at that. Holy *shit*.

I sat forward again. "What about Proloxus?"

Her expression changed into a thin smile, so hard and cold it could have been carved from ancient cometary ice. "Oh, I think he'll come back to you when he's good and ready. He has… plans."

"So he's one of yours."

The woman shrugged. "I'm sure you'd like to know. After all, if one of your Masters was a Stillness agent this whole time, well, that would be quite the revelation, wouldn't it?"

"Do you want your money or not?"

"Sorry, but leaving that question hanging open is worth four and a half million just for the anxiety and unrest it's going to cause your pathetic little Guild." She tilted her head to the side. "Besides, you wanted your two Masters, and I've answered you. One is dead, and the other is—somewhere, I honestly don't know where."

Unfortunately, I once again believed her. Of course she wouldn't know much about Stillness operations, outside of her own cell. That was how these scummy organizations worked. If an agent didn't know something, they couldn't reveal it.

"I will sweeten our deal, though," she went on.

"We have a deal?"

"That's up to you. I can tell you the last place Proloxus was."

"And why would you do that?"

"Because I sense that you're about to pull the plug on this conversation and abscond with my money. And that inbound Peacemaker isn't here just by coincidence; it's another threat to this deal going in a direction I can't allow. So I'm trying to make life easier for both of us." She leaned forward and dropped her voice to a conspiratorial whisper. "Between you and me, I don't care one bit about Proloxus or what happens to him. But I do have a job to do, on behalf of a client, who wants that Venera probe. So I'll tell you the little bit I do know, you'll keep my money, and

I'll get that probe. In the meantime, you can go and do—whatever it is that Peacemakers do that makes them feel so morally righteous."

I glanced again at Torina and Perry. This time, they both nodded. They were obviously thinking the same way I was.

"Alright, let's hear it," I said to the Stillness agent.

"The last I heard of Proloxus, he was on Spindrift."

I offered her an appreciative nod. "Okay, then."

"So do we have a deal?"

I stared back at this woman for a moment. She suddenly seemed almost... collegial. Like she and I had had a meeting of the minds and weren't bitter rivals. For a moment, I wondered if I might be able to cultivate her as an enduring channel on Stillness operations, or maybe even nudge her in the direction of becoming a double agent.

But then I thought about how much blood she might have on her hands. The Stillness were vicious, remorseless criminals and murderers. They'd stymied the best efforts of the Peacemakers to bring them to heel for decades, maybe centuries.

More to the point, I thought about Gramps, wasting away in some hospital bed, festooned with wires and tubes and beeping machines.

Maybe it had been cancer.

But maybe it hadn't.

This was for you, Gramps.

"Sorry, I don't make deals with the devil. It always seems to come back and bite you in the ass," I said and flicked the comm channel closed.

There was a moment of silence until Perry finally broke it. "So,

Van, should I add her to our list of bitter enemies alphabetically or chronologically?"

OUR SUCCESSION OF TWISTS—ANVIL Dark to Proloxus's homeworld, and then to Starsmith, and then to Halcyon—seriously depleted our fuel. We needed to make a refueling stop, but I wanted to throw any possible pursuit if I could. That meant staying away from twists to obvious places, like Spindrift, Dregs, or Crossroads. If we had to suddenly twist away, we couldn't, because one more transfer would leave our antimatter tanks dry.

Fortunately, Netty had a solution.

"There's an out-of-the-way refueling stop at Groombridge 1618, better known as Bullseye," she said, highlighting the system on the star chart. The box-out of data told me that Groombridge 1618 was a K-type main sequence star, about two thirds the mass of Sol, but only about six percent of its brightness. Still, the dim orange star had a super Earth originally named Se'grit orbiting it, a planet that on the face of it seemed like a perfectly habitable one. Any settlement would definitely need some sort of reliable backup power to offset the lack of heat and light, but it still had liquid water and a breathable, if cold, atmosphere.

But that's where the name Bullseye came in.

"It says here that the planet was hit by an asteroid?"

"Almost a hundred years ago, yes. It was an event on the same scale as the impact that wiped out the dinosaurs on Earth sixty-five million years ago."

As Netty spoke, she played footage obviously captured from high orbit, depicting a big hunk of rock whipping into the frame, then vanishing in a dazzling flash. When it cleared, a fierce shock wave of fire and debris swept rapidly outward from the impact site, a growing ring that would eventually engulf the entire planet. It had hit an ocean basin and released so much energy that it left an entirely waterless circle of shattered oceanic crust a thousand klicks across, surrounding a seething pool of glowing magma a hundred klicks wide. The concentric circles of devastation did, indeed, resemble a gigantic bullseye target.

I watched as the planet's climate became fire and shook my head.

"Wow. How many people were killed?"

"None."

"Really?"

"The planet had only a few settlements on it, and they were evacuated," Netty replied.

"You mean there was no way of stopping this from happening? Diverting that asteroid, or destroying it, or something?"

"Oh, there were ways. The impact was seen coming decades in advance, in fact. But there was general consensus it would be useful to study a large impact in real-time detail."

"I remember watching that footage when I was in school," Torina said. "Had to write an essay about it, in fact."

"What kind of grade did you get?" I asked.

Torina waggled her hand. "I took some liberties with my verbiage. I used the word *boom* a lot."

Perry snickered. "As we speak, I am searching all known records for this cultural artifact."

"I was eleven when I wrote it, you barbarian."

Perry was unruffled. "Irrelevant. When I find your Ode to Boom, or whatever you titled it, I'm having it stenciled on this ship."

I held up a hand. "I'll stop you there. While I appreciate petty aggression—"

"Thank you," Perry said, dipping his beak.

"We aren't painting my ship unless it's flames. Or maybe a dragon."

Torina lifted her eyes, and Icky snorted.

"They let a planet die as an experiment. Cold, but… efficient," I said, both impressed and repulsed by that kind of desire for knowledge.

But the wounded planet now filled another purpose. It was being subjected to terraforming to determine what it would take to bring a planet scoured by impact fire back to life. And, unlike the so-called terraforming operation from which we'd recovered the identity claiming to be the Nesit Erflos Tand, this one was legit.

Which brought us to the supporting infrastructure, an orbiting star port and refueling depot known as the Needle. It earned its name from its literal appearance as a long, slender central hub, surrounded by four rings. Needle was the logistics base for the ongoing terraforming, while also functioning as a port for ships plying the galactic spinward of known space.

"Looks like the perfect place to gas up. Netty, if you please."

"Way ahead of you, Van," she replied and started configuring the *Fafnir* to twist to Bullseye.

20

THE BIG PLANET was wounded but far from dead. The atmosphere was still hazy from suspended dust and other chemicals, the residue of the massive impact. And the planet gleamed with ice as massive glaciers sprawled away from its poles. The impact had plunged Bullseye into an ice age, except for the site of the asteroid strike itself. The crust there had been pulverized into gravel, pretty much right down to the planet's upper mantle, allowing vast eruptions of magma from deep in its interior. The result was a hotspot, shrouded in nearly permanent mist, spawning powerful storms and slowly building up new land as lava poured onto the surface and cooled.

"Looks like hell down there," I said as we approached Needle to dock. I was glad to be watching it all from a few thousand klicks up but still shivered a little at the terrible majesty of the ravaged planet.

"So I take it a trip down to the surface isn't on the schedule," Icky said.

I glanced back at her. "Hey, feel free. Just don't be late getting back to the *Fafnir*."

But Icky didn't immediately respond, which was odd for someone who I'd come to know as an inveterate wiseass. "Icky, everything alright?"

I'd thought she'd realized something was wrong with the *Fafnir*, but that wasn't it at all.

"Not entirely, no. I don't know about you guys, but I'm starting to find the *Fafnir* pretty… cramped."

As she spoke, she shifted uncomfortably in the small and hard jump seat, trying not to knock into her engineering panel with a stray hand or elbow as she did. And considering she had four of each, it was an extra chore for her. Add onto that the fact that she was as big and heavy as a linebacker, and I got her point.

"We do intend to upgrade the *Fafnir* sometime soon, so that should make a big difference," I replied.

She nodded but apparently still wasn't satisfied. "Actually, Van, if you don't mind, I'd like to run with this a bit. If it's okay with you, I'd like to talk to Papa. I've got a couple of ideas to run past him."

"Hey, you do you, Icky. If you come up with something interesting—and affordable—let's talk about it."

We docked, waited for the airlock to equalize, then stepped out into the arrival concourse of Needle. Like Spindrift, Crossroads, and Halcyon, it combined airport lounge with shopping center, all of it overlain by a distinct techno vibe. Unlike those busier ports, though, this didn't have the same sort of frenetic bustle. There were maybe a few dozen others here, all quietly going about their business. In fact, the place seemed downright clean and orderly compared to what I'd gotten used to in larger spaceports.

What immediately caught my attention, though, was a storefront across the concourse, behind a bank of elevators that ran up and down the central core of the Needle, giving quick access to any part of it. The shop was decked out in rococo golden filigree, all curlicues and cherubs, against a background of off-white. The sign over the door, just as ornate, proclaimed the place to be *La Maison Loin de Chez Soi*.

I did a double take at that. I'd traveled enough back on Earth to pick up a smattering of several languages, basically enough to order a meal or a drink, hire a taxi, or be directed to a restroom. One of them was French. I was able to translate this as being something about a house, or home, and being at it. But what it actually meant wasn't the real question.

The real question, of course, was why the hell a restaurant, or bar, or whatever this place was, had a French name to begin with. We were, after all, about sixteen light-years away from the closest part of France, Quebec, or anywhere else that actually spoke the language.

"Okay, I've *got* to check that out," I said, leading the way. Torina, Icky, and Perry followed me. It had to be an expat human, someone from Earth, and I wanted to know more.

We entered a combination restaurant and bar that could have sat alongside the *Champs-Élysées* in Paris, all French provincial furnishings and more of that intricate baroque ornamentation spilling across the walls. Musette-style accordion music, the stereotypical tunes played over every establishing shot of Paris in every movie ever, played softly in the background. A vintage cigarette machine, which looked as though it had been lifted straight from the

Right Bank sometime in the 1930s, even vended *actual* Gauloises cigarettes.

I stood and stared, taking it all in. It took a moment, but I finally found my voice again.

"You know, I have seen other stars, planets ranging from balls of rock to gas giants, spaceships of every size and type, super-intelligent machines, and more alien beings than you can shake a stick at. But I have to say, *this* is now officially the strangest thing I've ever seen in my life."

"Ah, bonjour, mes amis, bienvenue à La *Maison Loin de Chez Soi!*"

I turned to the speaker, expecting her to be clad in a slim, slinky dress with a floppy art deco hat and maybe a slender cigarette holder, like a character from an Agatha Christie novel. Instead, I got a roughly two meter tall slug deftly balancing atop a sphere roughly the size of a basketball, upon which she rolled about in a way that seemed to utterly defy gravity.

Again, I just stared. "I stand corrected. *That* is now the strangest thing I've ever seen in my life."

"Ah, human, and recently from Earth, no? Mais oui, I can tell by your accent."

A slug. On a ball. That sounded like a woman strolling through the shadow of the Eiffel Tower on her way to some sidewalk café with checkered tablecloths.

Torina stepped forward, smiling and nodding. "It's a pleasure to meet you—I'm sorry, I didn't catch your name."

"That is because I have not yet given it to you, silly one. I am Countess Henriette Eugenie de Gauthier-Francois."

Of course it was.

"And I'm very pleased to meet you, Countess—"

The creature waved a sticky tendril in a way, so help me, that had a touch of Gallic disdain to it. "We need not stand on ceremonies, yes? You may call me Retta."

"Well, it's very nice to meet you, Retta. This is Icrul, and this handsome metal construct is Perry."

Perry bobbed his head. "Handsome metal construct. I like that. I think that's how I'd like to be introduced from now on."

Retta turned to me. "And who is this mysterious stranger who stands as silent as Pierrot on the stage of *le Théâtre des Funambules?*"

I blinked. "As quiet—I'm—what?"

The slug laughed in a delicate, dryly tasteful way.

"Pierrot, le célèbre personage played by the great Deburau until his passing in 1846? No?"

"I'm sorry, I don't get to 19th century France very often."

Torina leaned in. "This is Van Tudor. And you're right, he's from Earth."

"Magnifique! I have had so few patrons from le berceau de l'humanité, the cradle of humanity. Please, you must sit, and I will bring you wine."

"Actually, we're here—"

"No, no, I must insist. I will not hear of you refusing my hospitality!"

She ushered us to a small table—not decorated in a checked tablecloth, of course, because that would have clashed with the much more Renaissance feel of the place. Retta bustled off atop her ball, and I looked at Perry.

"What the hell is going on? Why am I suddenly a character in a Claude Monet painting?"

"Ooh la-la, check out le mécène des arts."

"You speak French?"

"Naturellement. Je parle couramment le français—"

"Perry!"

"Sorry. Yes, I speak pretty much every Earthly language. Again, long days in that barn with nothing else to do. And as for what's going on, no idea. All I know is that Retta shows up in the Peacemaker archives as an occasionally handy source of information."

Retta came rolling back to the table before I could ask Perry to elaborate. Her sense of balance astounded me. Not only did she somehow stay perched atop the ball, but she also managed to carry a carafe of wine and three delicate glasses on a tray and smoothly place them onto our table.

"I'm assuming this is French wine," I said.

"Mais oui! It is Château Beychevelle 1989, an excellent year. Please enjoy."

On impulse, I gestured to a seat. "Retta, why don't you pull up a —er—"

"I am happy to join you, of course. Tell me, have you ever been to France?"

"I—yes. Yes, I have. My grandfather took me there when I was thirteen, to tour some old battlefields. We spent a lot of time around Ypres—"

"Ah, you test me, of course. Ypres is in Belgium, no?"

"You're right. It is. But he took me to France, too, around Arras, the Somme, the Argonne, Verdun—"

"Ah, c'est magnifique. Such beautiful places."

I exchanged a look with Torina, who just smirked. I turned back to Retta. "Well, they are now, considering their history. But I'm curious, Retta. Have *you* ever been to France?"

She sighed. "Only in the réalité virtuelle. I do hope to someday visit there in person."

And I would *love* to be there to see that, I thought, imagining Retta rolling along the Champs-Élysées, maybe passing beneath the Arche de Triomphe. But my mind quickly turned to a far more pressing question.

"Retta, considering where we are, I—well, I'm wondering—why France?"

"There is a country you prefer?"

"Well, I love visiting Italy—but that's not really my point. Why are you so interested in France, a country on Earth?"

"Pourquoi pas? Why not? It is a place of beauty, of art and culture, and of such very fine wine," she replied, sipping at the glass she'd poured with something crossed between a mouth and a proboscis.

I nodded, sensing it was all the answer I was going to get, at least for now. I paused to sip the wine, which was actually *very* good. I don't often drink wine, usually only with meals, and then mostly on special occasions, like Thanksgiving or Christmas. But this stuff was, I had to admit, really, really good.

"So, you are a Peacemaker, yes?" Retta asked.

"I am, yes. Perry's my combat AI, Torina's my Second, and Icky over there is my Engineer."

Icky, who'd been silent since we entered, finally spoke up. "Hey, how do you stay on that ball?"

I winced. So did Torina. Icky's isolated upbringing still showed.

But Retta merely laughed. "With great difficulty, of course. It is a thing the Thurk, my people, must learn and master if they are to be considered les adultes, yes?"

"That's amazing," Icky replied.

It was. As Retta—sat, stood, perched, whatever the right term was—by the table, I saw her making constant tiny adjustments, jiggling the ball around with her—again, I wasn't sure what to call it. Tail? Foot? In any case, it fascinated me watching the sheer dexterity and coordination it must have required. Even then, it would have to be pretty much autonomous, so she could do it while carrying on conversations about things like wine and famous French actors of the past.

"So you are here searching for les criminels? Those engaged in le méfait, the wrongdoing?"

"Actually, we're not. We're really just here to refuel our ship." I looked at her sidelong as I spoke. Perry had said she'd provided the Peacemakers with information in the past. So I decided to take a shot.

"But we are involved in a case," I went on, then explained the labyrinthine schemes that somehow seemed to link stolen identities, illicit trade in artifacts, missing Peacemaker Masters, and shady terraforming operations. I saw Perry looking at me, and he even spoke up, in my ear bud.

Van, are you sure you want to give this much away?

I just kept talking. Perry gave a pointed sigh but didn't interrupt any further.

When I finished talking, I waited for Retta to respond. Not surprisingly, I'd never tried to work out the facial expressions or body language of a slug before, but I can attest to the fact it ain't easy. For all I knew, she hadn't even listened to a word I'd said. And as the silence drew on, I found myself shifting uncomfortably and glancing at the others. Had I offended her somehow? Had I bored her to the point of her going completely dormant?

But I perked up when she finally did reply.

"This is most interesting. I am... not unfamiliar with les délits, the crimes of which you speak," she said.

"You're not unfamiliar? How so?"

"Because I know of those who have been threatened with l'usurpation d'identité, the theft of who and what they are."

Now I was leaning toward Retta. So were Torina and Icky. Even Perry seemed to perk up.

"Retta, if there is anything you can tell us about this, it might be very helpful in our case."

"Do you know anyone whose identity has been stolen that way?" Torina asked.

"Ah, vous n'écoutez pas. You do not listen. I know of those who have been *threatened* with this terrible thing, or have come to believe they are threatened with it."

"How? *How* do you know about them, Retta?" I asked.

"Ah, well, they tell me, yes? And then, je les aide à disparaître."

"Sorry—?"

"Ah, pardon. I help them to disappear."

I SAT BACK, stunned. Retta was not only claiming that she was in touch with people who risked running afoul of the identity thieves, but that she helped them to avoid them, apparently by making them disappear.

"I'm kind of glad we ran low on fuel. Retta, we could really use some help."

"I would be glad. I do not like les criminels. So it is that I make many friends, all over the known space, and listen to the things they tell me. And some of them are… very helpful to me."

"You're saying you have contacts all over known space?"

"Mais oui. Everybody, they think I simply serve very good food, and even better wine—and I do, yes—but that is an advantage. I am not, as you say, la personne célèbre. I am just a humble restaurateur."

We talked for the next hour. It quickly became clear that Retta had more than simply *many friends all over the known space*. She was, in fact, the hub of a sweeping information network, practically a spymaster. And as much as she played up being a humble restaurateur, it was apparent that she made very good money wheeling and dealing with that information. She also had the means of making people who wished to vanish do so. I'd crossed paths with a couple of so-called erasers back on Earth during the course of my various excursions into the dark web. They'd seemed like little more than thugs—specialized ones, but thugs, nonetheless.

Retta was no thug. A slug, yes, but not a thug. She was erudite, urbane, and ever-so-slightly disdainful in a very Gallic way. We left with a mutual promise to help one another.

"And when we come back, it'll be with… gifts. And maybe something more." I smiled at her. "Retta, I think this is the beginning of a beautiful friendship."

"Ah, *Casablanca*! Un film merveilleux! Bogart and Bacall, and Morocco, so romantic, n'est ce pas?"

I shook my head, my smile widening. She got the reference.

Because of course she did.

WE LEFT Needle having made an unexpected, intriguing, and admittedly weird friend. The fact that I came from Earth and had actually been to France seemed to impress Retta deeply. She asked me about the trip I took with my grandfather, trudging across old battlefields in both sun and rain. Despite mostly looking at fields of millet or rye that had once been trench lines, or busy forests shrouding bits of broken concrete that had apparently been bunkers, I'd had a good time and remembered it fondly, so it was easy to speak to Retta in warm, glowing terms about France.

Of course, it also meant ignoring my last trip to France to attend a pop-up white-hat hacker conference in Paris about two years ago. I'd just meant to do it as a stopover on a trip back from Prague to the States, but it ended up being three days of drunken hell-raising. On the last night, I'd fallen asleep in a cab, and the driver had happily taken me on a tour all over Paris, then stuck me with a bill for eighty Euros. I also missed my plane and had to shell out for another day of accommodations, plus a change fee on my ticket home. Yeah, I didn't bother telling Retta about *that* version of France.

"Do you think she's going to be able to help us? I mean, she didn't actually *tell* us anything we could use, did she?" Icky asked.

I nodded while scanning the tactical overlay. This was a pretty empty system traffic-wise, but that somehow made me more nervous —there are times that quiet has an ominous weight. Like just then. "I think she will. She agreed to follow up on a few leads we thought might be interesting, so we'll see what comes of that. But, yeah, I think she's decided she can trust us."

"More like *start* trusting us. In her sort of business, trust is a process, at least to build. It's like spun sugar when it comes to breaking it, though," Perry said.

I gave him a sideways glance. "The voice of experience?"

"Everything's the voice of experience, Van, insofar as everything that happens is based on all the things that happened before it."

"That was a touch pedantic for my taste, bird."

Perry shrugged. "Every now and then I need to remind people that I'm more than just a sparkling wit. I know things. Like, most things."

"Van, we've got an incoming comm message. It's from Icky's father," Netty chirped.

I tensed at that. We'd helped Urnak resolve the bitter legacy of his failed marriage to Icky's mother, who also happened to be a major criminal involved in our identity-theft ring—mainly by killing his ex-wife during a firefight. We hadn't had much to do with him since then. Moreover, long-distance comms like this weren't cheap, especially to a ship that might be located anywhere in known space. Maybe it was the complexity of the case and the pervasive nature of our shadowy adversaries, but having him call unexpectedly put me on edge.

I braced myself. "Put him on."

Urnak's image appeared on the screen between the pilot and copilot's seats. It was fuzzy, his voice slightly distorted by the twist relays carrying it from wherever he was.

"Hi, dad!" Icky said, leaning in between the seats.

"Hello, Icrul. You are well?"

"Awful. Van and Torina beat me and make me do all the work."

"Glad to hear it! Anyway, I was thinking about our last conversation, when you mentioned how cramped you all are."

Icky glanced at me, looking a little sheepish. "Yeah, sorry, Van. I vented to my dad a bit about how we're jammed together all the time."

"Hey, that's okay. I'm not a big fan of sleeping with my knees bent all the time either." I turned to her father. "Trouble is that we're still a long way from being able to afford any upgrades to the *Fafnir* that will actually make her any bigger than she is."

"It's not just that, Van. The only permanent base we've got, aside from Anvil Dark, is your farm in I-whoa," Icky said, rolling the state name on her tongue.

"I-woah—oh, Iowa. Yeah, that's true. I guess the only places we have to really put out our boots to dry is there and Anvil Dark."

Torina looked bemused. "Put out our boots to dry?"

I shrugged. "One of my grandfather's sayings. Anyway, it'd be nice to have another permanent base to work from, but we can't afford that either. Well, maybe on some out of the way planet, or asteroid or something, but even then—"

"Why bother going planet-side at all?" Urnak asked.

I frowned. "Well, because it's that, or the *Fafnir*, and we've already covered the situation with her, right?"

"You're missing a perfectly good third option. Do what I did, and get yourself a big old battleship."

My frown became a little thoughtful as I thought about Urnak's own battlewagon, the long-ago decommissioned *Nemesis*. He and Icky had, by themselves, managed to make her space worthy again, automating all of her critical systems and making it Urnak's home.

But that had been a *lot* of work, and the thing was enormous. It had to have the interior volume of a good-sized factory. I couldn't imagine it was cheap to run, either.

"I appreciate the suggestion, Urnak, but we haven't got years to refurbish some big ol' derelict," I said.

"Ah, but you don't have to. Here." He touched a control offscreen, and the image flicked to that of a massive ship, blocky and dark, sporting a multitude of turrets and a series of masts I now recognized as bristling with scanner arrays and fire-control sensors. Most of the turrets looked empty, but the ship looked intact. Moreover, a subtle detail hinted at her being more or less intact inside, too—lights speckled her flank, gleaming through viewports.

"So what am I looking at, besides a battleship?" I asked.

"That's *The Morass of Despair*. She's a former Ynlithi battlecruiser—so a fair bit smaller than a battleship, but with better acceleration. She was only decommissioned a few years ago, when the Ynlithi decided to downsize their fleet. This one got sold surplus, but she's been in a mothball orbit in the Tau Ceti system ever since. If I had to guess, the current owners are just looking to flip her and make a quick profit."

I curled my lip. "*The Morass of Despair*? Isn't that a little—I don't know, dark? For any ship, not just a warship? They're usually named things like Illustrious, or Enterprise, or Conqueror, not something that sounds like a bad marriage."

"It *is* a touch emo," Perry added.

"What's an emo?" Icky asked.

"You know how I said Santa was complicated? Well, brace yourself. This isn't just complicated. It's also about teenagers." I turned back to Urnak, tapping my chin. It was an intriguing idea. The advantage of a ship over a planet-side base was that a ship could travel. It also meant we'd be less beholden to any particular jurisdiction. On the other hand, it was a big ship, in what appeared to be decent condition, but still probably needing a lot of work. It would be that, plus the price to make her spaceworthy again, plus how much it was going to cost us to operate her that would be the deciding factors.

I allowed myself a sigh. Science fiction made space seem so exciting, all thrills and adventures. It had definitely glossed over the bookkeeping. You never saw the hero pause amid a space battle to consider taxes and valuation.

"So this thing is for sale?" I asked.

"So the listing on the registry says."

"Are you planning on buying? Or maybe stealing?" Torina asked.

"Depends on who holds the keys." I glanced at the entry on the sales registry, a more or less universal listing of all ships for sale in known space. It was more or less because a lot of sales happened privately. That this one was listed publicly suggested it was at least *somewhat* legit.

But Perry squawked a laugh. "Those names listed, for the current owners? They're Salt Thieves. Three of them, all brothers from the same nest, so to speak, and all bad news."

"You sure about that?" I asked him.

"Van, for the umpteenth time, AI bird here, remember? Of course I'm sure. Their names come up in the archives for about twenty different investigations."

I sat back. "Hmm. Well, it's intriguing. I'm not anxious to try and make deals with the Salt Thieves, though. I seem to recall our last encounter ended with them swearing to wreak terrible vengeance on us."

"Actually, all of our encounters with bad guys seem to end with them swearing vengeance on us. They're all starting to blur into one big smear of promised retribution, in fact," Torina said.

"That might not be as big an issue as you think," Netty put in. "I've checked the registry, and those three seem to be freelancers, not dedicated Salt Thieves. They've resold a dozen ships over the past couple of years."

"So part-time Salt Thieves," I said.

"That's right."

"So maybe they'll only deliver terrible vengeance to us during certain hours," Icky put in, grinning.

I cracked my knuckles. "You know what? I'm just intrigued enough to give this a try. Thanks for the tip, Urnak."

I turned to the others. "We've got some time, so let's go do some negotiating, shall we?"

Torina touched the fire-control panel, bringing it to life and ensuring it was green right across. The Salt Thieves had been implicated in the illegal strip mining that had ravaged her family's lands the first time, so I knew which of *buy* or *steal* she probably preferred. She turned to me with a fierce grin. "Yes, let's. Negotiating is my favorite thing."

"Van, if we do end up... *acquiring* this ship, I have a request," Icky said.

"What's that?"

"We change its name. I looked up emo while you guys were talking, and yeah, *Morass of Despair* is *pure* emo."

I smiled and nodded. "Way ahead of you, Icky. I don't do emo."

21

Space is big. Very, very big. So big, in fact, that a sprawling, bustling venture like the Tau Ceti Breaker Yard could operate in what was probably the busiest system in known space and never even remotely get in the way.

The Breaker Yard, or just the Breaker, was a defined volume of space, delineated by marker buoys that itself orbited Tau Ceti in the system's outer reaches. At its heart was a rambling shipyard, a series of connected platforms and stations spanning nearly twenty klicks. Old ships and ship components were brought here to either be refurbished or, if they were too far gone, scrapped altogether. Even an old ship could contain valuable parts—a fission reactor, for instance, might have years of useful life left in it, even if the ship around it was a crumbling wreck. Add to that all the cabling, conduits, structural ribs, hull plating, control systems, and the myriad other things that made up a ship, and even a derelict junker could end up fetching a tidy profit.

It was, I thought, not too different from a scrapyard I used to visit near Des Moines when I needed parts for my beater of a first car. I had fond memories, actually, of combing through the yard for bits and pieces, mirrors and headlight bezels and the like. It had been a sort of scavenger hunt, with that surge of satisfaction you get when you find that *exact* headrest or tailpipe bracket you need—and without having to pay the exorbitant price of a new one.

In other words—*score!*

I imagined this place was the same. If you needed a part for a spaceship—and there were a lot of standardized parts, as it turned out—this was the place to come comb through the junkers and mothballed ships, looking to make that same *score!*

As it turned out, though, the yard did more than just strip and break down old ships. It also leased out long-term storage, ensuring a ship would be parked in a safe volume of space and kept secure. That's why the *Morass of Despair* was here. We checked in with the yard traffic control and told them the ship we were looking for. I had to thumb a waiver, then a bored voice came back, giving us the coordinates, as well as the data for a safe lane to follow to get to it. That was another bit of fun about this place, as we found out traversing the yard toward the *Morass*.

Something clunked, hard, against the *Fafnir*. We all jumped in our seats.

"Netty, what the hell was that?"

"A portside retaining strut for the fusion reactor of a Model 980-AS workboat, if I'm not mistaken." As she spoke, she put up the image of a slightly curved hunk of metal tumbling off toward the distant stars.

"Didn't you see it coming?"

"Yes, but I decided you all needed a good scare."

I stopped and stared at the panel. "Really?"

"Of course not, Van. An object that small would normally be deflected by our nav shield. But traffic control specifically told us not to activate it because even a tiny nudge to a ship we happen to pass can grow, over time, into a serious problem."

I scowled at that. The nav shield was one of those systems you only thought about if it wasn't working. It was the closest thing to a ship-mounted forcefield, the classic shields of sci-fi. But it was only intended to shove aside small objects, mostly rocks and dust, that could degrade or even damage a ship traveling at high relative velocity. Apparently, work was feverishly underway throughout known space to develop a more powerful version that would work in battle. Whoever got there first would, in a moment, be among the most wealthy people in history.

"So how the hell are we supposed to avoid smacking into things like that?" Icky asked, obviously still shaken by the impact.

"That's what these clear lanes supposedly are, lanes regularly swept free of debris. I guess they missed that retaining strut. If it's any consolation, though, we hit it at only about forty meters per second, so it did no damage."

"So let's put up the nav shield and make *sure* things like that do no damage," I snapped.

Perry interrupted. "Uh, Van, if we do that, we'll be in violation of the waiver you signed."

"What?"

"It's there, in paragraph 8."

I sighed in disgust, then frowned. "Nobody reads those things before they accept them."

Torina smirked. "I'll bet it also says the yard isn't liable for any damages."

"Paragraph 11," Perry replied.

I turned on him. "Well, you're supposed to be my legal expert. From now on, I want you to review every agreement like that before I sign it, so I know if it contains anything that's a problem."

"What, exactly, constitutes a *problem*?"

"I... guess it depends on the agreement." I spread my hands in defeat. "Fine, we'll both review them."

"Fair enough. Title, *An Agreement to Access the Tau Ceti Shipyard, Corporation Number TC-109383200E2*. We good so far? Any problems?"

"Well, no, but—"

"Paragraph One. *The parties to this agreement, hereafter known as the Shipyard and the Entrant respectively, undertake to agree to the following provisions of the—*"

I held up a hand. "Fine, I get it." I managed to glare at Perry. "Aren't you supposed to be on our side?"

"I am on your side, Van. But I can't read your mind."

We bickered along for the remainder of our crawl among the derelict ships, some of them reduced to little more than skeletal remnants. We finally settled on a few ground rules for what Perry would look to flag in any user agreements and the like. It left me feeling ornery, wondering just which asshole had introduced cryptic, text-dense interstellar user agreements for everyday things to Earth.

Or had we been the ones to inflict them on the galaxy instead?

We finally found the *Morass of Despair* without anything else smacking into us. She was every bit as chunky as her image suggested, a spaceship obviously not intended to ever enter an atmosphere. She had few rounded corners or edges. If anything, she resembled a dumbbell, except all planes and sharp angles, the larger section at the bow being the bridge and crew habitat, and the one at the rear the engineering and drive section. The narrower connecting section mounted most of her firepower—three big laser batteries and two missile arrays on each of its top and bottom. She had another laser-launcher combo mounted on her bow and stern, and a half-dozen point-defense batteries. Add all that in shades of space gray, and she presented an ominous outline that said, in no uncertain terms, *warship*.

Except, of course, she was toothless. All but two of her point defense batteries had been removed, probably under liens. Perry and Netty had explained the system of liens to me right after I'd discovered an interstellar spaceship in Gramps' barn. They were just loans from other parties to buy stuff, with that stuff serving as collateral for the loan until it was repaid in full. The trouble was that liens could be called in at any time, which made those who used them vulnerable. The *Fafnir* had, in fact, been a larger, more capable ship than she was now when Gramps flew her, but he'd taken out liens and most of her upgrades had been seized when he'd died.

I was determined to not let that happen. If I couldn't pay for something in full upfront, I'd live without it. I'd run my pre-Peacemaker life much the same way, paying off my credit cards every month. So I wasn't about to start immersing myself in debt now, especially if some of those debts were owing to what amounted to complete scumbags.

We found a ship docked on the *Morass*'s towering flank, a small workboat. We'd already downloaded the stats for the old battlecruiser, and they looked pretty good. She still had her powerplant and all of her drives, including her twist drive. Most of her control systems were intact, as were her navigation scanners. Everything that had been stripped from her was either weapons or things otherwise related to battle.

We got a ping on the comm. I found myself looking at something similar to an anthropomorphic capybara, who introduced himself as Kaa.

He was immediately suspicious. "When you called to meet up and look this ship over, you never mentioned you were a Peacemaker."

"Is that a problem?" I asked.

"I don't know, is it?"

"Why would it be?"

"What does a Peacemaker want with an old battlecruiser?"

I gave him a thin smile. "Are we going to stop talking in questions at some point?"

"I notice you haven't answered any of mine."

I grinned. "Ditto. But—and bear with me for another question—why do you care who I am? As far as we can tell, everything about this ship is legit. Or is there something you haven't disclosed?"

The screen abruptly flicked off. I turned to Torina. "Well that was rude."

"Does that mean they're not interested in selling to us?" she replied.

I held up a finger. "Don't you start with the questions now."

She laughed but cut it off when Kaa came back on the comm.

"My brothers and I would be happy to have you come aboard and take a look around. That is, as long as you're genuinely interested in buying and aren't just kicking the thrusters."

"Trust me, there are lots of other places I could be right now. If I wasn't actually interested in purchasing, I wouldn't be here," I fired back.

"Fine. Docking port four topside. It'll be the one with the beacon."

I let Netty handle the approach and docking. I'd meant to bring everyone, but something about Kaa prompted me to leave Torina here, with the *Fafnir* powered up and ready to fly. Ironically, despite only being a fraction of the battlecruiser's mass, the *Fafnir* had her outgunned by a wide margin.

"Use your best judgment," I said to her as I unstrapped. "If you even sense a hint that you need to disconnect and move the *Fafnir* off, then you and Netty do just that. We can sort it out later."

She gave me a salute. I rolled my eyes at her, and she stuck out her tongue back at me.

Icky, Perry, and I piled into the airlock. We were suited up but lugged our helmets on our harnesses. I'd strapped on both The Drop and the Moonsword, while Icky brandished a new acquisition of her own, a boarding gun. It was essentially a big-assed shotgun that could fire solid or explosive slugs, or nasty clouds of flechettes. It was designed to do minimal damage to, say, a ship's interior during a firefight.

"Torina seems to be in a better mood," Icky said as the outer airlock door opened. We were immediately hit by a reek of hot electronics, something oily, and a strange, musky scent I was starting to associate with well-used spaceships. It was as though the smells of things like food and sweat somehow soaked right into a ship's structure, never to fade away.

We were met by three essentially identical kinda-capybaras, a race called the Trinox. As their name implied, they lived and worked in groups of three. The summary I'd read about them said that the number three permeated their society and even had spiritual significance to them. Spiritual or not, though, none of their three-ness stopped them from consorting with Salt Thieves.

This particular trio had apparently given themselves the grandiose crew name, the Scavenger Elite. One of the Elite now stepped forward. "I am Kaa. These are my brothers, Voktu and Duxar. Welcome aboard the *Morass of Despair*."

We greeted them, and they launched into a bizarre sales pitch. The pitch itself wasn't bizarre—it was the way the three Trinox presented it. One would start a sentence, and then one or both of the others would continue or finish it. I'd found it off-putting back on Earth, but even more so here because this wasn't some cute couple who'd been married for fifty years doing it. This was three rather sleazy criminals. Moreover, Kaa hadn't had trouble carrying on a conversation with me over the comm without his brothers being involved, so I wondered if it was just an affectation, something to throw off other parties in a negotiation.

"You will note that the main power bus—"

"—that traverses the length of the ship is—"

"—relatively new. It was installed—"

"—only a year before the ship was surplussed by the Ynlithi."

I turned around and around, chasing the conversation among the three of them. Icky's face had shaped itself into an ominous scowl. Perry was—

Well, he was Perry. He might not have taken any notice of it, or it could be driving him crazy. There was no way to tell.

The three Trinox kept up their sales chatter as we walked the *Morass*. My attention kept switching between them and the ship. I was keenly aware that these three had been implicated in a succession of crimes, albeit in indirect and peripheral ways. They'd be the sort to be a lookout during a heist, or the ones who cased a place for a robbery but didn't actually take part in either. It was as though they wanted to be crooks but didn't really have the heart or balls to follow through with it. It made me wonder why they didn't just switch to flipping ships, something they actually seemed pretty good at.

As for the ship, well, she definitely needed work. She needed to be cleaned and painted, she had some components that needed to be replaced, others that needed to be pulled, stripped down for a good refit, then replaced, and she just overall needed work. But she offered tons of space in her crew habitat in her forward module, and she had an engineering plant, reactors and drives, that made Icky gasp in delight.

"This stuff is *great*," she said, tapping at consoles and checking readouts. "It all works, but it all needs work. It's an engineer's dream!"

"Leave it to Icky to find joy in stuff that isn't working right," Perry muttered, hopping onto a console beside her and studying the displays. "Seventy-six percent? Really? That's the fusion reactor's efficiency? It's a glorified car battery," he said with perfect disdain.

But Icky shook her head vigorously. "No, no, it's not. I could get that over eighty with about ten minutes work and have it over ninety in a day or two if I can get a few parts, magnetic flow controllers, some servo-valves, and I'll need an alignment gauge—oh, and probably a new inducer unit—"

She kept muttering away to herself, happily absorbed in the laundry list of things the ship needed to be spaceworthy—and of a standard that we demanded.

For my part, I was pretty much sold, at least in principle. She was perfect. Absolutely perfect. She'd provide a firm base for our operations, one we could move around as needed. If we could get her rearmed, then she'd also be a formidable addition to any ops that might involve combat. I envisioned the reaction of the Stillness, as the *Morass of Despair* twisted right into their faces, bristling with firepower—

But first, there was the matter of the price.

I smiled at Icky, who'd slung her gun and was tapping away at controls while arguing with Perry about how much and what sorts of work the ship needed. Then I turned to the Elite and crossed my arms.

"Well, she's thrilled, but I'm not so sure. This ship needs a lot of work, and she's almost completely unarmed. What are you asking for her?"

One of the Elite—I think it was Kaa, but it was hard to keep track—spoke. Or, at least, he started the three of them speaking.

"Our price is a very reasonable one. It is—"

"—one hundred and nine million—"

"—three hundred and fifty thousand bonds."

"Okay, thanks for your time. Come on, Icky, let's go."

She gave me a look like a kid being pulled away from a toy store by her parents. I returned a wry smile and a shrug, then turned—

To find myself staring down the barrel of a howitzer.

22

Okay, it wasn't really a howitzer, of course, just a slug pistol. But jammed into my face from about a meter away, it sure as hell looked like a howitzer. And considering how effectively it would kill me dead, it might as well *be* one, too.

I held up my hands. "Okay, guys, there are high-pressure sales tactics, and then there are—"

"We are not interested in selling to *you*, Peacemaker Van Tudor—"

"—because once we recognized you, we knew that the Salt Thieves have—"

"—placed a very lucrative bounty on your head."

"And we will collect that bounty—"

"—and still have this excellent ship to sell—"

"—and the Salt Thieves will be rid of you."

"A lucrative bounty on my head?" Actually, that did take me aback, at least a little. I guess it was no surprise that the Salt Thieves would stick a bounty on me, considering how much of a thorn I'd been in their backside. But the idea that someone, somewhere out there had sat down and actually worked out that bounty, then advertised it—that was both rather cool and deeply horrifying.

I tried to remain casual, even as my mind raced through and then rejected possibilities. All three of the brothers were armed, one covering me, another Icky, and the third Perry. If any one of us did something to spook them, we all stood to die in a quick but decisive hail of shooting.

"Well, if the bounty's on my head, I guess you should shoot me somewhere else, huh?" I went on.

Which was stupid, I knew. Really just a lame, straw-grasping attempt to get him to shift his aim to another part of my body, where I at least stood a chance of taking the hit on my b-suit. If I'd had my helmet on, I'd have just launched into them. But I didn't, so I couldn't.

Well, hell.

I guessed that Perry might be calling Torina, but it would take her far longer to get here, all the way back to engineering, than I'm sure these three assholes would allow. And while she could shoot holes in the *Morass*, she couldn't do much more from outside. I even thought of using Perry's broad-spectrum jammer to flood the ship with noise, or light, or *anything* to create a disturbance. It had worked great in the past, but I doubted it would stop Kaa, or at least I thought it was Kaa, from just pulling the trigger and blowing my head apart.

We needed something else, something completely unexpected, and we needed it in the next few seconds. The fact these three hadn't killed us yet suggested the Salt Thieves wanted us alive, but if we didn't soon back down and submit, I was pretty sure they'd just settle for whatever reduced bounty my corpse would net them.

I swallowed a curse, letting my mind work through the rather limited set of options we had. It was a short list, so I was done in a matter of seconds.

The clock was running out. Kaa gestured with his head toward the exit, presumably to force us back to his ship. I took a step in that direction—

And then that unexpected thing I'd been desperately hoping for happened. In one smooth motion, Icky picked up Perry and threw him at our three captors. Perry squawked and flapped his wings wildly, servos whining, as he tried to assume some half-assed sort of controlled flight. The storm of wings turned to shouts, then shrieks, as each of the Elite tried to pull away from Perry's frenzied flapping.

I recovered from the surprise before Kaa did, then I reached out, yanked away the gun with one hand, and slammed a fist into his capybara face with the other. My fist landed with a satisfying crunch that only comes from a perfect punch.

Icky howled and charged. She bowled over both of the other brothers, then snatched one in one of her bigger, more muscular arms and slammed him back against the deck. At the same time, she lashed with two of her other arms, landing one hard with a meaty *thunk*. By then, Perry had recovered and landed on one of them, the slightly painful pressure of his claws on his chest calculated to make it clear he could press *much* harder. Icky, likewise, had one of them thoroughly pinned beneath her impressive mass. That left me facing —Kaa, I'm pretty sure it was Kaa, although even if it wasn't, what difference did it make? For our purposes, these three were literally interchangeable.

In any case, I wrestled mine down and persuaded him to stay there by getting to my knees and drawing the Moonblade with a metallic hiss. A bit of light caught on the blade, throwing a wedge of illumination that fell across the alien's eyes in a bright smear.

I glared down at Kaa, or whoever it was, past the upraised blade. The light from my Moonblade stayed in place, a nice theatrical touch that I played for maximum effect.

"I think you were bargaining in bad faith, my friend—"

"You *threw* me!"

All of us, criminals and good guys, froze and looked at Perry. He glared amber fury at Icky. It was a good thing his eyes didn't emit laser beams—which they could, although it was a pricey upgrade.

"You *threw* me! At these miscreants!"

I smirked. "Miscreants? Perry, turn your thesaurus off," I muttered, and he turned on me. I held up a one-handed surrender.

"Sorry, my bad. I'll stay out of it—"

"I threw you, yeah. And?" Icky answered, sounding bored.

"And? *And?* I'm not some sort of—*distraction*. You throw cats at people for that. Or chickens. Not cutting-edge combat AIs!"

Icky shrugged at Perry. "What can I say? You were handy. Those other things weren't. Anyway, what *is* a cat? Or a chick—what? Chick-something, anyway—"

I interrupted before this escalated to what the video gamer in me would call PVP. "Guys, time and place, right? Let's deal with our miscreants here—"

"I will have some kind of vengeance, you ruffian," Perry muttered.

"Again with the thesaurus? Anyway, then you two can—do

whatever it is a robot and a giant alien would do to work out their grievances."

Perry brightened. "Traditionally, they would trash Tokyo."

Icky let out a snort of laughter. "I can't wait."

Icky just wanted to space them, but capital punishment seemed a little excessive for their crimes. Still, I didn't immediately say no to her suggestion as we marched the Elite—now disarmed and cuffed—back toward the bow of the *Morass*.

The lingering uncertainty helped loosen their tongues, especially after I pointedly spoke back to Icky.

"They *were* intending to kill us."

"No, no. Hand you over—"

"—to the Salt Thieves, in exchange for—"

"—our lives—"

One of the others hissed at the speaker, who bit off his words. I raised a finger.

"Aha! You're not in perfect sync. There is some individuality in there. Well, I might be convinced that you should be treated as three individual assholes, rather than one big one."

I heard Icky make an *ewww* sound. In retrospect, I had to agree with her.

"Anyway, finish persuading me to accept that you each deserve to be judged separately, which would mean having to take you into custody instead of being flung out that airlock Icky mentioned," I said.

So they did. Their rapid-fire chatter cycled around and around among them. Somehow, they had crossed the Salt Thieves and owed them a lot of money. Because the Salt Thieves don't particularly care about the welfare of the freelancers they hire from time to time, the Elite got little sympathy from their occasional employers. When we arranged this visit and they recognized me, they pitched a proposal to the Salt Thieves—we'll capture him and turn him over to you, and you wipe our debts.

"But now, we've failed, and—"

"—we're as good as dead already—"

"—because we've got no other way—"

"—to pay them off."

We reached the airlock to the *Fafnir*. Torina welcomed us with her slug rifle.

"Perry called ahead. He said you guys might need help. He sounded pissed, too. What was that about?"

"She *threw* me. Me, a complex, artificial person with superior combat ability. She *threw* me."

"Let's—just say that we brought some baggage back with us, and it ain't just these three miscreants—"

Perry glared at me. Yeah, no laser eyes for him.

"—here, in our custody." I turned to one of them.

"How much do you owe? And don't bother lowballing it, because if it was just thousands of bonds, they'd have never been interested in dealing with you. So I know that it's millions." I leaned closer. "What I'm really asking you, of course, is how much of that hundred and nine million and change was profit."

"We owe them—"

They admitted defeat by essentially sighing in unison.

"—forty-two million bonds."

Anvil Dark

"Oh. Wow. You bastards *are* greedy. And ballsy. Staring death in the face, and you still want to make, like, a hundred and fifty percent markup. Kudos, to you gentlemen."

A new voice spoke up. It was Netty. "It gets even better, Van. Torina and I got hooked into what she has left of that ship's computer system. Everything from before her sale was wiped, of course, but she's had a bunch of flight logs, performance records, and the like recorded since. It seems as though the last legally registered owner of this ship is a shell corporation licensed in the Seven Stars League. It's controlling shareholder is another holding company, and so on, that ultimately leads to a Quiet Room account used by the Salt Thieves."

"*What?* So you guys stole this ship? From the Salt Thieves? And then you were going to sell it to cover your debts to said Salt Thieves? This is—well, I've got to admire your bravado," I said, shaking my head in wonder.

Perry bobbed his head. "Yeah, have to admit, I've seen a *lot* of criminals, literally *thousands* over the decades, and this is an astonishing reach for a whole organization, let alone three idiots on the back end of nowhere."

"How the hell were they going to get away with that? The Salt Thieves'll hunt them to Andromeda and back," Icky said.

Torina smiled. "With that kind of money, they'd be able to disappear if they really wanted to."

I turned to Perry. "Perry, do up a sales agreement for these guys to sign. I get this ship for the total price of one bond."

"And there. I'll upload it to your data pad," Perry replied.

One of them gasped and shook his head. "That's insane—"

"—we won't sign—"

"Actually, I think you will," I cut in. "I think you will because then I'm going to let you go. You can board that ship of yours and go wherever you want."

All three stiffened in horror. "We won't last more than—"

"—a day out there. The Salt Thieves—"

"—are expecting us to deliver you—"

"You know, it seems to me that you gents are trying to somehow make *your* problem into *my* problem. If you no longer have the financial means to pull your little disappearing act, that's on you." I smiled as I handed over the data pad for each of them to imprint their paw on the sales contract. I briefly wondered what would happen if one of them refused. Did they vote?

None of them did, though. They each, in miserable turn, touched the screen.

"There, was that so bad?"

"You call us criminals. You gave us the choice of—"

"—do what you want, or death. You are—"

"—no better than the Salt Thieves."

I spread my arms. "Did I threaten you directly? No. That would be immoral and unethical, not to mention illegal."

"You said—"

"—you would!"

"No, Icky suggested it. The only thing I said was, you were intending to kill us. Which you were, now weren't you?"

"You have killed us anyway—"

"—because we can't escape the Salt Thieves!"

But I shook my head. "Actually, I think you can. In fact, I think you can do your disappearing act after all. That's because I'm going to let Anvil Dark know that you'll be arriving there to turn yourselves in. You are going to hand over every particle of criminal intelligence you can, and then you'll probably go to prison for sundry crimes for, ah, some length of time. And then, if you're good and helpful, the Guild can just make you vanish. New lives, the whole deal."

I gestured toward their airlock.

"Right that way, gents, if you please. After you leave, it's up to you. Me, I recommend you show up at Anvil Dark sometime very soon. You proving yourselves valuable to the Peacemakers might just be what saves your sorry lives."

As they stalked toward their ship, I stopped one of them and fished a five thousand bond piece out of my b-suit, part of the emergency cash I carried in it. I stuck it into a pocket on his jacket.

"That'll ensure you have enough fuel to twist to wherever you're going to go." I leaned a bit closer. "Seriously, I'd make it Anvil Dark. And don't say a Peacemaker never gave you anything."

The three Trinox shuffled morosely into their ship, and the hatch sealed behind them, shutting away their angry and frustrated glares. I turned back to the others. Icky and Torina both began to clap. Perry raised and lowered his wings in salute.

"What?"

Torina came over and stood in front of me. "That was the most elegant display of being almost but not *quite* corrupt I've ever seen."

"I guess I almost but don't quite thank you."

"WELL THEN. GUESS WE GOT OURSELVES A—" I looked at the

bulkhead, liberally scaled with superficial corrosion. "A rust bucket, I guess."

Icky wiped a finger over the bulkhead. "I don't think all of this is rust."

"What is that smell, though?" Torina asked, wrinkling her nose.

I nodded. "Yeah. It seems to be confined to the forward part of the ship, in the crew hab."

"I suspect I know what you're smelling," Netty put in.

"What's that?"

"Those three were living aboard this ship, and have been for some months."

"Ah. Right. And the waste reclamation system is basically offline," Icky said, her lip drawing up in a disgusted sneer.

My mind went exactly where hers had. "So we had what amounts to three giant rodent brothers on the run for who knows how long." It was my turn to look disgusted. "We bought a floating litter box. With guns."

"Um. Eww," Icky added helpfully.

"Well, if you want to try moving her, I've gotten into the bridge command unit, and the flight controller. As an aside, it's got an autopilot with the intellect of a wrench," Perry said, every word that of a judgmental AI.

"Will it follow us?"

"If it can, it will. As long as it's got a position fix, a destination, and the fuel to make the twist, it'll do what you want it to," Icky answered.

"Speaking of fuel, how much is there?" Torina asked.

"Enough to twist once to nearly anywhere in known space. Not that the previous owners were planning on going anywhere, but it was enough fuel to simply power the ship, keep the heat on, and keep the air breathable for years," Netty replied.

I turned to Icky. "What do you think? Is this thing safe to fly?"

"Pfft. You should have seen the shape the *Nemesis* was in when we first started on her. Half her compartments were open to space." She looked around. "Give me a day to check out the critical systems, and I'll let you know if she can fly as-is, or if she needs any work."

"The question is, where do you want to go?" Torina asked me.

"Starsmith. Netty, tell our new autopilot friend to prepare to make that twist, please."

"I'll walk him through it just to make sure he does it right."

"Much appreciated."

"Okay, follow-up question. Why?" Torina persisted.

"Because Linulla's got exactly what we need for a cleanup job like this before we get to the restoration."

"He does?"

I smiled, recalling the multitude of young that had spilled into Linulla's forge and briefly turned the place to chaos. "Yup. Bored teenagers. I'm going to teach them how hard work is actually *building* character."

She nodded. "I wonder if any of them are emo."

"If teenagers are as universal as everything else seems to be, then yeah, some of them are bound to be emo."

"So they're going to hate your building character thing."

I raised a finger. "Which is, itself, building character, now isn't it?"

23

WE SET out to travel to Starsmith, or at least tried to. Icky and I both traveled aboard the *Morass of Despair*, while the rest flew in the *Fafnir*. It was *tried to* because every time the big ship's twist drive spooled up, it shut right back down as its controller perceived some instability or other and slammed the safeties shut. Icky finally traced the problem to some gizmo that connected the infinitesimally brief but titanically potent burst of power that drove the thing, and the part that actually did the twisting. There was far more to it than that, of course, involving not just fantastically complicated math and engineering, but an AI controller that could tweak and balance and rebalance things, all while on the fly.

As the fault alert sounded yet again, though, aborting yet another twist attempt, I leaned on a console and sighed. "So I guess it wasn't the—what did you call it? The power injection trajectory limiter?"

Icky scowled at the engineering panel, one fist raised over it, like she was going to smash it. I wasn't sure whether to intervene and save the panel or let it fend for itself in the face of her rage. But she lowered her meaty hand again.

"I did. And it was. That's what I spent an hour doing, jammed into that little access space—and by the way, what tiny species built this damned thing, anyway? All this extra space"—she gestured around the dimly lit bridge—"ain't worth squat if you have to fold yourself in half to get at anything."

Now she sighed. "Anyway, yes, I fixed the damned thing, but this is the same damned fault." She raised a hand over the panel again, but this time just to give it a morose wave. "If the burst of power from the primary source—sorry, the matter and antimatter doing their thing—if it's not precisely configured, we could blow up the ship, or at least damage the drive."

"You had me at *blow up the ship*. Is it the AI controlling it, maybe? Netty said it was about as smart as a circuit breaker."

"Well, that ain't helping. Maybe if it was more on the ball and faster to react, it could balance the power flow properly. But I think the trajectory limiter is just screwed."

Not for the first time, I gave myself a hearty pat on the back for bringing such a gifted engineer onto the team. Without Netty, we'd have to have a repair crew from the shipyard come in and help us—which raised a noteworthy point.

"Well, we are in a shipyard that specializes in parts. Can't we just get a new one?"

Icky looked at me. "They're about a hundred thousand bonds new. Even refurbished, you're looking at fifty or sixty thousand."

"Could you refurbish one yourself?"

"I—well, sure, I guess I can. Before you ask, though, no, it's not just a case of refurbishing the one we've got. It's worn out." Her eyes narrowed. "But if we could find one with, say, no more than ten thousand twist cycles on it…"

I nodded and turned to the comm. "As you guys might have guessed by now, we're still having trouble over here."

Torina came back immediately. "Yes, Van, I know. That's why we're still sitting here. But that's okay, Perry's been explaining to me how Icky threw him at the bad guys, and how terrible that was."

I blew out an exasperated sigh and turned to Icky. "Would you apologize to him already? Otherwise, we're never going to hear the end of it."

"He's a hysterical little device, isn't he?" Icky said.

"You do realize this comm channel is still open, and I can hear everything you're saying, right?" Perry's voice said.

Icky winced. "Oh. Shit. Look, Perry, I'm sorry that I threw you, and I'm sorry that I just called you hysterical. But it did save our asses, right?"

"Not the calling me hysterical part."

She rolled her eyes. "Yeah, that was uncalled for. So I'm double sorry for that one. Are we good now?"

"Do you promise not to throw me at things anymore?"

Icky frowned for a moment. "How about this. No, I don't, if it means saving our butts again. But I promise I won't throw you around casually."

Perry didn't answer right away. I decided to finally throw in my own take.

"Perry, I have to admit, if it's a choice between saving our lives or your dignity—"

"Fine, alright. But I want every other solution exhausted first."

"We'll keep that in mind. And now we'll call that matter closed so we can get on to our current problem," which I then went on to explain.

We finally contacted the shipyard and explained what we were looking for. Sure enough, they offered to sell us a reconditioned part for sixty-two thousand bonds. Thinking back to my fond memories of hunting for parts for my old junker of a car, I countered that we'd find one ourselves aboard whatever ships they'd let us search, then pay them twenty thousand for it and recondition it ourselves.

"Deal," the yardmaster replied and sent a list of ships that could be scavenged, including location coordinates and details about what systems aboard them remained more or less intact. Icky scanned the list and narrowed it down to three candidates.

"Okay, let's go get ourselves a new power trajectory thingy," I said as Torina moved the *Fafnir* back to dock with the Morass again.

Icky snorted. "Thingy? Oh, no, please, Van, enough with the complex technical jargon. You're losing me."

THE FIRST TWO ships we visited, an old class fourteen bulk freighter whose entire bow had been disassembled and a former Ynlithi light cruiser that looked as though it had collided with something big and lost most of its port flank, turned out to be a bust. The first one still had the part, and although they were now more or less standardized, this one dated from a time when they weren't. Icky took one look at it and shook her head inside her helmet.

"Nope, not even close. Besides, it's probably a hundred plus years old. The one we've already got is in better shape."

We had higher hopes for the Ynlithi ship. Since it was another of that race's decommissioned warships, we assumed the parts were standardized. And they were, and this one indeed had the correct part. But whatever had slammed into this ship and ripped off most of its port side had not only left it alarmingly unstable, but it had also blown out the entire twist drive with some sort of uncontained power surge. The trajectory limiter had been caught in the failure and partly reduced to slag.

We retreated from that wreck and set our hopeful course for our last candidate, a Yonnox fast freighter seized in some trade dispute that was pretty badly beaten up in the process. She'd been sold for scrap, and here she was. Her twist drive was the same model as that of the *Morass* and was apparently still installed and intact.

Icky glared at the Yonnox ship as we coasted toward it. "Intact. Yeah. The drive on that first ship we looked at was labeled *intact*, too."

I shrugged as Torina brought us to a relative stop, then eased us toward the docking port. "I think one more try is worth saving forty-odd thousand bonds, don't you?"

"I guess."

I exchanged a smile with Torina. Some of Icky's petulance was just that, petulance. But we'd started to realize her grumpy, pessimistic nature was a bit of a ploy not uncommon to engineers. Always assume the worst case, then under-promise and over-deliver. It was a quality that made for excellent engineers—and grumpy companions.

Still, grumpy was better than being dead due to ship malfunction, a compromise I was only too willing to make.

We thunked against the flank of the Yonnox ship, and the light turned green, indicating a hard dock. Icky and I checked ourselves over. None of these derelict ships were kept pressurized, not that many of them could be, being full of holes and all. This one displayed gaping wounds, some with the seared and melted edges characteristic of laser fire, others with the neat puncture of mass-driver slugs or the more ragged ones of missile shrapnel. She'd definitely been in one hell of a fight—

Huh.

"Hey, this isn't one that we took out and sold off for scrap, is it?" I asked over the comm. If it was, we'd already made some salvage money off it.

But Netty burst the bubble on my bit of imagined cosmic symmetry. "Sorry, Van, if the logs for this ship are to be believed, this is the result of a dispute between rival cartels trying to lock down illicit trade in certain pharmaceutical substances."

I sighed at that. Yeah, some things really were universal, and that included the things that sucked.

LADEN WITH TOOLS, power cells, and other bits and pieces Icky thought we might need, she and I picked our way through the battered interior of the ship. I stopped to darkly admire an almost perfectly circular tunnel that had been drilled by a mass driver slug completely through the ship, and at a pretty shallow angle yet.

"That must have been one *hell* of a rail gun," Icky said, touching the edge of the hole. The slug had essentially vaporized the alloy, leaving a smooth edge that looked polished to nearly a mirrored finish.

"Yeah, it was," I replied. We exchanged a look. The thought of such a potent weapon being in the hands of some drug cartel seemed to make her as nervous as it made me.

We carried on. The ship had no internal gravity, so we could pull ourselves gingerly along the corridor, carefully working past wreckage. Some of it was pretty jagged, and while my b-suit could probably resist tearing, Icky's standard vac-suit might not. We'd ordered a b-suit for her, but not surprisingly, four-armed suits tailored to Wu'tzur bulk weren't exactly a standard stock item on Anvil Dark. The last time we checked, it would be ready in another couple of weeks. Until then, she had to make do with body armor.

I led the way, following the map of the ship's interior downloaded from the yard's database. We had one more corner, and then we should be at—

"Engineering," I said, gesturing at a sign alongside a sealed blast door.

Icky moved past me and checked the door's control panel. "I wonder why this is still sealed."

"Maybe they got access another way?"

"Maybe." She opened the panel and connected leads from a power cell on her harness to power it up. An experimental press of the door control did nothing, though.

"Yeah, the door's drive motors probably require a lot more juice than this cell can put out. Van, give me that spare you're carrying."

I did, and she rigged it into the panel, fiddled a bit, then tried opening the door again. It moved, jerked sideways about half a meter, then jammed again.

Icky shrugged and disassembled her jury-rigged door opener. "Tight squeeze."

"Uh, can you even fit through there?"

She tried. No way.

We pulled all the bits and pieces off her harness. She still didn't fit.

"Well, either I take this armor off, or I talk you through getting that part," she said.

I didn't like either option. "Netty, can you confirm if there are any holes shot through the engineering section that we could use to get in from outside?"

"The biggest one I recorded on our fly around of this ship was only forty centimeters across," Netty replied.

"Well, shit. So we've got better access here," I said, and Icky nodded, then began pulling off her armor.

I held up a hand. "Icky, why don't we do the talking-me-through-it thing? I'm really not comfortable with you taking off your armor."

"Why? It's not like there are any bad guys aboard. Or, if there are, they're probably freeze dried into old leather by now."

"Indulge me."

She shrugged and fastened her armored vest again. "You're the boss, boss."

I pushed my way through the gap—I had to remove The Drop and the Moonsword to do it—then paused to strap them back on, on the other side. As I did, I took in my surroundings, trying thermal imaging first. But that came up a blank bust because everything in here was ambient temperature. So I turned on my helmet lamp and shone it around.

It was the usual sort of engineering space, about the size of a typical high-school gym, filled with the bulk of the power plant, the main fusion drive, and the conduits and cabling that connected them to one another and other parts of the ship. The twist drive sat on its own. Considering they could literally twist space-time to briefly bring two distant points in the universe together, twist drives had always struck me as surprisingly small. This one was several interlocking cylinders about the size of a midsize car. I made my way toward it while Icky watched on her heads-up through my helmet cam.

"Okay, Van, you need to get around to the far side of it, where the antimatter containment conduit enters it," she said.

"On my way," I replied, pulling myself to a protruding strut. I looked for the next landing point and selected a console about three meters away. The trick to getting around in zero-g, I'd discovered, was to take it in small, carefully controlled bounds. I'd planned and timed this one perfectly and would have made it with no trouble at all if, at that moment, I hadn't been shot in the face.

BACK IN MY ARMY DAYS, one of my NCOs was a crusty old Sergeant First Class who'd once been in the armored corps. As a young soldier, he'd served in Iraq during the Second Gulf War, crewing an M1A1 Abrams tank. One of the stories he told was being inside his tank when it was hit by the 122 mm round from an Iraqi T-72. The Abrams' stout armor deflected the armor-piercing shot, but the crew inside had been left shaken by *one God awful hell of a bang*, as the Sergeant had put it.

That's what happened to me. There was *one God awful hell of a bang*, then a shrill whine that seemed to flood my brain with dumb noise. My helmet's visor was suddenly shot through with a spider's web of cracks, and my suit's heads-up sounded a shrill warning I could barely hear.

Van!

I could barely hear the word over that damned shriek still filling my brain. But I ignored it and instinctively pulled myself behind the bulk of my handhold—a strut that spanned some thirty centimeters or more.

"Van!"

It was Icky.

"Yeah. I'm—here."

"What happened? It looked like something shot at you!"

"It looks like something shot at me," I slurred. At least that whine was receding. But my suit alarm wasn't. My suit pressure was dropping, slowly, but inexorably. I had no more than ten minutes of breathable air left. Whatever had just blasted me had hit me in one of the only parts of the suit that couldn't seal itself up, my faceplate.

"I'm coming in!"

"Icky—wait. Just—wait. Don't you get shot."

By then, Perry, Torina, and Netty were frantically calling. I guess the damage to my suit triggered an alarm aboard the *Fafnir*. For a few seconds, everything chattered at once, their words tripping over one another.

"Everyone just shut up!" I snapped, then peered around the bulky whatsit machine I was using for shelter. I had a brief glimpse of something metallic and spider-like clinging to a structural beam overhead, then another round sparked off my cover. The spider then moved, but where and how fast I had no idea, because I took cover again.

"There's something in here. It looks like—shit, Icky, it looks like that thing you and your dad had, the spider-thing."

"Bucky?"

"Yeah. Him."

"*Oh.* Dad based his general design on a medium-weight security bot. If that's what's in there with you, then we have a problem."

I looked cross-eyed at the web of cracks in my visor, then at the *pressure-loss* alert. "*Now* it becomes a problem? What was it *before* now?"

The worst part was that I had no idea where the damned thing had gone. I couldn't see it, it didn't show up in thermal imaging at all, and I couldn't hear it as we were in a hard vacuum. All I could do was clutch The Drop and wait for it to come to me.

And I had just under nine minutes of breathable air.

"Guys, we need a solution to this other than *wait here until I die*," I said.

"Van, I'm coming in," Icky said again. And again, I stopped her.

"You won't be wearing armor, Icky. That thing'll take you out with a single shot."

"I'm not just leaving you in there to die, Van!"

"And I'm glad to hear it. How about using that big engineering brain of yours to come up with a solution?"

Torina cut in. "Van, Perry and I are on our way."

It had taken Icky and me nearly fifteen minutes to get here as we worked our way past damaged and wrecked sections of the ship. Even hurrying, they'd never do it in less than ten, which meant they'd arrive in time to retrieve my corpse.

"That's nice. Don't suppose you could hurry that up, huh?"

"We could try disconnecting the *Fafnir*, then using the laser to cut open access big enough to let Torina and Perry in that way," Netty said.

"How long?"

"Five minutes, perhaps a little more."

"It's worth a try, I guess. Go for it. In the meantime, Icky—"

A flash just to my right marked the impact of a slug that missed me by centimeters. Spider-thing had scuttled into view atop the housing for the powerplant, outflanking me and stripping away my cover. It was a clever little bastard, even given the limited combat options in our space.

By way of greeting, I raised The Drop and double-tapped two rounds at it. Both missed, and it instantly ducked back, out of sight.

"Take *that*, you mechanical prick," I muttered. I tried to make it sound defiant, but honestly, I was starting to feel like I actually might not get out of this one. Which sucked, not just because I'd be dead, but because I'd have been killed not by some nefarious bad guy, but by a security system nobody had remembered to deactivate. It would be like charging the enemy, anxious to come to grips with them in tense, face-to-face combat, only to end up tripping and impaling yourself on a garden rake. For sheer comedic value, it was brilliant, but I had hoped for a less ignominious death.

"Van, my big engineering brain has come up with an idea," Icky said.

"I'm all—"

I stopped to fire two more rounds at the spider, which had scuttled back into view. One clanged off its bulbous hull, but it landed a shot on my b-suit that rendered my left shoulder numb. Too bad it hadn't hit me there the first time. I wouldn't have had—

Holy shit, I had just over seven minutes of usable air now.

"I'm all ears, Icky," I said as I spotted a position behind a conduit emerging from the powerplant, about three meters away. Taking a breath, I pushed myself to it. The spider popped back up and punched out another couple of shots. I did the same mid-flight, which was dumb, because the recoil just pushed me off-course. One of the spider's rounds hit my right foot. Again, the b-suit protected me, but the impact added a numb foot to my numb shoulder.

I landed wide of the spot I'd selected and pushed myself into it. My air was down to just over six minutes. Damn. That fifteen seconds or so of exertion had cost me a minute of air.

"Van, I'm rigging up the two power cells to generate a rather potent EMP. That's an electromagnetic—"

"I know what an EMP is. But you're talking about a bomb."

"Pretty much, yeah."

Okay, so a bomb.

"Will it be strong enough to take out my spider friend out there?"

"Only one way to find out. I'll be ready in about two minutes."

Perry cut in. "Van, where are you? We don't want to start shooting holes in the engineering section without knowing where you are."

"Can't you see my suit beacon?"

"Nope. That section's the most heavily shielded of the ship, for obvious reasons. We can't read your beacon."

Of course not. I glanced around. Fortunately, it let me see the spider-thing clambering across the engineering section, trying again to outflank me. I raised The Drop and banged out the rest of the magazine, hoping to get a lucky hit. I did manage to land one, but again, it just bounced off, then the spider vanished again.

I swallowed the coppery taste of raw fear. "I'm pretty far forward. If you shoot further aft—"

"Wait, before you do that," Icky cut in. "We're assuming the antimatter tanks were purged, but if there's any left in them, you might blow the whole ass end of this ship to bits."

"We'll wait two minutes, then we're coming in," Torina said, her voice tense.

I exchanged fire with the security spider twice more. It hit me both times, in the lower right leg and a glancing hit that clacked off the top of my helmet. I finally managed to clip a leg, leaving it dangling and at least slowing the thing down.

"Okay, Van, I've got this thing ready. You'll need to take cover," Icky said.

"Way ahead of you on that, Icky."

"When it goes off, the pulse will probably knock our suits offline."

She left that hanging. Hers, undamaged, would almost certainly just reboot, because it was designed to do that. So was mine, but mine was now far from undamaged.

"Do what you gotta do, Icky," I said, glancing at my heads-up. I had a little less than four minutes of air. Torina and company were going to start shooting in about thirty seconds.

"On the way!" Icky shouted, and a bundle comprising the two power cells and a bunch of other bits and bobs sailed through the gap in the blast door. It flew past me, and I scrunched myself down into a tight ball behind the powerplant housing, hoping that damned spider didn't choose this instant to start shooting at me again. Given the way the day was going, I more or less expected that.

A dazzling flash pulsed around me. I was surprised that my suit didn't even flicker.

I stifled a curse. Did that mean it hadn't worked? It hadn't produced a strong enough EMP to even affect my suit? Because if so, my remaining hopes hinged on Torina in the *Fafnir* shooting an opening into engineering without inadvertently blowing us up, then—something, I wasn't even sure what. Come in like the cavalry, guns blazing, I guess.

I unfolded myself from my fetal ball and was stunned to see Icky, totally unarmored, pulling herself toward me.

"Icky, shit, it didn't work, get back—!"

"Take it easy, Van. It worked fine." She gestured toward the back of the engineering space. I peered that way and, sure enough, saw the spider slowly turning in midair about five meters away.

"It came loose from that conduit over your head. I think it was going to sneak up on you that way." She eyed the conduit. "Yup, you had about ten seconds before it was right on top of you."

"And it's dead? But the EMP didn't work. My suit never went off-line."

She patted the housing of the powerplant. "This is some of the thickest shielding anywhere on the ship. Ain't no EMP getting through it, short of a big nuke."

Icky uncoiled her emergency air line from where it was stored in the small of her back and plugged it into my suit. The pressure alarm went silent, but the time remaining, 3:36, kept blinking, determined to remind me I no longer had a reliable seal on my suit.

I read the display again. "Over three and a half minutes left? Hardly even exciting."

Icky cut her eyes at me, then pushed a piece of debris away with one thick finger. "Next time, we'll cut it even closer. That is, if you're in the mood for drama."

I shook my head. "Let's avoid that. I've got goals other than dying in a dramatic fashion."

"Really? Like what?"

I paused, thinking. "I'd prefer old age."

24

It had been far more of an ordeal than any of us had expected, but we got the part for our twist drive, Icky installed it into the *Morass* and configured it, and it had happily responded as green across the board. While she was doing that, I'd taken up the matter of having a firefight with a still-working security system aboard one of their ships, but they'd just pointed to the waiver I'd signed.

Perry gave me an apologetic shrug when I turned to him. "Sorry, Van, but they've probably had two hundred years and probably a million bonds of legal assistance to put into that waiver. Unlike your b-suit, it's pretty airtight."

I shot him a glare. "Ha-*ha*."

"Sorry if you think I'm being a *miscreant*."

We locked gazes for a moment, but for me, it was like trying to stare down a couple of Christmas bulbs. I finally surrendered. "Touché, bird."

Speaking of my b-suit, a quick examination of it just cemented for me how good the damned thing was. B-suits were definitely the unsung heroes of the Peacemaker Guild. This one had taken repeated hits from what amounted to a high-powered rifle, and none of them had gotten through. Sure, I had bruises, including a nasty one on my foot that left me limping.

Corresponding to that hit was a chunk missing from my boot. The suit had shrugged off the other hits, but my helmet needed a complete rebuild. Still, it had kept me alive after having been shot in the face. I could imagine how much this lightweight, form-fitting, and virtually impregnable spacesuit would be worth on Earth. Of course, then I thought about who'd end up using them, and why. It wouldn't just be good guys, which is why the suits were rigorously controlled, and why they weren't just keyed to a particular user—but had a password to operate. That way, at least, if the Guild ever lost one, its use by ne'er-do-wells would at least be limited.

"Okay, Van, we're ready to try this again," Icky said.

She and I once more stood on the bridge of the *Morass*, watching as the twist drive spooled up. We both stared at the relevant panel, waiting with held breath to see if any of the indicators would go red, followed by the damned abort sequence.

But they didn't. This time, the drive controller indicated *Activating*, followed immediately by that wrenching sense of discontinuity that characterized a twist.

Icky and I shared a triumphant look, which immediately faded. "Okay, so we twisted, but to where?" I asked.

We puzzled over the navigation panel, a separate station on the *Morass* and not integrated right into the flight controls, as on the *Fafnir*. It just declared it was *Obtaining a Fix*.

"Holy shit, is this thing ever slow," I grouched.

"Yeah, if we're going to actually fly this thing around, it's going to need a bunch of work—"

The sudden change of the nav screen to a star chart showing our current location cut her off. I tensed and took in the data. Hopefully, we hadn't ended up in a different spiral arm.

But we hadn't. We were at Starsmith, a fact confirmed when the *Fafnir* twisted in a few seconds later.

"You're here," Torina said, relief evident in her voice.

"Yeah, except Icky and I have been merged into a single being," I replied.

"Lucky you."

I frowned. "What about Icky?"

"She's tough. And she always complained about not having enough hands."

I envisioned us as a merged being, arms all waving different wrenches. "We would be *unstoppable*."

Icky didn't want to risk bringing the *Morass* into orbit around Starsmith. She didn't trust the ship's surviving dumb-as-a-nail AI to do it, and didn't feel we had sufficient control over the big ship to do it manually, at least not without a full crew. For now, we just left her in a parking spot, trusting the AI to at least keep her there, or close by—not that she could drift so far away that we had trouble finding her again.

A crew. That was another issue. We convened back aboard the *Fafnir* and headed for a landing on Starsmith. Netty informed me that a ship of the *Morass's* class normally had a crew of between forty and sixty, depending how she was outfitted. Cut that in half to eliminate the crews of the various weapon systems and other functions not directly related to flying the ship, and that still meant she normally flew with a minimum crew of twenty. Netty figured we could probably get away with twelve to fifteen, but that would be the bare minimum required to fly her, while also taking care of her critical systems like powerplant, life support, and drive.

"Icky, you and your dad wired that big ol' battleship of yours, the *Nemesis*, to run with only two of you aboard. Can you do that for the *Morass*?" I asked.

She gave a noncommittal shrug. "With the current automation, probably not. If we had something like Netty aboard, it would be a lot easier. I mean, we'd still have to network a bunch of systems through dedicated controllers, and the AI would have to oversee all of it. But, if we could do that, you could probably fly the *Morass* with a crew of one or two."

"Not while meeting interstellar safety standards for ship operations," Netty put in, her tone a slightly scolding one.

"So, legally not so much, but it's technically feasible," I said.

Icky shrugged again, but this time in a *why not?* sort of way. "Sure. It'd probably take, oh, a week, ten days, something like that. And we'd need parts—new optical cabling, some programmable controllers, junction routers…"

She trailed off. I could see her already working on the problem, making lists and things in her head. But Torina spoke up.

"Icky, didn't you say that would work *if* we had an AI as good as Netty installed on the Morass?"

She blinked. "What? Oh. Yeah. Right. That AI installed right now would never be able to handle it. Honestly, I wouldn't even trust it with any more twists."

"So we need a new AI," I said.

"Pretty much. I hope these Starsmiths are okay with us parking the Morass here for now, because she ain't going anywhere for a while."

I smiled. "Not a problem, since that was the plan, anyway."

We hit Starsmith's atmosphere a few minutes later, and a short time after that we were back on the ground, on our way to meet Linulla.

"What she needs before anything else is a good cleaning," I said, throwing myself aside to avoid one of Linulla's rambunctious offspring. Most of them listened attentively, though, and one of the older hatchlings immediately scuttled after the one that had nearly bowled me over, corralling him—or her, I had no idea which.

"I think my brood can handle that," Linulla said. "We'll get them sent up to your ship and started right away."

He turned to one of the older hatchlings and engaged in a brief conversation, basically putting this one in charge of the rest, then proclaiming that to the whole bunch of them. There were a few protests, but Linulla silenced them with a dangerous swivel of his eyestalks, a gesture he only brought out on occasions where his parental authority had no room for negotiation.

I turned to Torina, Icky, and Perry. "And while they're doing that, we'll try and crack the problem of controlling our new ship so she doesn't end up a permanent fixture here on Linulla's doorstep."

Perry spoke up, but it wasn't about upgrading the *Morass of Despair*. "Van, there's a legal issue that worries me."

I raised a hand. "I know, minimum crewing standards under interstellar law. Netty thinks we can get around it, though, by claiming an exemption under—"

"No, that's not what I'm talking about."

"Okay..."

"Van, the *Morass* is stolen property. You knew that when you bought it. And that's, well, not a good thing."

I shrugged. "So?"

"So, the original owner, the holding company those three little jerks at whom I was unceremoniously flung—"

"Perry, get over it and move on already."

"Fine. Anyway, they stole it from that holding corporation. They could file a claim of restoration to have a lien put on it, then have it seized and returned to them."

"Again, so what?"

"Um—am I not making myself clear? Before you sink a lot of time and effort and, oh yeah, *money* into that ship, you might want to think about that."

"I already have."

"Really? Because it doesn't seem like it to me—"

"Perry, who's behind that holding company?"

"Another holding company."

I sighed. "Yeah, okay, it's holding companies and shell corporations all the way down, but the trail eventually leads to the Salt Thieves, right?"

"Well, yes it does. But—"

"And if we contest their claim of restoration, it's going to have to go to a magistrate, probably from Tau Ceti, since that's where the sale of these so-called stolen goods occurred, right?"

"Sure. But—"

"And Tau Ceti is a big, busy system, with lots of media, and lots of people to read it, or watch it, or whatever—right?"

If Perry could have narrowed his eyes in suspicion, I suspect he would have. "Wait. Van, I'm starting to get the sense that you *want* them to file a claim."

"Well, it'll be easier if they don't. But, if they do, then we'll contest it. I'll do my best to ensure that the media finds out all about it. More to point, I'll counter-file a claim of proof, which—"

"Which will entitle you to examine their corporate records, to establish proof of ownership."

Torina grinned. "And it's probably going to turn out that the holding company doesn't own the ship, they just lease it from another holding company, which is wholly owned by a shell corporation, and so on and so on."

I nodded. "In other words, typical corporate shell games, yeah. So if they want to come and file a claim for their rust bucket of a ship, let 'em. It just opens their books to us. And, you know what? I don't think they're going to want the whole galaxy to see just what comes wriggling and squirming off the pages."

"Impressive. Someone's been doing their homework," Perry said.

I shrugged. "Believe it or not, this ain't my first rodeo. One of the things I got hired to do the most back on Earth was chase down the identities of people who didn't want them to be revealed. That usually meant digging through business registers and articles of incorporation and similar such bullshit, until I hit bottom. Except for the fact that this involves an interstellar-capable battlecruiser, it's not really that different."

"So it's a win-win for us," Torina said, giving me an appreciative smile. "Very clever of you, Peacemaker Van Tudor."

"Hey, I'm not just another pretty face."

"That's for sure," Perry muttered, but when I glared at him, he just shrugged.

"Sorry, must be a glitch in my voice processor. I'll get that looked at as soon as we get back to Anvil Dark," he replied.

I gave him a bland look. "Throw yourself into that, won't you?"

TORINA GOT CALLED AWAY to take a message aboard the *Fafnir*. Icky and I exchanged an uneasy look over that. It might be good news, but it was probably way more likely to be bad news. I sent Icky along with her because I needed a few minutes alone with Linulla anyway.

He took me into a storage archive that, honestly, could probably qualify as a wonder of known space. The shelves were lined with all sorts of fascinating items. I marveled at ingots of alloys almost certainly unreproducible with current Earthly technology—for instance, how do you make an alloy of titanium, chromium, ammonia, and organic compounds similar to tar? Because when you did, you ended up with a porous material stronger than steel but as light as plastic foam. There were also bins of exotic scrap, ancient mechanisms of incredibly intricate design, and myriad blades that glowed or shimmered or just sat there, as ominously dark as night. Along every shelf were crates and bales and cases of things that were

Anvil Dark

wholly unrecognizable—and a few things that I knew right away. Overall, the collection left me feeling small, and more than a bit overwhelmed by the enormity of the stars.

Linulla scuttled along, his claws scraping in chitinous rhythm across the floor, and stopped at what looked like a large storage locker. He waved a claw through a pale beam, and the locker opened. Inside, securely stored in downy-soft packing material, were the two Vanguard satellites.

"They are absolutely as you gave them to me. Incidentally, they were hard to reproduce," Linulla said.

"How come?"

He swiveled a pair of eye stalks at me. "I assume your species has discovered nuclear power."

"Yes. Well, reactors and bombs, anyway. And some use in medicine—why?"

"Because, when I first copied these, I didn't realize that you've obviously had some terrible nuclear accidents, or else you've been detonating a lot of nuclear weapons in your atmosphere."

I shrugged. "A little from column A, and a little from column B. Why, is that a problem?"

"Any metals manufactured on your planet since you began contaminating it with radioactive isotopes will have incorporated them into their structure. That was probably why your other forged spacecraft—Venera, correct? Anyway, that was probably why it was determined to be a fake. I hadn't realized that, so it didn't contain those radioisotopes. And neither do the forged versions of these Vanguard probes."

Linulla's tone was slightly aggrieved. I could only shrug.

"Sorry, Linulla, it never occurred to me that that was even a thing."

Although, now that he brought it up, I did seem to recall reading a blurb to the effect that sunken World War One warships were valuable because they were made of metals that predated nuclear tech on Earth.

"Yes, well, just keep that in mind if you attempt to do anything else with the Vanguard forgeries. In the meantime, what do you want to do with these, the originals?"

"I'm going to take them right now. If you could arrange to have them loaded aboard the *Fafnir*, that would be great."

"I sense that you have some specific purpose in mind for them."

I gave him a wintry grin. "I do indeed."

PERRY COCKED his head at me as I settled into the *Fafnir*'s pilot's seat. "Okay, Van, I'm confused. Are we not returning those two Vanguard probes to Earth orbit? I thought that was the plan, anyway. But now you want to sell them?"

"I do," I said, strapping in.

"For cash?"

"Well, I suppose I could sell them for buttons or bottle caps, but cash would be better."

"And you want me to find a buyer for them."

I nodded. "I do."

"The originals. You're selling the originals, and not the fakes that Alic still has," Perry said.

"That's right."

He made to go on, but Icky pushed her way into the cockpit. "Those kids of Linulla's are just tearing the *Morass* up. They're cleaning behind bulkheads and in access panels. They're cleaning in places I don't think dirt could even *get* to."

"That's great."

"It gets better. Linulla's decided to get *them* to rig up the Morass for an undersized crew to fly. And I have to admit, they're pretty damned smart. When I left them, they were already mapping out how they were going to run all the control cables and splice all the systems into them." She sniffed and shook her head. "They might be Linulla's kids, but they actually seem to mostly be smaller, more rowdy versions of *him*."

I chuckled but peered past Icky into the cramped crew hab behind the *Fafnir*'s cockpit. Torina still hadn't emerged from her cabin, and I was getting worried.

But something else snagged me, and I turned back to Icky. "Wait. I thought that the current AI over on the *Morass* wasn't up to any of this."

"It's not."

"So we still have to get ourselves a new AI."

Icky looked a little smug. "Nope."

I had to narrow my eyes at that. Icky wasn't usually the cryptic sort, so her playing coy meant she was dancing around something that she really enjoyed. Something that, once she revealed it, would be an amazing, *holy shit* moment.

"Okay, I'll be the dumb fish and take the bait. How we working around the AI problem, Icky?"

"Simple. Netty?"

"Hello, Van," Netty said.

I stared. If this was a big moment, I was missing it entirely. "Uh

—hello, Netty." I turned back to Icky. "What am I not getting here?"

Icky's look of triumph peaked. "You're not talking to Netty aboard the *Fafnir*. You're talking to Netty aboard the *Morass*."

"I'm—what?"

"Actually, that's not quite true," Netty put in. "We've rigged in some of the *Fafnir*'s spare logic and processing modules, Icky has done some reconfiguring, and now there's an instance of me running on the *Morass*."

"There's—what? Two of you now?"

"Kind of. The system that Icky cobbled together over here doesn't have the speed, processing power, memory, or other minimum requirements to actually run me. All that we've cloned over to here is a core logic package. Most of my outright processing is still happening on the *Fafnir*."

"Oh. Okay. So you're like a stripped-down laptop, one that has limited functionality until it's plugged into the internet," I said, realizing I was now having that *holy shit* moment but not in the way Icky probably envisioned. I'd become so used to relating to Netty and Perry as other people that moments like this, when I suddenly remembered I wasn't and was talking to a machine, made me go *holy shit*.

"It's not a permanent solution, though. For one, that strapped together system I've got working over there isn't what I'd call reliable. Those Ynlithi systems and the *Fafnir*'s components don't play nice together," Icky said.

"Also, it's not feasible to operate this way over interstellar distances. It would mean constant twist-comm contact between the two ships, and even then, I would never attempt to operate the

Morass's twist drive this way. For that matter, I doubt that I even could. Twisting is something that has to be done in real-time, and by real-time, I mean nanosecond by nanosecond," Netty added.

"So the *Fafnir* and the *Morass* would need to stay together for this to work?" I asked.

"And within virtual touching distance to be able to operate the twist drive. I'd say no more than one hundred kilometers. More than that, and the error-correcting that starts to creep in just slows things down too much," Netty replied.

I had to shake my head at that. Considering the infinitesimal delay this would entail, it gave me a new dose of respect for what Netty did under the hood to keep the *Fafnir* operating.

"So we need to upgrade the systems over there to handle a complete instance of her. I'll need parts to do it, but it'll be way cheaper than buying all new hardware and software," Icky added.

"So we'd have two Nettys? Netty, are you okay with that?" I asked.

"There would only be two instances of me from your perspective. Whenever the *Fafnir*'s away from the *Morass*, each would simply seem to be me. And whenever the ships are together, both copies of me would automatically synchronize, essentially becoming one again. I could also synchronize from time to time via twist comms. But again, from your perspective, there would just be me."

"So, in summary, this is entirely doable, it's cheaper by far, and it would mean Netty would end up controlling both ships," I said.

Icky nodded.

Netty put in, "That's right."

"So what's the downside?"

"You have to put up with me aboard both ships," Netty said.

I laughed. "I think I'm okay with that—"

I broke off as Torina suddenly appeared at the back of the cockpit, picking her way to the seat with the kind of dignified pace that meant she was deep in thought.

"You okay?" I asked her. When she faced me, her expression was complicated, then it brightened, and the woman I knew was back—warm, steady, engaging.

"I've had a bit of time to think, after that call. About home, and what... what we need to do. What I need to do, really. This is my family problem, and I—"

"Stop right there," I said, my words firm, but not hostile.

"Stop? Yes?"

"Your problem, as you've understated it so well, is *my* problem," I said.

"Mine too," Icky added. ""And the bird and the robot, I think—"

"I am *not* a robot, you glorified wrench-turner," Netty protested. "But yes. It is my problem as well."

I looked at Torina, my hands spread. "See? *Our* problem. Which brings me to the simple question—how do you feel?"

She smiled—a real, if brief, smile. "Not bad."

"Oh. Okay, that's—that's great. So that call you got was good news then? They've made progress undoing the damage to your lands?"

"Oh, no. It's been slowed to just a few centimeters a minute, but it's still spreading."

"So someone has figured out how to stop it and is working on that right now?" Icky asked.

"Nope. It's probably going to take the Synergists to repair it. Everything else is just a bandage over the wound."

I exchanged another look with Icky, who just shrugged. "Alright, I'm stumped."

"Wait, I know what it is. You're drunk!" Icky said.

But Torina shook her head. "Not a drop. And before you ask, no, there are no pharmaceutical compounds involved. And, just so I'm not entirely misleading you, things are grim back home. But I discovered a treatment for that, if not a cure."

"And what's that?" I asked.

Torina smiled. At least, it was *technically* a smile.

"Revenge."

25

"Okay, so let me get this straight. You want to go and force this hard-assed mercenary, Pevensy, to reveal to you who hired him to oversee the original illegal strip-mining operation on your homeworld in the first place. How am I doing so far?" I asked her.

Perry had come back aboard by then and resumed his place between the seats. Icky, in turn, had boarded the *Morass*, where she would stay to supervise the ongoing cleanup, repair, and upgrading operation by Linulla's kids. We'd cast off the *Fafnir* but only moved a few hundred klicks away. I'd intended to go to Anvil Dark, check in with Lunzy, Steve, and Bester, and maybe even Groshenko, pick up the latest intelligence, and possibly get some work done on the *Fafnir*. But I wanted to hear Torina out.

"That's about it, yes," she replied.

"I—can think of so many things that can go wrong."

"Oh, so can I, believe me."

I sighed. "Torina, look. I really want to help you. In fact, I'm working on that right now. But this—"

"Is stupid. There, I said it, because Van didn't want to. This is astonishingly stupid," Perry said.

Again, Torina just shrugged. "You're probably right."

Just as Icky had a short while ago, Torina had a smug, knowing look, like she would soon reveal something earthshaking, and to my surprise—

I was annoyed. I hated it when characters in movies did it. For instance, a character knew that a bomb was a dud but just let everyone stress out and panic while the timer ticked down to zero. Then, when nothing happened, it was a moment that was supposed to be—funny, I guess? All I could think, though, was *what an asshole*. He could have just told them the bomb wouldn't go off and saved the artificial tension.

Torina must have seen the irritation on my face, so she relented. "My father and uncle called in some favors and got some feelers out. A few hours ago, they got a hit. Pevensy flies *way* under the scanners, so he's always just a name with no face. That's why people hire him for especially risky or sensitive jobs—like poisoning someone's childhood home, the bastards."

She snapped out that last bit, letting a bit of the anger seething inside her leak out.

She went on. "Anyway, my father finally got a hit on him, or at least how to find him. There's an asteroid on the edge of the Spindrift system, and by on the edge, I mean right on the edge, practically a third of the way to the next nearest star. It's mercenary central. It's apparently neutral ground, where they can meet, make deals among themselves, do training, rehearse operations, and do whatever sorts of other things mercenaries do."

"And no one knows about this?"

"Oh, the authorities on Spindrift probably do, and I'm sure they're well paid to make sure it stays off the charts and regular traffic is routed well away from it. It's also stealthed up to a crazy degree and really, really heavily defended. Like a fortress, but with bad motives behind it.

I turned to Perry. "And the Peacemakers didn't know about this?"

Perry shook his head. "There's nothing in any available archives, no—the operative word being *available*."

"If they pay off Spindrift, they can probably pay off the Peacemakers or anyone else they need to. Mercenaries make *good* money," Torina said.

"Or some do. Some are just blundering morons," Perry replied.

But I sat back, remembering something Gramps had told me.

There's good value in inept, careless, or just generally oblivious people, Van. Everyone pays attention to them and not the boring, faceless people in the background. They're the really *dangerous ones.*

He'd said it in a way that suggested he had experience with it. And, considering his line of work, the darkest of spec ops, it probably wasn't surprising.

I turned back to Torina. "So what are you suggesting here, my dear? That we go and crash this secret, stealthy, heavily defended base full of brutal, thuggish, professional soldier types who just want to be left alone?"

She nodded. "Yup."

"Have to admit, I'm not loving this idea, Torina, and I don't think Van is either," Perry said.

"Sorry, Torina, but I'm with Perry on this one. And yes, I know what happened to your home is awful. But we've been over how complicated a crime it is, and that the Seven Stars League has jurisdiction—"

She held up a hand. "You're right. I'd be asking you to take on an incredibly dangerous mission just to help me out."

"But?"

"But this is also connected to our case. Somehow, Pevensy is linked to the identity theft ring."

I sat up. "How?"

"Do you remember Jeanette Ruiz-Rocher?"

It took me a moment to shift mental gears. The name was familiar, but I couldn't immediately place it. But Perry, thanks to his perfect recall, did.

"She was involved with Emil Hoffsinger, the old guy we snatched from his home in lovely suburban Chicago. She and a Yonnox, Kuthrix, had a ship called the *Lawful Windrunner* that we ran down and seized. But she and Kuthrix got away."

I pointed at Perry. "Yeah, that. Anyway, what about her?"

"She is, it seems, one of Pevensy's most frequent employers. In fact, she contracted him for something just over a month ago."

I sat up even straighter. "Huh. Now that *is* interesting."

As soon as Perry placed Ruiz-Rocher, I remembered being stung at having her in our grasp but letting her slip away. She and her

Yonnox sidekick, Kuthrix, had been in the stellar wind ever since we seized their ship. We'd kept an eye on the incoming intelligence reports for any hits on her, sightings or even just mentions, but there'd been nothing. For all we knew, Ruiz-Rocher and her minion hadn't even survived their flight from us, and their bodies were now on their way to Andromeda, desiccating to freeze-dried beef jerky aboard their escape pod.

"How much do you trust these sources, Torina?" Perry asked.

She shrugged. "I admit that I'm going by what I've been told by someone who was themselves told about it by someone else."

"We call that hearsay."

I nodded. "Sure, but we also call it intelligence, right? If I remember my Army training, we assign scores for impact and reliability to every piece of information, and base what we do off that. So this would be high-impact and, what, plausible, I guess, right?"

Perry gave me a hard stare. "Actually, Van, you're right. But if you're now planning on flying to Sirius and trying to infiltrate these guys, or worse, take them on head-on—"

I raised my hands. "Hey, even I know when I'm out of my depth. I was offered a few hacking jobs that I took one look at, then backed slowly away. They were way beyond me."

Torina looked a little stricken and started to open her mouth, but I cut her off, too.

"Having said that, though, I'm not suggesting we just drop this. I can't help feeling Ruiz-Rocher is a bit of a linchpin in this identity-theft bullshit, at least when it comes to Earth. But we can't take this on ourselves, no. We need some help."

"I'm not even sure bringing other Peacemakers in is going to be enough. As good as Alic and K'losk and the others are, we're still talking what amounts to a semi-professional military force," Perry said.

I nodded my agreement. "You're right. And that's why we need to go talk to someone who's more likely to know his way around the shadowy world of mercenaries."

Torina and Perry spoke in unison. "Who?"

"The man who, along with my grandfather, was a seriously professional soldier back on Earth and probably did some freelancing of his own. Netty, let's make that trip to Anvil Dark we planned." I turned to the others. "We're going to see our friend, the good Master Groshenko."

THE PROBLEM LOOMING with us in the cockpit was simple—could we trust Groshenko? There were only seven Masters, of whom one was dead, and one was missing, both because of some epic corruption. We knew that a third was clearly involved in some shady dealings, like the bogus terraforming operation Urnak had been involved in. That left four, and we admittedly had misgivings about Groshenko, even if we didn't have outright reason to distrust him.

He wouldn't be the first otherwise decent person to find the allure of power, and the attraction of others to it, too tempting to resist. Far from it. And it made me wonder again about Gramps and his firm decision to turn down a seat at the Masters' Table. Was it because he wanted to focus on being a Peacemaker and combating wrongdoing—or was it because he didn't trust himself to indefinitely stave off corruption of his own?

After going back and forth about it on our way to Anvil Dark, we finally decided to go ahead and seek Groshenko's help. It was another solid lead in our case, when those were in short supply. And Torina was all for it, of course, because she just wanted to come to grips with Pevensy and extract from him the identity of whoever had strip-mined and poisoned her homelands.

When we arrived, we left Netty to take care of getting the *Fafnir* refueled, and we headed for the massive station's hub, where the Keel, the Masters of the Guild, maintained their sanctum. Max, the many-tentacled, multi-individual creature that acted as the Masters' receptionist, started to dissemble about us meeting Groshenko. That was, of course, Max's job, but I leaned on the circular reception desk and looked deep into one of the unblinking eye clusters.

"Max, this is important. We wouldn't have come all the way back to Anvil Dark if it weren't. Please, tell Master Groshenko we're here. We have a major lead, but we need his help. Please."

Max stared back at me—since there was really no other word than *stared* that fit a cluster of unblinking black orbs that served as eyes—then relented. "Fine. Have a seat. He really is in a meeting, so you may have to wait a while."

"Thank you," I said and moved to some nearby chairs with Torina and Perry. The chairs, which were designed to accommodate a wide range of appendages, tentacles, fronds, pseudopods, and other exotic anatomies, configured themselves as we sat down.

Torina leaned close. "What if Groshenko won't help us?"

Perry spoke through our ear bugs. *That's not what worries me. What does worry me is that he helps us, but turns out to be compromised and hangs us out to dry.*

I nodded and shrugged, both at once. "I seem to recall a very smart bird once telling me that the universe is risky."

Actually, I think I said a cold and uncaring place.

"Close enough. Anyway, if we can't get help here, then—" I shrugged again but didn't include a nod this time. I wasn't sure where we'd go from here if Groshenko couldn't or wouldn't help us.

The inner doors to the reception area slid open, and Groshenko stepped out. "Van, please, this way. I'm sorry to keep you waiting."

"No worries, Master Groshenko. And I'm sorry to disturb you."

He led us down the hall, into the Keel, the Masters' Sanctum. Ironically, the only Master I'd ever seen in here was Groshenko himself. I knew the other Masters by name and reputation only but had never actually met, or even seen them.

"So, I understand you have something urgent you want to discuss with me," Groshenko said, offering us a drink. My body was telling me it was morning, but I knew that didn't mean a lot to Groshenko. Sharing a drink was intended as a collegial way of opening a meeting, regardless of the time of day. So I accepted, as did Torina, and we sipped a silent toast to start. Then I put my drink down as we sat around his gleaming meeting table.

"We need your help," I said without preamble, then I went on to explain the situation.

Groshenko listened attentively, but his expression and body language offered no real cues to what he was thinking. He was spec ops, after all, and that sort of advanced soldiering both requires and cultivates a flat, noncommittal demeanor on-demand. Still, I couldn't help thinking I kept catching glimpses of something else, something he was trying to keep hidden. But it wasn't something necessarily nefarious. It seemed more that he was simply tired.

"So we've got this lead, both in our case and regarding what was done to Torina's homeworld—"

Perry cut in. "Itself a crime, I might point out. Maybe the strip-mining skirted the edge of legality and took advantage of some administrative loopholes, but deliberately introducing a dangerous toxin into a planetary environment violates several interstellar conventions—"

"I know, Perry. I know," Groshenko said, holding a hand toward him. But the Master kept his expression on me. "So what are you asking me to do here, Van?"

"Honestly, I'm not sure. At least offer some advice, I guess. Maybe hook us up with people who can help us. I mean, your background is military through and through. I find it hard to believe you wouldn't have contacts in that world," I replied.

Groshenko kept that flat stare on me for a moment while slowly turning his nearly empty glass of vodka around and around on the table. I could tell he was thinking hard about something but couldn't even begin to divine what. If he should help us? How could he help us? How he could *pretend* to help us, or further his own interests—?

Without warning, Groshenko stood and walked toward a screen on the wall near the meeting table that was currently depicting a star chart of known space. He stopped and stared at it in silence.

I glanced at Torina and Perry. They both gave shrugs. Torina was starting to look anxious, and I sensed her edging toward speaking, saying something to Groshenko. I was inclined to let her. I wasn't sure what the man was thinking at all, so maybe she'd be able to gain some insight.

Before she could, though, Groshenko spoke, while still facing the star chart.

"Van, did your grandfather ever tell you about an operation in—it doesn't matter where. What does is that he almost died. He and his team had been fighting for hours, they'd all been wounded, at least one was dead, and he was partially through his last magazine. When it was gone, their position would be overrun, and that would be that."

"No, he didn't. He never told me much about the things he did in his, uh, line of work."

Groshenko turned back and gave a thin smile. "No, of course he didn't. He didn't do the sorts of things that are suited for polite dinnertime conversation."

"From what you've said, neither did you."

"No, neither did I. Anyway, I happened to be part of the team that went in and rescued him and what was left of his." Groshenko's smile turned a little more genuine. He took a step back toward the table but stopped again, as though suddenly recalling something.

"That was only the second time we'd met. This time, he wasn't trying to kill me. Oh, and as for how I ended up being part of his rescue—" He looked at me and shrugged. "It's complicated but not that uncommon. Anyway, afterward he thanked me, and then he confided in me that he had accepted that he was going to die."

His gaze had wandered off, but it flicked back to me. "Incidentally, his biggest worry was about you, and what would happen to you."

That caught me off-guard, sending a pang of unexpected emotion through my body. "Really?"

"Yes. Really. He didn't name you by name, but he said his grandson, and as far as I know he's only got one, yes?"

"As far as I know, too, yeah. But—wasn't he a Peacemaker by then? Surely he must have had some Peacemaker tech he could have used to escape."

"No. He divested himself of all Guild technology and assets when he went back to what he called his day job. Imagine if he'd been killed or captured and it had fallen into the wrong hands."

I had to nod at that. "Yeah, good point. I might be getting a touch used to the idea of technology beyond my wildest dreams. Oh, and aliens and interstellar travel and—you get the idea. Might be tough to take a step back to another life."

Groshenko inclined his head politely. "It would be good to remember that. Anyway, I thought about what he'd said, that he'd accepted he was already dead. I asked him how that made him feel. His reply stuck with me. *I definitely don't want to die, but if it's going to happen, I want it to be like that, doing something I think is important.*"

My throat clamped down more. Considering how he had died, wasting away connected to wires and tubes—it was a shitty, ignoble way to go. Not for him. Not for anyone, really, but not for someone of his character. His worth.

Groshenko went on. "I ended up in similar situations more than once, and it happened to me, too. Between one breath and the next, I realized that I was going to die. And just like Mark had, I realized it was—well, not okay, but it was an inescapability. And, like your grandfather, I took great comfort in knowing I'd die doing something I genuinely thought was important, something that would make a difference."

I opened my mouth, but I was still having trouble getting words to form around the lump stuck in my throat. Torina came to the rescue, asking the question I wanted to ask.

"Why are you telling us this?"

Groshenko looked at her and smiled. "Because I'm dying, Ms. Milon. That's why."

We sat in stunned silence.

Groshenko finally returned to the table and sat back down. "I have six months, maybe a year to live. And the last days or weeks of it will be spent bedridden, probably on increasing amounts of life support."

I blinked. "I—I'm sorry," was all I could think to say.

Groshenko waved a hand. "Don't be." But he suddenly gave me a hard look. "Unless you're the one responsible, that is. Are you responsible, Van? Are you admitting your guilt?"

"Am I—what?"

Groshenko laughed. "Ah, you're as gullible as your grandfather was." His laughter faded, though, and he went on.

"I have had a long and very interesting life. So I have no regrets—today."

"Today?"

"It broke my heart to hear how Mark died, partly for him, but also partly for me. I have faced some terrible things, literally life-and-death situations, potentially fatal decisions that have to sometimes be made in fractions of a second. But none of that truly scared me, especially after Mark described how he was ready to die doing something he thought was important."

His eyes went far away, sifting a lifetime of memory I couldn't see. "This, though. This does scare me. It scares me to the very foundation of who and what I am. The idea of just wasting away—"

He shook his head, as though in firm denial. "No. For me and for Mark, I won't allow it." His focus returned to me. "So yes, Van, I will help you. There are some people I can talk to who will help you in turn. And then I will accompany you on this mission and continue helping you to achieve it."

That left me stunned. Torina likewise just stared at Groshenko. Even Perry seemed taken aback, albeit in his own mechanical way—a small series of wing flicks that were well out of his usual stillness.

"You're going to accompany us?" I glanced at Torina. "Well, I'd love to have your skill and experience, but—" I shook my head. "I don't even know how to say this."

"Am I just embarking on a deliberate suicide mission," Groshenko said flatly.

"Yeah. I mean, all due respect, but I don't really want to be part of that."

Groshenko again just waved it away. "Of course you don't, nor would I presume to force something like that on you. This will be my last mission for the Guild, no matter what happens. If I do not survive it, well, I accept that. But if I do, then I will… go somewhere else. *Do* something else, in some other place. Something important."

I slumped back in my seat. "Wow. And here I'd been hoping for a contact or two."

"Well, there will be those, too. But don't get too excited too quickly, Van. It's not like I can requisition the *Righteous Fury* on a whim and take it into what might very well be battle. For that matter, that would be a terrible way to approach this situation anyway. This doesn't call for brute force. It calls for finesse." He leaned back. "Pevensy is human, I know that much, but I've never met the man. Still, he is a mercenary…" Groshenko narrowed his eyes in thought.

"You sound like you have an idea."

"Hmm? Oh, several, each a different possible course of action. Now, we must examine them, weigh them against each other, and determine the best—" Groshenko suddenly stopped, as though catching himself. "I'm sorry, Van. I don't want to usurp your authority. For the purpose of this mission, I'm not a Master, just another Peacemaker like yourself. And since this is your mission, well, I'd like to offer some of that advice you asked for."

"Please, yes, by all means."

Groshenko leaned forward and started talking. As he did, I finally got some signals from his body language. That faint but pervasive fatigue I'd noticed in him earlier had receded. It was still there but largely displaced now by a clear, almost eager sense of purpose.

And with that, any lingering concerns about the Master faded away like water through sand. Groshenko wasn't corrupt. He'd just realized that the end was coming and had been desperate for something to give him purpose, a sense of accomplishment, when it did.

And we'd just given him that.

I smiled as I listened, but not because of Groshenko this time. This time, it was because of my grandfather. Groshenko and I both had the same feeling, I knew, deep inside. We were doing this for us, and because it was the right thing to do.

But we were also doing it for Gramps.

26

Groshenko proved to be just the help we needed. Left to our own devices, I wasn't sure how we'd have approached trying to breach the secretive, heavily fortified mercenary base on the far fringe of the Sirius system. From the way Torina's contact had described it, it probably bristled with military-grade weaponry that would leave the *Fafnir* hopelessly outgunned. More to the point, just destroying the place wasn't our objective. Even if we could find some legal justification for it, it would just end up killing or chasing away any possible leads.

What we needed to do was infiltrate the place and get close to Pevensy. We might even be able to do it without any violence. Not that I thought for an instant that Pevensy would help us out of the goodness of his heart, or for any other reason, for that matter. But he was a mercenary, and mercenaries are, in the end, motivated by money. Of course, he was also a high-end mercenary, with the sort of ruthlessly effective reputation that comes with a hefty price tag.

Moreover, Torina wasn't exactly in a give-and-take negotiating mood when it came to Pevensy, so her tolerance for dealing with him was going to have some hard limits.

But none of this mattered unless we could get close to him, and that meant getting close to Bulwark, the combination of fortress, clearinghouse, and neutral rest stop for much of the mercenary community in known space. And Groshenko made it clear that Bulwark wasn't the sort of place to which you could simply fly up, knock on the door, and expect to be welcomed. In fact, if you weren't already an established mercenary with some credible operations under your belt, you weren't going to get anywhere near the place.

"Which is why we need the assistance of my good friend S'lana," Groshenko said as we brought the *Fafnir* to a relative stop with his own ship, the *Nevsky*. A heavily upgraded Dragon, the *Nevsky*—named after the legendary sixteenth century Russian hero, Alexander Nevsky—was a formidable near-warship in her own right. She was still no match for an actual purpose-built warship, though, such as the one now on-station from us, about twenty klicks away. She went by the grandiose name *Wellspring of Lamentations* and was commanded by said S'lana, who was a Yonnox, which I admit I found kind of surprising. Every experience I had dealing with that race to date had been a variation on *sleazy used car hustler*.

"I guess I just have trouble envisioning a Yonnox as a reputable, competent mercenary," I said. Perry immediately pounced—and, in retrospect, rightly so.

"Oh, Van—are you branding an entire race, literally billions of individuals, with qualities based on interacting with just a few of them? There's a word for that. Something about music, I think...?"

Torina frowned at him. "Music?"

"Yeah. Music. Stereo—oh, right. *Stereotyping*, that's what it's called."

"But stereotyping has nothing to do with music," Torina replied.

"It—I—" Perry shook his head. "I know that. Pardon me for trying to be cute."

Torina laughed and touched Perry's head. "Oh, don't worry, little bird, you *are* cute. Adorable, in fact."

I cut in. "You know what? Perry, you're right. *Mea culpa* for tarring an entire race of people with the same sleazy brush. Actually, it'll be refreshing to meet a different sort of Yonnox."

Netty cut in with a call from Groshenko. "Van, you, Torina, and I are invited to board the *Wellspring*. They're sending a shuttle around to pick us up."

"I notice my name conspicuously absent from that list," Perry groused.

"Sorry, Perry, but S'lana's rules are quite clear when it comes to having things like advanced combat AIs aboard her ship. Same with weapons. You'll need to go over there unarmed, and the truth is, you *are* a weapon," Netty said.

Mollified, Perry flicked his wings with great dignity. "While my protest remains in place. I find it refreshing to be recognized as the lethal threat that I am."

"Never said you weren't a badass, friend. Just a bit… mouthy," I told Perry, who dipped his beak in acknowledgement. "However, that doesn't change the reality of us going over there without our absolute best combat ability in place."

"Will you go, boss?" Netty asked.

The answer tumbled out unbidden. "We go."

THE SHUTTLE that picked us up was piloted by a grumpy Nesit. She brusquely told us to strap in, then cast off from the *Fafnir* and jaunted across to the *Nevsky* to retrieve Groshenko. The idea of both Nesit and Yonnox mercenaries together in the same company ratcheted my wariness up a notch, frankly. But the pilot was all business and flew the shuttle with a deft touch that even Torina admired.

She leaned toward me. "I think she zeroed out the velocity at the same instant she hit the docking adapter," she whispered.

"Damned right I did," the Nesit replied, having obviously overheard. "Anything else wastes reaction fuel, and that shit costs money."

"Still, that was some fine flying," Torina replied.

The Nesit actually seemed taken aback at the compliment. "Oh. Well—thank you. Anyway, the Colonel's waiting to see you, and she does *not* like to be kept waiting."

Groshenko grinned as he unstrapped. "No, she does not."

I glanced at Torina. Groshenko and this mercenary, S'lana, obviously had some sort of history. I only hoped it would work in our favor.

We clambered through the airlock, into the belly of the *Wellspring of Lamentations*. I had another cognitive disconnect. Most ships that I'd boarded to date were either passably clean or incrementally more and more grimy to the point of being truly disgusting. The exceptions were Peacemaker ships, especially the *Righteous Fury*, the Guild's battlecruiser-pretending-to-be-a-police-boat. That had been the closest to a genuine space-going warship I'd been aboard so far.

The *Wellspring of Lamentations*—a name that *still* made me roll my eyes—was therefore the first genuine warship I'd ever boarded, aside from Earthly ones with my father. As it turned out, the *Wellspring* wasn't all that different from any of those. Every ship my father had brought me aboard had been cramped, starkly utilitarian, and insanely clean. The lack of disorder had a kind of weight, as if dozens of inspectors with white gloves could burst through a door at any minute—and find nothing. Not one bit of grime, or dust, or wayward grit. It was a true monument to fastidiousness, from the floor to ceiling and everything in between.

I clearly remembered my father's carrier, the *Abraham Lincoln*, with its gleaming paintwork, stout watertight doors ready to slam shut on undersized portals, and labels everywhere, describing what every pipe, cable, and conduit was with a glance. This was no different, really, except for the cryptic alien markings and everything being generally higher-tech. Although, I had to admit, some of the pipes looked as though they could have been bought from a regular Earthly supplier. All they were missing was a label I could read, and maybe the scars from a wayward wrench or two. But... maybe the pipes *had* been sold by earth suppliers. They sold booze to aliens, so why not something as mundane as pipes?

We were met at the airlock by a slender Yonnox who was accompanied by a male human and a Wu'tzur. All three wore charcoal grey uniforms sporting just a few small badges that made them less *plumber's apprentice* and more *possibly military*. They had tactical vests strapped overtop of them, laden with things that looked like submachine guns and pouches for extra mags—their overall readiness was excellent. Just from their body language, it was clear who the superior was here, and who the subordinates were.

"I'm Colonel S'lana, Commander of the Dire Legion," the

Yonnox said, her voice clipped and sharp. She gestured to her two companions, starting with the human. "This is Captain Meyer, Master of the Wellspring, and this is Kurcal, my Operations Officer."

Groshenko nodded gravely, then turned to the human, Captain Meyer.

"Permission to come aboard your ship, Captain."

"Permission granted."

As soon as Meyer said it, the tense formality seemed to drain away. All three of them relaxed, and S'lana's face lit with the grimace I recognized as a Yonnox smile. It seemed genuine in a way that I'd never seen on a Yonnox's face before—another reminder that I had to be less hasty judging an entire race on encounters with a few individuals. I sure as hell wouldn't do it back home, so why do it here?

"Petyr, it's good to see you," S'lana said, greeting Groshenko with a sunny grin.

"S'lana, a pleasure, as always," he said. They embraced briefly, the gesture warm and genuine, then S'lana led us forward, accompanied by both Meyer and Kurcal, the Operations Officer. As we passed members of the crew, they smartly came to attention—or generally stiffened up their anatomy, anyway. I puzzled over the nature of this mercenary company, given that it seemed to consist mostly of the crew of the *Wellspring*. So it was a—naval sort of mercenary company? A mercenary ship, as opposed to ground troops?

I decided to dare asking.

S'lana turned her head but didn't stop striding along. "With the exception of a small number of personnel permanently assigned to critical operations, such as bridge and engineering, every member of this crew is as adept at extra-vehicular and ground combat as they are at fighting this ship."

I exchanged a glance with Torina, who just looked impressed. We continued through a maze of corridors until we finally arrived at a cabin just behind the bridge. It consisted of an outer room, obviously intended for planning meetings, and an inner one, probably S'lana's personal quarters. The planning room was dominated by a large 3D viewer that currently held a slowly rotating, insanely high-res model of the *Wellspring* herself—presumably a really fancy screensaver.

S'lana waved a hand through the image, dismissing it, then gestured for us to sit around a conference-style table.

"Now, then, Petyr, I understand you're looking for some assistance with a delicate op," she said.

Groshenko nodded. "I am. And I'm going to call in some favors to get it."

She grimaced her smile again. "How many favors?"

"All of them." His answer was instant and certain. "Everything I'm owed, all called in at once. A clearing of the table, if you will. I think I've earned it, no?"

S'lana said nothing, she merely tapped a stubby finger against the table. Finally, she sat back.

"You've done a lot of things for me over the years, Petyr. I think that includes keeping me out of prison."

"Twice, in fact. There was that affair in the Wolf 424 system, involving the ore-pirates, and then there was Dregs, when that Skanax trader with the big—"

"Yes, I'd forgotten about that one, thank you very much," S'lana said.

I knew exactly what Torina was thinking because I was thinking the same thing. The big *what*, exactly?

She leaned forward. "You must be after something very big." The mercenary glanced at Torina and me. "Something involving these two, obviously. And if you're willing to call in all your favors for them—" She cocked her head slightly. "Petyr, are you dying?"

Groshenko chuckled. "I'd forgotten how quick that mind of yours is, S'lana." He nodded. "In a word? Yes. And since those favors you owe me are going to go *pfft* when I do, I figured I might as well cash them out."

"What do you want?"

"I want access to Bulwark. In particular, I want access to Pevensy."

S'lana looked at us again, then turned back to Groshenko. "Why?"

Groshenko opened his mouth, then turned to me. "Actually, I'm going to let Van explain it."

"The short, gruesome version is this... Pevensy and another vile creature named Ruiz-Rocher have been hijacking people, loading them into chips, and letting them be used for purposes beyond any horror you can imagine. There's no escape from the... the prison, the chip... and this prick Pevensy is doing it for money. Do I need to go on, or is that reason enough to see this guy roasted?"

S'lana dipped her head to me, eyes bright. "I'd say you're wholly justified in this... pursuit."

I held up a finger. "It doesn't end there."

"Busy boy, this Pevensy. Go on," S'lana said.

"He's part of a mechanism that's turning Torina's homeworld into a howling wasteland, and we're all one bad break away from the plague—because that's what this is—jumping offworld and going rogue. You understand? Everyone is at risk. Not just us," I finished.

S'lana listened without even a flicker of change in her expression. When I was done, she laced her fingers together on the table.

"So what, exactly, do you intend to do once you have access to Bulwark and Pevensy? Flash your Peacemaker credentials and try to get Pevensy to cooperate? I can guarantee you that it won't carry much weight."

"Actually, I was hoping to buy information from him," I said.

S'lana stared back at me for a moment, then asked her two colleagues to step out. They did, but not without some pointedly questioning glances.

When they were gone, S'lana turned back to us. "It is rare in the extreme for me to not have my Operations Officer glued to my hip, and Captain Meyer, too, when I'm aboard his ship."

"So why are you doing it now?" Torina asked.

"Because Pevensy isn't just a problem for you. He's a problem for me as well. For all mercenary outfits that operate through Bulwark, in fact."

I leaned forward, both intrigued and alarmed at the direction this was suddenly heading. Friction between S'lana and Pevensy might work in our favor, sure. But did we really want to get involved in some spat between professional killers?

"Why? What's Pevensy doing that you don't like?"

"There are nineteen mercenary companies that use Bulwark as a base, or at the very least as neutral ground to pick up jobs or even just spend some downtime. It's a pretty firm rule that the station is supposed to be a weapons-tight zone. Even if we end up fighting one another somewhere—and we do, all the time—when we're back on Bulwark, the guns get put away. Doesn't stop the fists and feet and other appendages from occasionally doing some talking, but it's neutral ground. It's meant for the benefit of all of us."

"Okay. And?"

"And, of those nineteen mercenary companies, Pevensy now exercises effective control over eleven of them, and he's moving on another two. He ultimately wants to run the whole show and turn Bulwark into something it was never intended to be."

Even Groshenko had leaned into her words. "And what's that?"

"A base of conquest. Pevensy wants to set himself up as a new stellar power, and he wants to use a ready-made army, all those mercenary companies, to do it."

A WEEK LATER, after a quick and unscheduled visit to Torina's homeworld, we returned to a rendezvous with the *Wellspring of Lamentations* and its no-nonsense owner and ultimate commander, S'lana. True to his word, Groshenko was already there.

I stopped in the back of the cockpit before disembarking the *Fafnir*. "Okay, Icky, Perry, you guys know what you need to do, right?"

They looked at one another, then Icky sighed. "Take the *Fafnir* back to Starsmith and finish up the work on the *Morass* while Perry finds a buyer for those two junky old satellites, yeah." She held out her arm. "You sure you don't want to tattoo all that, all that long, complicated list of instructions on my flesh, boss?"

"Nah. Perry'll remember."

Perry looked from Icky to me. "Remember what?"

I gave them a grin and a wave, then clambered out of the *Fafnir* with my go-bag, essentially a backpack with some essentials stuffed into it, plus The Drop. I'd given my b-suit a woebegone look as I'd closed up my cabin, because I wouldn't be bringing it or the Moonsword along this time. For the purposes of this next op, Torina and I, along with Groshenko, were no longer Peacemakers. We were just nondescript members of the Dire Legion, S'lana's mercenary outfit.

S'lana and Groshenko met us as we came aboard—after asking permission from the Officer of the Watch, of course—then immediately led us the opposite direction we'd taken last time, rearward instead of forward. We navigated the stark, nearly sterile corridors, and finally arrived at a cabin. It contained four bunks with lockers and a small desk-terminal setup.

I stared at the bunk. It might have a few centimeters on my rack aboard the *Fafnir*. Maybe. I sighed.

"I *really* need to get back to Iowa, spend a few days in a real bed."

Torina nodded. S'lana and Groshenko both looked amused. Considering some of the places they'd probably slept during their careers, this was probably palatial to them. Which was fine, but my own creed had always been, *any asshole can be uncomfortable.*

S'lana gestured around. "These are standard NCO quarters. The three of you will billet here. Technically, you're part of Headquarters Platoon, which nominally puts you under the command of

Lieutenant Forlax. But since you're not actually part of the Legion, and you're only aboard for a single op, you can consider Kurcal, my Ops Officer, your immediate superior."

She walked away, leaving the three of us to do what little unpacking and settling in we needed to do. As we did, I extracted a pouch from my go-bag and attached it to the tactical harness I'd been given, along with a uniform and body armor, by the Dire Legion.

Torina lifted an eyebrow. "Do Perry or Netty know that you brought that?"

"Nope."

That caught Groshenko's interest. "I'll say it again. What you're contemplating is illegal in at least several different ways. Clever, maybe even brilliant, but illegal."

I glanced at him. We'd been through this at length when we worked out our plan of attack several days ago. "So shouldn't you be stopping us from doing it?"

"Should I? Yes. Will I? No. Honestly, I'm sure that talking with Pevensy isn't going to work, and I don't think you're going to be able to buy him, either."

"Which just leaves arresting him—" I started, but Torina's derisive snort cut me off.

I went on. "—outsmarting him, discrediting him, or killing him. The second is going to be tough, considering his reputation. And I can't imagine trying to kill the most powerful and influential guy among a cadre of highly skilled and ruthless warriors is going to work out too well either. Plus, it doesn't get us the information we want. So I'll say it again. If you can think of something better, please, I'm all ears."

Groshenko shook his head, smiling. "This is exactly the sort of plan Mark would have come up with—ballsy to the point of ridiculous—but like I said, also clever. Maybe it'll even work. And if it does, the *Nevsky* will be there to pull our asses out of the fire. She's been prepositioned at Spindrift and will start heading for Bulwark as soon as the *Wellspring* arrives there."

I sat down. "Which means that now, we wait."

27

WE DIDN'T HAVE to wait long, the *Wellspring* sounding her twist alarm less than an hour after we boarded. I jumped at the harsh blare of the klaxon in a way that made both Groshenko and Torina laugh.

"Sorry, I'm used to Netty's gentle, dulcet chime, not that air-raid siren," I groused. In fact, my own military experience, as limited as it was, had all come rushing back to me. Things in the military were rarely soft, gentle, or quiet unless they had to be. Hard, angular, brash, and loud were the order of the day. We even joked that the pillows weren't filled with feathers, but with beaks and talons.

It pushed my already raw nerves from merely being on edge to teetering on the very brink. What we were contemplating was insane. We were going to slip into this nest of mercenaries, then deliberately create a situation that not only allowed us to force them to do what we wanted, but also shield us from their wrath afterward, until we were able to escape.

It all hinged on one critical assumption—that the mercenaries, and particularly Pevensy, were as motivated by money as we hoped they were. If it turned out they actually had *loyalties*, or any sort of *ideology*, well, then we were screwed.

AT LEAST WE got *to* Bulwark without incident. It was, I had to admit, an impressive place, a sprawl of modules of various shapes and sizes built upon, and extending from the craggy surface of a large asteroid. It bristled with weaponry, including two of the largest rail guns I'd ever seen, and all of that was backed up by the firepower of a dozen ships—and what amounted to warships, at that. Even if we pulled together fifty Peacemakers and their ships, this place would still have us outgunned by at least two or three to one. There was a menace to the place—a hum of purpose that was purely destructive, and out in the open. This was a base made for war, and little else.

As we boarded the Wellspring's shuttle, Groshenko fell into place beside me. He didn't look at all out of place in his uniform and tactical harness—if anything, he filled it out better than I did. The old soldier in him was on clear display.

He leaned close to me. "The *Nevsky's* on her way, about two hours out. We've got that long."

Two hours. I didn't like that kind of window for error, and my stomach went tight as I set an internal clock, counting down the endless seconds between us and action. Time is an enemy, even when it's on your side. In this case, two hours felt a lot longer, sprawling ahead of me in uncounted seconds. I set my jaw and settled in for the ride to Bulwark, determined to stay sharp.

Groshenko sat directly across from me, with Torina two spots to my right. The other ten or so passengers, all soldiers of S'lana's Dire Legion, joked and prodded fun at one another in the way soldiers do, especially when they're on their way to some shore leave. One of them looked at Groshenko and narrowed his eyes.

"Hey, new guy. Aren't you too old for this sort of shit?"

Groshenko nodded. "Aren't you too young to harass a grandfather?"

The soldiers burst out laughing at that, touching their helmets in little signs of respect. Groshenko became one of them at that moment—battle tested. Accepted.

When we reached Bulwark, those of us who were new to the place were given an orientation tour complete with flashing signs and colored emblems painted at intersections in the myriad passages. It was all very organized and reminded me of the tour groups I'd seen visiting dad's ships whenever they were in port. Bulwark was, in fact, not much different than a warship writ very large, with the same slickly clipped, sterile cleanliness of the *Wellspring*.

These people *definitely* had their shit together.

"And this is food production," our guide, a dour Nesit NCO, was saying. He'd led us among rows and rows of all manner of crops, including a few I actually recognized.

Torina touched my arm and whispered, pointing at some green stalks. "Isn't that corn?"

"It—is. See, it doesn't just grow in Iowa," I said, trying to sound flippant. But my heart pounded away like an autocannon. In the next few minutes, we'd have to make our move, or else abort and quietly return to the *Wellspring*—

There. Right *there*. That was my target.

I angled toward a large tank, into which water was gushing from a recycler. From this tank, pipes led among the crops, keeping them watered. They weren't hydroponics, which would have been a deal-breaker, but it turned out it was easier to make soil by pulverizing asteroid rock you were excavating anyway, then adding the necessary things to make it fertile. It was a lot cheaper, which was the point.

I peered into the tank. As I did, I reached down, opened the pouch on my harness, and slipped my hand into it.

"It's water," a voice said from my immediate right. I jumped and had to take a second to find my voice. It was our tour guide.

He gave me a hard stare. "Jumpy sort, aren't you?"

"Sorry. I just—" I hesitated, not sure what to say next. I just what? Groshenko came to my rescue, though, miming taking a drink.

"I just want to, you know, get a drink. It's been a while."

The Nesit stared a moment longer, then nodded. "I hear that. But this orientation's mandatory for all first timers here. And you still have to sit through the safety briefing." He leaned closer. "Don't worry, I've learned how to make it quick, 'cause I only get about thirty seconds of everyone's attention anyway, am I right?"

I gave him the knowing look of a tired soldier. "If that."

He turned back to the group. As he did, I grabbed a handful of what was in the pouch and tossed it into the water tank.

To most people, it was plain old dirt. To me, it was *opportunity*.

We carried on with our tour and safety briefing—which was another instance of something on Earth and in outer space being much the same. In this case, vital information that could save your life was presented in a tedious way, devoid of any flare or personality. It was as if driver's safety courses and an insurance seminar joined forces in order to put people to sleep, a feat I knew to be rather easy thanks to my own years in both school and the army. Before we were dismissed, though, our Nesit NCO told us to wait, then left and returned a few minutes later with a gruff, older human male. The NCO, who'd been sharp and switched-on, had fallen into an unmistakably servile posture. I didn't even need to see the man's name tag to know who this was.

Pevensy. Well, wasn't this convenient.

Groshenko, sitting nearby, casually raised his hand and splayed his fingers twice, as though stretching them. Ten minutes until the *Nevsky* arrived. I hoped none of the controllers of Bulwark's fearsome weaponry got trigger happy at the approach of a Peacemaker ship, despite both Groshenko and S'lana assuring me it was well in hand.

Pevensy launched into what was ostensibly a formal welcome to Bulwark. What it really was, though, was an outright recruiting pitch for his own outfit, the not-so-subtly-named Red Slaughter. It struck me as presumptuous as hell to try and poach mercenaries from other companies, especially in such a blatant way. But Pevensy radiated diamond-hard self-assurance, a sort of brashness, bordering on bluster, that often characterized excellent soldiers but asshole human beings. He finished his impromptu pitch with a time and place to show up and sign up, whereupon I looked at both Torina and Groshenko and scratched the side of my nose, twice.

It was time.

I saw Groshenko touch his comm. I took a deep breath and stood up.

Pevensy had started to turn away but saw me and grinned. "Look at this, folks, we have someone who can't wait to sign with the Slaughter. Be where I said to be when I said to be there, and we'll hook you up."

I had to take an even deeper breath. I itched, like dozens of laser dots crawled across my skin from dozens of readied weapons. This *was* insane.

But, as Caesar said crossing the Rubicon, *Alea iacta est*, "the die is cast." It was very, *very* much cast, in fact.

"You've got it all wrong, friend." My voice was low and even, no small feat among a throng of people who chose a unit name like the *Red Slaughter*. Arrogance, I can tolerate. Unoriginality I cannot, and these idiots featured a lot of both.

Pevensy just turned and started to walk. "Pass it up through the chain, son—"

"No, this message is for you specifically, Pevensy."

He stopped, then turned to face me, his face gone mulish and tight. Whatever he was, his instincts were superb—and he knew a threat. "Is it now?"

I blinked once, then rolled the dice. Without taking my eyes from his, I unsnapped the pouch from my harness, opened it, and dumped it out. Fine, dry dirt poured onto the floor in a pale, billowing puff of dust.

"Recognize this?" I asked.

I saw just a hairline crack appear in Pevensy's iron demeanor. "Congratulations, troop. You've just identified dirt," he snapped, then nodded to the Nesit NCO, who moved toward me. Pevensy headed for the exit.

"Correction. It's dirt from Helso," I said, my voice utterly devoid of emotion.

He stopped. So did the NCO, who looked from me to him, eyes hooded with uncertainty.

"You know, the dirt you and your—people—poisoned with the nanobot agent. The one that kills planets, and everything on it? To me, that feels like an interstellar crime. The kind that gets you locked up for good." I gave him a measured look. "Or worse."

Pevensy stopped again and glared at me. "I don't know who the hell you are, and I sure as shit don't know what you're talking about. What I do know is that you need some time in the brig to learn your place—"

"I tossed a handful of it into the water supply for the crops you grow here," I said.

That got a reaction. Pevensy spun on me, a look of horror etching his face. "You did *what?*"

Bingo. I could feel a sudden shift in the room as the focus switched from me to Pevensy. I pounced. "For someone who doesn't know dirt, you sure seem... concerned? Let's call it concern, although you look like you're shitting yourself right about now. Awkward for someone from a crew called the Red Death. Or whatever."

Pevensy turned on the NCO. "Clear this room and get security in here—"

"There you are," a new voice said as S'lana strode into the room, a half-dozen of her own Dire Legion troops following her.

Almost right on cue.

She looked at Pevensy but pointed at me. "These bastards managed to slip themselves aboard my ship as new recruits. Turns out they're not legit—" She stopped and pretended to look puzzled. "What's going on?"

Pevensy said nothing until the Nesit NCO had ushered everyone out of the room. Torina and Groshenko came to my side.

"What's going on is this asshole infected my homeworld with a toxic, self-replicating plague that's wiping out all of the plant life." Torina leveled a truly poisonous smile on Pevensy. "So we returned the favor. I'm pretty sure that by now that agent is now infecting the soil you use to grow your crops, which means that you're going to be running low on food out here very soon." She laughed, a bright and uncomfortable sound—for Pevensy, anyway. "Better get ready to tighten that belt. Lean times on the way."

"Can't they just buy food?" I said. "Seems easy enough for an outfit like the Red Death."

"Red Slaughter, you asshole, and—" Pevensy spat, but Torina cut him off, lifting a professorial finger.

"Cost a fortune, I'd imagine. You'll have to put anything even resembling a profit right back into sustaining this place—and even *that* might not be enough. Hungry people make for bad teammates. Actually, the only good thing they are is enemies. And that doesn't take the supply line into account." Torina whistled softly. "Wouldn't want to be the one paying to protect *that* little venture."

Groshenko looked around as if seeing the place for the first time. "Kind of makes this a lot less imposing, doesn't it? Hungry troops, shitty chow. Oh, and money. You'll bleed money like atmosphere through a missile hit."

S'lana wheeled on Pevensy. "Is this true, Nigel? What they're saying?"

Pevensy ignored her. "Tell me why I shouldn't just space you right now," he hissed.

"Because we have a countermeasure. We've developed it and tested it, and it works. And I think you're going to want it," I said, then shrugged. "Of course, your bosses, the ones who paid you to run security on that illegal mining operation on Helso, have a countermeasure of their own that they'll give you—right? They do, don't they?"

I held my breath, face impassive. This was the one lingering uncertainty. The biochemists and nano-engineers Torina's parents had hired to study the damned thing were pretty sure there *was* no countermeasure to it, aside from the labors of the space-hippy synergists. The extortion scheme attached to its infection of Helso was probably just another cash grab for an antidote that didn't work.

But we weren't sure of that.

Or, we weren't until I saw the rapid-fire stream of emotions sweep across Pevensy's face. Most satisfying of all, it ended on nervous uncertainty. The full realization of the damage we'd done to his precious base for future campaigns was sinking. Fast.

His gaze flicked from us, to S'lana, who just stood with her hands on her hips, waiting for him to speak. He looked back at us.

"What do you want?"

I think I finally managed to take a full breath, and it was sweeter than honey. We weren't out of this mess, but there was light on the horizon. I pressed my case without hesitation. Pevensy was a bully and a shit, but inside him, there might be a core that knew living to fight another day was better than the alternative.

"The names of whoever employed you on the Helso job. Plus, we want to know the significance of one Jeanette Ruiz-Rocher, who seems to have a history of employing you on other jobs. We especially want to know where she is and who *she's* associated with."

"I want the counter-agent," Pevensy snapped.

"And you'll get it, or instructions on how to get it, once my colleagues and I are safely out of range of Bulwark's weapons."

"So that explains the inbound Peacemaker ship," S'lana said.

Pevensy's ire switched to her. "Why was *I* not informed there's a Peacemaker ship en route?"

S'lana just crossed her arms. "I don't know, Nigel. Maybe if you weren't in here trying to steal my soldiers, and those of every other company that works out of Bulwark, you'd be more in the loop. Stop being a ruthless prick, and you'll be stunned at how much better our relationship could be." Her smile was cloying, and Pevensy winced, his anger at being outplayed turning into that cold, ugly realization that there was nothing he could do.

She turned to us. "There's also the matter of you infiltrating my company. You just expect to get away with that, too?"

This was an act, of course. But Groshenko went off-script and stepped forward.

"I'll be surety. You can hold me until they deliver on their promise."

Pevensy studied Groshenko with narrowed eyes. I waited for a glimmer of recognition, but there was none, and he finally just nodded and reached for his comm. "Fine."

But S'lana stepped between them, raising a hand. "No, he's

going to be *my* prisoner. Nobody sneaks into my company like this and just walks away." She nodded to the armed detachment she'd brought with her, who surrounded Groshenko.

I exchanged a look with Torina, but she seemed as puzzled as I was. Groshenko and S'lana must be up to something, but whatever it was, we'd never been brought into the loop on it.

I decided to forge ahead, reasoning that Groshenko could take care of himself long enough for all of us to get to the *Nevsky*. So I turned back to Pevensy.

"Well?"

If Pevensy's glare was any more toxic, I'd die on the spot. He was beyond angry. He'd been outplayed, and that was something he hated more than a simple loss. After a moment, he began to grind out words, as if each one cost him a year off his life.

"Fine. I can answer both of your questions at once. Ruiz-Rocher is the one who hired me for that job on Helso. It wasn't *just* her, but I've got no idea who else was involved. She was the face I dealt with, her and that grubby Yonnox sidekick of hers. She was involved in biomedicine of some sort back on Earth, so she was one of the principles behind that thing that infected the soil on your homeworld." He sighed and scrubbed a hand across his face as the enormity of his fall sank in. "I have no idea if they've got an antidote."

Torina muttered something that included the word *bitch*.

"As for where she is, I have no idea," Pevensy went on. I drew a breath and started to open my mouth, but the mercenary held up a hand. "Her Yonnox partner sets up the meetings. It's all done in person. He's on Dregs for the first three days of each month and works out of a dive bar called Wasted. And that is all I can tell you.

Now, do we have a deal? Because if we don't, I've got nothing to lose by tossing you out an airlock."

I nodded. "We do. You're going to let that Peacemaker ship dock here, and we're going to board it and fly away. Like I said, once we're out of weapons range of this place, we'll send you what you need to know to undo your little problem."

He took a step forward. "If you double cross me, I swear I'll hunt you to the edge of the universe itself."

"Yeah, see, that's where you and I differ. I'm not the sort of scumbag that would poison the environment of an innocent world and the people who live there. I'm Peacemaker Van Tudor the Third, and I'm good for my word."

Despite everything going on, the stress, the tension, and the danger, Torina snickered. She glanced at me sidelong. "Sorry, Van. That sounded pretty—"

"Cheesy," Groshenko finished. "Right down to the rhyme."

I scowled. "We'll talk about this on the way home."

WE BOARDED the *Alexander Nevsky* under the watchful glare of mercenaries from several companies. Pevensy personally escorted us to the airlock. I was surprised at how quickly word had got around Bulwark about what we'd done, but I also wasn't. The only thing on the battlefield that travels faster than a bullet is a rumor.

"Remember, even a whiff of double cross, and I'll have enough firepower that you'll end up with your atoms scattered right across known space. There will be *nowhere* you can hide."

I nodded gravely. "I understand."

He stepped back, and the door slid closed. Torina and I both slumped against the airlock wall.

"Well, that was fun," she said, smiling.

"Yeah, next time I have a plan like that, kick me, hard and repeatedly."

A new voice cut in. "Welcome back aboard, Peacemaker Tudor. I presume you'd like to get underway as soon as possible."

I nodded at the female voice that sounded like Netty's but with a touch of a Russian accent. "Even sooner, if we can, Svetlana, thanks."

We made our way to the cockpit, reveling in both the sheer volume of empty space aboard Groshenko's ship and the lack of laser-like mercenary glares. By the time we'd gotten there, the AI, Svetlana, had already cast us off and started a high-g acceleration away from the menacing bulk of the mercenary station. That was good because I still had an itch between my shoulder blades that felt like the targeting point of a shot from one of those big-assed rail guns.

A chime sounded, an incoming message on a tight comm beam.

"Impatient, isn't he?" I said, meaning Pevensy, but when I answered, it was Groshenko and S'lana.

"Van, it worked," Groshenko said.

"Well, thanks to you two. Do you think we made Pevensy look bad enough? And in front of enough soldiers? We need him hamstrung, not just wounded. The bastard won't stop if he thinks he can still get us."

S'lana grimaced. "Oh, yes. His credibility took a major hit. I, along with several other company leaders, am already working on exploiting the gap you made. We think we can keep Pevensy in check, at least for now. More importantly, we can pick off the best talent and keep him weak that way—a bunch of hardass soldiers will always go to the top, and for now, that's not Pevensy."

"Good. The fewer guns he has at his disposal, the better." I glanced around, then back at the screen. "And don't worry, we'll try not to scratch the *Nevsky*."

"Actually, Van, I won't be needing her back. I've already resigned my post as Master and my credentials as a Peacemaker. I need you to take the *Nevsky* back to Anvil Dark and hand her over to Lunzy. She'll be decommissioned, and various parts under lien will go to the lienholders. That will leave a few components above and beyond the normal configuration of a stock Dragonet. Those, I'm giving to you."

I fought the urge to say no, but asked a simple question instead. "Why? I mean… thanks, but… why?"

He gestured around him. "I'm doing it. I'm staying with S'lana's Dire Legion as her new Special Operations Officer. She's got contracts lined up that will keep me busy—oh, and all of them on the right side of the law and, well, for the most part, the right side of morality, too."

As he spoke, I saw the truth in Groshenko's eyes. He was going to die as a soldier.

He seemed to read my thoughts and offered a warm smile. "Don't worry, Van. Your grandfather is going to be right there at my side the whole time."

"I—thank you. I hope you find what you're looking for, Petyr."

"As I do you, Van."

He smiled once more, then the screen flicked off.

WHEN WE WERE WELL clear of Bulwark and clearly had no one tailing us, we called up Pevensy and gave him the antidote to the infection.

"They're called the Synergists. They're from a planet called Arminsu-el—"

"I know who they are! They're glorified actors with chemistry sets. Are you shitting me? *That's* your version of a bloody antidote?"

I shrugged. "They might seem a little odd, but they do good work. Lots of singing, too. You'd be surprised at—"

"Bullshit. You're done. I'm not just hunting you. I'm putting bounty money on your ass. I'll make sure your head has a price on it until—"

"Pevenesy, I know you're pissed. But take a leap of faith and believe in the, uh, space hippies. Truly. They can do the work. I know, I put my own money up against their promises, and I'm all in," I said with my oiliest tone.

"You—"

I cut him off and looked at Torina.

"Another bitter foe bent on terrible vengeance?"

She nodded. "I'll add him to the list." But her smile faded.

"Thank you, Van, for… all of it. It was very, very cathartic, seeing Pevensy backed into a corner the way he was. The only thing that would have made it better was a large gun and a great deal of blood."

I smiled back but couldn't help feeling that large guns and great amounts of blood could very well still be in our future with Pevensy. He didn't seem the forgiving kind.

But then again, neither was I.

28

We were about to twist back to Anvil Dark when yet another comm message interrupted us. This time, it was from Icky and Perry aboard the *Fafnir*.

"Still in one piece? Huh," Perry said.

"Well, I'd expected a tone of relief when you found out Torina and I were still alive, but I guess surprise and disappointment are good, too. Tell me, how much was your bet with Icky that we wouldn't survive?"

"Van, I'm shocked. Appalled, even, that you would suggest—"

"Perry."

"Not a very big one."

Torina rolled her eyes. "What does an AI need with money, anyway?"

"Bragging rights, but that's not important right now. Van, are you still at Spindrift?" Perry asked.

"We are, but we're just preparing to twist back to Anvil Dark."

"Don't. We're on our way to you. We've got a buyer for the two Vanguard satellites, and he's waiting there for us."

I FIDGETED in the *Fafnir*'s pilot's seat, glaring around me. Our brief opportunity to sprawl aboard the comparatively vast expanse of the *Nevsky* had spoiled me. I was glad when we docked at Spindrift and I was able to disembark. I wasn't all that happy that we were still in the Spindrift system, since Pevensy and his mercenary gang weren't too far away. But S'lana had insisted she'd arrange to keep him and Bulwark occupied to give us some breathing room.

Which allowed us to take some time with our buyer, a shambling mass of limbs and hair that emanated a distinct reek of ozone, the smell of a thunderstorm. He took his time examining the Vanguards, but it didn't bother me because they were the real satellites, and we were selling them in good faith. If anything, what bothered me was just generally hanging around Spindrift. How long could S'lana keep Pevensy occupied?

We finally settled on a price—12.275 million bonds. The buyer offered cash, which I eagerly and quite loudly accepted. And that was that.

"Okay, Van, let's get to The Quiet Room's branch here, and you can have them turn all that cash into a secure transfer note," Perry said.

"Nope. We're going back to the *Fafnir*."

"With nearly thirteen million bonds in cash."

"That's right."

"Are you trying to make yourself a target—wait. You're *trying* to make yourself a target, aren't you?"

We strolled along, me keeping The Drop and the Moonsword, which I'd left aboard the *Nevsky* before transferring to the *Wellspring of Lamentations*, prominently displayed. The sort of people whose attention I was trying to attract weren't the ones likely to take a stab at mugging me on the Spindrift docking concourse.

"Might I point out that while you paint that big ol' target on yourself, it kind of spills over to Icky, Netty, and I," Perry went on.

"Well, I can call up Torina and have her come pick you up in the *Nevsky*, if you'd feel safer that way."

"And leave you without the benefit of my knowledge, skill, and experience? That would almost be a crime in itself."

"Um, seems to me we just did that, on Bulwark, and it worked out okay."

"You got lucky."

We strode on a few paces, then I glanced down at Perry. "Although, I did miss having you there at my side."

"Damned right you did."

We made it back to the *Fafnir* without incident, then departed Spindrift, also without incident.

The same couldn't be said for the outbound trip. It happened with *lots* of incident.

WHICH STARTED when we were about half an hour out from Spindrift. Netty spoke up, although I'd already seen the ping on the tactical overlay.

"We've got a class ten, corvette following us at high acceleration. They left Spindrift only a few minutes after we did."

"Yeah, I see them. I was kinda hoping they were on business of their own."

"I think they are, actually. And we're that business."

"Yeah, and—okay, incoming message. Getting tired of this comms traffic. None of it's been good news." I sighed. "This day could be better. First Pevensy, and now this." At least I'd managed to don my b-suit, which felt a lot better than that mercenary outfit.

"Get it all over with at once," Perry said, his logic grim but flawless.

I answered the comm. A Yonnox appeared on the screen, one decidedly more of the sleazy, money-grubbing sort than the slickly professional S'lana. Standing beside him was none other than Master Proloxus.

"Peacemaker Van Tudor. You're making quite a name for yourself," the Yonnox said.

"I don't seek fame, it seeks me. Anyway, how can I help you?"

"Well, by cutting your drive and handing over that fat wad of cash you've got aboard."

I gave a thin smile. "Guess you saw that, huh?"

The Yonnox grimaced that smile of theirs. "We see everything."

"We being—the Stillness, right?"

"Very good. You didn't think we'd just gone away, did you?"

"Was kind of hoping that, yeah."

"Well, here we are. Anyway, if you cut your drive, we can conclude this transaction without any need for shooting or dying or any of that unpleasantness."

"And if I don't?"

"Then said shooting and dying and similar unpleasantness will, I'm afraid, be inevitable."

Proloxus spoke up. "Tudor, listen. You have to do what they say."

"Why? For your sake? You're going to need to give me a better reason than that. Oh, by the way, your family says hi—or they would, if you hadn't killed them all."

"It's not that simple—"

I cut him off. "It never is, is it?"

"Please! They said they'd let me go if you hand over that money. Then you'll have me as a permanent… contact. I know people. I know things. Things you'll want to know!"

I hesitated for an instant. Proloxus probably knew a great deal. But the moment lasted only a fraction, maybe a single heartbeat. I made to throw an answer back in his face—

Whereupon the Yonnox raised a slug pistol and blew a chunk out of Proloxus's head. The former master vanished from the frame like a dropped rock.

"Actually, there's lots he could have told you," the Yonnox said, holstering his weapon. "If only he'd kept his mouth shut. So, back to our business."

Icky, who'd occupied the copilot's seat while Torina was with the *Nevsky*, just shook her head. "That was—holy shit."

"It was. So let's avoid any repeats of that and just hand over that money, shall we?" the Yonnox said.

I frowned, curled my lip, appeared to think about it for a moment, then turned back to the screen. "If I may? Another option? And this is so simple, it can't be misunderstood. Go. To. Hell."

I snapped off the comm.

"They've illuminated us with fire control scanners and will be in weapons range in just under ten minutes," Netty said.

"You *did* want to be bait, Van," Perry said.

"Yeah, I did, didn't I." I sighed. "When are you people going to stop me and my brilliant ideas?"

"When they stop working. Of course, we'll be dead, but that's going to put an end to them anyway, isn't it?"

THE *FAFNIR* SHUDDERED as another missile detonated close by and showered us with shrapnel. We'd taken several near-hits and had a half-dozen system failures. Netty and Icky were doing their best to keep up with the damage, but the inexorable laws of space travel were working against us.

We couldn't twist for another half hour.

We couldn't outrun the pursuing Stillness ship because it had a slight edge on us acceleration-wise.

Torina was on her way to help, but she'd had to reverse course in the *Nevsky* and couldn't possibly get here fast enough.

If only I'd been thinking ahead and had her and the *Nevsky* accompany us instead of sending her back to Anvil Dark. I'd told myself I'd put her in enough danger today, but, in retrospect, Groshenko's ship easily had the firepower to keep these bastards at bay.

But. If.

"This is only going to end one way," I said, staring glumly at the system failures flashing across the *Fafnir*'s status board. "They're going to catch up to us, and we can't stop them."

"I'm afraid so," Perry said.

Icky popped her head into the cockpit. "Van, we've just lost two applique armor plates, port rear quarter and underside. Leaves us with no armor on our ass. Mind you, they might give us some cover, but—"

I sat up. "Icky, take over," I said, unstrapping and standing. "When I give the word, I want you to cut the drive and let these assholes catch up to us."

"Why?" she asked as she pushed her way past me into the pilot's seat. "We giving up?"

Perry shook his head. "Nope. Van just had another idea."

"Aren't we supposed to stop him? Didn't he specifically say that?" Icky asked, taking the controls.

"Van, is this going to save our asses?" Perry asked.

I grabbed my b-suit's helmet. "Maybe."

"Good enough for us."

As soon as Icky cut the drive, the Stillness ship rapidly overtook us. I saw it while peering around the edge of a loose applique armor plate that was drifting along in company with the *Fafnir* about twenty meters away. It was on a slowly diverging course, but that wouldn't be a problem because this would work, or I'd be dead long before it became one.

The Stillness ship braked, its exhaust flaring to bring it to a stop relative to the *Fafnir*. Over the comm, repeated from the *Fafnir*'s cockpit, I heard the Stillness giving curt instructions to Icky. At the same time, thrusters puffed, nudging the Stillness ship closer.

I waited, sweating inside my b-suit. I felt naked as hell. Sure, I had an applique armor plate between me and the Stillness ship, but there was nothing but the void everywhere else.

First confronting Pevensy, then this. Two existential crisis situations in one day.

I needed a drink. No, *two* drinks. And then, many more.

The Stillness ship had closed to within ten meters of the *Fafnir*. That was close enough. I took a breath, then gripped the armor plate and pulled myself around it. It felt as solid as a rock outcrop under my fingers, my relatively paltry mass tiny compared to its considerable inertia. As soon as I'd made it to the side facing the Stillness ship, I kicked off.

A long, *long* ten seconds ensued, with me watching the Stillness's point-defense batteries intently, waiting for one of them to slew around, track me, and bring this whole desperate little venture to an end.

But they didn't. I was probably too close for them to even detect me, much less lock. It was a safety feature intended to prevent the weapons from targeting, say, a ship's own debris, and it had just saved my life—a *true* safety feature.

I stopped myself against the flank of the Stillness corvette and grabbed an antenna mount for support.

"Okay, let's see just how sharp you are," I muttered and drew the Moonsword.

In its previous incarnation, a short, stabbing blade, it never would have penetrated both a ship's outer and inner hulls. I could only hope that in its new lengthened form, it could.

Bracing myself, I drove the sword point-first into the hull, just as the ship was about to dock with the *Fafnir*. It sank hilt deep with surprisingly little effort. And when I pulled it out, a satisfying stream of vapor erupted from the small rent.

Good enough.

I could imagine pressure warnings suddenly blaring in the Stillness ship. But she was too close to the *Fafnir* to engage her with weapons or light her main drive and try to accelerate away without a collision. Of course, her crew would be suiting up, but there was nothing to be done about that—

Especially since her hull chose that moment to fail. A sudden split raced away from my small cut in both directions, then her entire atmosphere vented all at once. Bits and pieces of debris, as well as a few bodies, were cast into the void in a silent cataclysm that filled my vision with violence.

And I was a part of that violence. One moment, I was clinging to the Stillness ship; the next, I was spinning crazily away, clutching the Moonsword as I narrowly missed slamming into the armor plate that had sheltered me just a minute before.

ALTHOUGH I FELT like I was speeding off into the unknown reaches of deep space, in reality I was moving at a good jogging pace, nothing more. The Stillness ship, mortally wounded, now drifted, while Icky brought the Fafnir along in pursuit, easing her close enough for me to finally grab and stop my wild gyrations. By the time I was aboard, the Stillness ship had started to make way again, but that was when Torina finally got within range. She was obviously tired of this day and just wanted it to be over, too, because she cut loose with every weapon the *Nevsky* could bring to bear. The resulting fusillade of fire shredded the Stillness corvette, leaving it a lifeless, drifting wreck.

"Just think, it's all thanks to the Moonsword," I said, tapping the blade where I'd propped it against the *Fafnir*'s pilot's seat. "It was *just* long enough to get the job done."

Torina sniffed over the comm. "Men and their swords. Always worrying about whether they're long enough or not."

I managed a tired grin. "And, with that, I have a name for our spiffy new battleship. We'll call it *The Above Average*."

EPILOGUE

Torina's father stared at the money, all twelve million and change bonds sitting on a table near the veranda that overlooked the ravaged wilderness of Helso.

"You're… giving this to us?"

"Well, I'd like the case back," I said.

He looked up at me, dumbfounded.

"What—" He stopped and shook his head. "What are the terms?"

"No interest and no payments."

"No, I can't—"

"Yes, you can, because I do have one term. Do you have a family banker?"

"Of course."

"Then I'd like you to send them to the Srall. They've got money and nowhere to put it."

Torina's mother, who was standing nearby with Torina, laughed and wiped her eyes. "Oh, he'll love that. That's his favorite kind of money. Available."

While her parents secured the money and started contacting the necessary people—including the space hippies—Torina and I wandered onto the terrace and stared out across the grey, lifeless landscape.

"It'll be green again soon enough."

She took my hand. "I know it will. I can already see it."

OKAY, so we didn't rename the *Morass of Despair* to the *Above Average*. In fact, there was really only one name that made sense for her, and I carefully stenciled it onto the rear bulkhead of the newly cleaned and rewired bridge. I'd avoided letting anyone know my true thoughts about the name—up until now.

"Iowa?" Icky asked, smiling as she pronounced the word with ease. She may have practiced.

"Yeah. She was an old ship, with a great lineage, and it's my home state. We'll honor both with our new home." I gestured around. "Or, if not home, then a place to which we can return if we need to."

Torina, who'd been puzzling over the new single-pilot bridge with Perry, glanced back over her shoulder at me. "I think you've earned a trip home, Van."

I stepped back to admire my handiwork. I had to clean up the W a bit, but the rest of *IOWA* looked pretty damned good. "Maybe. But we have somewhere else to go first."

"Where?"

"France."

"France?" I saw Torina ponder that, moving her finger. Finally, she nodded. "The one beside Germany."

"Very good!"

"Why there?"

"Because we owe our friendly Francophile, Retta, some wine."

She moved to join me, looking at the new name of our ship. "So is France like Iowa?"

"Replace the corn with romance, yeah." But I shrugged. "Although I'm sure France has corn, and Iowa can be quite romantic if it needs to be."

Without warning, Torina turned and kissed me.

"Perry, we need to go do that… thing. You know," Icky said.

"Wait. I want to watch this—"

Icky scooped Perry up and unceremoniously carried him off the bridge.

"She *grabbed* me!"

The bridge door sealed, cutting him off. Torina finally pulled back, smiling.

"I think I like romance better than corn."

Amazon won't always tell you about the next release. To stay updated on this series, be sure to sign up for our spam-free email list at jnchaney.com.

Van will return in LEGACY OF STARS, available now on Amazon.

GLOSSARY

Anvil Dark: The beating heart of the Peacemaker organization, Anvil Dark is a large orbital platform located in the Gamma Crucis system, some ninety lightyears from Earth. Anvil Dark, some nine hundred seventy years old, remains in a Lagrange point around Mesaribe, remaining in permanent darkness. Anvil Dark has legal, military, medical, and supply resources for Peacemakers, their assistants, and guests.

Cloaks: Local organized criminal element, the Cloaks hold sway in only one place: Spindrift. A loose guild of thugs, extortionists, and muscle, the Cloaks fill a need for some legal control on Spindrift, though they do so only because Peacemakers and other authorities see them as a necessary evil. When confronted away from Spindrift, Cloaks are given no rights, quarter, or considerations for their position. (See: Spindrift)

Glossary

Dragonet: A Base Four Combat ship, the Dragonet is a modified platform intended for the prosecution of Peacemaker policy. This includes but is not limited to ship-to-ship combat, surveillance, and planetary operations as well. The Dragonet is fast, lightly armored, and carries both point defense and ranged weapons, and features a frame that can be upgraded to the status of a small corvette (Class Nine).

Moonsword: Although the weapon is in the shape of a medium sword, the material is anything but simple metal. The Moonsword is a generational armament, capable of upgrades that augment its ability to interrupt communications, scan for data, and act as a blunt-force weapon that can split all but the toughest of ship's hulls. See: Starsmith

Peacemaker: Also known as a Galactic Knight, Peacemakers are an elite force of law enforcement who have existed for more than three centuries. Both hereditary and open to recruitment, the guild is a meritocracy, but subject to political machinations and corruption, albeit not on the scale of other galactic military forces. Peacemakers have a legal code, proscribed methods, a reward and bounty scale, and a well-earned reputation as fierce, competent fighters. Any race may be a Peacemaker, but the candidates must pass rigorous testing and training.

Perry: An artificial intelligence, bound to Van (after service to his grandfather), Perry is a fully-sapient combat operative in the shape of a large, black avian. With the ability to hack computer systems and engage in physical combat, Perry is also a living repository of

Glossary

galactic knowledge in topics from law to battle strategies. He is also a wiseass.

Salt Thieves: Originally actual thieves who stole salt, this is a three-hundred-year-old guild of assassins known for their ruthless behavior, piracy, and tendency to kill. Members are identified by a complex, distinct system of braids in their hair. These braids are often cut and taken as prizes, especially by Peacemakers.

Spindrift: At nine hundred thirty years old, Spindrift is one of the most venerable space stations in the galactic arm. It is also the least reputable, having served as a place of criminal enterprise for nearly all of its existence due to a troublesome location. Orbiting Sirius, Spindrift was nearly depopulated by stellar radiation in the third year as a spaceborne habitat. When order collapsed, criminals moved in, cycling in and out every twelve point four years as coronal ejections rom Sirius made the station uninhabitable. Spindrift is known for medical treatments and technology that are quasi-legal at best, as well as weapons, stolen goods, and a strange array of archaeological items, all illegally looted. Spindrift has a population of thirty thousand beings at any time.

Starsmith: A place, a guild, and a single being, the Starsmith is primarily a weapons expert of unsurpassed skill. The current Starsmith is a Conoku (named Linulla), a crablike race known for their dexterity, skill in metallurgy and combat enhancements, and sense of humor.

CONNECT WITH J.N. CHANEY

Don't miss out on these exclusive perks:

- Instant access to free short stories from series like *The Messenger*, *Starcaster*, and more.
- Receive email updates for new releases and other news.
- Get notified when we run special deals on books and audiobooks.

So, what are you waiting for? Enter your email address at the link below to stay in the loop.

https://www.jnchaney.com/backyard-starship-subscribe

CONNECT WITH TERRY MAGGERT

Check out his website
http://terrymaggert.com/

Connect on Facebook
https://www.facebook.com/terrymaggertbooks/

Follow him on Amazon
https://www.amazon.com/Terry-Maggert/e/B00EKN8RHG/

ABOUT THE AUTHORS

J. N. Chaney is a USA Today Bestselling author and has a Master's of Fine Arts in Creative Writing. He fancies himself quite the Super Mario Bros. fan. When he isn't writing or gaming, you can find him online at **www.jnchaney.com**.

He migrates often, but was last seen in Las Vegas, NV. Any sightings should be reported, as they are rare.

Terry Maggert is left-handed, likes dragons, coffee, waffles, running, and giraffes; order unimportant. He's also half of author Daniel Pierce, and half of the humor team at Cledus du Drizzle.

With thirty-one titles, he has something to thrill, entertain, or make you cringe in horror. Guaranteed.

Note: He doesn't sleep. But you sort of guessed that already.

Made in United States
Troutdale, OR
08/07/2025